RACING THE DEVIL

Also by Charles Todd

The Ian Rutledge Mysteries

The Bess Crawford Mysteries

Other Fiction

RACING THE DEVIL

An Inspector Ian Rutledge Mystery

Charles Todd

wm
WILLIAM MORROW
An Imprint of HarperCollins*Publishers*

RACING THE DEVIL. Copyright © 2017 by Charles Todd. All rights reserved. Printed in the United States of America. No part of this book may be used or reproduced in any manner whatsoever without written permission except in the case of brief quotations embodied in critical articles and reviews. For information address HarperCollins Publishers, 195 Broadway, New York, NY 10007.

HarperCollins books may be purchased for educational, business, or sales promotional use. For information please email the Special Markets Department at SPsales@harpercollins.com.

FIRST EDITION

Library of Congress Cataloging-in-Publication Data has been applied for.

ISBN 978-0-06-238621-2

17 18 19 20 21   LSC   10 9 8 7 6 5 4 3 2 1

For our beloved Smokie, a character to the end.

And for sweet Ditto, who gave love on his own terms.

Rescues who brought joy to our lives and captured a place in our hearts.

There's always room for one more . . .

But Bash, dearest Bash, preferred her independence outside, and all who knew her loved her deeply just the same.

I

Late June 1916

It was a way of daring Fate. Of spitting in the eye of the devil.

On the eve of what was to be the worst battle of the war, the coming Somme offensive, all leave had been canceled, and men who had anticipated at least a few days in rotation were ordered to return to the line before midnight.

In a more or less sturdy French barn that had somehow escaped the lot of the heavily shelled farmhouse connected to it, an enterprising sergeant had set up what passed for an officers' mess. The food was appalling—he had learned to cook in Bodmin Gaol, although it was anyone's guess whether he'd been an inmate or hired staff—but he had come into possession of the contents of an abandoned wine shop (or so it was said), and word had got around that what he served was of fairly decent quality.

The seven officers seated around the scarred, three-legged table had drunk bottles of his best claret, and the bleak mood had changed to a sober acceptance of what they would soon be facing. Verdun was in trouble, the French desperately holding on by a hair, the death toll rising. Britain was mounting a flanking attack to prevent a German breakthrough, and it looked to be a bloody shambles. None of them expected to survive.

The bombardment that they now knew to be the prelude to tomorrow's attack had been going on for several days, rattling nerves but with any luck leveling the German trenches they would have to attack at dawn. And the Germans, forewarned, would be waiting, if the artillery barrage had left any alive.

The seven men were strangers, had never served together. But they soon discovered that before the war they had lived within a hundred miles of each other along the southern coast of England. They had one other thing in common: an enthusiasm for motorcars. Three of them presently owned one. The other four spoke pensively of what they would buy if they lived to see the war's end. Candles danced and sputtered in rusty tins, a feeble light that made it easier for tired men to say whatever was on their minds.

It was then that the name of Randolph Graves came up. He had driven in the Grand Prix de Monte Carlo not once but twice, and had come very close to winning both events. One of the seven had known him, but the others knew of him. Anyone mad about racing knew who Randolph Graves was.

"Bought it at Ypres," the Captain who had known him said. "I went to see his widow when I was last in London. She took it hard, poor lass. She'd been at school with my cousin. Not much I could do but say the usual. Died for his country. Brave as hell. An example to his men. I doubt it was much comfort."

"You never know," the only Major present commented, finishing his glass. "My father, now, says much the same sort of thing about lads I've grown up with. As if," he added sourly, "sacrifice is a fine end. I'd much rather survive, thank you very much."

"What will you do when it's over?" the Lieutenant queried, passing the nearly empty bottle. "Stay in the Army?"

"God, no," the Major said as he sent it on. "I had my eye on a Rolls before that damned Archduke got himself shot. My father talked me out of buying it. Made a certain sort of sense that summer. But if I live, I'll have it now, and I'll drive it to Monte Carlo to watch the race."

That led to a discussion of model, speed, and cost.

"There'll be new chassis designs when this is over," another Lieutenant put in. "Bound to be."

"At least between Paris and Monte Carlo, there's been no fighting," the Major added, a touch of yearning in his voice. "The Grand Prix should commence again without too much trouble. Unless of course the roads haven't been maintained."

"If there are any men left who can drive in it," the Captain retorted bitterly, shifting in his chair. "It'll be down to us, more's the pity. And none of us have that skill."

"I say. Let's make a bargain. One year after the war is over, let's meet in Paris. With our motorcars. And race each other to Nice. Not the Grand Prix. An affirmation that *we* survived. Something to measure our future by."

Surprisingly, they grasped at the straw offered, agreeing with the enthusiasm of men who knew they were doomed and didn't want to believe it. The sergeant brought out another bottle, still dusty and quite old. They finished it, serious now, laying out the details of their future, the hotel where they'd stay in Paris, the hotel where they'd celebrate their arrival in Nice, how to bring the motorcars across from London, what route to follow south.

It was taunting Providence, but they didn't care. Something to hold on to, when tomorrow dawned and they were in the thick of whatever was to come. A talisman.

As they walked back through the dark to their respective sectors, the guns were still at it, lighting up the night sky, shaking the earth beneath their feet.

"I don't envy the poor devils under that," someone said quietly.

"No. But the more of them killed tonight, the fewer we have to face tomorrow or the next day," the Lieutenant replied grimly.

What they didn't know was that the shelling would not penetrate the German trenches. Could not. They had been built far better—and much deeper—than those in the British lines.

And so on 1 July, when the first charge went over the top, they were met with a taste of hell.

The South of France, Above Nice, Late Autumn 1919

Andrew Brothers watched the sun set over the hilltops and took a deep breath. He was tired now, and the lamps were being lit in the isolated villages clinging to their perches where the central massif ran down to Nice and the sea. They beckoned, promising food and possibly even a bed. But he couldn't stop. The others hadn't, he was sure of it. And he wanted very much to reach the Promenade des Anglais first. Not to best the others, but for his own sense of accomplishment, a way to end his own war. He hadn't been able to do that in the past year. It still haunted him in ways he'd never expected. And so he'd come to believe that this race would put paid to the trenches and all they represented. Proving he was a whole man at last.

He wondered how many of the others felt the same way.

There were only five now. Dobson had bought it on the Somme, some said cursing the Germans as he died. Everett had developed gangrene after a skirmish near Passchendaele, his foot shot off and infection creeping up his leg inch by inch. The doctors had done what they could, but there had been no hope from the start. He'd written Brothers a rambling letter, mostly claiming that even without his foot, he would ride in the motorcar with them by turns and smell the sea as they ran down to Nice. He'd been dead by the time Brothers got that letter, and there was something macabre about it, the certainty Everett had felt that he would survive to make the journey.

Truth be told, none of them had expected this week would come. Not after the Somme, where they'd all realized they were living on borrowed time, walking dead. For one thing, they'd been more than a little drunk that night in late June, Midsummer's hardly past, the days long and warm. Drunk and a little mad. Defiant.

The odd thing was, he could recall it clearly, as if it were yesterday. The scavenged tables and chairs, whatever cups and mugs could be found in the ruins of shelled villages, a dented coffeepot, a saucepan or two, and a few skillets. The sergeant was nothing if not enterprising. He himself had drunk his wine from a porcelain cup with lilies of the valley painted on it. The Major, he remembered, had had a child's silver christening mug.

They'd been daft even to think it might be possible. And yet it *had* seemed possible somehow. The barn had still smelled of horses and, oddly enough, of chickens. Nothing like the trenches, where the stench of urine and sour sweat and death seemed to permeate the muddy footpath and the scarred walls.

At the time it all seemed to make perfect sense. They'd toasted each other and wondered what the girls were like in Nice, and ignored the coming battle. The night was quiet, except for the shelling and, closer to, a cricket in one of the stalls. They'd laughed and passed the bottles, all of them a little drunk.

By the time he was back in the lines, he was cold sober and wishing he weren't.

He'd had to borrow his brother-in-law's motorcar to keep his rendezvous at the Hôtel Ritz in Paris.

William hadn't been happy about it, but he'd relented in the end. And so Brothers had walked into the hotel, found the other four in the bar, and endured the good-natured chaffing about being the last to arrive. "But not the last in Nice," he'd told them, and realized he meant it.

There was no prize for winning. Only a bottle of the best French brandy they could find. If the winner chose to share it with the others, all well and good. If he didn't, no one would raise an objection. Being alive—and whole—was all that mattered.

Brothers also recalled—far too clearly—standing in the trench at dawn on 1 July three years before, waiting for the signal that the attack would begin. And thinking that he had hardly known the men he'd made the pact with. He'd decided that it was for the best. Their deaths wouldn't touch him. He'd lost enough friends. He didn't care to make new ones.

And yet, with each attack he survived, he'd told himself, *I'll race to Nice after all. By God, I will!*

That had become his mantra, and he told himself that if he lived, it didn't matter about the others. He'd make that drive alone. To prove he was still alive. If he had to beg, borrow, or steal a motorcar.

They weren't meant for racing, any of the vehicles the five men had brought to Paris. Nothing like the low, sleek Grand Prix models that swept around the curves and dealt easily with tight corners. Randolph Graves would laugh. But none of them cared. They had lived through the worst that life had to offer. It had taken their youth and their nerve and their joy. And still they had survived.

He shook himself, staring ahead. Tendrils of mist were beginning to swirl in front of his headlamps, and as he came into the next turn, he realized that he could see nothing to his left—where the long drop had been until now—but a sea of white. With the setting of the sun, mists had crept up the cliff faces all along here. Lost in the past, he hadn't noticed, but now they were moving toward the heights above him, and in a matter of minutes he was going to be swallowed up.

He didn't know this road. They had all been warned that the descent into Nice was dangerous, a series of twists, turns, and switchbacks with nothing between the motorcar and plunging into ravines but a man's skill. Bad enough to drive it in the dark, but in a mist? Madness!

He began to slow, leaning forward to peer through the windscreen at the road. It was vanishing one instant, reappearing the next. And then without warning there was a clear patch, and he took the bend holding his breath, uncertain what he'd find as he rounded it.

A flash of light behind him distracted him for an instant, but he had no time to glance at his mirror. As it was, he almost missed the next turn as mist eddied at the last possible second. Swearing, he gauged his speed and kept to the right, so close to the cliff face that he felt the scraping of branches against his wings.

William, he told himself grimly, would be cursing if he knew.

The mist thinned a little, revealing a straight stretch of road for about twenty yards, and he drew a breath of relief. He couldn't see the drop on his left, although he knew it was there, but he sped up a little to take advantage of the easier run.

Something tapped his motorcar hard in the rear, catching him completely unprepared. For an instant, Brothers nearly lost control, reflexes kicking in even as he veered left and fought to bring himself right again. Risking a look back, he could see a vague shape in the mist behind him. No lights—whoever it was was running without lights.

But the next bend was already on him, and he had no time to think about that. He edged around it, working the brake, and then he was hit again.

Shouting at the other driver, he kept his attention on the mist-shrouded road, hunched over the wheel, gripping it with both hands.

Who the hell was behind him? And what was he trying to do?

The next time Brothers was struck, he nearly went over the edge, his tires spinning in the loose grit and underbrush. Yelling, he felt himself sliding, the left rear seeming to lean into the void, and then almost miraculously, he was back on the road.

Fully alert now, he gunned the motor to earn him some space, skidded in the dust toward the drop as he took the next curve at speed despite the mist, and thanked the gods watching over him that there was no one else on the road. Another bend loomed, and he almost misjudged what he could see in the brightness of his headlamps, for the ruts were deep and treacherous, filled with shadows. It was a sobering moment. But it was a risk he'd have to take.

The other car was behind him again, and this time when it struck him, it sped up, pushing him, in spite of the possibility that in sending him crashing over the edge, the other driver might fail to disengage in time to save himself.

Brothers had a moment's clarity. If he stayed on this road, he'd surely be killed. He didn't know why or by whom, he only knew that if he didn't do something soon, either the mist or the man behind him would win.

And then he saw it. As the mists shifted a little, there was a broadening in the road. Lights, blurred by the white curtain, high above his head. A village perched on a promontory—like so many others he'd passed during the late afternoon.

Was that a turning? Yes, and it was wide enough for him to swing in a loop off the road and come back just behind his tormentor. Without signaling, at the last possible second, he whipped the wheel to his right—and then pulled it hard left, praying that he hadn't overshot the turn. He flew into the street, listening to the scream of braking behind him, fully intending to turn the wheel again, finishing the circle. And then his danger registered.

Half hidden by the mist was a narrow bridge, low stone walls looming on either side. Too narrow for his motorcar. His brother-in-law's motorcar, he reminded himself in a panic. The bridge was too close to miss. He was headed straight toward it, and there was nothing he could do.

He gripped the brake, pulling hard, sideslipping on the loose grit, bracing himself for the unavoidable shock of collision. Fast as he'd been going, he was going to wreck William's motorcar and kill himself.

He never knew what had saved him—bald luck, his own skill, or the excellent brake. The motorcar came to a sudden juddering halt that threw him against the steering wheel so hard he thought he'd broken ribs.

Stunned, pinned there and helpless, he turned his head to look for his tormentor. But the other motorcar had been swallowed up in the mist. Even the rear lamp was only the faintest glow that vanished as he watched.

He sat there, his hands shaking on the wheel, his chest feeling as if breathing were impossible.

And then he got out, walking to the bonnet to look.

He didn't think there was a coat of paint's space between the wing and the stone abutment.

It took him a good ten minutes to collect himself again. The certainty that he was going to die had rattled him—and then cleared his head as it had done in battle. Now it was lost in such a surge of anger that he was shaking with it. Anger that someone had brought back what he had been most ashamed of in France, that courage had not come naturally to him, as it had seemed to do for many other men. Finally an overwhelming relief that he and his brother-in-law's motorcar were safe.

He left the motorcar there, crossed the narrow bridge on foot, and started up the rutted lane that climbed to the village above. The mists were heavy here, and he had to watch where he was walking. A twisted ankle wouldn't do—and he had no way of knowing how the land dropped off to either side. At length he found himself passing a house to his right as the lane narrowed into a street with buildings on both sides. A church—shops—a turning that led even higher—more shops and houses—and then he was abruptly stopped by a low wall. The mist roiling up from below enveloped him, cool and damp. But for the wall, he'd have gone straight over before he knew the precipice was there.

He swallowed hard.

Surely the damned village had a bar of some sort? He badly needed a drink, and his flask was in the motorcar God knew how far away.

Brothers turned back the way he'd come. And then someone

stepped out of a door to his left, and he saw what he wanted—a few tables, chairs, and a wall of bottles. He nodded to the man who had just left, went through the open door, and realized that he wasn't sure what language these people spoke, whether his French was sufficient.

"Cognac," he said, and the proprietor, a heavyset man with a beard, answered. Brothers wasn't sure whether it was a greeting or a question.

He shook his head, and the man pointed to several bottles. He recognized the label on the second one in line, and nodded.

He had two stiff drinks before paying the man and walking back to the motorcar.

Dutch courage be damned. He was going to have to drive on to Nice, like it or not, and the mists were no better, the road ahead no straighter.

He was startled to see that he'd left the motor running. Getting behind the wheel, he sat there for a full minute, letting the brandy warm him. And then he reached for the brake, let in the clutch, and after reversing, drove on.

It was a test of endurance, the next few hours. At times he had to feel his way around the bends, judging them as best he could. And always in the back of his mind was the worry that the other motorcar had pulled over somewhere to wait for him.

When he finally came out on the straight stretch of road that ran on toward the city of Nice, he barely noticed the bright lights of the villas and hotels ahead of him. He couldn't have said just when he'd run out of the mist. Two miles back? Three? Almost as if it had done its worst, failed, and finally had given up without any warning.

He found the Hôtel Negresco without difficulty. It stood on a corner overlooking the Boulevard des Anglais. It had been a French hospital during the war and was only just recovering. A room was waiting for him. He asked the man at the desk to see to his motorcar, walked on to the lift, and went up. He didn't want to speak to anyone else, no half-drunken postmortems of the drive, no celebration of victory. What he needed was sleep. Being first to reach Nice no longer seemed to matter.

The next evening, Brothers walked into the hotel bar, prepared for the welcome and a riotous night.

What he found were three other drivers sitting around a table, their faces gloomy, their shoulders slumped, as if they'd been in the same chairs for hours.

Brothers crossed to their table without speaking, and they looked up, at first startled and then delighted to see him. Slapping him on the back, calling for another glass. But it was a strained welcome.

"What? What's the matter?" he asked as champagne was poured into his tall, elegant glass. A far cry from the makeshift cups so long ago on the Somme . . .

"We'd just about given you up," he was told. "Haven't you heard? There was a terrible crash up in the hill country last evening. One of the worst stretches. There was fog, you see, and he missed the curve. Someone reported it at first light, and they went up after him. The rescuers. Took hours to reach the site. Motorcar a shambles, of course. He's alive. That's all we know. They won't tell us any more than that."

Brothers barely heard the rest of it. He wanted to ask if there had been another vehicle involved, but something in their faces held him back.

And he wasn't certain that he wanted to know. More to the point, he couldn't bear to relive what had happened to him. Not this soon. Besides, these men were strangers, really. Nice enough and all that, but he never expected to see any of them again. Better to leave it. He took the chair pushed out for him, downed his champagne, and listened to the jumbled account they had been given of what had happened.

And wondered if he'd been meant to go over the edge as well.

But who the hell could have done such a thing? And in the name of God, *why?*

He wanted to search their faces, he wanted to know if winning had mattered so much to any of these three survivors that they would kill to be first. Hard to believe.

Still, just how well did he know any of them?

It wasn't until much later that another thought came to him.

What if the motorcar that went over the edge had been the one trying to send him into the ravine?

2

East Sussex, November 1920

There was a heavy rain that evening, wind-driven into vast curtains. The roads leading to the cliffs were passable—just—if they were negotiated with care, although traction could be nasty where the mud was thick. When it mixed with chalk and whatever rubble had washed down in the storm, it was slick and unpredictable.

Not a night fit for man or beast. Even the sheep had huddled in the lee of the hedgerows, wet and miserable. The long, steep, winding road down into the Gap was particularly treacherous, but it was seldom used, and the locals knew to avoid it in bad weather.

It was just after dawn when a farmer by the name of James, who had a holding near East Dedham, went out to the cliff meadows to see how the sheep had fared. It had rained heavily well past five o'clock, dark clouds coming in from the west and sweeping on toward Dover. He had stood by the window watching the downpour, anxious to be on his way. Then the wind shifted and the rain settled into a cold drizzle that swept over the chalk headlands from the sea. Ten minutes later, he set out, not waiting for his breakfast, worried about the sheep.

Two hours later, James walked into Burling Gap, the closest village, to seek out Constable Neville.

"From the look of it," James said, describing what he'd found, "he didn't know the road, and like as not, blinded by the rain, he lost his way. What happened next I can't say, and there's no way of telling when he came to grief. The motorcar rolled, you'll need horses and ropes to right it. He was thrown clear. I saw him there just beyond the boot. Dead, of course. There's no question."

"Who is he?" Neville asked, dreading to hear it was one of his neighbors.

"Damned if I know. I didn't recognize him, and there's a good deal of blood about. I didn't care to turn him over. You'll have to bring him in and see for yourself."

There was no doctor in Burling Gap. The nearest surgery was in East Dedham, which had expanded after the war, while Burling Gap had been fighting the encroaching sea. High as they were here, the cliffs still gave some access to the narrow strand below, and men of the Gap had made their living from the sea and the shipwrecks along this part of the coast for generations.

Neville found a lad to take a message to Dr. Hanby, and after that collected half a dozen men and four horses. He led them to the long sloping road that came down into the Gap, and even before he reached the motorcar, he could see it, on its side like some wounded beast. It wasn't until he was some twenty yards from it that he could make out the body lying facedown in the grass, half hidden by the bulk of the vehicle. The man's hat, sodden with rain, lay just beyond, almost within reach of his hand.

"That's Captain Standish's motorcar," Harvey Bainbridge said suddenly.

Neville turned to him. "Are you certain of that?"

"Certain enough."

It had been a long climb up the headland, but they were used to it. Reaching the scene, they went in silence to stand near the body. Neville kept them back as he stepped forward and leaned over for a closer look.

"Dead," he confirmed, and behind him there was a shifting of feet as the others accepted the news. Neville knelt then in the wet, bruised grass to study the body.

The motorcar hadn't rolled over it. He could see that much. A man, wearing a heavy coat, his hair still wet with rain and dew. No indication that he'd been badly injured and had tried to crawl to the shelter of the vehicle. A quick death, then. That, Neville told himself, was one mercy. *He* wouldn't have wished to lie out here the rest of the night, life dwindling, waiting for help that never came.

Reaching out, he gently turned the body over so that he could see the face. Behind him there was a sharp indrawing of breath.

The onlookers had glimpsed the clerical collar even before the dead man's face came into view.

"It's not Captain Standish," James said, and watched as Neville brushed the wet hair out of the dead man's face. "It's Rector," he added then, in a stunned voice. "But what's he doing here in Captain Standish's motorcar?"

There was a deep gash at the hairline, blood caked across the pale, lifeless face, but Neville knew that James was right. "It's the Rector," he confirmed. "Mr. Wright."

Wright had served at St. Simon's in East Dedham for some years, except for the four years of the war, when he'd been chaplain to one of the Sussex regiments.

"We can't leave him here," someone was saying, and walked back to the horses to fetch the stretcher while Neville went through Wright's pockets in an effort to confirm his identity. One of his more unpleasant duties, he thought as he did it. Clearing his throat, he opened the dead man's purse and said, "There's money here. And his identification."

He put them away again before getting to his feet and brushing at his wet knees.

Turning to look at the motorcar, he made a note of the crushed wing, the broken windscreen, and the smear of dark green on the dark red boot. The driver's door was standing wide and at an awkward angle. Neville thought it was likely that as Wright was thrown out of the vehicle, the door swung back and caught him in the head.

He was nearly sure that Wright had been alone in the motorcar—there was no sign of a passenger, and no blood in the interior to indicate that someone else had been injured. Any passenger surely would have been as the motorcar rolled and he was tossed about inside. And if he had survived unhurt, undoubtedly he'd have come for help. It wouldn't have been the farmer, James, who discovered the wreckage.

Satisfied, Neville nodded to the men with the ropes and horses, and they moved forward to begin the task of righting the vehicle. Harvey Bainbridge was already helping another man to lift the Rector's body onto the stretcher. He was lashed there with the extra lengths of rope, and Bainbridge turned just as the motorcar jerked and swayed and then crashed back on its wheels again, raising a shout from the men guiding the horses.

Neville went to look it over once it had stopped rocking, jotting information into his notebook as he studied the vehicle. He knew very little about motorcars, but he could see the damage done and judged it to be fresh. But then Captain Standish would be able to confirm that.

"What shall we do about it?" one of the men with the horses asked. "Not like it's flotsam on the beach."

This raised a chuckle from another man, and the first turned to glare at him.

But Neville was walking up the road some distance, casting about for any reason why the driver had lost control.

What he found instead was a second set of tracks, at one point overlapping those of Standish's vehicle.

He followed the second tire marks for a distance, realizing that both were often on the grass, not the packed chalk and earth surface of the road. And he didn't like what he saw.

Keeping his thoughts to himself, he walked back toward the now-upright motorcar.

"Anything?" Harvey Bainbridge asked, meeting him partway.

Neville shook his head. "I wonder if he fell asleep at the wheel."

Bainbridge shook his head. "In that storm? Not very likely."

"Well." Neville nodded to the men who were to carry the stretcher. "All right, then, to Dr. Hanby with him."

James said, "What shall we do with the motorcar?"

"Take it to Trotter's garage. If anyone can find out what went wrong, he's our man."

"I don't think it will run," one of the men with the horses said. "Pull it, then?"

"Just be careful of the horses on the hill."

"Not to worry," the other man said.

They set off, the stretcher bearers in front, Neville bringing up the rear.

James fell back to walk beside him. "Not the best of starts to the day."

"No."

"Will you be handing over the inquiry to Constable Brewster?"

Neville stopped, forcing James to halt as well. "The body was found in my patch. I reckon that means I'm in charge."

"But Wright's from East Dedham," James said.

"Not that it matters," Neville replied, walking on. "I'm sending a message to the Chief Constable, asking him to bring in Scotland Yard."

"Is that really needful?" James asked, surprised.

Neville glanced at him. "Do you think Constable Brewster would be any happier than I am, dealing with Captain Standish and the Rector's Bishop?" Still seeing uncertainty on the farmer's face, he added, "And we don't know what it was that made Rector borrow the Captain's motorcar."

"Surely he had a sound reason?"

"I'm not eager to pry into the Captain's affairs. Or the Rector's. I'd rather hand it on than take it on."

James shook his head. "To tell truth, I hadn't given it any thought."

"No, I expect you hadn't," Neville said, "but I had. It's my duty."

James considered him for a moment. "Still. Scotland Yard."

"Nothing wrong with Scotland Yard," Neville answered blandly. "By now they must be accustomed to being caught in the middle. You'll be required to give evidence at the inquest. I'll have to do the same." He nodded toward the men ahead of them, struggling to keep the motorcar on the road. "And so will they."

James fell silent, considering that prospect. "You must do as you think best," he said finally, and with a nod walked on to join the stretcher bearers and their sad burden.

Neville watched him go, satisfied. He had no great belief in Constable Brewster's ability to do more than keep the peace in East Dedham. Better the Yard, indeed. And he himself had seen enough to know that there was more to the Rector's death than a motorcar losing control in a night of wind and rain.

Walking on toward East Dedham, watching the stretcher make its way toward the doctor's surgery, he could see the rainwater dripping out of Wright's clothing and through the canvas.

Poor soul. It was not a suitable end for a man of the cloth. But then Wright had been much more than that. And God willing, Scotland Yard would send someone capable of dealing with what very well might be murder.

D r. Hanby confirmed that the Rector's neck had been snapped, most likely by the blow from the vehicle's door as Wright had been thrown from the rolling motorcar. "It was quick," he said, looking up at Neville. "He wouldn't have suffered."

"I'm relieved to hear it. He lay out there all night."

"I'll have a look at the rest of him, cursory of course, but necessary. It will have to wait until later in the day. But I expect no surprises."

"Nor I," Neville responded.

Hanby gestured to the bruised face. "You're satisfied with the identification? Or do you want his housekeeper to be sent for?"

"I shouldn't worry Mrs. Saunders with that. It's Mr. Wright, no doubt about it. And those are his belongings." He indicated the ring of keys and the dead man's wallet. "Trotter has the motorcar for the time being. Do you know of any kin?"

"He never spoke of any family," Hanby said, covering the body with a clean sheet. "A private man, the Rector. But I expect Mrs. Saunders will know who to send for."

Shortly afterward, Constable Neville went on to the rectory of St. Simon's Church. It was set back from the road on the far side of the churchyard, well out of sight of the cortege that had made its sad way to the doctor's surgery. In the Middle Ages, wool had built East Dedham and enlarged its church before the market declined. Still, during the Great War, the demand for uniforms and blankets had seen a small resurgence in income here and elsewhere, although not enough to bring a return to real prosperity. Close to, even East Dedham was showing the cost of war.

He made his way up the path to the rectory's door. Like the church, the house was built of flint, sturdy and rather attractive with its stone facings and peaked roof. But while the church had Norman antecedents, the rectory was much later. It had been renovated early in Victoria's reign, and a later Rector had set out gardens, softening the severity of the flint in spring and summer. Now the beds showed only the last bare spikes of late autumn amid withered leaves.

Neville stood at the door for a moment before lifting the brass knocker and letting it fall. Listening for footsteps, he tried to arrange the words he would have to use when the housekeeper opened the door. But it was hopeless. He wasn't a man who found it easy to express sympathy. He'd have given much for a pint before coming here, but one didn't deliver bad news while reeking of strong drink.

It was several moments before a woman with graying hair put up in a bun on the top of her head opened the door to him.

"Constable," she said, nodding to him. "If you've come for Rector, he's not returned yet," she added apologetically. "He was supposed to be back late last night, but he'll be here in time for services. I hope it's not urgent business brought you here."

"Might I come in a moment? It was a walk from Burling Gap. I could do with a glass of water." He hadn't meant to begin that way, but he found it hard to tell her, bluntly and on the doorstep, what he'd come to say.

"Yes, of course." She moved back, allowing him to enter the cool dimness of the hall, then led the way to the kitchen. "What was it you wanted with Rector?"

He didn't answer straightaway. As she busied herself fetching a glass and pouring water into it from a jug kept cool in the pantry, he looked around at the plain, old-fashioned kitchen. It was built to hold a large family, like the house itself. Two infant chairs stood on either side of the door to the back stairs leading to the upper floors. Nearer to him, the Welsh dresser gleamed with patterned china, large platters and serving dishes handed down from generation to generation. The table itself, in the center of the room, could easily seat ten at a pinch.

Mrs. Saunders handed him the glass, and he drank a little before saying, "I expect you'll be wanting to sit down." And without waiting for an invitation, he pulled out one of the straight-backed chairs and held it for her before taking one for himself.

She was alarmed now, although he'd tried not to let her guess what he'd come to say. There was nothing for it but to come out with his news and then give her time to take it in.

"There was an accident up on the Gap," he said slowly. "The steep part. Motorcar went over off the road and rolled, killing the driver instantly."

"Oh, my dear," she said softly, and he realized that she thought it was on behalf of the dead man that he'd come. "Anyone we know?"

"The driver was Rector," he said, and watched her face change.

"Rector?" she repeated. "Surely you must be mistaken. He doesn't own a motorcar."

"It was borrowed. But he was driving. There's no doubt about that. And as far as we can tell, he was alone." Neville picked up his glass and then set it aside.

"Oh, my dear," she said again, and this time her voice dwindled into a sigh.

"He didn't suffer," Neville repeated, trying to reassure her. Then, fiddling with his helmet, he said, "Whose motorcar would he be likely to borrow? Do you know?"

"But he left here on his bicycle just after two o'clock. He was calling on that farmer whose son is dying of his wounds. Dicky Melford."

Neville knew Melford. And his farm was nowhere near where the motorcar had gone off the road. Nor was there a bicycle in the wreckage.

She was saying, "Poor lad, he was in hospital for months. They brought him home to die. The wound in his chest wouldn't heal, and finally turned septic. There was naught to be done for him. A nice lad, grew into a nice young man."

Neville said gently, "Let me get this straight. Rector went to the Melford farm on his bicycle. Was he intending to go somewhere else from there?"

"He never said. But he did ask me to leave his supper, that he might be home late. He'd often stay until the undertaker had come. It was never touched, his supper. I found it this morning, just where I'd set it."

"I see." Changing the subject now, he said, "Is there anyone I can bring here to keep you company?"

She shook her head. "I'd rather be alone, at least for now. I might go to my sister's tonight, if that's all right. First I'll need to lay out clothes for the undertaker."

"There's no family to be notified?"

"Rector never spoke of any. His mother died when he was young, and his father while he was in seminary." She looked around the kitchen. "He loved this church. I expect he'd want to be laid to rest here."

"Is there a will? Anything that might tell us what his last wishes might be?"

"If there was, he said nothing of it to me. You'd have to ask his solicitor. Mr. Edgecombe."

Neville resigned himself to traveling back to the Gap in the dark. The days were short now, and it was already nearly nine o'clock. There were many more calls to make, and the message to be sent to the Chief Constable as well. He sighed.

He stayed a little longer with Mrs. Saunders out of kindness, eating the bit of cake she'd insisted on offering him, the hospitality of the rectory. And afterward he posted a notice for her on the church door, telling worshippers that there would be no service. In the vestry, he left a message for the church warden and the sexton that the Rector was dead.

The Rector's solicitor had chambers in a narrow building with a dark green door, set between the tiny stationer's shop and the greengrocer's. When Edgecombe's clerk was located, Neville was informed that the solicitor was in Pevensey for the day, and wouldn't be back until late afternoon on the morrow.

So much for that. Disappointed, Neville went on to the pub. Avoiding all questions, he begged paper and an envelope, and sat down at a table in a corner to write his request to the Chief Constable. That done, he went around back to where he'd heard a brewery van offloading the week's supplies of beer and ale, and persuaded the driver to carry the letter to Arundel, where the Chief Constable lived.

"Mind you hand it directly to his housekeeper," Neville told him. "Not to a housemaid."

His next call was at the police station to inform Constable Brewster of Wright's death.

He found Brewster half-asleep at the table that served as his desk, his helmet set to one side and his feet on the blotter. As Neville recounted the morning's events, Brewster shook his head. "There's a loss. He was well liked, Rector was. But what was he doing driving on the Gap road?"

"God knows." Neville told him what he felt Brewster ought to know, then waited for the other man to think the matter through.

"Here, this should be my inquiry. You should have sent someone for me."

There was a querulous note in his voice now.

"He died in my jurisdiction," Neville countered. "But there's doubt about why he was there. According to the housekeeper, he was going to the Melford farm yesterday. On his bicycle. But he hasn't been back to the rectory since."

"Are you certain it's Captain Standish's motorcar? He's not likely to be lending it, even to Rector."

"Certain as can be." He paused. "The general opinion is, this is a matter for Scotland Yard. My advice is to leave them to it."

"Why? It appears to be straightforward enough."

"But what if it isn't?"

Brewster stared at him. "Do you know something I don't?"

"There's nothing to know. Except that Captain Standish won't be best pleased that his fine motorcar is at Trotter's. Mark me, he won't take to using a bicycle."

"No," Brewster said slowly. "But as you say, it's your patch, not mine."

Closing the door of the police station, Neville wished for his own bicycle. He could have asked the loan of Brewster's, but he'd have had to explain why.

The church clock was just striking two as he turned toward the Melford farm.

It was a good three-quarters of an hour before Neville reached the house, set in a fold of the land and protected by half a dozen trees that leaned with the prevailing wind, their tops like shrubs set on nearly bare trunks. The light was already fading, and the temperature was dropping as he came up the track to the house. Like many of its neighbors, it was built of flint, long and rambling, nestled into its setting. He stopped to button up his tunic again—the pace he'd set himself had been warm work—and then went on to the door.

It was hung with black crepe, and there was no answer when he knocked. He stood there, waiting patiently, but no one came.

Finally, nursing a stiffening knee, he walked around the house to the kitchen door. Through a window he could see Mrs. Melford sitting at the wooden table, staring into space.

He startled her, even though his knock was hardly more than a tap. For an instant he read hope in her eyes as she opened the door. Then she said, "It's Constable Neville, isn't it?"

"Yes, from over to the Gap. Is your husband at home today?"

She moved aside to allow him to step in. "He's gone into Seaford to speak to the undertaker. I thought at first you might be from there, come to tell me—he's taken it hard. The boy's death."

He could see her clearly now as she lit the lamp. She looked tired, a tension about her eyes that told him she wasn't sleeping well. He thought perhaps she had had a long battle with hopelessness, even before her son's death.

"I'm sorry to hear he's gone," Neville said. "He was always a good lad, Dicky."

"It was a blessing," she said, but there was doubt in her voice. "Watching him waste away—but the house seems so empty now. I listened night and day to his breathing. You could hear it anywhere in the house. I don't know that I can bear the silence."

Not knowing what to say that might bring her comfort, he went on gently, "Actually, I've come to find Rector. His housekeeper told me he was planning to call on you yesterday."

Her eyebrows went up in surprise. "Rector? He's not been here. I've been expecting him all the day long, but we haven't seen him."

"When was he last here?"

"It's been four days, I should think. Yes, I'm sure of it. He stopped by often, looking in on Dicky. It was a comfort to all of us."

He nodded in sympathy, uncertain whether to tell her that Wright too had died in the night. "There was a motorcar crash last night," he said finally. "Rector was killed. I'm that sorry to have to be the one to tell you."

Her hands to her face, she stared at him. And her first thought was for her late son. "But who will bury Dicky now?"

"I don't know, Mrs. Melford. The Bishop will send someone, I've no doubt."

"I can't get over it," she said. "Rector dead too." Tears filled her eyes as if this was the final blow, and Neville stood there, unable to think of anything to say.

Rousing herself, she said, "I'm forgetting myself, Constable. Could I offer you a cup of tea? I was just about to make one for myself."

But she had been sitting there lost in thought, not starting to make tea or cook the evening meal. He thanked her for her courtesy and asked if she'd be all right, left alone, waiting for her husband and the undertaker.

"Yes, I'll be fine," she said, and accompanied him to the door.

He stood by the window, watching her walk back to the table and sit down again, lost in her own grief.

Despite his stiff knee, he set himself a fair pace back toward East Dedham. There he encountered a dozen people who asked him if it were true, about Rector.

He'd intended to go home, fetch his bicycle, and continue to Captain Standish's house. Instead, cursing the steady climb up to the scene of the accident, he looked again at the torn turf and the bruised grass. Finding what he was after, he took out his notebook. He squatted where the two sets of tire tracks converged. The light was going fast now, but in the afterglow, he could just see the patterns where the mud from the road had marked the place where two vehicles had driven onto the turf, their tracks overlapping. He began to sketch what distinguished the sets, then made certain he got it right in each case. Already the distinctive marks were harder to see, and he cursed himself for not coming back here before he went on to the Melford farm. As he rose from his cramped position, his knee reminded him why he had not come sooner.

Standing there, notebook in hand, he looked around. It was as if he were alone here at the ends of the earth, only the wheeling gulls overhead, coming in from the sea and adding their calls to the ever-present sound of the wind. Not a single other soul in sight, not even the sheep, who had moved on. He shivered, for no reason that he could think of, and snapped his notebook shut.

On the long walk back to the Gap and the remnants of his own village, he found himself thinking that the cottages here, even though they were made of the same flint, couldn't hold a candle to those at East Dedham. The roofs were still in need of repair, even two years after the war had finished, and several could use a little paint around windows and doors. But there was no money to put toward repairs. Perched as it was on the very edge of the great chalk cliffs, where it had stood for centuries, Burling Gap was slowly crumbling into the sea. Since 1905 he'd watched the decline, watched the houses of neighbors crash down in winter storms that ate at the cliff faces. How many were gone already? He recounted the names of those who had lived here. One or two had tried to rebuild a little farther inland, but the rest had moved on, taking what they'd managed to salvage with them. For there was little enough work here as it was.

But it was his patch, and he liked it. As long as one house remained at the top of the cliff, he'd not be leaving it.

The first stars were just showing as he limped to his door and stepped inside. He wasn't sure he could make it to the chair by the cold hearth, his knee threatening to buckle first.

He was too old to walk as far as he'd done today. Come to that, he was close to being too old to pedal, but he dared not complain to anyone. Since the war's end there had been talk of closing the police station at Burling Gap and adding the hamlet to the jurisdiction of East Dedham. To Brewster's jurisdiction, a man too lazy to care.

Sinking at last into his chair, he leaned his head back on the cushion.

If the Chief Constable agreed to his request to bring in the Yard, Neville prayed that whoever they sent owned a motorcar. Unlikely, of course, but it would make short work of distances and be a blessing.

A man could always wish for something, couldn't he?

3

Inspector Ian Rutledge finished his testimony and waited for questions. But the coroner had none.

Dismissed, he stood, nodded to the coroner, and walked to the door of the stuffy upstairs room of The Boar, letting himself quietly out into the passage. There he took a deep steadying breath. The crowded room, dark-paneled and low-ceilinged, windows tightly closed against the cold November rain, had nearly driven him mad, his claustrophobia pinning him in the witness chair because it was the only open space available. He'd been amazed that his voice had remained calm, his evidence clearly presented, when he felt the walls closing in on him, and the faces of the avidly curious villagers seemed to stare intently at him, hanging on every word as he described the finding of the body and the subsequent investigation into the shoemaker's death.

He stood there for a moment, absently listening to the voices he could just hear through the closed door, waiting until his pulse had slowed and his breathing was back to normal.

The inquest would bring in a charge of murder against Eleanor Hardy. The evidence was too strong; she would have to be bound over for trial. A pity, he thought. She had killed a man who was a predator, but justified or not, murder was still murder. It would be up to a jury to decide her fate.

Rutledge turned toward the stairs, and was halfway down them when someone called, "Inspector? Mr. Rutledge?"

He looked to his left as he descended the last half-dozen steps and saw the innkeeper, Boils, coming around the desk in Reception. "Yes, what is it?"

"A telegram, sir. For you. From the Yard." He leaned one hand on the carved figure of a boar that capped the newel post. "I left it in your room."

Rutledge thanked him, climbed the stairs again, and went down the passage to the room he'd taken for the duration of the inquiry. The telegram was lying on the table that stood by the window, clearly visible in the circle of lamplight. He picked it up, opened the envelope, and spread out the single sheet inside.

Constable Neville is expecting you tomorrow in Burling Gap, by Beachy Head, Sussex.

His next assignment. He read the single line, frowning. Acting Chief Superintendent Markham, a Yorkshire man of few words, was not given to explanations. Rutledge would have preferred to return to London. He had spent ten days here in Guildford. Surrey had been stormy and cold by turns, and a traveler had told him that there had been a dusting of snow on the higher elevations in the far north.

He glanced at his watch. The inquest would be over in less than an hour. His valise was already closed and standing by the door, and the motorcar had been filled with petrol early this morning, for the journey to London. A Thermos of tea and a packet of sandwiches waited for him in the kitchen.

Rutledge remembered seeing a dog-eared *Guide* in the lounge downstairs, likely left by a traveler several years before the war. He ran lightly down the steps and crossed Reception in long, brisk strides. It took him only a matter of minutes to find Burling Gap in the index.

He knew Beachy Head. Far too well. He had once stood on the cliff's edge, staring down at the new lighthouse below, and considered how easy it would be to step over the last few inches of wiry grass and plummet to the spreading arc of flints washed in by the last high tide. It had seemed an easy death, but he had not taken that last step. Afterward he'd never been sure why he hadn't.

Burling Gap was not far away. Nearer, even, to the now-defunct Belle Tout light.

The *Guide* spared only a few words for the hamlet: *Once a wrecker's haven before the Belle Tout light put paid to this activity, the hamlet sits on the crumbling edge of the cliffs, and on the South Downs Way, a walk along the southern coast. Indications of Iron Age man at excavations nearby.*

Hardly a hotbed of crime?

Rutledge flipped to the title page of the book: 1901, before the lighthouse there had been decommissioned.

Perhaps the war had changed the hamlet for the worse.

He put the *Guide* back on the shelf by the hearth and was just turning to go up to his room when he was summoned to the inquest once more to answer a few questions about his earlier evidence. From the nature of these he surmised that Mrs. Hardy was being given the benefit of the doubt. She would still stand her trial, but in every likelihood, she would escape the gallows. As he gave his answers, he felt a sense of relief. Justice, he thought, has many faces, but they don't always include mercy.

It was shortly after noon—he'd heard the clock in the church tower strike the hour as he was walking out of his room—that he was at last free to put The Boar and the house where Mrs. Hardy had lived behind him and turn the bonnet of his motorcar toward the south coast.

He spent the night in Newhaven and arrived close on to ten the next morning on the high downs above Burling Gap. The sun was a watery disk in the cloudy sky, but the rain had held off for the time being. Passing through East Dedham, he saw only sheep on the downs until he came to a crossroad that climbed steeply to his left. He made the turn for Burling Gap instead, running down toward what must be the Belle Tout light and the edge of the cliffs overlooking the sea. Staying to his right, he found himself among scattered cottages that for the most part looked their age. The police station was in the front room of one of the cottages facing what passed for a road. From what he could see, there was no inn, no church, no town hall, only a general store and a tiny pub called The Seven Sisters. A faded sign swinging on rusted hinges showed a sailing ship coming to grief below a long undulating line of high chalk cliffs. Far below where he stood, the sea ran in and out, a whisper almost lost in the wind. Farther out, the water was a gray-blue under heavy clouds.

Resigning himself to the inevitable, he left the motorcar in the road and walked into the police station.

The man behind the worn wooden table looked up, looked past him at the motorcar, and suppressed a grin.

"You must be the man from London. Constable Neville, sir."

"Inspector Rutledge, Scotland Yard. You sent for me?"

"Sir, I did." He rose and indicated the chair. "Would you care for a cup of tea while we talk?"

"That would be very kind."

Neville nodded and disappeared into another part of the house, where Rutledge could hear him setting the kettle on and opening a cabinet to bring out cups and saucers.

As he worked, Neville said, "There was an accident on the Saturday night. Out there on the road that comes down to Burling Gap from the direction of Eastbourne. If you came from London, you passed the turning after you left East Dedham."

"Yes, I saw it. Quite steep and twisting, and not in the best of conditions."

"That night there was a very hard rain, a good deal of wind, and it's likely that the man driving couldn't see his way very well. It must have been quite slippery, and the verges aren't that straight. The motorcar came to grief, and the driver was thrown clear, but his neck was broken when the driver's door caught him as it swung to." He stepped back into the front room as he waited for the kettle to boil. "A tragedy, but nothing, you might say, out of the ordinary."

"No," Rutledge agreed. Neville disappeared again, and a minute later returned with a tray holding a teapot, milk jug, and cups. These looked as if they might have belonged to his mother or perhaps his wife, treasured bits of good china kept for visitors and Sundays.

Neville carefully set the tray in front of Rutledge and went back to his chair behind the table.

Rutledge poured two cups, passing one to Neville, and sat back to wait for the rest of the story.

"The dead man was the Rector at St. Simon's in East Dedham. You will have passed through it on your way. A prosperous village. The problem is, the motorcar Rector was driving wasn't his. It belongs to Captain Standish, who lives in a large house a mile or two inland from East Dedham. I went to call on the Captain, to explain what had happened. And he tells me he hadn't lent his motorcar to Rector or anyone else. He'd been away visiting friends in Brighton, and only got home late Sunday evening, the night after the accident."

"How did he travel to Brighton? If he didn't drive himself?"

"As to that, sir, it appears that he went with a friend. She's a widow, husband was killed in the war. He's helped her from time to time with her husband's affairs."

"Any idea why the Rector had borrowed the motorcar—or why he'd needed one?"

"No, sir. His housekeeper thought he'd gone out to the Melford farm—their son was dying, and the Rector had been stopping in to offer comfort. But he hadn't been there. Not for days."

"How well did Mr. Wright know Captain Standish?"

For the first time Neville seemed to be at a loss. "I can't say, sir.

I should think they were acquainted. But as to how well they knew each other, you'll have to ask the Captain." There was a pause. "I'm a Chapel man myself, sir. I don't attend services at St. Simon's. I can't tell you if Captain Standish does or not."

"And the motorcar?"

He was clearly on safer ground here. "It's with Trotter, sir. He's turned the smithy on the outskirts of East Dedham into a garage. He was ground crew for aeroplanes during the war, and set up as a mechanic when he came home. Coming things, automobiles. I was to speak to him today, to see what he'd discovered. Now that you're here, we might call on him together."

"So far I see a mystery of a sort, but no reason to call in the Yard."

"No, sir. Still, there was another motorcar on the scene the night of the accident. I found two sets of tracks, crossing each other up there on the Down." He reached into his pocket. "I sketched them, sir, in the event they might be important."

"And the other driver never stopped or went for help?"

"Not to my knowledge, sir, and Constable Brewster over in East Dedham knew nothing about the accident until I stepped in to speak to him."

He found the pages in the notebook with his rough sketches and passed them across the table.

Rutledge set down his cup, took the notebook, and studied them. The treads were very similar, the type to be found on most motorcars, including his own. But the second drawing showed a small tear in the outer rim of one tire, small but distinctive.

"You're certain that this is an accurate drawing?"

"Yes, sir. I grant you it was much later in the day, and the light wasn't the best as I worked, but I noticed that mark in the morning, when I first discovered the second set of tracks. At that time I wasn't sure what to make of them. I came back later because I knew they'd be gone soon enough and I couldn't think of any other way of preserving what I'd seen."

"Yes, well done." Rutledge looked up at Neville as he returned the notebook. He thought to himself that Neville was the sort of man who would have made a very good sergeant in the Army. He was nearly Rutledge's height, strongly built, and clearly quite capable. But his graying hair and a limp that he'd tried to disguise as he walked indicated that he had probably missed the Great War. What was he doing here in this backwater? "This puts a different complexion on the accident. I think we should pay a visit to Captain Standish and see what he can tell us. But first I'd like to see where the motorcar came to grief." He set his cup back on the pretty tray and rose.

Neville said, "I'll just carry this to the kitchen, sir."

Rutledge went out and turned the crank, and by that time Constable Neville had joined him.

"I must say, this is an easier way of getting about than my bicycle, sir," Neville said as he closed his door.

Rutledge had owned a bicycle in his early days at the Yard, and he'd taken omnibuses and even cabs as he crisscrossed London. But of course here the terrain was very different from city streets.

Still, before the war he'd been content to travel by train to wherever an inquiry took him. The touring car had been more or less a personal decision, and it had proved its worth from the start. Often he'd made better time cross-country than he would have done waiting for the trains, and he was his own master, independent of timetables. More to the point, being buried alive during the war had left him with severe claustrophobia, and the thought of traveling by train now—crowded carriages, airless and smoke-filled, shut up cheek by jowl with other passengers—was anathema. Where the motorcar had been an indulgence before, it had become a necessity. He was sure that some at the Yard, possibly including Acting Chief Superintendent Markham, considered it an extravagance, even an affectation, but he couldn't really explain without telling them more than he wanted them to know about his war.

As he and Neville reached the point where he could look up to where the road curved, following the steep incline of the Down, Rutledge could see that in the dark, in the middle of a rainstorm, in an unfamiliar motorcar, and on a road he might not have known well as a driver, the Rector of St. Simon's could have found himself veering off onto the verge, and realizing his mistake, he might well have jerked the wheel in a panic and set in motion the accident that he'd been trying to avoid.

Rutledge drove slowly up the long, twisting road to the spot where Neville said, "Just here, sir," and in the same instant he saw the torn and bruised turf, the white bones of the chalk underneath showing through. Pulling to the other side of the road, Rutledge got out and went over to walk the ground.

Neville, coming up beside him, pointed. "The motorcar was lying on its side here, where you see the worst of the torn turf. Rector was lying over there, facedown. By the looks of him, he never stirred, never came to his senses." Moving forward, he added, "It was up here, well before the crash, that I found the second set of tracks." He cast about for a moment, then went on. "Just as I'd feared. There's no sign of them now, nor of the Standish motorcar's tire marks. Well. You'll have to take my word, sir, that I saw them, clear as day."

"No, I don't doubt you," Rutledge said, squatting for a moment to look for any trace of what Neville had seen. But it was useless. He rose, standing for a moment to consider the road in both directions. As a quiet place to commit a murder, it was ideal. But how had it been set up? Had the second driver followed at a distance, waiting for his chance? Or had he held back, with an eye to keeping out of sight until the two vehicles reached this stretch of road?

And where had Wright been coming from? Eastbourne? Hastings? Even Rye?

There was of course another possibility, another explanation for the two sets of tracks crossing each other: the second motorcar had not been involved in the crash, but had come upon it in the midst of the storm. Had the driver stopped, got down, and come hurrying to where the body lay, discovered that Wright was dead and that there was no one else in the overturned vehicle?

Then why hadn't he driven directly to the police station in East Dedham, got the local man out of his bed, and brought him back here to recover the body? Why had he simply vanished into the storm, leaving Wright to be found by someone else?

What did he have to hide?

Rutledge finally turned to Neville. "All right, thank you, Constable." Together they walked back to the motorcar. Underfoot the road was rough, slippery, rutted, and in places the verges were not very well defined.

At the crossroads, Rutledge drove on toward East Dedham.

"Tell me about Wright."

"He's been—was—Rector here for some twelve years, and I've never heard anything ill of him. He was liked even by us who go to Chapel. East Dedham was lucky to have him, from all reports. This is an out-of-the-way parish, for one thing, and a small church. That often means the least experienced man or one who's already been shunted from parish to parish. He was in the war, you know. Chaplain to a Sussex regiment. By all accounts he came home a changed man. Quieter, keeping to himself a good deal of the time. A good man, all the same, one you could turn to in a time of trouble."

Many of the chaplains had had a bad war. They comforted the wounded, gave last rites to the dying, prayed for the dead, and tried to make sense of killing at a rate that no one had foreseen. More than a few had suffered a breakdown. Telling a weary, dispirited soldier to return to the battlefield for King and Country, assuring the frightened that they would fight bravely when the time came, listening to the horrors told by haunted men who had already seen too much and sometimes preferred to die than witness more carnage—

Without warning Rutledge was nearly overwhelmed by his own recollections of Corporal Hamish MacLeod. He shut down the memory with a harshness that must have shown in his face, because Neville,

glancing his way, repeated uneasily, "He *was* a good man." As if this
stranger from London doubted it.

"Yes, I'm sure he was." He wasn't certain whether he was talking
about Hamish MacLeod or the Rector.

Collecting himself, he said, gesturing toward the square tower of
St. Simon's just coming into view, "Tell me about Mrs. Saunders, the
housekeeper. Was she devoted to Wright—would she have lied for him,
if he'd asked her to?"

"I shouldn't think so," Neville answered, striving to keep the shock
out of his voice. "From all reports, she's served him well, and the Rector
before him. Constable Brewster tells me she keeps the rectory spotless,
always had Rector's meals ready for him, and isn't above reminding
him to eat when he's come in from a long night with a parishioner, or
has been out in all weathers."

"He wasn't married?"

Neville frowned. "I don't know the whole of it, but I've been told
there was a girl before the war he was keen about. Brewster says she
wasn't suited to a country rectory."

"Was he wounded in the war? Wright?"

"He was. He was a great one for comforting the dying, no matter
where they were, and he carries a bit of shrapnel in his hip and has
other scars to show for doing his bit. Carried," he corrected himself.
He cleared his throat, as if uncertain whether to continue.

"Yes?" Rutledge asked, glancing his way.

"There's one odd thing I ought to mention. Rector wasn't at the
Melford farm when their son died of his wounds. And that wasn't like
him. What's more, he'd told Mrs. Saunders that that was where he was
going. But the Melfords hadn't seen him for three or four days. Rector
must have known that Dicky's time was near. The lad had been in and
out of hospital for two years, but the doctors never got all the infection,
and they finally sent him home to die. There's another thing: Rector
wasn't one to sit still. I'd see him out walking the cliffs or digging
around in the Iron Age ruins, if he wasn't about his duties, going all

over the parish on his bicycle. I couldn't help but wonder sometimes if he was hurrying as fast as he could go because there was something at his heels. I can't tell you why it struck me that way, and it takes nothing away from him as Rector."

But Rutledge could understand fleeing before the hounds of memory. He'd come back to the Yard for that very reason, haunted by a dead man who was not a ghost but whose presence in his mind was as vivid as if Hamish MacLeod had taken up residence just behind his right shoulder—where he had so often stood in life. Corporal Mac-Leod, one of the many young Scots he'd led in countless battles. One of the hundreds if not thousands he'd sent to their deaths on orders from the high command, orders it was his duty and responsibility as an officer to carry out to the letter. However ridiculous they might seem to men in the line. However many men were sacrificed to gain inches and not yards.

But he had had to execute Corporal MacLeod, a man he'd re-spected, whom he'd stood dozens of night watches with, waiting for the Germans to attack. The Battle of the Somme in July '16 had been a bloody disaster. In the midst of that long and horrifying nightmare—it had in fact lasted for weeks—the young Scot had refused to lead an-other charge across a No Man's Land already littered with their dead. Please God they *were* all dead, those bodies scattered among the shell holes and the barbed wire. He'd dreamed about them often enough, of their calling out to the living. And he, Rutledge, had had to order Hamish's execution for disobeying a direct order, though he'd tried repeatedly to convince Hamish to relent.

And no sooner had the shots been fired and he'd given the coup de grace than a shell from his own artillery had buried them all alive. By the time help had come, he had been the only survivor, ironically saved by a small pocket of air between his face and Hamish's body. The living and the dead locked in a macabre embrace in the thick, unspeak-able, enveloping mud.

Since that night, the voice in his head had always been there, his own mind refusing to leave Hamish in his grave in France, bringing him home in the only way he could. Unable to face what he'd been forced to do in the name of military necessity. Haunted by the guilt felt by those who had lived while so many had died.

They were in the village now, people on the street turning to stare after them. Rutledge took a deep breath to keep the strain out of his voice and said, "This Captain Standish. What do you know about him?"

"Four Winds is quite a fine place, I'm told, but I got no farther than the kitchens. The rest of the staff was off, since the Captain had gone to Brighton, and so the cook offered me a cup of tea, because I'd come so far and it was quite late. Before long she was telling me about coming to work for his mother, the late Mrs. Standish, what a fine lady she'd been, and what Standish was like as a boy. But she didn't have much to say about his time in France or his coming home. Except that he never spoke of the trenches. Come to that, I don't know many who did talk about them. Not if they'd been there."

"How well did he know Wright?"

"The cook didn't think there was more than a nodding acquaintance between them. The Captain attended services at St. Simon's—as a duty, she thought, more than a question of faith—but he'd never had Rector to the house to dine. His mother, now, she had invited him every other Sunday to have dinner there."

It was the duty of the local squire—in this case very likely the Standish family—to invite the Rector to dine. After all, the Rector, the doctor, and the squire were the leaders of the parish.

"Did the cook have anything to tell you about the motorcar? I doubt she'd have known what had transpired between Wright and the Captain."

"That was the odd thing, sir. She was certain it was in the old stable over behind the house, where the Captain always kept it. When I'd finished my tea, I took out my torch, and she and I walked out there to have a look." He glanced across at Rutledge. "The door was closed. But the motorcar wasn't inside."

After a moment Rutledge asked, "Is there other staff at the house?"

"Two maids and a housekeeper. But the cook—her name is Mrs. Donaldson—hadn't chosen to take that weekend off because she wanted to attend a christening in Eastbourne on the next Sunday but one. Her nephew's boy. And Captain Standish agreed to the change."

"Then we must ask Standish about any arrangement he had with Wright. There must have been one. Wright knew where the motorcar was kept, and he would have no reason to alert Mrs. Donaldson that he'd come as expected. When did Standish return to the house?"

"That Sunday night, sir. I expect the staff have already told him what's happened."

"Then very likely he's already been to East Dedham to speak to Brewster."

Neville was pointing out an old smithy set well back from the road. Half flint, half wood, the wood weathered to a silver-gray.

"That's Trotter's garage, sir. Where the Captain's motorcar was taken. You'll turn left at the fork coming up."

"Is there any chance that Wright was drunk that night? Or was he tired? Worried enough about something that he couldn't keep his mind on his driving?"

"I never heard it said he liked his drink," Neville answered. "But he might in private. As to what he could have been anxious about, sir, your guess is as good as mine."

4

Half a mile farther on they took a lane that veered left. Following that, they came to a stand of trees on both sides of the road. They'd been planted as a windbreak many years before, for they were mature, but like most of the trees so close to the cliffs, they were shaped by the wind. A low flint wall on the far side of the road, enclosing part of the wood, led to a pair of gateposts topped by stone pineapples, the symbol of hospitality. A bronze plaque on one of the posts gave the name of the house—FOUR WINDS. Passing through them, they were led up a drive to a house set on the slope of the Down, which was not as steep here as it was at Burling Gap, and the house seemed to fit into the land comfortably. Surprisingly, it had not been built of the omnipresent flint but of brick, which had no doubt been brought here at great expense. Late 1700s, Rutledge guessed. It was tall, three stories in the square central block, with lower wings to each side. The steps leading to the door were white marble, like the columns that held up the small portico. The door was black with polished brass fittings.

As manor houses go, it was not very large compared to many Rutledge had seen. But it made up in style for what it lacked in size. And it boasted very fine windows with stone surrounds.

There was smoke coming out of the clusters of chimneys, and from somewhere in the back came the rhythmic sound of an ax chopping wood.

The two men walked to the door, and Rutledge lifted the heavy brass knocker.

It was several minutes before the door opened and a gray-haired woman in severe black greeted them.

"Captain Standish," Rutledge said. "Inspector Rutledge and Constable Neville."

But she had already recognized the constable, and her mouth was a grim line as she stood aside to allow them to step in.

"The Captain is in his study. This way."

She led them down the passage on their left to a room at the far end and announced them. Instead of the dark paneling and rows of floor-to-ceiling bookshelves found in most studies, this one was full of light. The walls were covered in a light green watered silk, with small, exotic birds flitting through stylized branches of what appeared to be willows. The several bookcases, in a rich walnut, were only breast-high. On the polished tops was a fine collection of small jade figures.

Rutledge, seeing it, wondered which of the Captain's ancestors had been a collector. Possibly the one who had built the house?

Captain Standish rose from behind the desk where he'd been working on what appeared to be accounts and said, "Inspector. Constable. This is about my motorcar? Yes, I thought so. I can tell you straight off that I didn't lend it to anyone. I've no idea why Wright should come and take it. Unless it was urgent business?" He was slim and fair, with good features and dark blue eyes.

Rutledge could also see that Standish's left hand was missing. He said, taking the chair that his host had indicated, "We haven't discovered just what his business was. We'd hoped you could tell us."

"He left no message as far as I could discover. Not with my cook nor in the stable, which I've converted to house the motorcar." He resumed his seat. "Not that I object to his borrowing it, you understand, if he was desperate—if it was urgent, a matter of life or death."

"Perhaps he intended to tell you when he returned it."

"Yes, I'd like to think so." He hesitated, then asked, "I understand he was alone in the vehicle when it crashed?"

"As far as we can determine."

"As far as . . . ?" Standish prompted.

"There wasn't a second body in the motorcar. And no indication that there had been anyone with him."

"A blessing then that no one else was killed," Standish replied.

"I must ask. Is there anyone who could vouch for your time in Brighton."

"I'd hardly wreck my own motorcar," he answered shortly. "But if you must know, I was calling on the mother of an officer, a friend I'd served with. I wrote to her when he was killed, and now she's dying. Her daughter came to collect me. It was a distressful weekend, but it was a duty that I felt strongly about."

Standish looked across to Neville. "Is there any date set for getting the motorcar back to me? There will be legal issues, I expect. I haven't seen it myself. It was quite late when I got in from Brighton that Sunday evening, and at the moment I have no transportation to this garage. I don't keep horses any longer, and I can't manage a bicycle. I've never used Trotter. Does he know his business or should I have the vehicle taken on to my man in Eastbourne?"

Constable Neville hadn't taken the seat that Standish had offered. Instead he stood just behind Rutledge, his notebook in his hand.

"Trotter is one of the best I've seen," Neville said now. "But if you would prefer to have your own people take over, I'm sure it could be arranged."

Standish frowned, showing the first signs of irritation. "Thank you, Constable, but if traveling to Trotter's garage is a problem, Eastbourne would be impossible."

"I'm sure Trotter would be happy to come for you, sir, and show you what's needing doing."

"Thank you, Constable." He turned his attention back to Rutledge. "This is all very unusual. That's to say, we're speaking of the Rector at St. Simon's. I find it difficult to believe any of this. Are you certain he was driving my motorcar—that he wasn't walking on the road and was struck by it?"

Rutledge could sense the constable stirring behind him, but he forestalled Neville's answer by saying, "We've only just begun to look into his movements that day. I have no idea what our inquiry might turn up in regard to Wright. I was hoping you could shed some light on the matter."

Standish shook his head. "It's as much of a mystery to me as it is to you."

"How well did you know Mr. Wright?" Rutledge asked. "Well enough that he might feel he could borrow your motor and explain at a later date why he needed it?"

"I attend services from time to time at St. Simon's. As a matter of duty. That's the extent of my acquaintance with the Rector. My mother was more religious than my father or I." As if that closed the matter, he went on in a different vein. "I've not asked how severe the damage is. After all, there's been a death as well. But I'd like to know."

"Fairly extensive, sir," Neville said. "I'd not lie about that."

Standish took a deep breath. "You're saying I shall be buying a new motorcar."

"When it went off the road, it rolled, sir. But you'd best speak to Trotter, sir."

"God."

Rutledge stood up, preparing to take his leave. "If—when—we have more information, I'll call on you again. For now, I'm afraid you know as much as we do about what happened. But if you think of anything we ought to be told, you can send someone with a message to Constable Neville, here. He'll see that it reaches me."

Standish glanced from Rutledge to Neville, then said, "No reflection on your abilities, Constable, but I should have thought this was a matter for Constable Brewster. The Rector lived in East Dedham."

"Since the accident occurred in my patch, sir," Neville said with deference, "it was decided that I should deal with it. If you have no objections, sir."

But Rutledge, acutely aware that Neville was standing where Hamish generally stood, could feel the other man stiffen as Standish hesitated.

"Yes, good thinking, Constable. I'm sorry I can't be more helpful. It was rather a shock coming home to this news."

Standish walked with them to the door. There he said, as if he had put it off as long as he could, "If you'll send this man Trotter to me, Constable?"

"I will that, sir."

Neville went to deal with the crank and then climbed in beside Rutledge.

Instead of driving back the way they'd come, Rutledge sat for a moment, listening to the motor ticking over. "It appears that Wright took the motorcar without leave. For all we know, he was driving as fast as he could to reach the stable and return the vehicle before anyone was the wiser. But the question remains, how did he know that Standish was away?"

"Overhearing gossip at the church? Mrs. Donaldson could have spoken to someone about the christening, and the Captain allowing her to shift her days off."

"It's possible," Rutledge answered. "Does Standish have any family?"

"I knew his elder brother, a little. He was nearer to my age. Both lads were sent off to school when they were seven, nor did I see much of them during the holidays. Mrs. Standish often took them to visit her parents in Yorkshire, and there was never any chance of local mischief making, if you follow me. And no sooner had the Captain come down from Cambridge than he enlisted in the Army. August that was, of '14. I never had any reason to call on Mrs. Standish."

"Where is the elder brother now?"

"He drowned, sir. The summer he was twelve. The family had gone to Wastwater on a walking holiday. What I heard was, young Nigel went swimming and had a cramp. By the time they got to him and pulled him out, it was too late."

"Why do you think Standish would have preferred to have Brewster to you?" He let in the clutch and turned down the drive.

Neville rubbed his chin. After a moment, he replied, "In a word, sir, East Dedham is more to his liking than the Gap. We're the poor stepchild."

Rutledge smiled grimly. "And Brewster is more—amenable, shall we say?"

Neville hadn't expected the question. "I—he's more inclined to see the obvious."

"I'll bear that in mind. Did you think Standish was telling us the truth? Or making certain that he can't be connected to Wright's death?"

"I don't know. I couldn't put my finger on it, sir, but I had the feeling he was wishing it had never happened. And not just because of the damage to his motorcar."

"Who manages his land for him?"

"He has tenants, sir. They ran the estate while he was in France, although they were hard-pressed to do it with all the able-bodied men off to war."

"Do any of his tenants live near enough to have seen Wright come for the motorcar?"

Neville shook his head. "The farms are some distance from the main house."

"Wright would have known that, wouldn't he? The more I learn, the more I feel he thought he could return it before anyone was aware of what he'd done. And he almost made it. Who saw to it that he didn't?"

R utledge stopped at the forge on his way back to East Dedham.
The great anvil still stood in the lean-to that formed a porch
where horses could be shod, and an ancient bellows hung above the
cold fire pit.

Inside, there had been a reincarnation. Benches lined two of the
walls, tools laid out on them in orderly fashion. A few of them were
left over from the era of the smithy, but most, Rutledge noted, had to
do with motorcars. Half a dozen oil lamps hanging from hooks in the
ceiling did very little to penetrate to the far corners of the large shed.
And there was still straw on the floor, to absorb oil and other fluids,
although a distinct smell of horses lingered.

Rutledge and Neville had walked almost to the center of the shed
before a short, dark man loomed out of the shadows behind what had
once been a motorcar.

"Who are you?" he asked belligerently.

"Rutledge, Scotland Yard."

"Ah." The man relaxed and came forward. His coveralls were
grimy, and his hands gave the impression of never having been clean,
for grease and oil seemed to be ingrained in his skin. There was a black
stubble of beard on his cheeks, hardly distinguishable from the grime
there, and he gave the illusion of living like a troglodyte in the shadows
of the garage when not working on motorcars.

But his voice when he went on was educated.

"You've come to see the ruin. What happens to a perfectly fine motorcar that has been driven off the road with careless abandon. Or so it
would appear. Step over here and look for yourself."

Rutledge joined him by Standish's vehicle.

It had been a lovely touring car very like Rutledge's own. But the
chassis was twisted, the top torn, the wings bruised and crushed, the
bonnet dented like dimples. The steering wheel was cracked.

There was still blood on the leather of the upholstery, black now.
It appeared as if someone had tried to clean up the worst of it, and
failed.

"Small wonder no one survived. You see the vehicle—imagine the man."

Rutledge could.

"Why did it go off the road?"

Trotter shook his head. "God knows. I've found nothing mechanically wrong that could explain it. But look at this." He walked around to the rear. "Look here, just below the boot. Now, they brought the motorcar here directly from the site of the crash. And I can tell you there's nothing between there and my door that is the same green you see on that paint."

In the dark red of the body, the green was not clearly visible, but Trotter reached behind him on a bench, brought up a torch, and shone it on the area.

At some point in time, the wing of a dark green motorcar had scraped the boot and rear of the Standish vehicle.

"Would the other vehicle have suffered damage?" Rutledge asked.

"It would show, yes."

"How fresh is this paint?"

"Fairly. You can see, there's no rust where it struck Captain Standish's motor. And I would willingly wager that the other motorcar struck it several times. Look there."

"Do you think that that's what drove this motorcar off the road and caused it to roll?"

Trotter sighed. "Depends. Whoever he was, he'd have had to come up from behind fast, to keep the element of surprise. It would have been risky. He might have lost control as well. Remember, there was a storm that night. The roads were wet. Slick too. And there was a wind, blowing hard from the southwest, coming up over the cliffs. But it could have been done, if he'd kept his nerve. The other driver. And if Mr. Wright wasn't as familiar with the motorcar as Captain Standish might have been."

Rutledge tried to picture the second car coming up behind, catching Wright off guard, and in the end, causing him to lose control. It was possible, he decided.

"There's no specific damage to this motorcar to indicate it was interfered with?"

Trotter shook his head. "Not that I can see. Not in the usual places. But then it's a wreck, isn't it? And that means that someone clever enough to have planned to cut a hose or do something to the linkages, even weaken a tire, would have had to know that these would be looked at closely. The wonder is, that corner is intact enough that we can see the paint. What I can't tell you is when it got there."

"Nor which motorcar it came from." He was willing to accept Trotter's word that no one had tampered with the vehicle. Still, taking the torch, he walked around it, bending down to look more closely at various vulnerable areas. All the damage he could see appeared to have been related to the accident. Satisfied, next he examined the vehicle's tires.

Unless it was where they rested on the shed floor, he couldn't see that odd corner that Neville had sketched in his notebook. Which meant there were indeed two motorcars on the Down that Saturday night.

"No. Not a chance," Trotter was responding. "Green is too popular. That's not to say we might not be lucky enough to find one with dark red paint on a wing."

"An interesting thought. If I brought you a prospect, could you tell if it was the motorcar we're after?"

"I could do, depending on whether or not he's seen the paint and scraped it off and how well he did it. Whoever it was might have thought of that. He's clever."

"What rate of speed was Wright going when he lost control?"

"Fairly high, at a guess. He was fighting to regain the road, and that's when he pulled too hard, sending him over. There was nothing more he could do after that but pray."

"Are there any dark green motorcars in East Dedham?"

"Captain Standish has the only motorcar. There's a lorry at the sheep farm, but it's not green."

"How good a driver was he? Wright, I mean."

"Difficult to say. Mind you, I've never seen him drive a motorcar, but he must have done somewhere. France, perhaps. At any rate, he got to wherever it was he was going, didn't he, and nearly managed to get back. Still, that bit of road can be tricky in the rain. He might not have been expecting it to be quite so bad."

"How well do you know Wright or Standish?" Rutledge had finished examining the tires, and he looked up just in time to see a change in expression on Trotter's face.

"I know who they are." He glanced at Neville. "I'm a Chapel man myself, not one of Rector's flock. As for the Captain, he's never brought his vehicle to me. If that's what you're asking."

Rutledge said, "It's a lonely stretch of road. I doubt it was heavily traveled that night, not if the storm was as fierce as I'm told. Blinding sheets of rain, wind gusting. A driver would be concentrating on staying on the road. How likely is it that the other motorcar didn't see Wright until he was on top of him?"

Neville asked, "Then why didn't he stop? Why didn't he find out if Wright was alive or dead?"

"For all we know, he might have done. And decided there was nothing he could do. He was well out of it, if he drove on." Rutledge reached out to touch the green smudges. He gestured to the empty space around him. "If there are no motorcars in East Dedham, where does your business come from?"

Trotter shrugged. "Newhaven. Eastbourne. I have my own lorry out back. I usually go to wherever the motorcar lives. It's a start, and I've built a reputation for good work. This . . ." He looked around at the hanging lamps, the benches filled with tools. "It's what I could afford when I left the Army. I looked all along the south coast, mind you. Rents were too high. The business will grow. And then they'll come to me. Meanwhile, if you're asking me to tell you if I see a motorcar with dark red paint smudges, I will."

Rutledge thanked him, and they went out the broad door—wide and tall enough to bring in a good-sized horse.

Neville saw to the crank again, and Rutledge was about to pull out into the road when he glanced up. Trotter was standing in the doorway they'd just passed through, watching them. After the briefest pause, he nodded and went back inside.

As Rutledge drove away, he wondered what was on Trotter's mind when he came to the door. Making certain they were leaving? Remembering what Neville had said, that the man had serviced aircraft in the war, he didn't discount the possibility that Trotter could conceal damage as easily as he could detect it.

"If he's as good as he says he is, why did Trotter start out in East Dedham? Regardless of what he just told us, Hastings or Eastbourne or even Brighton would have been a better choice. A small shed to start—something grander as he built up his clientele."

Neville said, "I can't give you an answer to that. But I've heard nothing against the man. You might ask Constable Brewster if he's heard any talk."

Slowing as he drove down the busy street, Rutledge saw several women with baskets over their arms, going about their marketing. With them were a clutch of small children in leading strings and in prams. Babies born after their fathers came home. Even so, there were far too few of them—and more women still wearing the black of mourning. The men they'd hoped to marry hadn't come home, or had come home too severely wounded. By the town hall he counted three men on crutches with legs or feet missing, others with empty sleeves. Hamish had left behind the girl he'd wanted to marry. Fiona. He'd called to her as he lay dying and Rutledge had leaned down to deliver the coup de grace.

He hadn't heard what Neville was saying. Something about Trotter? About his smithy-cum-garage?

Rutledge managed to say, "What is Trotter hiding from?"

Neville glanced at him. "What makes you think he's hiding from something?"

"He hasn't married. He's chosen to do business where there is none. He travels to other villages or towns, where he's known for his skill and not necessarily for who he is. And somehow he's been able to make a living."

Hamish, who blessedly had been silent all morning, said clearly, "Aye, verra' like you."

Startled, Rutledge swerved, then caught himself.

Neville stirred uneasily. "I never thought about it either way." After a moment he said, without turning toward Rutledge, "Are you all right, sir?"

"A cramp in my leg," Rutledge managed to say. "It will pass."

5

Their next call was at Dr. Hanby's surgery.

He was a small, wiry man with glasses and a steady air.

He welcomed the two policemen with a nod, saying, "I'd heard someone was being sent down from London." He waited until they were settled across from him, then picked up a sheet of paper lying on his desk. "There were a number of injuries. The fatal one should have been a severe concussion that must have occurred when he was thrown from the motorcar. But the blow itself broke his neck. He was probably dead before he hit the ground. I'm told the motorcar rolled a number of times. That would account for what I found in the way of scrapes and bruising. Otherwise he was healthy enough to have lived to a good age. I found three war wounds, cleanly healed. Nothing life-threatening, but nasty enough. He'd never spoken of them to me, and I'd had no reason to examine him closely until now."

"Do you know what sort of war he had?"

"Suicide? Is that what you're suggesting?" Hanby shook his head. "Why should he take his own life in a borrowed motorcar? He need only walk to the cliffs and let the wind pull him over. A revolver or a razor would have done the deed with more certainty. If he'd survived the crash, he might have lived on as a paralyzed invalid. Surely not the best of outcomes."

"Perhaps he didn't want his housekeeper to find his body. Or as a clergyman, might not have wished to be seen a suicide."

"Yes, I understand." Hanby toyed with the letter opener lying on the blotter before him. He smiled wryly. "If we're playing at conjecture, I might suggest that while the concussion from colliding with the motorcar's door knocked him unconscious, the blow might not have accounted for the fact that his neck was broken. The gash on his head was neither deep enough nor in the right place to have caused the neck to snap. But then I didn't see how he landed on the turf. That might well explain everything."

Neville spoke for the first time. "He was lying facedown when we found him."

"That may or may not be relevant." Hanby put down the letter opener. "Unfortunately there are many ways to end a life. A boating mishap at sea? Climbing the fells in Cumberland? Simply walking out into a London street without looking? Hard to prove or disprove whether it was an accident or intent. A doctor might wonder sometimes, but he says nothing because he can't prove anything and therefore silence is the better choice."

"And how many murders have you suspected and couldn't prove?"

The doctor's gaze sharpened. "My share, I expect. At least three over the course of my practice. But there was nothing I could point to and ask the police to investigate. Simply an uneasiness that one can't explain away, but still nags at one, leaving an unpleasant feeling in the back of the mind. Like the newlywed couple who stood on the edge of the cliffs out there, watching the sun set. The grass and chalk crumbled under his feet, and he plunged to his death on the beach below. He was twice the bride's age, and wealthy. She was distraught, made herself sick with weeping. And yet I couldn't be sure it was sincere."

"I don't remember that," Neville said, surprised.

Hanby smiled grimly. "It was before your time, or I wouldn't have spoken of it even now." He turned to Rutledge. "You're asking me about this because you feel that Wright's death was murder."

It was a statement, not a question.

Rutledge answered him with equal honesty. "Uneasiness is a very good way of expressing it. If Wright hadn't borrowed Standish's motorcar, if he'd been driving his own, for instance, I would feel more comfortable about his death. There's an oddity here that makes no sense, and I feel an obligation to get to the bottom of it."

Hanby nodded. "I understand," he said again. "But I can think of no explanation that would satisfy either of us."

"Precisely."

Neville opened his mouth and then shut it smartly.

Rutledge thanked Dr. Hanby, and they left.

Neville said, as they got into the motorcar, "What do you make of that?"

"You were right to summon the Yard." It was evading the question, but Rutledge wasn't ready to discuss the possibilities with Neville.

One issue that had been at the back of his mind since their call on Standish was the distance between the rectory and Four Winds. Hamish had questioned it when Neville had described his interview with Mrs. Saunders, but Rutledge had had no time to consider it until now.

The housekeeper had told the constable that Wright had left the rectory on his bicycle. It wouldn't have taken all afternoon to reach the Standish house. Or had he prudently arrived early enough to observe the house, making certain that it was empty save for Mrs. Donaldson, that the Captain was indeed away and the staff had taken their day off?

But where was that bicycle? Not in the converted stable where the motorcar was kept, or Neville would have seen it and reported it. Not in the wreckage.

Still, it behooved him to have a look at that stable for himself.

And he preferred to do it alone.

He interjected, before Neville could say more, "There's no inn in Burling Gap. Where would you suggest I stay?"

"There are a few cottages that offer rooms to summer visitors. Mostly people walking the South Downs path. I'm sure they would be happy to oblige."

But Rutledge didn't want to share a house with anyone. Not when he couldn't be sure when the nightmares would come—when the war returned and he woke shouting to his men or to Hamish. "Perhaps a more public place would be better. I often come and go in the small hours, and it would disturb the family."

Neville regarded him doubtfully. "The only other possibility is here, in East Dedham," he said slowly, as if he couldn't bring himself to lie but would have preferred not to tell the truth.

"Then I'll take you back to the police station, and find a room there. Where is it?"

They hadn't passed it in their travels.

"Down that lane," Neville said, pointing. "It's a pub. But there are rooms upstairs. The Sailor's Friend, it's called."

He'd stayed in pubs before.

Neville began to open his door. "I can walk from here, if you like."

"It's no trouble," Rutledge said, and let in the clutch. He had no wish to find Neville loitering in the vicinity.

The winter day was closing in by the time Rutledge got to the Captain's house. It was darker under the trees than it had been in the open. He'd have preferred to be there a little earlier, but on the Downs there were few places to conceal his presence if he lingered in the dusk for another hour. What's more, he wasn't familiar enough with the comings and goings in East Dedham to be certain he wouldn't be discovered. The last thing he needed was to be reported to Constable Brewster, drawing attention to what he was planning to do.

After taking his torch from the boot, he left his motorcar in the shadows of trees some distance from the gates and walked back to the drive.

Hamish said, "'Ware. There might be dogs."

Rutledge answered him: "I saw none when I was there."

"Still."

As he went up the drive, he could see that lamps had already been lit in the house. He approached warily, for the drapes had not been drawn in a small, elegant room. The walls were a pale blue, the trim was white, and there was a fire on the hearth. Keeping to the shelter of the rhododendrons in the plantings by the house, he moved closer.

Pausing just outside, he could see the Captain pacing the floor. Someone came to the door of the room, and he stopped in midstride, spoke to whoever it was, and waited until the door had closed. Then, instead of pacing again, the Captain strode over to the hearth and stood with his hand on the mantelpiece, looking down into the flames. Rutledge could see the ruddy glow of the fire on the man's face.

Curious, he was tempted to stay and watch a little longer, but it would not do to be caught there, peering in windows.

He moved away again, and rounding the house at a little distance, he soon found the small horse stable at the back of the kitchen garden, separated from it by a tall hedge and a half-dozen apple trees. Almost at once he realized that there would be a problem opening the large double doors without making enough noise to alert the household that someone was poking about. And yet this was the best way to test the theory that Wright had come here in the dark and no one had seen him or heard him.

Working slowly and carefully, he got the door open wide enough to step inside, and shielding the torch with his hand, he cast the light around the empty interior. There *was* a bicycle at the far end, leaning against a bale of rotting straw, but on closer examination, he realized that it was rusted and probably hadn't been used in years. Too small for a man, it had probably belonged to one of the Standish sons when they were young.

He looked around the stable but found nothing else of interest. If Wright had come here and taken the motorcar, he'd done it with the same stealth as Rutledge, except for finding a way to open the outer doors wide enough to drive through. But if that storm was coming up, with any luck it would have covered any strange sounds from the back garden. Especially if Mrs. Donaldson was a sound sleeper.

He flicked off the torch and stepped outside again. The wind had picked up. He stood for a moment looking at the house as he pulled up the collar of his coat. He could see that the windows of the servants' floor looked in that direction, but the trees and the hedge, designed to shield the house from the sight—and smell—of the stable, had grown tall enough to hide any intruder, even winter bare as they were. But how had Wright known that the Captain didn't keep a dog? Most people living in the countryside did. Had he come here before that night to reconnoiter?

Rutledge discovered as he started back in the direction of the house that a rough track had been put in, circling the hedge and the trees. He'd come the opposite way round the house and had missed it. Following it, he saw that it connected with another track that debouched onto the road some thirty yards from the gates. That would explain why the cook hadn't heard the motorcar leaving.

He still didn't know how Wright had reached the house.

Making his way back to the gates, he tried to shut out Hamish in his head.

"Ye know the how. But no' the why."

The moon had risen, shining down the road now. Rutledge had almost reached his motorcar when he realized that something was wrong. The dark shape was more settled on one side than the other, and even leaving it close in by the trees didn't explain the difference.

He didn't need Hamish to tell him what had happened.

While the motorcar had been standing in the road unattended as he walked into the grounds of the house, someone had come along and punctured one of the tires. He shone the torch on it, and saw that the puncture was well above the tread, deliberate, with no intent to conceal the damage by choosing to cut on the side half hidden by the trees.

He swore.

Hamish said, "Be grateful he didna' slash all four."

It was no consolation.

Rutledge was adept at changing his tires. Driving the rutted, uneven roads of England had seen to that. It was the responsibility of each parish to keep roads in passable condition, but the war years had put paid to proper upkeep—there was no money and no workmen to see to it.

He moved the motorcar to a flatter stretch of ground, on what he judged to be a fairly sound patch of earth. Still, he watched the jack wobble dangerously in the omnipresent ruts. He waited for it to decide to grip or sink, and it finally appeared to plumb into harder soil beneath it.

He finished replacing his tire, and then more closely examined the damage on the one he'd removed. Deep and very efficient. And manmade. He folded up the cloth that had kept him reasonably clean as he worked, wiped off the tools he'd used, and stood back.

It might have been an act of sheer vandalism. Most especially if word had got round that he represented the Yard and was looking into the Rector's death. Someone who simply resented a police intrusion into the quiet world in which he lived?

It was possible. Even the sleepiest villages held secrets.

By the same token, it could have had other ramifications. A warning, a way to slow the pace of the inquiry, or just a bloody-minded attempt to distract him.

But why here—all but on the doorstep of the man whose motorcar had killed the Rector? When he, Rutledge, was already inside?

He found a rag to clean his hands, looking at them ruefully afterward. It hadn't done much good.

Hamish, who had been hovering at his shoulder throughout his work on the tire, seeming to be intrigued by it—he was a Highlander, he'd had no motorcar of his own—startled him by saying softly in his ear, "There's a watcher."

Rutledge began to fold the rag, walking purposefully back to the boot.

"Where?"

"Twenty-five paces left, past the log."

He dropped the rag into the boot and stretched his shoulders, letting his gaze sweep the thin wood on this side of the road. Hamish had always had very good hearing and vision. If he said someone was there, then someone was.

The log was large enough that he found it easily where it lay rotting in the deeper shadows of the woods. Even as he spotted it, Rutledge thought he saw something move just behind it.

He let his gaze drift on, sliding up into the trees, in no particularly hurry, then he turned and shut the boot. He debated whether this was the vandal, waiting to see how his handiwork had succeeded, and then decided against it. And now he was curious. Walking back toward the bonnet, he said, raising his voice only a little, "Want to come and have a closer look? I don't bite."

There was silence. He thought he caught a bit of consternation in it, and stood with his back still toward the trees as he reached over with his elbow to buff an imaginary spot on the gleaming dark red paint.

As he moved on toward the crank, still not looking back, he heard the light thrash of dry weeds and stalks as someone else moved as well.

He tensed, but made a point of appearing to ignore the sound and reached for the crank with no intention of turning it. Out of the corner of his eye he saw a thin, tallish boy in coveralls, a coat too large for him, and a battered straw hat covering short, straw-colored hair. He was carrying a sack of what looked like potatoes. Twelve, possibly? No more than thirteen, not less than ten.

Straightening, he said, "Hallo, there. Want to see how it's done?" He grinned on purpose and turned toward the figure that had stopped at the edge of the road.

They stared at each other for a few seconds.

The boy said gruffly, "I don't deal with strangers."

"Ah," Rutledge said, keeping his voice bland, showing only some little surprise. "Smart, that. Where do you come from?"

He didn't answer. Rutledge thought, possibly from one of the tenant farms on Standish's land or a neighbor's. The clothes the boy had on were clean enough but worn. There wasn't a lot of money about, then. Or—perhaps not a tenant's child but one of the farm laborers one of them employed.

"Someone messed about with my tire," he said, thoughtful now. "Not you, surely. But I wonder if perhaps you'd seen anyone here, around the motorcar."

The silence had a different texture, as if the boy had seen someone but either didn't know who it was or didn't want to give a name.

"Well. I must go." He bent toward the crank. The boy sidled up the road toward him for a better view. "It's not easy, you know," Rutledge went on instructively. "Catch it wrong and it will break your arm for you. Ever had a broken elbow?"

"One of my brothers fell out of the apple tree and broke his arm."

"Painful, that. How many brothers do you have?"

"Two. They were killed in the war. There's only me, now."

He straightened, looked at the boy again, and said, "I am sorry. Hard for you, hard for your parents."

"My father's dead too. I'm the man of the house now. Are you going to turn that thing or not?"

Rutledge laughed. He reached down, caught the crank just right, and the motor turned over. Folding the crank away, he said, "Looks easy. But it takes practice. You can tell the other lads you've seen how it's done in London."

"London?" the boy said sharply.

"Yes. That's where I live."

"Then why are you here, in Sussex?"

"Calling on Captain Standish."

"Oh."

"While we were exchanging a little news, someone punctured that tire." He gestured with his hand toward the right rear. "That's why I asked if someone was mucking about here when you came along."

No answer.

"Hmm." He opened the driver's door. "Shall I offer to drop you somewhere? Or are you close enough to walk home?"

"I told you. I have nothing to do with strangers."

"Right, then." He hesitated. "My name is Rutledge. Just in the event your mother asks who kept you. Good evening."

He had put one foot into the motorcar when the boy came forward again. It was clear he was torn between seeing more and remembering his mother's warnings against strangers.

And in the same instant it occurred to Rutledge that this lad, possibly mad about motorcars, with no way to own or even look over one, might know something more, if it were possible to dig out the answers he wanted.

"All right, then. A compromise. I left my driving gloves at the house. I must walk back to fetch them. As long as you don't touch anything, you can look at the motorcar. Fair enough?"

The boy stood his ground, glaring.

Rutledge ignored him, shoved his gloves into a pocket without the boy seeing, and started back toward the drive.

The boy didn't move—Hamish would have warned him—until he himself was well out of sight. He circled back toward the far corner of the low wall, where he could watch what the lad would do, taking his own stance behind the thick trunk of a tree, from which he could observe without being spotted. For the boy kept casting quick glances toward the drive even as he circled the vehicle, touching this, touching that, but always with care.

He leaned in Rutledge's door, which he'd purposely left standing wide, and saw the little mirror on the windscreen, paused, put his knee on the driver's seat, and looked right into it for a moment, before brushing his grubby hands over the smooth leather. Lightly, almost with a caress. Then, startled by something, he backed out of the door.

Satisfied that the boy had had ample opportunity to do more damage, if he'd been the vandal, Rutledge worked his way back to the drive.

When he came through the gates a minute later, slapping his leather driving gloves against his palm, he found the lad standing where he'd left him, as if he hadn't stirred.

With a nod, he walked on to the motorcar and got in. As he did, the boy shifted his weight a little, and Rutledge saw the slim ankles in the old, heavy shoes that had belonged to someone else.

He remembered the caressing touch on the leather of the seats, the brief stare into the small mirror.

Was the lad actually a girl? Even in the moonlight, it was hard to tell.

And that presented something of a problem. A boy could find his way home—he must often ramble far afield in search of adventure or at least respite from his chores. Rutledge had a qualm about driving away and leaving a girl there.

Not after the tire had been cut by person or persons unknown.

He looked at the child again, uncertain. She, if she were a she, played the part well.

He said, "I've a long drive ahead of me. But not so long that I can't drop you at the end of your lane. In London, it would be thought discourteous not to ask."

For an instant, yearning loomed in the child's eyes, and was ruthlessly squashed.

"I know," he said with resignation before the lad could speak. "I'm a stranger. But you do know my name, after all, and you know I called on Captain Standish. And that I'm from London. Enough to scrape acquaintance for five minutes of driving?"

The temptation was too much, and that worried him. The child was desperate to ride in the big London motorcar, torn about her mother's strictures—and he understood them very well, now—possibly even fearing a whipping if the news got home somehow.

If not Rutledge's motorcar, someone else's might come along . . .

He said, intentionally harshly, "Look, my lad, I'm being kind. Nothing more. And you might as well know one other thing about me. I'm a policeman. Scotland Yard."

The expressive eyes, dubious and beginning to send signals of flight to the limbs, stared at him.

"Constable Neville can vouch for me." He let in the clutch, allowed the motorcar to move a few inches. "Come along. Or not, as you like."

She was across the road like a rabbit, before his hand could touch the brake. He leaned across and opened the passenger door, listening to the growl of disapproval from Hamish, just behind him.

Leaping in with that boyish grace, she settled in the seat without looking at him, waiting for him to drive on.

He was suddenly amused. Her theory of safety was that he could do her no mischief as long as he was fiddling with the mysteries of driving. Amusement passed into pity.

"What's your name, lad?" he asked, watching her face as she leaned into the movement of the motorcar.

"Jim," she said roughly.

"You mentioned strangers. See many of them about, do you? I'm looking for a friend of mine—he drives a green motorcar. I'd planned to have lunch with him today, but he was late and I couldn't wait any longer."

He slowed and threw the motorcar into reverse, surprising a smile and buying himself a little time.

She said, "A few strangers come this way. Usually they're lost. I haven't seen another motorcar today. Not even a green one."

There was the slightest emphasis on *motorcar,* as if she had seen someone on foot or a bicycle.

"Who was passing by as you came along?"

She shrugged. "I don't know. A man."

"What did he look like?"

She shrugged again. He wondered if she had stayed well back, worried about being seen and discovered.

He purposely gunned the motor, sending the big touring car leaping down the road, and she hastily suppressed a squeal of surprise and delight. And then she was jabbing her finger toward a lane just ahead, turning off to his right, and she was out of the door as soon as he'd slowed enough for her to get down safely.

Sack in hand, she bucketed down the tangle of dry weeds and brambles that filled the overgrown lane, and vanished around a bend that made him wonder if she would stop just out of his sight and look back. If only to be sure he'd not try to follow.

He drove on, giving her a brief salute from the horn before disappearing from her line of sight.

She was safe enough now. At least he thought it very likely. From two older brothers, never mind that they were buried in France, she had learned well how to be man of the house.

He drove on. Jim. Jem? Jemima? Beatrix Potter, Jemima Puddle-Duck. Quick thinking, that. Or had she been named for the story? It was very popular.

It didn't matter. Someone would know.

Rutledge stopped at the police station in Burling Gap, on the off chance that Neville was still on duty. But there was only the small night lamp burning on a table by the door.

However, light shone from the windows of the house next door, indicating that someone was at home, and he knocked. They would surely know where to find the constable.

The man himself answered the summons, surprised to see Rutledge standing on the doorstep, saying with alarm, "Is there anything amiss, sir?"

"No, sorry, I've been driving through the countryside to learn the roads. How many men can you raise to search for a missing bicycle?"

"Missing?" he repeated. His suspenders were down, his shirt open. Wafting from the kitchen in the back of the house came the smell of frying sausages and potatoes. It reminded Rutledge that he hadn't eaten since breakfast.

"If Wright took the motorcar, he didn't walk all the way there. There must have been a bicycle. Where is it?"

Neville looked back in his memory, then said, "There wasn't one in the stable, sir. Well, not one anyone could use."

"Then where did Wright leave it?"

Neville cleared his throat. "I'll have a half-dozen men out in the morning. We'll search the park at the house, and any rough land around the village. But, sir, we still can't be sure how the Rector knew the motorcar was there and the Captain wasn't. It's a long way to go on the off chance that he could take the motorcar without being caught. Mrs. Donaldson is a fragile link."

"He wasn't likely to stumble across it. He had to know where to look for it," Rutledge agreed.

"I'll send word to Constable Brewster if we find anything. Is there anything else, sir?" Suddenly aware of his suspenders, Neville pulled them back in place. A woman's voice called from the nether regions. Neville flushed. "My neighbor offered me dinner. I had nothing in the larder, and I accepted."

Rutledge had intended to ask about the child he'd met, but almost at once thought better of it. There were other ways of finding out, and the last thing he wanted to do now was draw attention to her presence on the road or what she might or might not have seen. The woman in the kitchen could be a gossip.

"No. Go and enjoy your dinner. Good night."

On his way back to the pub, Rutledge heard Hamish stir in the rear seat of the motorcar, where he usually sat while Rutledge was driving.

Or so it seemed, when the voice spoke in his head. He often felt that he need only turn a little to see the dead man sitting there. But of course that was nonsense. And yet, driving alone in the night, he could almost feel the presence at his back, the deep Scots voice itself had such reality to him.

"Yon Rector," Hamish was saying. "It's no' in his character to take another man's property just for a lark. But it wasna' a sudden decision— he must ha' planned it verra' carefully. What drove him to do sich a thing?"

"A good question," Rutledge answered aloud, then swore. Yet it was a habit he'd found very hard to break. "If he was meeting someone else, who was it?"

"It might be as well to ask yon housekeeper if there was anything that worrit him."

"I'll call in at the rectory."

But it was far too late for that. Mrs. Saunders had either gone early to bed or left for her sister's house before it grew dark, for there were no lamps lit in any of the rooms that he could see as he turned in by the church. In the moonlight, he glimpsed gravestones in the churchyard, outlined by the pale light. Their familiar shapes marched in irregular rows across the grass, punctuated here and there by bulkier darkness where a handful of table tombs reminded him of tanks in the company of infantry. And then a shadow moved across the face of the moon, casting the graveyard into darkness. After a moment, he reversed and went on down to the pub.

The corner room he was shown to was adequate—large enough not to be claustrophobic, one window overlooking the back garden and the other with a partial view to the street. He nodded to the middle-aged man who had taken him to have a look at it, and asked, "Do you serve dinner?"

"Yes, sir. Pub fare, you understand." He was apologetic. "The kitchen is still open."

Thanking him, Rutledge washed his hands, cleaned the mud from his shoes, and went down to the small dining room. It had been separated from the bar by a thin partition, and he could hear the drone of conversation and laughter from the other side, although not the words.

A couple sat at a table across from the door, older, dressed for an occasion, for she was wearing a pretty cameo pin in the frothy lace of her collar, and her hat was trimmed in fur, but of a style that was prewar. His collar was stiff and new. Next to the partition, two commercial travelers had their heads together, talking earnestly. Rutledge chose the table by the window, farthest from the drifting tobacco smoke, heavy and stale, that also found the partition no hindrance.

A woman came out from the kitchen and greeted him, handing him a menu. He thought she might be the wife of the man who'd shown him his room, for she was about the same age and she wore a wedding band.

"I'm Josie," she added with a smile. "Would you care for anything from the bar?"

"Not tonight," he said.

"Then I'll leave you to make your choice."

Both of them turned as the door opened and a well-dressed woman stepped in and looked around at the other diners. She hesitated as if uncertain what to do.

Josie said brightly, "We're busy tonight," and went to greet her, showing her to the table across from Rutledge.

"I'll just have tea at the moment," the newcomer said in response. When Josie had disappeared through the kitchen door, she sat back, trying to appear at ease.

Waiting for someone, Rutledge thought, and uncomfortable at being the first to arrive. She was quite attractive, wearing a dark blue walking dress with a white collar. It appeared to be the latest fashion. A pert hat was set on her carefully arranged dark hair. Slender, an educated voice, blue eyes.

Not the sort of woman who was likely to be staying at a pub, or was even accustomed to dining in one.

When her pot of tea came, she poured it, then looked up, a tentative smile on her face that quickly faded as the man who had shown Rutledge to his room stepped in and went to the table where the commercial travelers were seated. He said a few words, the younger of the two nodded, and he withdrew, shutting the door after him.

Rutledge had given his order and was halfway through his vegetable soup when the woman across from him got up, stepped out of the dining room, then after a few minutes returned. Josie, carrying a fresh pot of tea to the older couple, stopped and asked the woman if she was ready to order. With obvious reluctance, she did.

He had finished his gammon steak and was drinking the last of his tea when his neighbor summoned Josie and asked for her bill. She had only toyed with her food, pushing it about her plate in a pretense of eating, and now abandoned it entirely.

"No pudding, miss?" Josie asked. "There's a nice treacle tart and an apple crumble with custard." She received only a shake of the head in reply.

Rutledge had already settled his account and left the dining room before the woman, waiting impatiently, had dealt with her own.

Not ready to go upstairs, he opened the pub's outer door and stared up at the blackness of the night. The clouds had moved on, and in their place, the stars were sharp pinpoints of light arcing over his head. How many times had he stood watch in the trenches before a dawn attack and watched these same stars cross the sky? With the thought he felt Hamish stir, and he moved quickly away from the memory and the door, nearly colliding with the woman from the dining room, who had come up behind him.

"My apologies," he said, stepping aside.

She gave him an absent smile, then stood in the doorway herself, as if uncertain what to do next.

A man dressed in the uniform of a coachman came out of the darkness, startling her. "The carriage is this way, miss," he said with a little nod of his head. And still she seemed to hesitate. Then, as if coming to a decision at last, she stepped briskly out into the night, following the coachman.

Intrigued, Rutledge watched her go. Who had she been expecting? Hamish answered him. "Rector? Or yon Captain?"

Rutledge remembered something Constable Neville had said. That the Captain had ridden to Brighton with a friend in her carriage.

He turned and went back to the dining room, catching Josie just by the kitchen door as she was carrying his dishes away.

"Could you tell me the name of the woman sitting just across from me?" he asked pleasantly. "I'm sure we met the last time I was in East Dedham," he added. "I think it must have been at the rectory. But for the life of me, I can't recall her name. Embarrassing, really."

Surprised, Josie set her tray on the tall stand by the door, uncertain how to answer him. "I don't know her, sir," she said. "She doesn't live in the village. I'm sorry."

He thought she was telling him the truth. "She doesn't come here often?"

"No, sir, I don't believe she's dined here before. I'd remember." She smiled deprecatingly. "I do think I've seen her a time or two on market day. She dresses so lovely."

She picked up the tray and disappeared into the kitchen beyond, leaving him standing there.

6

Later that night, Rutledge lay awake for some time, his thoughts too busy to settle into sleep. And Hamish was awake as well, but silent. Waiting. It was always a bad sign.

Rutledge reached for the glass carafe on the table by his bed and drank. The water was tepid, with the flat taste often found in country wells. Setting it back in its place, he went over his conversation with Stapleton.

After dinner, too restless to go up to his room, he had fetched his coat and gone out to walk. St. Simon's rectory was dark, as were many of the houses he passed, but there was a light on in the police station. He decided to speak to Constable Brewster rather than wait for morning and Constable Neville.

Brewster was surprised to see him. "Inspector. Is anything wrong?"

"I was walking off my dinner," he said, giving no particular importance to his question, "and as I passed the rectory, I found myself wondering who had taken over for Mr. Wright while he was in France."

Brewster tried to hide his relief that the question didn't demand immediate action. He said readily enough, "That would be Mr. Stapleton, sir. He had the living in a church in Seaford before he retired, and he was willing to fill in for Mr. Wright."

"Then he doesn't live in the village?"

"No, sir, he has a cottage on the road just outside of the next village over. He's a gardener, is Mr. Stapleton. The finest peonies you ever saw. Bred them himself. He gave my wife a few cuttings one year, and I was amazed when they bloomed. A red dark as blood. I'd never seen anything quite like it." He paused, his enthusiasm fading. "Are you thinking of going there tonight?"

It wasn't very late. Rutledge was already considering the possibility of calling on Stapleton, but he had no desire to take Brewster with him.

"I'm sure it's well past his bedtime. Tomorrow, perhaps. Thank you, Constable. Good night."

He left the police station and walked briskly back to the pub. Turning the crank of his motorcar, he listened to Hamish, an undercurrent in his mind, and tried to ignore the persistent, deep Scots voice.

Driving out of East Dedham, he found the next village, and just beyond the last cottage he saw a small sign posted at the head of a winding lane.

PEONY LODGE

That must be it, he thought, and turned down the lane.

The cottage was larger than most, just missing being described as a bungalow. There were flower beds—dormant now—leading up the path to the door, and more under the cottage windows.

Peonies, surely, Rutledge thought, as the beds had been mounded over and the summer's growth long since relegated to the compost heap. It was obvious how Stapleton spent most of his time, for the beds weren't small.

There was a light showing in the pair of windows to his left.

Leaving the motorcar on the lane, Rutledge got out and went to knock on the door. The man who opened it was nearly as tall as he was, his hair a thick, snowy white worn a little long, as if he had no time for barbers. He could, Rutledge thought, pose for a portrait of one of the apostles, with his strong nose and chin. But his blue eyes were still sharp, and he examined his visitor briefly before inviting him inside, after Rutledge had given his name and identified himself as Scotland Yard.

The front room of the cottage was large and comfortable, with old, well-polished furniture and a worn Turkey carpet on the floor, where the original rich dark reds and blues lingered in patches. A fire burned on the hearth, and a wooden tray standing on sturdy feet held the remains of Stapleton's dinner.

"Come in. I was just about to pour myself a small sherry. Will you join me?" He led the way to the pair of chairs by the fire.

"Thank you, I will," Rutledge replied, although he'd have preferred a whisky from the decanter on the tall bookshelf by an inner door. "I've come about Mr. Wright, as I'm sure you've guessed. You have heard about the accident with the motorcar?"

"Yes, sadly, I have. Let me find a second glass, and I'll be glad to help in any way I can." He collected his dishes and carried them into the kitchen.

Rutledge listened to the sounds as the dishes were set into the sink, then of a cupboard door being opened and after a moment closed again. He found himself wondering if Stapleton had suggested a drink in order to collect himself and decide how to answer whatever questions this man from London might ask.

He rose and went to the doorway leading into the tiny kitchen. Stapleton was just wiping a crystal glass.

"I understand you served at St. Simon's while Wright was in France."

Stapleton didn't look up. "Yes, I'd retired some years before, but when he came to tell me he felt he was needed in the trenches more than he was needed here, I agreed to take over St. Simon's for the duration."

"What sort of man was Wright?"

"Young. More than a little idealistic. I think that's why he was drawn to serving in the Army. Unfortunately, his wasn't a very pleasant war—he spent a good bit of it in a base hospital, attending the wounded and dying. And then he volunteered to go forward. I was never sure why. A testing of himself? Or a need to reach those in direst peril? He told me later that if he'd known what was in store, he'd never have left St. Simon's. Certainly he came back a chastened man, but in many ways a better priest. I was glad to turn the church over to him once more."

Stapleton set the glass on a silver tray, then led the way back to the chairs by the fire, where he took a second slim decanter from the bookshelf and poured each of them a generous sherry. He handed Rutledge his and left the decanter on the tray, an invitation for a second glass. Settling himself, he turned to his guest.

"No one expected the war to last four years. I'd found it arduous, the last year or so. Never did take to the bicycle. And the influenza epidemic was more demanding than I had the stamina for." Stapleton smiled wryly. "Emotionally and physically. It was as if the plague had returned, killing everything it touched. Man, woman, and child. I did what I could, I gave comfort to the dying and to the living, and returned the next day to find that the living had become the new patients, and it was all to do over again. The sexton was cut down in the first month, and we were hard-pressed to bury our dead. I fell into my bed at night, weary to the bone and knowing that I'd be summoned before the dawn to watch more of my parish sicken and die. The miracle was, I never caught the infection myself. I often wondered why."

"Do you think Wright was suicidal? That his experiences in the war weighed too heavily on him?" Rutledge asked as the man across from him sipped his sherry.

Stapleton addressed the question seriously, gazing into the heart of the blaze before responding slowly, "I don't believe he was. Deeply wounded, perhaps, but not suicidal." He turned back to Rutledge. "In some way I can't explain, the war had honed him, made him tougher and thinner and far less idealistic. I felt it, you know, the minute he came through the rectory door. I hadn't seen him in four years, and I hardly recognized him. And if he'd wanted to kill himself, there are other, less dramatic ways of doing it. Wright was not the flamboyant sort."

"Why do you think he was driving a motorcar that wasn't his?"

"I don't have an answer to that. But if someone had needed him, he'd have found a way to reach that person. If Captain Standish wasn't there to give him permission to take the motorcar, he'd have taken it and offered his explanation later."

"The staff was there." Only Mrs. Donaldson, but Rutledge didn't clarify his comment.

"Perhaps he saw that as a waste of time. If it were an emergency."

"What do you know about Captain Standish? Would he at some time in the past have given permission for Wright to borrow his motorcar for church matters?"

"I doubt it. The Captain seldom came to Sunday services if he could avoid it—or to any others, for that matter. I daresay he and Wright were hardly more than acquaintances. And of course he was in France during my tenure at St. Simon's." He frowned. "I don't care to pass on gossip. As a rule, I would say nothing. But in the circumstances . . ." He looked away for a moment, then turned back to Rutledge. "Rumor has it that Standish's war was no different from that of most officers at the Front. He returned to England tired and dispirited, but soon recovered enough that he went out and bought himself a motorcar. He even took it to France with him on a visit about a year ago. When he came back from Paris, he was a very different man. It wasn't well known, but he seldom drove anywhere after that. If he couldn't walk to his destination, he stayed at home, or someone came to fetch him. I'm aware of it only because he was asked to chair a charity event in which I was also involved, and he agreed only if a motorcar or carriage was sent to collect him."

"I'm told he was in Brighton when the motorcar was taken. He traveled in a carriage belonging to someone else. A woman. Do you by chance know who she is?"

"I'm afraid not." Stapleton shrugged wryly. "Gossip hasn't come my way on that subject."

"Tonight I encountered a young woman in a pub in East Dedham. Attractive. Fashionably dressed. Dark hair, blue eyes. She'd come in for dinner, and it was clear she was expecting to meet someone—or was looking for someone she thought might possibly be there. Whoever it was, he or she never arrived. She left in a carriage. Could it be the same woman? Or is there someone else in this part of the Downs who might fit her description?"

"I can think of a number of young women. But I have never heard their names linked with that of Captain Standish."

Rutledge leaned forward and set his glass on the tray. Choosing his words carefully, he said, "Certainly the Rector died as a result of the crash. That's not in dispute. What we have reason to suspect is that he was deliberately run off the road, with the intent to kill the driver. As a result, this has become a murder investigation."

Stapleton stared at him. "I was beginning to wonder at the direction of your questions. And I can tell you that Wright didn't drink more than the occasional whisky. I'm sure Mrs. Saunders can confirm that. If it wasn't drink, and it wasn't the storm—and it wasn't suicide—the alternative must be murder." He shook his head. "That's a very unpleasant thought to live with. Wright didn't deserve to die that way. In spite of the difference in our ages, I counted him as a friend."

"Nevertheless. Who might want to kill Mr. Wright? Or was he not the intended target?"

The blue eyes were fixed on Rutledge's face, and for a moment Stapleton said nothing. Then he answered slowly, "I don't know. I might surmise. What could have happened here, in East Dedham, after he came home from France in the spring of 1919, that might lead to murder? I can think of nothing—what I know from four years of ministering to the parishioners of St. Simon's tells me that the cause must lie elsewhere." He moved in his chair so that the firelight caught his profile, emphasizing the resemblance to an apostle. "Men in great pain, men in fear of dying, often try to clear their consciences by confessing. Setting the record straight as a final bid for God's mercy, fearing that they'll be facing him soon enough. As chaplain, Wright must have been privy to many last words. And sometimes a man who thought he was at death's door survives. What if he realizes that Wright could expose him?"

That made a certain kind of sense. If Wright had borrowed the motorcar to go quite a distance—as far as Hastings or Rye in one direction and Newhaven or Arundel in the other, to name towns along the coast without even considering those inland—he would surely have needed a motorcar.

But what had precipitated that need to travel? Had someone contacted Wright? Or had he somehow heard a name he recognized? Even made a decision at last to act on what he'd learned?

Rutledge said, "If someone contacted him, there might still be some record of it. I'll go to the rectory tomorrow and search Wright's papers."

"I should like to hear what you discover. For my own peace of mind, to be sure it isn't someone I know. I shouldn't care to think it is."

Rutledge took his leave shortly thereafter, thanking Stapleton for the sherry and his help.

As for himself, he had come away from Peony Lodge with very little. Except for the information about Standish. And the possibility that Wright's death was connected in some way to his war.

Had Wright somehow learned that Standish didn't drive now? Was that why he was so certain that he could borrow the motorcar and return it without anyone being the wiser? It was an interesting point. The inhabitants of a village the size of East Dedham generally knew their neighbors' business. Had that included what went on in the Captain's household? Had Wright turned that knowledge to his own advantage?

Rutledge drove back to the pub, dodging a flock of sheep grazing along the road. They were slow to respond to his presence or his horn, standing there gazing at him, their eyes bright in his headlamps, before ambling out of his path, some of them choosing the opposite way from the one he'd expected, as if secure in the belief that he wouldn't run them down whatever they did. It occurred to him that sheep also grazed on the headland where Wright had come to grief. Had they somehow played a role in the motorcar's crash? Had the Rector found himself with another motorcar behind him, relentlessly pressing him, and a farmer's flock of sheep searching for shelter in front of him? It could have happened that way. It might even explain why the accident was so deadly. There might have been no room to do more than swerve off the road, only adding to Wright's chances of losing control.

The outer door of the pub was still unlocked, and he climbed the long flight of stairs to his room. As soon as he shut the door, he found it stuffy in spite of the chill night, and somehow claustrophobic. But it was late now and there was nothing more he could do until the morning. And so he undressed and got into bed, only to find his mind refusing to rest.

He heard footsteps on the stairs and recognized the voices of the two commercial travelers as they said good night and went into their rooms. He hadn't realized that they were staying at the pub, and he stared at the ceiling until the small hours of the morning, afraid to sleep, afraid to dream, afraid to wake up screaming.

Instead, he turned down the lamp and lay there listening to the voice in his head, the voice of Hamish MacLeod, until he got up and crossed the cold floor to sit by the window, watching a cat hunting for mice in the kitchen garden. When at last it too gave up and trotted away, Rutledge felt a surge of loneliness so strong he turned from the window and went back to bed. But not to sleep.

Hamish was still waiting for him, there in the darkness. As he so often was.

Although Rutledge described the woman he'd spoken with last night, the local man, Constable Brewster, shook his head.

"Doesn't ring a bell, sir." Rutledge had caught him in the middle of a very substantial breakfast, and Brewster looked longingly at his meal, clearly hoping the man from London would be brief and finish while the eggs and sausages were still hot.

"Josie, at the pub, tells me she sometimes comes in on market day."

"Before the war, now, I could put a name to everyone who lived five miles in any direction. But it's not the same, is it? People come and go, even on the farms, and then there are the day-trippers, come to see the Beachy Head light or to picnic along the cliffs."

Even on the farms . . .

Rutledge took the opportunity offered to ask, "Can you give me the names of the tenants living on the Standish property? They should be asked if they saw anything the night the motorcar was taken."

"There are three families, sir. The Tomlinsons, the Meadowses, and the Fieldings."

"What else can you tell me about them?" he asked, ignoring the longing glance Brewster cast toward his breakfast.

"The Tomlinsons are older, two grown daughters, one helping on the farm, the other married and living near Petworth. Lost their son in the war. Mrs. Meadows's husband died of his heart, then her two boys were killed in the same tunnel explosion as young Tomlinson. There's only her youngest left to help her. As for the Fieldings, they have three sons, ages fourteen, sixteen, and seventeen. Just missed the war. A bit of luck there."

Men from the same village often enlisted and served together—and died together. Witness the Tomlinson and Meadows sons. The Fieldings were indeed lucky.

He wanted to ask how old Jem was, but there was no reason he could think of to put the question to Brewster. And then he saw an opening.

"Mrs. Meadows has only her youngest son to help her? How does she manage? I should think Standish would have no choice but to hire farm laborers to help her."

"He hasn't so far. Jem's a little girl. And a handful, from what I hear."

"In what way?"

"Stays away from school to help her ma, and then sometimes disappears for hours on end. Mrs. Meadows claims she's still grieving for her brothers. In my view, her mother's too busy to keep a proper eye on her."

"How old is this child?"

"Going on twelve."

He thanked Brewster and left him to his breakfast.

From the police station, he walked to the rectory. Pausing outside the churchyard, he looked up at the board, where black crepe had been draped.

ST. SIMON'S CHURCH
NATHANIEL B. WRIGHT, RECTOR

He wondered if the members of the Vestry had seen to that, or the housekeeper.

Mrs. Saunders, a scarf over her hair and a feather duster in hand, opened the door to his knock. He recognized her from Constable Neville's description. Removing his hat, he gave her his name and held out his identification. She barely glanced at it.

"My sister heard you'd come," she said, looking straight at him. "But I don't see how Rector's death should warrant sending for the Yard."

Keeping his voice kind, he said, "He was in a borrowed motorcar. Naturally Constable Neville felt he needed a senior officer to sort out what had taken Mr. Wright away in such weather. There appears to be—um—a jurisdictional problem."

She stood aside to allow him to step in. "Constable Brewster couldn't manage to thread a needle without help," she said, "although Rector would tell me not to speak ill of him or anyone else. Still . . ." She left the sentence unfinished and showed him into the parlor.

Whereas Constable Neville had been taken to the kitchen, Scotland Yard, he realized, counted as a guest. Or else, uncertain of his status, she had decided to be safe.

He stopped her at the door. "Perhaps I should step into Mr. Wright's study instead. I don't think he'd mind our borrowing it. After all, that must be where he spent most of his time."

"It's just as he left it," she said, defensive. "I'm not sure he'd care to have someone poking about in there."

"I didn't know him. The study will help me understand the man."

She turned, reluctant still, and led him down the passage to a large, bright room overlooking the churchyard. There was a massive Victorian desk set against one wall, low bookshelves on either side, within reach, and by the hearth stood several chairs where Wright would have counseled or comforted parishioners. Ignoring the desk, Rutledge took one of the chairs and asked her to take the other, but she shook her head, remaining standing.

"I've hardly been able to do my work," she said, putting the duster to one side. "People coming to offer condolences or bring food or even asking who should take the calls from the parish. I've written a letter to the Bishop. He'll be sending someone. But he hasn't told me when to expect him or if he'd be staying here. I've laundered the sheets and remade Rector's bed, but I'd rather whoever it is would take a guest room. I'm not ready to watch someone step into Rector's shoes."

He could understand how she felt.

"Tell me about Mr. Wright. Why did he feel his place was at the Front, and not here in his parish?"

"So many young men were rushing off to enlist. And then the casualty lists came in, and it was enough to make the angels weep. Rector read the accounts in all the papers, and it kept him awake at night. He told me he was praying over what to do, but sometimes his bed wasn't slept in, and I think he paced the floor more often than not. Then one morning, when he came down to breakfast, he told me he'd made up his mind and was going to ask someone to take over St. Simon's until he came home again. I was that shocked, I can tell you."

Stapleton had called Wright idealistic, and Mrs. Saunders had confirmed that.

"What did his Bishop have to say to his decision?"

"I don't think there was much he could say. War fever had the country in its grip, and everyone was rushing about wanting to do their bit. And of course there was someone willing to step in."

"It's part of police procedure. I have to ask: Did Mr. Wright have any enemies?"

"I wish you wouldn't call him that," she said, and he could hear the tears in her voice.

"I understand," he answered gently. "Did the Rector have any enemies?"

"Not that I'm aware of," she said stoutly, defending him.

"Perhaps I should ask instead if there was anything that worried the Rector? Anyone he was concerned about. Anyone who took a dislike to him?"

She considered the question. Then she said, "I spoke to Constable Neville. I told him what I know. Surely you've asked him?"

"I have, but Constable Neville is a Chapel man. You knew the Rector as well as anyone in East Dedham. I can count on you to tell me the truth."

That worried her, his suggestion that there might be whispers neither she nor her sister had heard. As he'd hoped it might.

"How well did Mr. Wright know Captain Standish?"

"By sight, of course. Everyone knows who he is. But the Captain seldom came to services after his mother died, and then only out of a sense of duty."

"They weren't friends, they never got together from time to time to remember France? I've been told that many soldiers find it easier to talk about the war with each other, rather than with family or friends who weren't out there."

"Rector never spoke of his time in France to anyone, that I know of. I can't say for certain that they never met for a pint or two, but I'd be hard-pressed to remember an occasion when they might've. Rector had many calls on his time; he seldom enjoyed the freedom of doing something for himself."

A man who buried himself in his work, to forget? Stapleton had brought that up.

"What did he do, when he needed to renew his own reserves?" When she looked blank, he added, "Did he collect stamps? Grow roses? Tramp the district looking for rare birds?"

She stared at him as if he'd lost his mind. "Rector wasn't a frivolous man. When he had an evening to himself, he read." She gestured to the books on the shelves behind him. "He was a great reader. It showed in his sermons. They were very uplifting."

He tried another direction. "Was there anyone he counted as a friend? A confidant? A woman, perhaps, he felt close to?"

Her lips thinned with disapproval at the question. "St. Simon's was Rector's life. He wasn't one to have friends calling in every other week, distracting him. And if there was ever any gossip about Rector and a woman, I never heard it."

It was clear to him that Mrs. Saunders considered Wright something of a paragon of all virtues. In Rutledge's experience, this was often the way housekeepers viewed their unmarried charges. She took pride in what must have actually been his loneliness, because he was there to serve and not to live like ordinary men. She was the gatekeeper, the protector of his privacy, and as such, it must have given the Mrs. Saunderses of the world a status of their own.

Changing the subject, he said, "Did you cook dinner for the Rector?"

"I did. Even on my day off, that's to say Thursdays, I'd leave something for his dinner."

"Did he sometimes choose to dine at the pub, instead?"

Yesterday was Thursday, and the young woman who'd come to the pub was expecting someone to arrive . . .

"Not often. It wasn't a regular thing."

Then perhaps Wright was not the man the woman had come to see after all.

"Was there anyone else who seemed to seek out Mr. Wright, someone who perhaps upset him?"

"Now that you mention it, there *was* a man some months ago who came to the door asking for a handout. I was in the kitchen garden, fetching vegetables for dinner. I didn't know Rector had come in, and he went to the door himself before I could get there. I couldn't hear what was said, but as he was shutting the door, I asked, 'A summons?' Thinking I'd be holding his dinner for him. And he said no, just a poor ex-soldier needing a little money. But he looked ill, and I asked if he was all right. He said that it hurt him to see men who'd fought for England reduced to begging. And he went into his study, shutting the door."

"Did you see this ex-soldier?"

"No, but Rector has—had—a soft heart when it came to ex-soldiers."

"Had he reacted like this before, when someone came begging to the door?"

"I usually answer the knocker. I try—tried to take some of the burden from Rector." Suddenly, she turned away from him and bit her lip. "I don't quite know—I can't seem to come to grips about it. That he's gone. Or what's to happen next. No one's come to tell me. Still, I go about my duties as I always did. Rector would want that."

"I'm sure he would," Rutledge replied gently. He was about to ask her for permission to go through the Rector's desk, looking for anything that might be useful. But before he could begin, there was a loud knock at the door.

Mrs. Saunders looked at him almost in a panic. Then she stood up and walked resolutely out to the passage. Rutledge followed, standing in the shadows by the study as she opened the door.

There was a man in a clerical collar on the walk, his hat in his hand, his suit of clothes well made and well pressed. She stepped back as if he'd struck her.

"I'm Jonathan Barnes; I've been sent by the Bishop to take over Mr. Wright's work while decisions are made as to the future of St. Simon's." He looked at the small square of paper in his other hand. "Mrs. Saunders, I expect? The rectory housekeeper?"

"Yes. Won't you come in?" As he stepped past her, she remembered Rutledge, and in that same instant, Barnes saw the other man standing in the shadows. He said, "I'm sorry. I didn't know someone else was here." He came forward, not waiting for her to answer, and held out his hand. "Barnes's the name. And you are?"

"Inspector Rutledge, Scotland Yard. I'm looking into the events surrounding Mr. Wright's death."

Barnes frowned. "Yes, very unfortunate. I understand the Rector had not been given permission to take out the Captain's motorcar."

"That's the general assumption. We haven't determined whether that's true or not." Out of the corner of his eye, he saw Mrs. Saunders standing stoically by the open door, the cold wind moving her skirts slightly as she suddenly remembered the scarf over her hair and reached up to remove it, smoothing the strands that were out of place.

Barnes said, "The Bishop is of course very much interested in the outcome of your inquiry."

"I'm sure the Yard will see to it that he has a full report."

Barnes tugged at the lobe of his left ear. It was not the answer he'd expected.

Rutledge had taken a dislike to him. The man had shown the housekeeper no courtesy, expressed no sympathy for the loss of the man she had served faithfully. Instead, he'd walked in as if the rectory was now his and changes were in the wind. His fair hair, smooth as a cap on his head, looked as if he'd used macassar oil to keep it rigorously in place. His eyes, a dull gray, held no warmth, only a sense of his own importance.

Rutledge said, "I was just in the Rector's study, about to ask permission to look through his desk. I'm sure Mrs. Saunders will be happy to see you to the guest room."

She opened her mouth as if to object on two counts, then she must have decided that if anyone was to go through the Rector's desk, it was better for the man from London than this interloper.

"This way, sir," she said to Barnes, and started toward the stairs.

Barnes said, "I think I should be present while Mr. Wright's desk is opened."

Mrs. Saunders turned to Rutledge, panic in her gaze.

He smiled. It was cold. "This is a police matter, I'm afraid. If there is anything of importance, you will of course be informed."

It was Barnes's turn to object, but he thought better of it and with a curt nod followed the housekeeper up the stairs.

Rutledge took that as permission and returned to the study. He looked at the Rector's diary first, for it sat on the blotter, where he must have left it.

Going back several weeks, Rutledge looked for any reference to Standish.

Nothing. But he put the diary into his pocket and moved on to the main drawer of the desk. He found a ledger, a number of accounts, and a few letters from friends. He pocketed the latter as well. The other drawers offered little of importance until he reached into the back of the last one on the left. His fingers closed around a bundle wrapped in a soft felt, and he knew at once what it was, before he had drawn it out.

A service revolver. He debated unwrapping it, and decided against it, restoring it to the drawer.

He himself had kept his own revolver. It was his, after all, not Army issue. And it was there for the day—or night—when his own war was more than he could cope with.

Had Wright felt the same way? Or was the revolver only a souvenir? Had Wright ever used it in anger? Or need?

Rutledge could hear footsteps on the stairs, and he shut the drawer, rose, and was moving toward the door when Barnes came into the study, Mrs. Saunders at his heels.

"Any luck?" the man asked, and there was an avidity in the question, as if he'd hoped for a *yes* that would resolve the little matter of taking a motorcar without permission.

"Only what one might expect to find in the desk of a busy man of the cloth." He nodded to Mrs. Saunders. "Thank you for your patience with my questions."

She stammered a "yes, sir" and followed him to the door. Barnes remained in the study, clearly eager to perform his own search.

At the door, Mrs. Saunders glanced quickly over her shoulder. "Was it helpful to you?" she asked softly.

"If you are asking if there was something Barnes shouldn't have seen, I don't believe there is. Mr. Wright either kept no secrets or kept them elsewhere."

She nodded, then quickly shut the door as if afraid Barnes might overhear their brief conversation.

He walked down the path, his mind on the revolver.

Hamish said, "He died in a crash, no' by his sidearm."

And yet . . .

Had Wright kept his for the same reason Rutledge had?

7

Neville was in, his own breakfast finished hours before. There was a woman with him, a kerchief over her fair hair, work-reddened hands holding a battered box.

"He broke it open and took my savings. Every bit that I'd put aside for three years. Then he walked out. He said he was going to London. But I don't think he did, I think he's in Eastbourne. I want you to find him and I want him taken up for what he's done."

He nodded curtly as Rutledge stepped through the station door-way, then his attention returned to the woman in the chair in front of his desk.

"Why do you think he's in Eastbourne, Mrs. Grant?"

"Because there's a woman. I know there must be. And he's with her." There was venom in her voice. "*She* put him up to this. I know she did. Find her and you'll find him. And maybe what's left of my money."

It took Neville several minutes to convince Mrs. Grant that he would pursue her husband and the unknown woman. He walked with her to the station door and saw her out. Then he turned to Rutledge.

"I don't doubt she took a hammer to that box herself. There's always another woman, in her view." He shook his head. "I don't know how Grant puts up with her. Well, to be fair, I expect she would say the same about him."

Rutledge took the chair Mrs. Grant had just vacated and said, "How large is Standish's property?"

"Sizable, sir. And he has three tenant farms as well."

"If anything happened to Standish, who is his heir?"

"I don't know. He must have drawn up a will when he enlisted."

"Who is his solicitor, do you know?"

"I expect it would be Edgecombe and Edgecombe. They handle most of the village business, including Rector's."

"Where can I find them?"

"On the other side of the greengrocer's." Neville hesitated. "Are you thinking that whoever ran Rector off the road thought it was the Captain who was driving?"

"We can't ignore the possibility. It was his motorcar, after all."

He thanked Neville and drove back to East Dedham. He found the greengrocer's shop easily enough. To one side of it was a door with a brass nameplate beside it announcing EDGECOMBE & EDGECOMBE, SO-LICITORS. He opened the door to find a staircase leading up to the first floor, where there was a small antechamber. It was tastefully furnished, the wallpaper a hunting print and the carpet on the floor a dark green that matched the wallpaper's background. Two windows looked out onto the street, and there were several chairs as well as two small tables.

To his surprise, the clerk who poked a head around the door to greet him was an older woman. She was slim and dressed in black, complementing her dark hair.

She smiled at his reaction. "Mr. Edgecombe's clerk is unwell, and I've stepped in while he's recovering. How may I assist you?"

He gave her his name and told her that he'd come about the accident to Captain Standish's motorcar.

"Yes, of course. Mr. Edgecombe will be with you shortly."

And she was gone. In a few minutes, a man leaning heavily on a silver-headed cane opened the inner door and said, "Hallo. I'm Edge-combe the younger. Won't you come back?"

Rutledge followed him down a short passage to a large room with glass-fronted wooden cabinets and bookcases almost cheek by jowl around the walls. There was a hearth at one end with several chairs before it, and at the other an oak partner desk that looked to be very old.

Edgecombe gestured to the chair in front of the desk and then sat down behind it. "You've met my mother. Henderson—my father's clerk for many years—has had a stroke, and we failed wretchedly at finding even a temporary replacement. She insisted that she could do at least as well as the most likely candidate, and by God, so she has."

"It doesn't shock your clients?"

"Good Lord, no, they've all known her socially for years. No surprise to find her helping out in here." He cleared his throat, indicating that he was shifting subjects. "We're in shock over the Rector's death. A real tragedy for East Dedham. I am his executor, and I'll be seeing to his services when the body is released. Is that why you've come?"

"The body is still in Dr. Hanby's charge. I'd like to know how the Rector's will stands."

"As a matter of fact, it's very simple. The greater part of his estate has been left to St. Simon's, in trust to be used as deemed necessary by the Vestry for the maintenance and upkeep of the fabric of the church." Edgecombe smiled. "He was in a position to know the need for such sums. Who better? He also has left bequests to Mrs. Saunders for her many years of dedicated service, to the sexton, and to the Lifeboat station."

Very simple, indeed.

"Has he made any major changes in the past five years?" It was an arbitrary number.

"Actually, this will was drawn up in 1910. Two years after he came to St. Simon's. When he informed me he was enlisting, I asked if he wished to make any changes, but he told me he was satisfied with it as it stood."

"And there is no one who might challenge his dispositions?"

"Not to my knowledge." The solicitor regarded him. "Why do you ask?"

"It's not unusual for distant relatives to appear after a death, challenging a will when the chief beneficiary is a church or some charity or other."

"I don't know that there are any relatives, distant or otherwise. The Rector never spoke of his family. And as far as I know, no one has come to visit him." He stared out the window for a moment, listening to a dog barking somewhere nearby. "There was a rumor—oh, some years ago—that he was engaged, but the young woman wanted no part of such an isolated church and he chose to remain at St. Simon's. I have no idea how reliable that rumor may be. I pass it on for what it's worth."

"His must have been a rather lonely life," Rutledge commented.

"As to that, I think he found the church to be his family. I do know that St. Simon's was his first church, and he was well liked from the start."

Rutledge recalled Neville's comment—that Wright was running from something.

"Where did he live before he came here?"

Edgecombe was at a loss. "I don't believe I ever knew. That's to say, I don't recall the Rector ever reminiscing about his childhood. Or his family. Nothing like 'I remember as a boy,' or even 'my father and I used to do this or that.' I never thought twice about it, assuming he'd grown up in a city. London, perhaps. One's childhood there wouldn't be the same as mine, here in the country. I expect we were all surprised when Wright decided to enlist. It seemed so out of character—he appeared to be dedicated to St. Simon's. Of course he was young enough to feel the call to arms quite strongly. So many of us did. Myself included."

There was an undercurrent of regret in his voice.

How many of the young men who rushed to enlist had felt the same way? And yet without them, Germany might have succeeded in overrunning France . . .

Rutledge brought his attention back to Edgecombe, who was saying, "Is there anything else, Inspector? I'm at your service."

"There are some irregularities in the crash that killed Wright. The police would be remiss if we didn't consider every possibility. For instance, why he borrowed the Standish motorcar without permission."

Edgecombe shook his head. "I have no idea what happened there. I can only speculate that it was an emergency, and Wright did what he had to do at the time."

"But what sort of emergency would have required a motorcar? His parish was within walking distance, or within range of the Rector's bicycle, for the outlying farms. Did he rush someone to hospital? Or was it a personal matter that took him elsewhere?"

"I—if he took anyone to hospital, I have yet to hear of it."

Hamish said, "He didna' ask what irregularities were discovered."

Rutledge moved in his chair but said as calmly as he could, "What if Captain Standish had been driving? Who would have inherited his estate?"

Surprised, Edgecombe said, "You know I can't tell you that. You must speak to the Captain."

"Did he draw up his own will before enlisting?"

"As a matter of fact, he did. I recommended it and so did the Army. But as it happened, he survived the fighting." He adjusted the edge of a folder on the dark green blotter.

"Since his return from France, has he spoken to you about reviewing the provisions or even making changes to them?"

"He has not."

Rutledge thanked him and left.

There appeared to be no problem with Standish's will. What about his war?

It had ended two years ago. But a wounded man with vengeance on his mind might have only just left hospital. There might have been difficulty tracing Standish. There might not have been an opportunity to act until now.

There was one way to learn about Captain Standish's four years in the trenches. Whether he'd served on a court-martial or had reported one of his men or was himself disciplined. Anything that might have followed him into civilian life. Rutledge had connections in the War Department, but it would take time to sift through mountains of files, and he needed an answer sooner rather than later, if he was to eliminate Standish from consideration.

And that was the difficulty—time.

Aside from anything lurking in Standish's past, it had been quite dark that Saturday night, a stiff wind blowing heavy rain. Wright was wearing his hat and an outer coat, very likely with the collar turned up against the cold. While an onlooker might have recognized the Standish motorcar, it would have been nearly impossible to be sure who was at the wheel. Still, a very natural assumption would be that it was the Captain himself. After all, the residents of East Dedham could have sworn that they had never seen anyone else driving it.

Returning to his room at the pub, Rutledge sat down in the only chair and read through the Rector's diary.

It covered the year 1920, for the most part listing various duties, meetings, and events. Marriages were noted, and births, christenings, deaths, illnesses, and troubled hearts. An accounting was given of each Sunday's collection as well as the contents of the poor box. Reading through what had been recorded each day, Rutledge could see that the Rector of St. Simon's was a conscientious shepherd to his flock. There was very little about the shepherd himself, except for a brief entry on 20 September of a headache after Evensong, and the comment, *I had hoped to be done with them.*

There was an odd comment on 26 September. *I wish—but there is no turning back.*

Rutledge made a note of both dates. Setting the diary aside, he turned to the packet of letters.

An invitation for the Rector to attend a chaplains' reunion in London. A letter from a woman thanking Wright for his care of her mother during her last days. Three other letters in a similar vein, gratitude for his care of the living and the service he'd conducted for the dead. And an envelope with no return address, only a postmark from Portsmouth. There was no letter inside. Rutledge looked among the other correspondence, hoping to find it. He was nearly certain that he hadn't overlooked it in the Rector's desk. He even went back to the other four envelopes to see if the missing letter had been misplaced, without any luck.

Why had Wright kept the envelope but not the letter?

The date of the postmark was 19 September. Was there a connection with the Rector's comments about his headache and the remark about wishing for something?

"Ye're leaping to conclusions," Hamish said, startling him.

"True," he replied aloud. "There's the chance that it was the Portsmouth address he wanted to remember—perhaps a reminder not to open another letter from there."

The remainder of the letters offered no further insight into Wright beyond indisputable proof that he cared for his flock and was loved in return.

When Rutledge had finished, he carefully recorded in his notebook the dates of importance in the diary, and slipped the empty envelope in the notebook as well. Then he put the diary and the other letters in the drawer of the desk, wishing for a key to lock it. Changing his mind, he took them out again and stowed them in his valise.

Wishing as well for a key to what might have decided Wright to take the Captain's motorcar without leave.

He went to find Constable Brewster, who had just stepped into the police station after his rounds.

"Hallo, sir," he said as Rutledge came to the door. "Anything I can help you with?"

"Do you remember any strangers in East Dedham since—let's say the end of August? Not holidaymakers or travelers. Someone who stood out in any way? Who might have asked directions to St. Simon's?"

"Easy enough to see St. Simon's without asking. But come to think of it, there was a man who came into town late one afternoon. Military carriage. Walked with a limp. Drove a motorcar, and left it by the pub. But he never stayed the night there nor et his dinner there. When next I walked past on my rounds, he had gone. Where he might have been between his arrival and his departure I can't say."

Another question for Mrs. Saunders, but not today, not with Barnes poking about. He had seen the man prowling through the churchyard early this morning, as if it was his duty to separate the damned from the saved. Wearing a black coat that flapped about his legs, hands behind his back, head thrust forward, Barnes reminded Rutledge of an egret stalking frogs in the shallows of a river.

As if he'd heard the thought, Brewster said, "There was a clergyman outside the rectory today. Stiffish-looking man, not like Mr. Wright at all. Do you think he's to stay until the church finds a replacement for Rector?"

"I'm afraid he is. I was there speaking to Mrs. Saunders when he came to the door."

"Ah," Brewster said, but Rutledge was almost certain he'd broached the subject because he'd seen the man from London go up to the rectory shortly before the Bishop's man arrived.

"Barnes is his name. I don't think Mrs. Saunders is very happy about it."

"No, poor soul, she's hardly taken in Rector's death. And a stranger to do for, one with different tastes and wishes, that will be hard to face."

Rutledge agreed but he said only, "Can you think of anyone else who might have been here in the past few months or so? Someone out of place?"

But Brewster shook his head. "A few ex-soldiers—or so they claimed—looking for work. A tinker, sent about his business before he could set up. A girl seeking to be taken on as a housemaid, but she had a sly look about her, and I asked the constable in Newhaven if he'd seen her. He told me she'd got off the train there, claiming she was looking for her sister. The greengrocer's van was setting out for Eastbourne, and I sent her on her way."

Constables were very good at knowing their turf, who was to be trusted and who wasn't, who was likely to make trouble and who was not. In most cases they could spot the miscreant better than someone coming into the village from the Yard or the nearest large city. And strangers would be noted, their comings and goings watched until they either were explained away or left without causing problems.

And yet, Hamish was pointing out, Brewster had not known the name of the woman who had dined at the pub, even though she had very likely come to market day several times, according to Josie.

He left the police station and walked on, thinking. He needed to speak to Mrs. Saunders again, but not in Barnes's presence. Short of lying in wait for her to leave the rectory to go to market, there was no way to encounter her by accident or design.

Curse the man for coming today.

He reached the outskirts of the village and turned back. Just as he came within view of the pub from the main road, Barnes appeared and walked briskly up the steps, disappearing inside. Lengthening his stride, Rutledge walked past the pub and made his way up to the rectory. He had no idea how long he might have, and so he went not to the front of the house but to the back.

A startled face looked out at him from a kitchen window, and then Mrs. Saunders opened the door to him. "What are you doing out there, sir?"

"I didn't want to encounter Barnes. I have several more questions for you. Do you remember if the Rector received any letters from Portsmouth?"

"No, sir, but I didn't always collect the post before he did."

Had Wright been expecting such a letter?

"And you're sure no stranger came to the rectory looking for the Rector?"

She frowned. "No one, sir. That's to say, if you don't count a man come to the door about the church organ. He wanted to have a look at it. It's not all that grand, but he asked if Rector could tell him about it. He thought his grandfather had built it."

"And they went over to the church?"

"I think Rector was reluctant, but yes, he walked over with him."

"How long did they stay in the church?"

"I don't know, sir. It couldn't have been very long, for I went into the parlor to water the sansevieria, and I saw Rector standing alone in the churchyard. I remember thinking he looked like a man carrying the weight of the world on his shoulders, and then he turned and walked toward the road. I don't know where he might have gone from there."

"When he returned to the rectory, did he mention the man? Or have anything to say about the organ—how fine the man thought it was, whether it needed work?"

"No, sir, he went directly to the study and shut the door. I always knew if the door was closed, he wasn't to be disturbed unless there was someone in desperate need of him. And so I left him to himself."

The front door of the rectory opened and closed again. They stood there listening, and heard footsteps climbing the stairs.

Mrs. Saunders said in a whisper, "He didn't fancy what I was preparing for dinner. He went to ask what the pub was serving tonight."

"He's in the guest room?" Rutledge asked. She nodded. "Does the guest room look down on the back of the house or the front?"

"The front, sir."

"Then I'll go the way I came. Thank you, Mrs. Saunders."

"He'll do," she said in an attempt to convince herself more than to persuade Rutledge. "It will just take time, won't it?"

Walking as far as the pub, he considered what Mrs. Saunders had said about the visitor interested in the organ. Was it a very clever way to get Wright out of the rectory, where they might be overheard? He would have given much to know what the two men had talked about.

I t was quite late, after midnight, when Rutledge heard voices raised in anger. Shaking off the last remnants of sleep, he realized that they were outside in the street, not in the passage beyond his door. He got up and went to the window. At first he couldn't see them, and then he caught a brief movement to his left. They were standing in the shadows there.

He could just pick out Constable Brewster's tall helmet. He was speaking to someone whose back was turned toward Rutledge, but the other voice was unmistakably a woman's. Even as he watched, she walked away a few steps, then turned back toward the constable. He could see her now, clutching her coat about her. The weather had changed with sunset and a cold wind was blowing out of the northeast.

She shouted something at the constable, and then walked on, her shoulders hunched. Brewster stared after her, then set out for the police station.

Rutledge stood at the window for several more minutes before going back to his bed.

As he was coming down to breakfast the next morning, someone stepped through the hotel doorway, and before he could close it again, the cold wind seemed to sweep through Reception in a gust. The newcomer looked up, saw Rutledge on the stairs, and shook his head. "Not a fit morning for man nor beast."

Rutledge smiled. "It's been long in coming."

"Indeed. I came from Portsmouth last night, and the motorcar's heater was all but useless. Damned near froze."

"From Portsmouth, did you say?"

"Aye." He was taking off his hat and coat, preparing to walk on toward the dining room.

"Know anything about church organs?"

The man stared at him as if he'd run mad. "Should I?"

"I was expecting someone who did."

"Ah. Not me, I'm afraid. Visiting my sister for a few days." And with a nod he walked on into the dining room.

When he was out of hearing, Rutledge stopped the man who'd shown him his room, and said, "The gentleman who just came in— he's in the dining room now—do you know who he is?"

"Yes, sir. He's a regular visitor. Mr. Davidson. His sister lives here in the village. War widow. He looks in on her from time to time. If you'll excuse me, sir, we're expecting a crowd. It's market day."

Finishing his own breakfast, Rutledge collected his coat and a scarf and went out into the wind. Men and women were busy in the tiny square in front of the pub, putting up tables and tents, anchoring them against the weather before setting up their stalls. One woman was just taking a tray out of a basket, and it caught his eye. The pattern, violets on a cream background, was quite lovely, and violets were a favorite of his sister's. Frances was busy planning for her wedding, spending much of her time shopping with the friends who would be her attendants. She would take pleasure in the fact that he'd thought about her. He stopped long enough to buy the tray, chatting for a moment with the stall's owner.

Like everyone in East Dedham, she knew who he was, and commented on the Rector's death as she was wrapping the tray for him. "Such a good man," she said, shaking her head. "And so young. A shame, really."

"I wonder what took him out on such a night?"

"I saw him out on the headland Friday, near the Belle Tout light," she said. "That was in the afternoon, before the rain came up. He was talking to a man."

Was he indeed? Rutledge said, "Someone from Gap village?"

She shook her head. "I couldn't see him well, but I didn't recognize him. I thought it might be a friend of Rector's. But they didn't part like friends. I don't know that I ever remember Rector losing his temper."

"Was the man on foot? Or did he come by bicycle to Belle Tout?"

"He must have been walking. But then I can't say for certain, because he might have left a bicycle up by the lighthouse. I'd come here to ask Constable Brewster about help putting up my stall. My husband hurt his foot, and I knew I couldn't manage it myself."

"Where did you come from?"

"Eastbourne. I have a little shop there, but I come to market days whenever I can. This time of year, visitors are thin on the ground at the seaside." She smiled ruefully as she handed him the tray, well wrapped in brown paper and tied with string. "Keeps the roof over our heads and food on the table."

He thanked her and moved on. Three women sat in another stall, wearing kerchiefs against the wind. They were selling items made from wool, mostly caps and scarves and mittens, some of them knitted in brighter patterns for the Christmas trade. Beyond, a woman was selling embroidered pillow slips, and an older couple offered jams, jellies, and small jars of honey, done up with colorful ribbons. In the corner stall a man with a large whetstone run by a foot pedal sharpened knives and tools.

Rutledge continued to wander among the stalls, where sausages and loaves of bread, cheeses and dried fruit, bits of wood worked into small toys or pretty boxes were all for sale. Mrs. Saunders was there buying sausages for her dinner. She looked more than a little harassed, as if Barnes's continued presence was making her life difficult. He was about to speak to her when he glimpsed the woman who had come to dine in the pub.

He changed directions just as she moved on, and when he came around the stall at one end of a row, she had vanished.

Swearing under his breath, he circled the outer rows of stalls, but there was no sign of her.

Where had she gone? The pub door had been within his line of sight at all times, and he was certain she hadn't slipped in there. One of the other shops? But she wasn't in the greengrocer's or the baker's, the dress shop or the stationer's. Rutledge even took the stairs to the solicitors' chambers, but Edgecombe & Edgecombe was closed for the day.

And then he saw her walking up to the churchyard, and he went after her, threading his way through the marketgoers with as much haste as possible.

He found her standing by a gravesite, looking down at the stone, her face sad. He waited by the marker for a PARSON DARBY, THE SAILOR'S FRIEND.

At length the woman turned to leave, and he stayed there until she had almost reached the low wall surrounding the churchyard before catching her up.

Touching his hat courteously, he said, "I'm sorry—but I believe we've met before. I thought I recognized you the other night at dinner in the pub. My name is Rutledge."

She regarded him. "Rutledge? I don't know anyone by that name."

"But surely we met at the rectory?"

"I'm afraid you're mistaken," she said coldly. "I've never been to the rectory."

"But you have just visited a grave—"

"My grandmother. She died when I was only three. It's none of your business, but she left me her jewelry, and so I often come to pay my respects." She started to walk on to the gate in the wall.

"I'm from Scotland Yard, investigating the accident that killed the Rector of the church just there," he said flatly.

This time she stopped and stared at him. "The Rector? But—I thought—was someone else killed?"

"Only Mr. Wright."

She was clearly upset. "I should like a cup of tea. Is there anywhere we could go?"

"The pub."

She shook her head. "No, not there. Wasn't there a tearoom once in the old lighthouse?"

"Belle Tout? I don't think it's there any longer. The building is der-
elict."

"Oh."

"My motorcar is at the pub. Eastbourne isn't far."

"Are you really from Scotland Yard?" she demanded.

He took out his identification and showed it to her.

"Oh. Then, yes, Eastbourne is fine."

They walked in silence back toward the market stalls. He realized
he was still carrying the tray he'd bought for Frances. When they
reached his motorcar where he had left it next to the pub, he looked up
at the sign. "The Sailor's Friend. I just saw a gravestone where a parson
was also called the sailor's friend."

"I don't know where the name came from."

Rutledge set the tray in the boot and then opened her door for her.
After the briefest hesitation, she got in, and he went around to turn the
crank.

When they were well out of East Dedham, climbing the Down
where the accident had occurred, she looked away, as if she couldn't
bear to see the scene.

"Where is your coachman?"

Startled, she looked across at Rutledge. "He's in East Dedham, on
the far side of the green. I told him to enjoy the market. How did you
know?"

"I was at the pub's door the night you went there to dine. I saw him
come up to you as you were leaving."

"Oh." She took a deep breath. "He was the one who told me that
Captain Standish's motorcar had had an accident over in the Gap. He'd
only heard that someone had died in the crash. I—I couldn't find out
who was in the motorcar—if someone had been injured. The Captain
would have been driving, surely. But no one in my village seemed to
know. And I didn't feel I should speak to the constable."

"Do you know the Captain well? Why not simply call at the house?"

"We were engaged, when he came back from France. And then

he went to Paris to meet some friends who also survived the war. But when he returned from his visit with them, he was very different. In fact, he asked me to release him." She was staring out her window, her voice low. "I would have felt—it would have been awkward. Surely you see that."

"You still love him?" It was more a statement than a question.

"I expect I do," she whispered.

"And that's why you came to market day?" He glanced at her. "In the hope of meeting him?"

"Not—meeting. I just wanted to see him, to know he was all right. Alive."

"And the other night, in the pub?"

She took a deep breath. "I sent him a message, asking him to meet me there. I told him I needed to speak to him. But he never came. I ordered a meal, and it might as well have been chalk I was eating. Still, I thought—it was possible that he had decided not to come, and in the end might have changed his mind." She stopped, then went on in a rush. "I was so ashamed. I only wanted to be sure he was all right, you see. Then it occurred to me that he was too badly hurt to come. And I didn't know what to do."

"Standish wasn't driving that night. The Rector had borrowed his motorcar."

She closed her eyes. "Oh, thank God." He could see tears on her lashes.

Rutledge gave her time to recover. And then they were coming down into Eastbourne. The sea was rough, gray, driven by the wind, and she shivered in the raw cold.

"The hotel—just there—the large white one. There's a tearoom."

He found a place close by to leave the motorcar and they hurried up the long walk to the main door. The tearoom—mostly glass and palm trees—was to one side of Reception, and Rutledge found a table for them by the windows.

After they'd ordered tea, he asked for a plate of sandwiches and pastries as well. While they waited for it to be brought, she stared out the window at the sea. He thought she was still feeling the shock of relief that Standish was alive. There was no one on the Promenade, and the bandstand looked forlorn. Even the tearoom was nearly empty. But the water was wind-whipped, whitecaps rolling in toward the strand, and a pair of gulls were patrolling the surf.

"I don't know your name," he said after a while.

She turned, surprised, as if she had expected him to know it. "Emily Stuart."

Their tea came, and when the woman serving them had left, Rutledge told her about the accident.

"He had no idea his motorcar was taken?" she said in surprise. "I find that hard to believe."

"He was away. In Brighton."

"Ah." She bit her lip. "There's someone else, then."

He didn't lie to her. "A woman drove him there in her carriage. I thought it might have been you."

"No. Sadly."

Standish had told Rutledge he was calling on the mother of a friend killed in the war, but it had been the woman's daughter who had collected him, and there was no way to know whether the mother or the daughter was the reason Standish had gone there. And so he said nothing about it to Miss Stuart.

"Why do you think he broke off the engagement?"

Shaking her head, she said, "It was sudden, unexpected. He came back from Paris, and I waited for him to come to see me. But he didn't. I was just about to write to him when he appeared at my door, unannounced. I was so glad to see him that I didn't realize at first that he wasn't himself. He looked tired, worn. I was chatting away, making plans, overflowing with happiness, and he interrupted me. I don't remember what he said next. I was so stunned. Something like, 'Emily, listen to me. Please. This isn't why I've come.' And all I could do was stare at him, thinking I'd said something that upset him. In the silence he said, 'I would like you to call off our engagement. It's better that way. I won't mind if I appear to be the villain. You can say whatever you like. But we aren't well suited to each other, Emily, and the sooner we face it the better for both of us.'"

Her voice nearly broke on the last words, and then she got herself under control, and went on angrily. "No explanation. I asked him if there was someone else, and he swore to me there wasn't. I don't know whether I believed him or not. I asked if we could think it over, work out whatever the problem might be. And he said, quite baldly, 'No.' I felt—I remember flushing, my face going quite red. I could feel the heat in my skin. There was nothing more to say, and a thousand things to say. But my pride came to the rescue, and I thanked him for coming to speak to me in person, rose, and ushered him out the door. He said, 'I'm sorry, Emily. Good-bye.' And I shut the door before he could see me cry. I couldn't let him see that. It would have been the final humiliation."

She was very attractive: classic features, dark hair that curled about her face, dark blue eyes. She would turn heads wherever she went. What then, Rutledge asked himself, had caused this sudden change of heart on Standish's part?

He said, "I mean no disrespect. But was it a matter of money?"

"I thought of that. It would have been a fairly even match. Socially we were certainly equals. Someone else? I don't know. Perhaps he lied about that. I don't know why it would have hurt me more than *not* knowing."

He could understand that.

She concentrated on eating for a while, although he didn't think she was particularly hungry. It was more likely that she was being polite. She had, after all, asked him for tea.

And then, setting her cup down, she added, her eyes dark as she looked again into a painful past, "Something happened to his hand in Paris. I can't think how. There was nothing wrong with it before he left. And I didn't know how to ask."

8

Rutledge put down the sandwich he had just picked up and studied Emily Stuart's face.

"You said nothing to him about it?"

"I didn't notice it at first. I was just so pleased that he'd come. And he must have been trying to conceal it. He had his coat over his arm—usually he'd have given it to Thompson, but I thought he'd been that eager to see me. And then I glimpsed bandaging under the edge of his coat. Heavy, not the sort one put over a cut—grotesque. He tried to cover it, but it was too late. Before I could even ask what had happened, he told me that he wanted to be released. That drove it out of my head entirely."

"You said he was meeting friends in Paris. When was this?"

"Almost a year ago. He'd told me they were friends from the war, and that he had promised he would be there." She crumbled the edge of her untouched pastry and pushed the bits across her plate. "A cousin said something once during the war, that men who lived so closely together and faced such horrors each day shared a bond that had nothing to do with friendship or blood. They counted on each other to survive, and they depended on each other not to let the side down."

He said nothing, knowing all too well that the cousin had been right. And yet unable to explain it any better.

She was still speaking. "I remembered that, when he said it was a promise he had to keep. And I said good-bye without so much as a qualm, because I thought it was the right thing to do." She looked up at him, tears in her eyes. "I thought I'd have him for the rest of my life, and what did a fortnight matter against that?"

"He didn't tell you anything else about his promise, or what he and his friends expected to do while they were in Paris?"

"Only that it was something that mattered to all of them—to meet in Paris if they survived the war. It was very important to him, I could tell. Very personal. He didn't want to talk about it very much. I didn't press."

Then, without warning, Emily Stuart reached for her coat. "This was *wrong*. I shouldn't have told you these things. You listen too well— and I needed to talk to someone. But not to a stranger."

Signaling for his bill, he said, "Sometimes strangers are better."

She shook her head, struggling with her coat. "No. Usually I keep up a good front. After all, everyone thinks I jilted Roger, don't they? And I could hardly stop someone on the streets of East Dedham and ask. I couldn't even send Sewell—my coachman—to ask for me."

He took her coat from her and helped her into it. She was already walking to the door as he paid for the tea. He followed her, and they left the hotel in silence.

On the drive back to East Dedham, she sat huddled in her coat, staring out the window, hoping to discourage him from picking up the threads of their conversation.

It wasn't until they had nearly reached the Gap that Miss Stuart, goaded by her need, asked, "Have you seen the Captain? You must have done, if only about the motorcar. How is he? How does he look?"

"He's troubled by something, I think."

"I wish I was on his mind. But I don't expect him to care that much. I don't know why," she ended bitterly, "I should go on caring either."

She wouldn't let him take her to find her carriage. "I don't wish to have the staff gossip about what I do. Most of them are new employees—since the war. I don't know them well." She pointed to the pub yard, and Rutledge pulled in there. As he came around to open her door for her, she said wryly, "As it is, they think I'm mad to wish to spend so much time in East Dedham. Perhaps I am."

"Is there a way to reach you?"

"I don't expect there to be any need for that."

And with a nod she walked away.

He watched her until she turned the corner, thinking about what she'd said.

Hamish interrupted his thoughts. "It's all verra' weil, but what has it to do wi' the death of yon Rector?"

"I don't know," Rutledge said slowly.

It wasn't until he'd walked back toward the market stalls that he realized he'd answered Hamish aloud again. Why, he demanded of himself, couldn't he break that habit? But it wasn't a habit; it was far more deeply seated than that.

When Constable Neville came hurrying through the throng of marketgoers, looking for Rutledge, he stopped short as he saw the man from London's grim face.

"Is anything wrong, sir? Or have you already heard?"

"Heard? What?" Rutledge asked.

"Three of the local lads went up to Belle Tout. They'd nicked cigarettes from somewhere, and they wanted a place to do their smoking in peace. They climbed over the wall, out of the wind, and that's when they found Grant."

"Grant?" The name was familiar, but he couldn't place it.

"Yes, sir, Timothy Grant. His wife wanted us to find him. I thought it likely that Grant had had enough and taken off for good."

He remembered the conversation between the distraught woman and Neville.

They moved away from the marketgoers, Neville looking over his shoulder to be certain no one was near enough to overhear. "The man's dead, sir. I can't tell what killed him."

R utledge took the narrow turning to Belle Tout. The lighthouse was of the style that had living quarters attached. A wall encircled part of the grounds, high enough to keep the winds from scouring what must be a garden.

Neville was saying, "The lighthouse was built in 1832. I was always told my granddad had worked on the construction. They brought granite for the tower from Maidstone by oxcart. It must have been quite a sight. The keeper's cottage is local limestone. The problem was not the lighthouse, it was where it's built. Up here on the cliff? Ships at sea would be hard-pressed to see it in bad weather. It didn't stop the wrecks." He gestured to the end of what had been a rough track in. "You can leave the motorcar here, sir."

They walked to the wall, followed it closer to the house, and opened the gate.

The gardens had gone to seed, brambles and wildflowers crowding out whatever plants had been there before. But Rutledge could see the vague outline of the beds, and thought it must have been a sheltered place to serve tea.

By the far wall were three boys, no more than twelve or thirteen, reminding him of Jem. Pale, shivering, and chastened, they turned as one toward the newcomers, a look of relief on their faces. As Neville cut across the garden, one of them called, "Can we go now? Please?"

Ten feet from them lay the remains of a man, and they were studiously avoiding looking at him again.

"Not until you've told the Inspector here what you told me."

They began to speak all at once, and Rutledge held up a hand. Turning to the one who appeared to be the eldest of the three, he said, "What's your name?"

"Harry, sir. Harry Dixon."

"Tell me how you came to find the body."

He glanced anxiously at his companions but said, "Tom's brother is drunk, and we took three cigarettes off him as he lay on his bed. We didn't wish to be caught with them, and Gerald here suggested we come to the lighthouse. There's no one about to tell on us. So we came through the gate, and I spotted *him*." He pointed over his shoulder. "We thought he was drunk and might have a bottle on him still. And so we came over to have a look. What we saw was that." He stumbled away and was sick against the wall.

Gerald and Tom appeared to be on the verge of joining him.

"Is that what happened? Is Harry telling me the truth?"

They nodded vigorously, eager to be done with the inquisition.

"We didn't touch him," Tom said. "Nor go near him. We turned tail and went for Constable Neville. We didn't know what else to do."

Rutledge believed him. Shaken as they were, their mothers would have got the truth out of them soon enough. It would have been impossible to hide.

"All right, you may go. But Constable Neville will come around later to take statements from you."

The three boys nearly collided in their haste to be gone, running for the open gate. Once outside, they were as silent as they'd been while standing guard over the body. This lark had not ended well.

Rutledge watched them out of sight, then turned back.

One could see that it was a man, but the weather and the gulls had been at him. The clothes were working class: heavy shoes, off-the-rack coat and trousers. Cheap cotton shirt. Clothing that might be seen on half a hundred men within a ten-mile radius.

"He's been here for several days," Rutledge said. "Can you be sure it's Grant?"

"That belt buckle. It belonged to his father, and he always wore it. Besides, what I can tell of his hair fits as well. Dark, receding."

Rutledge could see the buckle. Heavy brass shaped like the head of an elephant.

"His father was a merchant seaman, sailed all over the world. He got that in Ceylon, as I remember. Brought his wife-to-be—this one's ma—silk from China to be made into her wedding dress. He'd send postcards from ports he stopped in, and his mother put them in an album. Everyone in Gap has seen those at one time or another. Very exotic, some of them were. Ah well, his wife won't be wondering anymore where this one is off to."

"Didn't she claim he'd taken money she'd hidden?"

"So she did."

They studied the body, but it was nearly impossible to be certain how or why Grant had died. For that matter, even the time of death. But Rutledge felt certain the man had never left Burling Gap.

"Any possibility that his wife tired of him and the trouble he brought her, and killed him?"

Neville frowned. "Her anger seemed genuine enough. It never crossed my mind when she was badgering me that he might be dead, and she the cause of it. She even asked Constable Brewster to search for him."

Rutledge had heard her.

He cast a glance at the sky. "Not many day-trippers this time of year, nor walkers on the south-coast track. He might have lain here for weeks before he was discovered." He gestured toward the belt. "If she killed him and left him here, she'd have been clever enough to take that belt buckle with her. That way the police would have no way of identifying him after a few more weeks."

"We get jumpers here, you know. People who come to throw themselves off the cliffs. If he'd been found on the strand, now, it would have appeared to be another suicide."

"But he might have been spotted sooner. Whoever left Grant here must have wanted him to disappear."

"That brings us back to his wife."

"So it does." Neville turned away, scanning the ground around the body. "Nothing to show how he came to be here—whether he was killed here, died here of natural causes, or was dragged to this wall after he was dead."

Rutledge had already scanned the ground. After the storms any tracks would have vanished, washed away in the downpours. "Did he drink?" he asked, remembering Tom's brother.

"Not enough to die from it, sir, if that's what you're thinking."

"And no known health issues?"

"Not that I ever heard about, but Mrs. Grant or Dr. Hanby can answer that."

They spent ten more minutes examining the scene, the torn face and scalp. Even the hands had not escaped the birds and small animals. But any information either the ground or the body might have offered before was gone.

They left it where it was and went back to the motorcar, driving to the village to speak to Mrs. Grant and then arrange for the body to be taken to the doctor's surgery.

Mrs. Grant sat down heavily when Neville broke the news.

"It can't be him," she said, pale as the pillow slip she was holding. She had been making up the bed when they came to the door, and her first question had been, "Well? Have you found the bastard?"

"We can't be sure," Neville said, avoiding mentioning the state of the body, "but he's wearing that brass belt buckle. I don't think he'd have let anyone else have it. Or that anyone could have taken it from him."

Her face crumpled. "No." And she began to cry, wrenching sobs that seemed torn from her.

The two men stood there, offering words of comfort, but it did very little good. Neville disappeared for a time and came back with a gray-haired neighbor he introduced as Mrs. Mitchell. She went at once to put an arm around the weeping woman and told them to go away.

"Do what has to be done. By then she'll be able to talk to you."

As they left the room, they heard her say in the voice one might use to a child, "There, there. Let me take you back to lie down, and then I'll fix us both a nice cuppa."

They found men to handle the stretcher and walked back up to the light with them. Coming from this direction, Rutledge could see how the cliffs must have eroded since the lighthouse had been built. It was barely fifty feet from the brink now. That would also explain why the lighthouse had not worked as planned, and why Beachy Head, right on the waterline, had been built some seventy years on.

It was not pleasant work, gathering the body up to place it on the stretcher. Rutledge left his motorcar in the hamlet and walked with the stretcher party to Dr. Hanby's surgery.

The doctor had gone out to one of the farms and would be back, his wife told them, in no more than an hour.

They had covered the body with a blanket so that the crowded market wouldn't see what they themselves had had to cope with.

Avoiding looking at it herself, Mrs. Hanby said, "Who is it? Do you know? The doctor will ask."

As the stretcher bearers set their burden down in one of the examining rooms, Rutledge said, "We think it's Timothy Grant."

"How sad," she responded. "His wife was here only yesterday begging the doctor to tell her if there was anything wrong with her husband. But there was nothing to tell."

They thanked her and were just leaving when Constable Brewster, coming at a run, met them at the surgery door.

"I just heard—a body," he said, out of breath as he stopped on the path to the door.

"Timothy Grant," Rutledge answered him.

"Good God. His wife was after me just last night to send out a search party. We had words over it. She couldn't sleep for worry, she said. It wasn't the first time she's come. What happened? Was he a jumper?"

"Early days," Rutledge said, nodding to the stretcher bearers to go on about their business. "We'll see what the doctor has to say."

"Best not to spread the word until we know for certain," Neville added.

Brewster turned to look at the crowded market in front of the pub. "Yes, best to say nothing." He turned back to Rutledge. "Perhaps I should have a look at the corpse."

"He was found on Neville's turf," Rutledge answered. "We'll wait for the doctor to come back."

Brewster frowned. "Nothing has happened in Gap for years, and now two bodies on Neville's watch."

To Rutledge's ears it sounded petulant, as if Brewster thought it unfair for Neville to be so fortunate.

"Thank you, Constable," Rutledge said, and ushering Neville ahead of him, he walked back inside to sit in the doctor's waiting room until his return.

Brewster didn't follow them.

They waited for more than two hours for Hanby to finish whatever it was that had taken him to one of the farms. Neville nodded off in his chair, chin on chest, his breathing softly sibilant.

Rutledge, sitting in the chair across the room, found himself going back over the conversation he'd had with Emily Stuart.

What had happened to Captain Standish's hand while he was in Paris? And why had he so abruptly broken off his engagement?

Nothing to do with Wright's death. And yet he'd learned long ago that anything that was out of the way was ignored at one's peril. Too many cases hinged on small details that appeared to be extraneous.

It was late afternoon when they heard voices in the passage, and the waiting room door opened.

Dr. Hanby said, "Sorry to keep you waiting. What's this I hear about Grant being found dead?"

"He's a patient of yours?" Rutledge asked, rising. Mrs. Grant had already told him as much, but he had his reasons for repeating the question.

"Yes. Healthy as a horse. His only problem is an eye for women other than his wife. I'd not have been surprised if he contracted syphilis, but he seems to have the constitution of an ox."

Rutledge told him how the body had been discovered and by whom.

"Well, then, give me five minutes to change, and we'll have a look."

It was not a pleasant examination. Between the elements and the predators, the body had been heavily damaged.

Hanby said, after a time, "I can't tell you how he died. He wasn't shot in the head, there's no sign of that. And at a guess, not in the torso either. I will have to look at the bones to see if there's any indication of a knifing or a bullet wound. But there's some indication that his neck has been broken. Any chance he climbed over the wall up there at the light? No? But there is a gate, isn't there? Then it was deliberately done." He straightened. "Naturally I won't know for certain until I examine his neck more closely. There's always the possibility that he was strangled first."

"Will you send word when you are sure about cause of death?"

"Yes, of course." He looked at the body again. "That belt buckle belongs to Grant. I've never had occasion to examine him fully—that is, to remove his clothes—and so I don't know of any distinguishing marks to look for. Scars, moles, tattoos. You might ask Mrs. Grant." He pointed to the ravaged face. "It would be best to ask, not to bring her in."

"No," Rutledge agreed.

Hanby pulled up a sheet, drawing it over the dead face. "I'll do what I can this evening."

They thanked him and left him to wash his hands.

Walking back to Gap, where Rutledge had left his motorcar, Neville asked, "What do you make of this?"

"Too early to say. It might be unrelated to what happened to Wright. But if Grant's neck was broken, we have to wonder if both men died by the same hand."

Neville turned to face him. "Are you saying that someone found Wright alive and saw to it that he didn't survive?"

"It's possible."

Neville whistled softly under his breath. "But why kill Grant?"

"Perhaps he saw something he shouldn't have. Or someone who didn't wish to be seen."

"Good God," he said. "Grant was a canny man. He'd be quick to see an advantage in a bit of knowledge. And a stranger wouldn't easily catch him off guard or lure him to a quiet, dark place like the lighthouse. Not if Grant intended a little blackmail. That tells me he must have known his killer. Someone right under my nose, so to speak."

"It could mean the killer was local, yes."

"Then it's possible Mrs. Grant did kill her husband."

Rutledge remembered something. He stopped.

"Walk on, and look in on Mrs. Grant. See if she's able to give us any information about her husband's disappearance. There's something I have to do first."

He turned back toward the market stalls.

But the woman who had seen Wright out on the Downs arguing with another man had already left. When Rutledge questioned the women in the neighboring stall, they said, "It wasn't much of a day for her. It's the weather kept people away."

"Do you know where I can find her?"

At their expressions, knowing who he was and why he was in East Dedham, he smiled and said, "I bought a tray from her. I wondered if she might have any more pieces with that same violet design."

Disappointment loomed in their faces. A bit of china was not much in the way of gossip. They had obviously hoped for more.

They didn't know where she lived, but she did have a shop in Eastbourne, they agreed on that. Only they weren't certain where the shop was.

"Not having been there," one explained.

He had hoped they would know. Eastbourne was a good-sized town. He would have to ask the police there to help him locate the shop.

"Where is the next market, do you know?"

But they were local women and they shook their heads.

A dead end. He thanked them, hiding his own disappointment, and went to catch Neville up.

Mrs. Grant had fallen asleep at last, the neighbor informed them.

"Let her sleep, poor lamb. It's been a rough time, not knowing where he was."

With a glance at Rutledge, asking permission, Neville said, "It's best not to ask Mrs. Grant, or take her to the doctor's surgery. Do you know if her husband had any scars—tattoos—anything that might help us make certain the dead man is Grant?"

Her eyebrows went up. "What's wrong with his face?" she asked, keeping her voice low. "Why doesn't the constable here tell you it's Grant?"

Rutledge spoke then. "It's routine, Mrs. Mitchell. The police always ask a member of the family to identify the body."

"Who identified Mr. Wright, then? Mrs. Saunders isn't family."

"It's a problem, isn't it?" he asked pleasantly, in response. "We must do the best we can."

"I don't know of any marks or scars," she said then. "Not even a chipped tooth."

Neville, consternation in his face, glanced at Rutledge, then said hastily, "Thank you, Mrs. Mitchell. We'll leave you to look after Mrs. Grant, and I'll call in later."

Outside, out of hearing, Neville said, "She's the village busybody, quick to pick up on anything if you aren't careful what you say in front of her, but she has a way with the sick and bereft."

"When you go back, ask her in as roundabout way you can think of how well he knew the Rector."

"Grant was a Chapel man. Like me," Neville retorted in surprise. "I doubt he ever spoke to Rector, no more than common courtesy if they met in the street."

Rutledge said only, "It never hurts to give a busybody an opportunity to spread gossip. The Mrs. Mitchells of this world are often a good source of information."

Unsatisfied, Neville said, "As you say, sir."

Rutledge left then, intending to speak to Constable Brewster. The woman he was looking for had come to East Dedham for help in putting up her stall. He might know where to find her in Eastbourne.

Instead, he decided as he came into the village that this was a good time to call on Captain Standish. Armed with what Miss Stuart had told him, he knew the man better now than he had done on his first visit.

He was halfway to Four Winds when he saw a child at the side of the road, hunched over as if in pain.

Slowing, he pulled to the verge. The child looked up, and Rutledge recognized Jem, her face wet with tears, and grubby now from her hands trying to wipe them away.

She started up in alarm, then subsided as she saw the motorcar and then the man behind the wheel.

"What's happened?" he asked in concern, opening his door to get out.

"I've lost the money my mother gave me to buy flour and things. I was kicking a stone, and I tripped. When I stood up again, I couldn't find the shillings." The last words came out in a wail.

"Surely she'll understand," he said.

"Sometimes there's no money at all, and we make do. How can I tell her I *lost* what she gave me?"

Heedless of his trousers, he sat down beside her. He saw then that one hand was scraped and one knee was bleeding a little through her hand-me-down coveralls. "Shall I help you look?"

"It's useless. I've spent hours searching. She'll be wondering where I am, and I can't go home."

He rose. "Show me exactly where you fell."

Jem got to her feet reluctantly. "Just there. My toe caught that rut."

He walked with her to the spot, then said, "I think you must have stubbed your toe on that stone. Do you see?"

"It doesn't matter. Stone or rut, the money is gone."

"Shall I make a loan of what you lost? Policemen do that sometimes."

"Not Constable Brewster," she scoffed. "He would send me home with a flea in my ear." She looked up at him, her face earnest. "And I can't take your money. There's no way to repay you. And debt is a bad thing. It leads to trouble."

Rutledge wondered if her mother or her father had taught her that. "You're absolutely right," he said. "How many shillings did you lose?"

"Two," she said.

"Let me fetch the torch in my boot," he told her, and walked briskly back to the motorcar. While he was out of her line of sight, opening the boot, he felt in his pocket for coins, found two shillings, and closed his fingers over them. He went back to where she was standing, forlorn and anxious.

"Here, cast about with the torch. It might reflect on the silver."

She began to search, her head bent, the torch barely bright enough on this cloudy day to do much good. He made a pretense of searching as well. And then he called, "Look here. I think I've found one." He knelt by a rut, and as she came up, he pointed.

"It must have rolled," she exclaimed, her face wreathed in smiles. "Now let's find the other."

With her standing so near him, he was hard-pressed to drop the second shilling, for fear it might bounce on his boot and give him away. Turning his back on her, he moved a little distance away and discovered the second shilling.

She pounced on it with glee, and said, her eyes shining, "You must have very good eyesight."

"I've always been told so," he agreed. "Now let me run you into the village before the shops close, and you can buy your flour. I'll run you back to your lane, and no one will be the wiser."

"No, I mustn't," she said. "Someone will see me and tell my mother. I'm not allowed—"

"—to speak to strangers," he said in unison with her. "What if I drop you where no one will notice? Will that do?"

Torn, she considered his proposition. "Are you sure you're a policeman?" she asked.

He solemnly took out his identification and passed it to her.

She bent her head to read it carefully, and he wondered how much schooling she might have had, taking her brothers' places in the household as she had done. Then she gave it back to him.

"Very well," she said, echoing her mother's voice, he thought, and walked back to the motorcar.

Rutledge managed to get Jem to the village without being seen, and was waiting when she came back.

"I thought you might have gone," she said, putting several sacks on the floorboard as she climbed into her seat. "It took so very long."

"A promise is a promise," he said lightly.

"It's quite far to drive," she went on, eager and yet trying to be polite.

"I'm on my way to call on Captain Standish. It's no trouble."

"You won't mention me to him?" she asked, alarmed. "He'll surely tell my mother. He keeps an eye on us. My mother thinks he's being kind, but I worry that we aren't doing our bit and he's waiting to catch us out."

Surprised at such adult wisdom, Rutledge said, "Is he not a kind master?"

"Yes, but even I know we aren't doing as well as we were when my brothers and my father were all working together on the farm. He's not blind, you know."

He had no answer for that.

They reached the lane where she'd got down before, and he pulled up to let her out. She had shut the door and was about to run down the track when she paused and said with a sweet smile, "Thank you. For finding the shillings too."

"Glad to be of assistance," he told her, and watched her until she was out of sight.

Surely there had been someone else to walk into the village for flour? But then he answered himself. There was only her mother, who had other work to do and couldn't spare the time.

But there was no way to help them without betraying Jem, and doing that would only cause more trouble for the family.

9

He drove on to the Captain's house and knocked at the door. This time Standish received him in the pretty room where Rutledge had watched him pace.

"What brings you here? News, I hope? I could use a little good news," the Captain said, gesturing to a chair.

"I just had a few more questions," Rutledge told him. "Have you been to see your motorcar?"

"No, I haven't," Standish replied curtly. "Mr. Trotter hasn't darkened my door."

"I'll be happy to drive you to Trotter's garage."

"I don't need your help."

"Very well. Do you know a man by the name of Grant, who lives in Burling Gap?"

"Grant? No, I don't. Who is he, and why do you think I might know him?"

"He was found dead this afternoon. In the walled garden at Belle Tout. Not far, in fact, from where the accident occurred that killed the Rector. It's possible that there's a connection between Grant's death and Wright's, even though they occurred in two different places. On Friday night Wright was seen arguing with someone. It could have been Grant."

"You think this argument precipitated the borrowing of my motorcar? I don't see how."

"Nor do I at the moment. But there's no doubt that Grant is dead. And it's possible that Wright was murdered."

"Good God," Standish said blankly. "*Two* murders? Is that what you're telling me? I can hardly remember when either village last saw one."

"Unfortunately, it could be true."

"But you told me that Grant's body was found today. Wright couldn't have had anything to do with his death."

"It appears he'd argued with his wife last Friday, and in a fit of temper, decided to leave her. That seemed to be a pattern in their marriage. Under the circumstances it was thought he'd simply gone missing, very likely with another woman. We can't be sure when he died."

Standish got up and walked to the windows. "Is there no end to this business?" he asked, staring out. The afternoon light had nearly faded, leaving patches of darkness where the trees were closest together. There had been stress in his voice, though he tried to conceal it. He stood there for a moment, not speaking.

Rutledge waited, letting him take his time.

Finally the Captain turned. "I would not have had any of this happen. I wish to God it hadn't. All right, I'll take you up on your offer. Let me find a coat, and we'll go to Trotter's garage."

He was back in a matter of minutes, and followed Rutledge out to the motorcar.

"She's a handsome lady," he said, looking over Rutledge's motorcar. "Quite like my own. I didn't know policemen drove touring cars."

"As a rule they don't. The Downs just here are not easy to get about in. As you know from your own situation."

"True. I'm buying a horse. It's the only thing I can think of doing until I know how long it will take to repair my own motor or to buy another."

They drove in silence to the garage. At first it seemed that Trotter wasn't in, but he finally came to the door and opened it. There was another vehicle in the interior now, sitting in the lamplight. Underneath it were a trolley and a torch, where Trotter had been working.

"I wasn't certain I'd heard your knock." Turning from Rutledge to Standish, he said, "I'm sorry to be the bearer of sad tidings, but your motorcar has sustained quite a bit of damage." As he talked, he led them toward the far side of the garage and lit another lamp so that the Captain could see what had happened to his vehicle.

"My God," he whispered, taking it in, walking around the outside, peering into the body and then under it. "How will it run, once you've done the necessary repairs?"

"Well enough. I shall have to order two new wings, and part of the bonnet is beyond repair. The roof I can deal with. The motor is still sound, for a wonder. But some of the linkages and the lines will need checking to be certain they still work properly." He went on describing the damage and what it would require to set the motorcar to rights again.

Rutledge stood to one side, watching the Captain's reaction. Ten minutes later, Standish thanked Trotter and gave him instructions. When he was finished making notes, Trotter started to hold out his greasy hand to seal the agreement, stopped, and said ruefully, "Well, better not to shake hands. But the Inspector here is our witness."

"Yes," Standish said, suddenly eager to be away. "Thank you. Please keep me informed." And he was out the door ahead of Rutledge.

On the road back to the house, Standish said, his feelings suddenly overwhelming him, "This is the second motorcar smashed in a year's time. It's as if I'm cursed. Or unlucky."

"You've had a crash yourself?" Rutledge asked, surprised.

"It's not important," Standish said, regretting his outburst. "Just—I can't believe this is happening to me."

But it *was* important, in Rutledge's eyes.

"Where and when was this crash?"

"Not in Sussex. Last year. I have told you, it's not important."

"Are you married?" Rutledge asked, willing to change the subject for the moment and taking advantage of an opportunity. He wondered if Standish would admit to having been engaged at one time.

"No. No, I'm not." It was final, closing the subject.

"Then you have no one else to consider but yourself."

"What? Yes. True."

When they reached the house, Standish got out and said good evening, making it clear that he didn't expect Rutledge to come in again.

The door shut firmly behind the Captain, and Rutledge drove away.

He'd told Standish more than he'd intended when he set out for Four Winds, but sometimes it was necessary. He was fairly sure that Standish didn't know Grant, and it was likely that there were witnesses to his visit to Brighton, proving where the Captain was when Wright died. That could be established in the course of the inquiry, but for the moment, it was not as important as the reference to another crash.

"Aye," Hamish said from his accustomed place just behind Rutledge's shoulder. "He didna' wish to talk about it. No' a good sign."

Just as Rutledge reached the main road, it was as if the sky opened up and the rain came down in heavy curtains, nearly blinding him. In the end, he had to creep into East Dedham. The market stalls had been abandoned, goods hastily covered over while the sellers took shelter in the pub.

It was busy and noisy when Rutledge walked in the door and took the steps to his room two at a time. The smoke from cigarettes seemed to wreathe around the ceiling, trails of it in the lamplight.

He found two messages shoved under his door, both of them in sealed envelopes.

The first was from Neville.

The search party hadn't turned up any sign of the Rector's bicycle. The final sentence read, *I can't think where else to tell them to look.* The second was from Dr. Hanby.

His neck was indeed broken. Quite efficiently. If I didn't know better, I'd say that whoever did this to Grant had also broken the Rector's neck. Make of it what you will. There are indications that Grant was in an altercation with someone before his death. His nose was broken, and there was tissue damage consistent with bruising. More difficult to break the neck of a man who knows you're there. Easier if he's unconscious. Time of death? Stage of decomposition suggests Friday last.

Rutledge read both messages, then locked them in his valise.

It was surprising that Neville's search party hadn't found the Rector's bicycle.

He could understand that Wright wouldn't have left it where it might easily be found before he could return the motorcar or speak to Standish about borrowing it. Still, it should have turned up. The men set to searching knew this country.

As for the doctor's message, it was one more convolution in an already complex situation. Rutledge decided to ignore the death of Timothy Grant for the moment and give his attention to the Rector's. Find the answer to that, and he might well have the answer to what happened at the lighthouse.

The rain was still coming down hard when Rutledge went in to his dinner.

He had the dining room to himself. It was too wretched a night for anyone to choose to dine out, and the bar was bursting with marketgoers caught by the rain and the stall owners who were still unable to do anything about their wares. He'd looked in, scanning the faces, hoping to find the woman who'd sold him the tray, but she wasn't there.

And then, as he was reading the menu, the dining room door opened and Barnes stood on the threshold, shaking his hat and removing his coat. Josie came in from the kitchen just at that moment and clucked her tongue at the resulting puddle, but said nothing as she showed the newcomer to a table.

Apparently dinner at the rectory was so little to his liking that he was willing to wade through the rain.

Rutledge felt a moment of sympathy for Mrs. Saunders.

Barnes recognized the man from London and said, as soon as Josie had returned to the kitchen, "You haven't returned any of the papers you took from Wright's desk."

"There was nothing of interest in them. At least that's how it appears at the moment. I'll hang on to them for a little longer."

"My Bishop won't approve," Barnes responded. "Nor will he approve of the theft of Captain Standish's motorcar. And the report I must send him on the state of affairs at the rectory will appall him."

Rutledge said curtly, "We don't know why the motorcar was taken, or what Wright intended to do about borrowing it, if he'd lived."

"That's splitting hairs," Barnes said officiously.

"And the rectory?"

"The present housekeeper is sullen, and her cooking is not fit to eat."

"She's grieving for a man she'd faithfully served for twelve years. And Wright never complained about her cooking."

"Are you sure of that? You've only just come to East Dedham."

Rutledge held on to his temper with both hands.

"This isn't London, Barnes. It's a small village, and that makes a difference in how things are done." He remembered the letters full of gratitude that had been sent to Wright. "I daresay the Rector cared more for his flock than he did for his dinner. His Bishop needs to take that into consideration as well."

"We shall see. But I would count it a favor if his papers are returned at your earliest convenience."

Rutledge rose. "That will wait for the police to finish their inquiry." He walked out of the dining room, shutting the door carefully behind him when he'd have enjoyed slamming it.

Fetching his coat and an umbrella, he walked out into the rain. It had not let up, and he was counting on the fact that it had kept Mrs. Saunders at her post, when usually by this time she would have left to stay with her sister.

He was quite wet when he arrived on the rectory's doorstep. Mrs. Saunders answered his knock with a sour expression, then it changed when she saw who was there.

"I thought he'd forgot his key," she said, opening the door wider so that Rutledge could step inside. "Oh, just look at you," she added as he furled his umbrella and moved into the circle of light cast by the lamp on the table. "Come into the kitchen. It's still warm, and you can dry your coat and hat a little." She ushered him, unprotesting, to the kitchen, and pulled out a chair for him.

He gave her his hat and coat, and she set the kettle on to boil. "You'll need something hot to drink. Have you eaten? There's Rector's dinner still in the cupboard. His high-and-mightiness refused to have any part of it."

He laughed at her name for Barnes. "Is he quite so bad?" he asked.

"He's a prying man, looking into everything, wanting to know this or that. I can tell you Rector kept his accounts in order. He took pride in it."

"What is Barnes looking for? Wright is dead—I'm sorry, but it's a fact. Why not simply bury him figuratively and literally, then get on with replacing him?"

"A good question, Mr. Rutledge. I've wondered myself. He went through the drawers of the desk in the study, went through Rector's bedchamber, and even took all the books out of the bookshelves. As if he's afraid something might escape him, and the Bishop will be dis-pleased."

But it sounded to Rutledge as if Barnes was expecting to find something. What was it? And then he thought he knew. Anything that might explain why Wright had been driving another man's motorcar?

Mrs. Saunders was saying, "Rector kept no secrets. He wasn't that sort of man."

"I did notice that among the letters from his parish, there was an envelope postmarked from Portsmouth in September. But the letter is missing. I wondered why the Rector kept the envelope and not the letter itself? Usually it's the other way around."

"I never knew him to mention friends in Portsmouth. He said once that most of his friends were killed in the war. I think it must be true. But then he never did have all that many visitors, even before the war. He told me his friends at seminary were busy with their own churches, and not likely to be calling on him. They did write often in the first few years, as I remember, but friendships grow cold with the passing of time, don't they? They must all be married now, and have families. He'd have little in common with them, a single man."

"Wright never married."

"No." She put his cup of tea in front of him and sat down across from him. "It was sad. He came to this church happy to begin the next stage of his life. And he stayed here because it was something he wanted to do." She looked away. "I never said. Rector was a private man, and it was long ago. But there was a girl once. He'd have married her if he could, I think, but she had better prospects than a clergyman." Looking back at Rutledge, she said, "I never met that young woman. But I don't think much of her."

He was reminded of Jean, who had been horrified to find him struggling to recover from a war that hadn't taken an arm or leg or eye from him, but had left him with invisible scars in the mind. Not an honorable wound, shell shock. He had released her from their engagement, allowing her to think she had done what was best for him, when he'd needed her support more than ever.

He was also reminded of something else. "Was she by any chance from Portsmouth?" An envelope kept—a letter destroyed . . .

"No, from Eastbourne. But she liked London, and she wanted a London life."

By the time Rutledge had finished his tea, Mrs. Saunders was pressing him to eat the Rector's dinner instead. "I'll only have to throw it into the bin," she said. "It's a sin to waste good food."

In the end, he let her serve him, if only to see if there was any merit in Barnes's claims.

There were potatoes, parsnips, and carrots roasted in goose fat, a roasted chicken with gravy and boiled onion, and a plum crumble "from plums I put up myself in the summer," she told him proudly.

"Why did Barnes prefer the pub's cooking?"

She smiled. "It's a small parish. He's afraid if he doesn't complain about it, the Bishop will leave him here. It can't be easy finding another Rector as caring as ours. And this one is accustomed to grander dishes, and invitations to dine with the gentry. East Dedham wouldn't please him at all." Her smile broadened. "I wonder what God thinks of that, now."

B y Sunday morning, the rain had dwindled to a few showers, although the ground was wet and pools stood here and there in ruts, ponding where they could.

The service at St. Simon's was full, everyone wanting to hear what the new man had to say, and what he might tell them about the late Mr. Wright.

Rutledge had gone out early, driving to Eastbourne to search for the woman's shop, and he couldn't be sure he'd found it. Still, in the window of one on a side street just behind one of the larger hotels, he saw the same pattern of violets that had attracted him to the tray he'd bought for Frances. This time they were on the backs of a mirror, a pair of brushes, and the handles of a set of combs and nail files as well as a round powder bowl.

He told himself it was unlikely that another shop would carry exactly the same pattern, and he looked for the owner's name so he could take it to the local police to ask for their help in his inquiry. But there was only the name of the shop: Past Perfect.

By the time he'd returned to East Dedham, parishioners were just leaving the church, and judging from their faces, they had been sorely disappointed in the new man.

He wondered if this was a part of Barnes's plan to be turned down for the vacancy at St. Simon's, or if he was the Bishop's assistant because he was better at administrative tasks than he was in the pulpit.

It was time, he thought, to try to reach the Yard. He needed someone to run down information for him.

He discovered that the telephone hadn't reached East Dedham. The nearest would be in Eastbourne, he was told, and very likely in one of the larger hotels catering to holidaymakers.

He located one on his first try. It was in the rear of the lobby and free at the moment. Most of the guests were in the dining room, ensuring him a modicum of privacy.

When the call went through, Sergeant Gibson answered. Apparently it was his turn at weekend rotation. A gruff man who was not so much Rutledge's friend as the former Chief Superintendent's enemy, the two had come to an uneasy alliance that had continued after Bowles's heart attack. Mainly, Rutledge had decided, because Gibson hadn't yet made up his mind about the Acting Chief Superintendent, who was not from the London ranks but from Yorkshire.

When it came to ferreting out information through what appeared to be endless contacts across half of England, Sergeant Gibson had no peer.

Pleased at his luck, he said, "Rutledge here, in Sussex. I'm in need of information."

"It's murder, then? The death of the Rector?"

"It appears to be. I have a list of names for you. Background, mostly. Captain Roger Standish. The Rector, Nathaniel Wright, who was a chaplain in the war. A priest named Jonathan Barnes, acting on behalf of his Bishop. A young woman, Emily Stuart, who lives in this vicinity, although I can't be sure of the village or town. And a Timothy Grant, here in Burling Gap."

"I'll do the best I can." He paused. "There was a call that came to the Yard for you. She didn't leave her name. And I didn't recognize the voice."

Not Frances, then. Gibson would have known her.

"How did she sound?"

"Educated, upper class."

Not Kate Gordon, surely. He could think of no reason why she should call the Yard seeking him. Someone like Emily Stuart, wanting to be sure he was what he claimed to be? He had a feeling that it could easily be Miss Stuart, having second thoughts after talking to him.

He thanked the sergeant and put up the receiver, glad to be out of the small telephone room that seemed to be closing in on him as he talked to the Yard.

Rutledge would have liked to add the name of Wright's correspondent in Portsmouth, but he knew it was unlikely that he would ever discover who wrote the missing letter.

And then a possibility occurred to him.

He drove back to East Dedham and went in search of Trotter.

He found the mechanic in the garage, where he seemed to work, eat, and sleep. When the man opened the door, Rutledge thought he could smell chicken cooking.

"Sorry to interrupt you on Sunday morning," he said before Trotter could tell him that the garage was closed, even to the police. "I need to know what was found in the Standish motorcar when you first examined it. Anything that might have belonged to the Captain or the Rector."

Trotter frowned. "The usual. A torch and an umbrella in the boot. And a rug. A Thermos of tea. I expect that was Rector's. A map, a fountain pen. A handkerchief. That's about the extent of it."

"The map. Was any place marked in particular?"

"It was just a map. I looked at it."

"No letter? I was looking to find a letter. Not an envelope, just the contents of one."

Shaking his head, Trotter said, "If there was a letter, it must have been in his clothing."

But Neville had looked through Wright's pockets, and there had been no mention of any letters, with or without envelopes.

Rutledge thanked Trotter and turned away.

No letter in the desk, none in the motorcar, none in the Rector's pockets. Had Wright burned it, after all?

It seemed more than likely.

The men and women who had brought goods to the market in East Dedham had arisen early and cleared away their stalls, their wares, and the water-soaked tents. A few scraps of paper scudded across the wet space that had been so lively yesterday, and a dog walking with his owner stopped to sniff the ground where the butcher's stall had been.

As Rutledge drove on to interview Mrs. Grant, he pondered the question of the bicycle. If Wright had left the rectory on it, he must have still had it when he reached the Captain's stable. The only solution Rutledge could think of was that he'd taken it with him, wherever he'd been going, perhaps expecting to need it, and for some reason left it behind. But where—and why? It was a long, wet walk from the Standish house to the rectory, with little protection from the storm most of the way. No man in his right mind would want to face the distance on a bicycle, never mind on foot, knowing he'd be wet to the skin before he reached his door.

Hamish said, "Unless, ye ken, he was expecting yon Captain to drive him back."

That was an interesting point. Had Wright expected to find Standish at home? But why would Standish leave for Brighton instead, and then lie about Wright?

Rutledge reached the cottage where Mrs. Grant lived. Someone had hung black crepe on the door, and a woman was just leaving, an empty bowl in her hands.

Inside, he found several more women sitting with Mrs. Grant, and there was an array of food on a table against the wall.

She looked up as he stepped through the door and her guests fell silent, staring at the tall policeman from London.

They seemed to be in no hurry to leave, and after offering his condolences a second time, he asked her, "When did you last see your husband?"

She sniffed, holding back tears. "On Friday it was. More than a week ago, now. We'd had words and he stormed out of the house. It wasn't until later that I found he'd taken the money from my box. And Constable Neville told me that Doctor now had his purse. He went to the surgery to ask about it, after I told him I was desperate to know what had become of my money. And he came back to say there was only a few pennies and a shilling or two. What did he do with it, that's what I want to know."

Rutledge had the feeling that the money mattered more than her husband. But then, with the breadwinner dead, it would help her through what was to come.

"We're taking up a collection for the undertaker," Mrs. Mitchell said, coming through from the small kitchen. "If you care to donate, there's a jar on the table."

He made a contribution, then asked, "Do you have any children, Mrs. Grant?"

"A son. He's working on the docks in Greenwich. Lois's husband has gone to Eastbourne to send him a telegram." It was Mrs. Mitchell who answered.

"Do you have any idea where your husband went when he left the house on that Friday?"

Mrs. Grant shook her head. "I thought he was with another woman. It was what we quarreled about, he and I. He had an eye for women, I've always known it. I thought he'd gone to *her*."

"Can you give me a name? I'd like to ask her what she knows about his movements after he left you."

"How should I know her name?" she wailed, burying her face. "I've never known the names of the hussies he's taken up with. But I've smelled their scent on him. There was one who favored gardenia. *She* lasted two years."

He thought she was lying to him, playing to the gallery of her neighbors, who were avidly listening to every word. As if to prove him right, they murmured sounds of comfort and commiseration.

After giving her a moment to recover, Rutledge tried another approach. "What did your husband do for a living?"

"He was a rag-and-bone man, wasn't he? Mostly in Eastbourne, but sometimes in Pevensey, and even as far away as Hastings. You'd be amazed what summer visitors and day-trippers throw into dustbins. He worked as a young lad on building of the Beachy Head light, and hurt his leg rather badly. After that there wasn't much else he was fit for. But he had a way with women, didn't he?" She turned to her neighbors again, and they nodded knowingly.

Mrs. Grant went on in an aggrieved voice: "He told them grand stories about how his leg came to be broken. Riding elephants in Ceylon, searching for lost tribes up the Amazon. He'd read about such things in the books he found, and you'd think he'd been there. Well, how was anyone to know otherwise, him and that fancy belt of his? There was one woman come looking for him, and that's how I know. She told me to my face I wasn't a suitable wife for such a fine man."

That proved his suspicion that she knew more about her husband's infidelities than she cared to let on.

There was a knock at the door, and Mrs. Mitchell hastened to open it.

Constable Neville stepped into the front room. "Begging pardon, sir. I saw your motorcar outside the door and thought you might need me."

Rutledge turned. "Mrs. Grant was just telling me about Mr. Grant."

Neville's expression was wooden. "I daresay you found it helpful."

"I have." He thanked Mrs. Grant and left her to the ministrations of her neighbors, walking out into the watery sunshine with the constable. Glancing up at a hazy patch of blue sky, Rutledge said as he got into the motorcar, "Was Grant ever in trouble with the police?"

"His wife complained of him," Neville said, resting a hand on the frame of the open window, "but no one else did. I daresay he sometimes came by the goods he sold in questionable ways, but there was never a householder who went to the police, nor a woman either."

"There was a woman I spoke with on market day who saw Wright arguing with someone out by the lighthouse. I've been trying to find her again. Apparently she owns a shop called Past Perfect in Eastbourne. Do you know who she is?"

"You'll have to ask Constable Brewster," Neville replied reluctantly. "I don't know any of the regulars. I make it a point not to go to the market. That's his patch, and he's not always happy to see me there."

"Then I'll speak to him."

Rutledge drove on, slowing as he crested the Down and turned toward East Dedham to allow several sheep to trot across the road in front of him. Their wool glistened with moisture from morning showers. He found Constable Brewster asleep at his desk, snoring softly.

He went back outside and knocked before reentering the police station.

Brewster, his feet swinging off the desk and his chair coming upright with a thump, cleared his throat and said, "Inspector Rutledge. How can I help you, sir?"

Rutledge described the woman he was seeking, adding, "She owns a shop in Eastbourne, I'm told. I need to find her."

Brewster frowned. "Did she cheat you over your purchase?"

"Not at all. But she came to see you earlier in the week about helping her with a space last Saturday. I'd like to ask if she saw anything that would help us with our inquiry."

"Ah. I've never been to her shop. But I do know her name. Patricia Sedley."

"Thank you." Rutledge turned to go.

"She didn't mention anything unusual when I spoke to her that day."

Rutledge said, "Possibly it didn't seem unusual at the time. But in hindsight it could be crucial."

He drove to Eastbourne and stopped in at the police station there to ask where to find Mrs. Sedley.

The sergeant at the desk wanted to know why Rutledge was looking for her, and he gave the same answer he'd given Constable Brewster. In the end he got what he wanted and found the Sedley house on a back-street not far from the Promenade.

Mrs. Sedley was at home and quite surprised to see him. "The tray?" she asked. "Is there anything wrong with it?"

"I've come about the two men you saw quarreling on the day you went to speak to Constable Brewster." He gave his name and showed her his identification.

"Ah." Reluctant to allow him in, she kept him standing at the door as she added, "I told you what I saw. They were quarreling."

"Would you know either of the two men if you saw them again?"

"Since one of them is the Rector of St. Simon's, I think not," she said tartly.

Rutledge smiled. "How did you know it was Mr. Wright?"

"He'd come to the stalls on market day," she told him, as if it were obvious enough that he should have known the answer before asking the question. "He'd walk through and speak to everyone, and he always knew what to ask. My husband had his gallbladder out, and he inquired about that, and how soon he'd be out of hospital. He'd ask Mrs. Templeton about her grandchildren, and how her daughter was faring, with Daniel killed in the war. He was a caring man. It wasn't hard to recognize him out there on the Down. I didn't see his face, of course, not at that distance, but I couldn't have been mistaken."

"And who was the other man?"

"I don't know. I don't think I'd seen him before, but then you can't be sure, always."

"What was the other man wearing?"

"Workman's clothing, I think. And a cap."

"Did you notice anything about him that would help us find him again?"

"I doubt it. But what's this about, why are you asking these questions?"

"We're looking for anyone who spoke to the Rector the last few days before his accident. A matter of routine, to establish state of mind."

"Do you think he crashed that motorcar on purpose?" she asked, shocked.

"It's usual police procedure in such a case," he replied, keeping his voice bland. "To be certain that all the facts have been brought out."

"Well, you're wrong," Mrs. Sedley told him roundly. "I can't think of anyone less likely to kill himself."

And yet by her own admission she had said she didn't know the Rector well, just as a visitor to her stall at the Saturday market. Was it only because he was a man of the cloth that suicide seemed unthinkable?

When he didn't respond straightaway, Mrs. Sedley seemed to feel this man from London didn't believe her, and that she needed to convince him of the truth.

"There's a young woman he's been seeing here in Eastbourne. He's taken her to dinner any number of times. I've seen them together and pretended not to notice. Well, it would be rude to claim acquaintance, wouldn't it, when he's only spoken to me on market day, out of kindness? But she's quite pretty, and I shouldn't have been surprised if there was a wedding in the offing. That's to say, if he'd lived." She clapped her hand over her mouth as she said the words. "Oh, the poor dear, I hadn't thought until now. I wonder how she's taken his death?"

No one, not even Mrs. Saunders, had mentioned a new woman in Wright's life. They had spoken of the London girl who hadn't wanted to be a country rector's wife, but nothing had been said about anyone else. Had he kept it secret, so that he could conduct his courtship quietly, without anyone the wiser if it came to nothing?

Hamish, stirring in the back of his mind, said, "Has anyone told the lass that he's deid?"

"Do you know her name?" Rutledge asked. "Perhaps there's something I could do."

She considered him, doubt in her eyes. "You won't upset her, will you? You won't talk about suicide?"

He promised.

"It's Elizabeth Wilding. Her father's a doctor. They have a house in the side street running down past the Grand Hotel. It's number seven."

He thanked her and left, but Mrs. Sedley stood in the doorway watching him go.

10

Rutledge had no trouble finding Dr. Wilding's surgery.

It was in one of the tall white houses that reflected Eastbourne's popularity with more affluent visitors to the seaside. And here, close by one of the finest hotels on the Promenade, a doctor's surgery meant a prosperous practice.

He drove past the house and found a place to leave his motorcar. Walking back, he wondered what sort of woman Elizabeth Wilding might be. Wright had not spoken of her to anyone in East Dedham, nor had he brought her there to meet any of his flock. Had he been afraid she might find it too provincial, as his first fiancée had done?

Or was Wright still deciding whether he was willing to allow himself to care for someone else again? Rutledge himself had learned that painful lesson. He understood the care with which Wright had managed this friendship. The question was, how many other secrets had the Rector kept?

He went up to the dark blue door and lifted the brass knocker. A young maid in a starched black uniform answered the summons.

"Miss Wilding, please."

"She's not in at present," the maid informed him.

"I've come down from London, and I'd like to speak to her. Do you know where I might find her?"

"She's walking on the Promenade," he was told. "She's got her dog with her."

Rutledge thanked her and continued to the Promenade. It wasn't far, but as he came out of the protection of the hotels facing the water, he felt the temperature drop. The wind was even colder here, coming in off the sea and blowing inland. It might as well, he thought, have been blowing across the arctic ice floes.

Hardly a place to choose for a pleasant stroll, this time of year.

He decided to start to his left, and walked briskly along the wide, handsome Promenade, with its arches and benches where summer visitors could sit and look at the sea without having to walk out onto the strand. He could see a bandstand ahead, and there appeared to be someone sitting in it.

As he drew closer, a large golden retriever half hidden by a woman's skirts raised its ears.

The dog growled as Rutledge approached the graceful white bandstand, and rose with head lowered and tail still.

The young woman had looked up, her face alight with surprise, and then, when she saw that it wasn't the person she'd expected, she rose, gathering the dog's lead, preparing to leave.

Rutledge took off his hat, and the wind ruffled his dark hair. Smiling, he said, "Miss Wilding? Your housemaid told me I might find you here."

"And you are . . . ?" she asked, a hand on the dog's head, the other holding a white fur muff. Mrs. Sedley had called her pretty, for she was fair and had green eyes. But her face was rather plain until it had lit with hope and joy, and then he would have called her pretty as well.

"My name is Rutledge. I'm down from London. I understand you're a friend of Nathaniel Wright's."

"He told you about me?" she asked, surprised. Then alarm replaced her amazement. "But he said—we promised we'd tell no one! Not yet."

"He kept his promise," he assured her. "Would you prefer to walk, or sit here in the bandstand, out of the wind?"

Uncertain, she hesitated. And then curiosity got the better of her. Drawing the dog closer to her skirts, she sat down. "It *is* cold," she agreed politely. "But Ginger here likes to chase the gulls, and so I bring her out for a run." She patted the dog's head again, then looked straight at him and said, "How do you know Nathaniel? And who told you about me?"

Rutledge turned slightly so that he could see the sea beyond the bandstand and not look directly into her face.

"I found out about you in rather a roundabout way," he said, choosing his words with care. "A shopkeeper here in Eastbourne saw the two of you dining together on several occasions. She spoke of it to me."

"But who is she? I've no idea why you should be gossiping about us with a shopkeeper." She was tense again, as if preparing to leave in a hurry.

He could postpone his news no longer.

"She often sets up a stall on market day in East Dedham. And Wright always made a point of speaking to the people who come there for it. A kind man, is the way she described him."

"Yes. He is very kind. But how is this woman connected to you?"

He said, keeping his voice low and gentle. "I'm from Scotland Yard, Miss Wilding, and I've been sent to Burling Gap to look into an incident there."

"I don't understand," she said, rising. "Get to the point, please, Inspector, or whoever you are." A thought struck her. "Did my father send you to spy on me? On us? Is that what this is about?"

"I traveled to East Sussex because there has been a motorcar crash, and the driver was killed."

"And the passengers?" Her voice rose with her anxiety. "Was Nathaniel one of the passengers?" She was leaning forward, staring into his face. "How badly is he hurt?"

"There were no other passengers, Miss Wilding. Mr. Wright was driving."

"But—I don't understand," she said again. "Nathaniel doesn't own a motorcar. He—" The sense of what he said reached her. "This is impossible. There has been a dreadful mistake."

"Mr. Wright is dead."

She sat down, her face a kaleidoscope of emotions. Disbelief, fear, uncertainty—and finally acceptance. She hadn't looked away, and he watched her eyes darken in what appeared to be a profound despair.

"No," she said, shaking her head violently. "This is some trick of my sister's. I won't have it." She got to her feet, unwittingly jerking at the lead, and the dog scrambled up as well. "It won't do." But before she turned away, he saw the tears in her eyes.

Rising as well, he put out a hand, taking her arm in a firm grip. "Scotland Yard doesn't lie about such matters," he said gently. "I'm afraid it's true."

She stood there, the ends of her scarf lifting in the wind, and tendrils of fair hair blew across her cheek, catching in her eyelashes. "Dear God," she whispered, and for a moment he thought she was about to faint because all color drained from her cheeks and she swayed. She was crying now.

And then, remembering where she was—in this very public place— she made an effort to control her grief. Lifting her chin, squaring her shoulders, she said, "Take me home, please." But her voice was ragged, and then it failed her altogether as she whispered, "I can't go home. They don't know, they won't—what am I to *do*?"

Rutledge did what he could to comfort her, and in the end simply held her in his arms until the worst of her sobbing became a soft keening. At length she raised her head from his chest and said, "I'm so sorry, please forgive me," and moved away.

He handed her his handkerchief, but she refused it. "When?" she asked.

"This past Saturday evening—into Sunday morning. In that storm. He went off the road. A farmer found him the next morning. Dr. Hanby believes he was struck by the door of the motorcar as it swung back toward him when he was thrown from the vehicle. Death was immediate. He probably never realized what happened."

"I can't . . ." She swallowed hard. "I can't believe it's true. I want to see him."

"I don't think you should."

Anger flared. "Someone is always telling me what to do." She walked to the steps, then thought of something. "Was he coming to see me? The night of the storm?"

"He was returning to East Dedham. We don't know where he'd been before that."

He hesitated. "Why do you think your sister had something to do with the news of Nathaniel Wright's death?"

"Because she doesn't want me to become involved with him. Her word, *involved*. Neither does my father. I can do so much better than a country parson. Margaret has. But I think she regrets her fine marriage now. She never seems quite happy."

It was an odd echo of what had gone wrong with Wright's first love.

As if she'd heard the thought, Miss Wilding lifted her hand in a gesture of despair. "My sister was engaged to Nathaniel, and she broke it off to marry someone else. I was only sixteen at the time, but I couldn't understand how she could have done such a thing. I thought he was wonderful."

Rutledge said nothing, and she went on, almost as if he weren't there.

"I met him here in Eastbourne, quite by accident. That was last summer. We've been seeing each other quite regularly since then. Always going to places where my parents weren't likely to find us. I was going to marry him." Tears filled her eyes again. "I don't want to *believe* it."

"Does anyone in your family drive? Do they possibly own a dark green motorcar?"

"Of course they drive," she said, taken aback at what she considered a trivial question. "And yes, both my father's motorcar and the one belonging to my sister's husband are a dark green. How can it matter at a time like this?"

"Does your sister live in Portsmouth, by any chance?"

"No, she lives in London. She has a large house there, and social position." Her voice was suddenly bitter. "That's all my mother talks about, how grand her house is, and who comes there to dine."

"I'll walk with you as far as the surgery," he said as she prepared to go.

"It isn't necessary."

"You've had a shock. I'd rather be sure you got there safely."

"I've no place to grieve." She turned to look at the cold waters of the sea, waves running in to crash on the strand, then hissing as they were sucked out again. "You can't stand guard over me every day, can you?"

"I don't think this is what Nathaniel Wright would want for you."

"Yes, he believed in an afterlife, didn't he? Now I'm not so sure I do. *His* God wouldn't have been so cruel. So perhaps He was only in Nathaniel's head, and not very real."

And she set out at a brisk pace, not waiting for him. He caught her up and walked beside her. "Would you like me to speak to your father?"

Hamish said, "It wouldna' do any good to speak to her father. He'd see yon Rector's death as a fine thing."

"No. It wouldn't make any difference," she told him, echoing Hamish's words.

When she went into the house and shut the door behind her, Rutledge turned away, but he was concerned for her.

He walked to the head of the street, where he could watch the house for a time, ignoring the cold wind that buffeted his shoulders. But Miss Wilding didn't come out again. And in the end he went back to his motorcar and turned toward East Dedham.

Wright had had everything to live for. Or so it would seem. No reason, clearly, for suicide. What, then, had gone wrong in his life? Had he killed Grant? He'd most certainly taken a motorcar without permission—and he hadn't borrowed it to call on Miss Wilding. Something had changed him. And not for the better.

B y the time he reached East Dedham, the streets were empty and the village appeared to be deserted. Only the lamplight visible through curtained windows gave any hint that people lived in the cottages and houses.

His mind was still on Miss Wilding as he made the turn toward the pub.

Had Wright really cared for her as much as she seemed to care for him? Or did he see their relationship as a way of getting back at the family that had rejected him years ago? Would he have married her out of spite, or out of love?

There was no way to know now. The man was dead, and what he felt had died with him. Still, however this inquiry ended, Rutledge hoped that Miss Wilding would never doubt Wright.

Tired, he drove into the yard by the pub and went up to his room.

No one was ever what he or she appeared to be, he thought as he climbed the stairs. Everyone had secrets—even he had them, hiding his shell shock from friends and enemies alike, from his sister as well.

Standish had them. And Wright. Grant too. But whether murder was among them, only time would tell.

He found a note pushed under his door, picked it up, and tossed it on the table by the bed. Going to stand by the window, he looked out. He could just see the churchyard from here, and a corner of the rectory. Even as he watched, Mrs. Saunders came into view, a basket over her arm and one hand keeping the hat on her head from the prying fingers of the wind. Her skirts blowing behind her, she stumbled once as the wind caught her, then recovered.

Rutledge was still wearing his coat. Retrieving his hat from the bed, he walked quickly to the door and went down the steps and outside in time to catch Mrs. Saunders up as she walked past the pub.

"Inspector," she said, surprised to see him.

"On your way to your sister's?" he inquired.

"Yes." She indicated the basket over her arm. "Mr. Barnes didn't care for my cooking again. If he stays on, I'll be let go as housekeeper. I can see that coming."

"If he has anything to say to it, he'll not stay."

"That's what keeps me from walking out now."

He let a silence fall between them before saying, "How often did the Rector go into Eastbourne?"

"Whenever he wasn't needed. It was good for him, I think. He always seemed to be happier when he came back."

"Do you know the names of anyone he may have called on there?"

She looked up at him. "He never said. And I didn't care to pry. It was his free time, you see. I thought perhaps someone he'd known in the war lived there. Or it was nothing more than getting away from East Dedham for a bit."

"Never a young woman?"

She smiled. "Heavens, no. I never had any notion he was seeing someone."

Wright had kept his promise, then. He'd said nothing, even to his housekeeper.

"How well did he know Timothy Grant?" Rutledge asked then.

"The one found dead up by the light? I shouldn't think he knew him very well at all. The Grants are Chapel folk."

Rutledge remembered something that Mrs. Grant had said. That his work often took Grant to Eastbourne and beyond.

Had he seen the Rector with Miss Wilding? And had Grant threatened to make what he'd seen public? He owed no loyalty to the Rector. A spot of blackmail might have seemed tempting to a man who scraped a living picking up rags and bones and the unwanted scraps from the houses of those better off than he was.

"If that was the ragman having words with the Rector," Hamish said, his voice clear in spite of the wind, "it doesna' bode well."

But Mrs. Saunders was saying, "Here we are at my sister's. Good evening, sir."

He realized she'd stopped in front of a tidy cottage on the far side of the green.

He wished her a good evening, tipped his hat, and walked on.

There were sandwiches for dinner that night, for the kitchen staff had Sunday evening off. Josie brought them up when she heard him climbing the stairs, a cloth over them, and a Thermos of tea in the other hand.

"You weren't here to pick what you'd like," she said in apology. "But there's egg and pickle, gammon and cheese, and a bit of chicken as well. A sponge for after."

He assured her that the selection was fine, and took the tray and the tea from her.

It was then he remembered the message he'd found under his door. Opening the envelope, he took out the single sheet and unfolded it. It was from Trotter.

I came home to find someone had been in my garage, poking about. I think you should know.

The sandwiches forgotten, Rutledge pulled on his coat, took up his hat, and went down to the yard, where he'd left his motorcar.

When he reached the garage, he drove slowly into the bare ground in front of it, looking around. But there was no sign of anyone about.

Getting out, he walked to the large door.

Hamish said, "'Ware!"

Instead of knocking, he called, "Trotter? Are you there? It's Rut-ledge."

He was beginning to think this might be a trap, and he stepped to one side, in the shadows near the rear of the motorcar.

After a moment the door opened slowly. There was only darkness inside, but the brightness of the headlamps picked out the steel barrel of a shotgun.

"Stand in the light, where I can see you," Trotter ordered, and Rut-ledge did as he was told.

"All right, you can come in, then."

The shotgun's barrel vanished, and a lamp was lit, casting heavy shadows around the inner room. "Come in. Took you long enough to get here."

"I was in Eastbourne much of the day," Rutledge answered, step-ping through the door. Trotter closed it behind him and barred it, then went to light another lamp. "How did you discover that someone had been here?"

Trotter set the lamp down on the workbench, and as the light touched his face briefly, his features were cast into relief, giving them a sinister look.

"Look around you. I have a goodly number of expensive tools. A thief could sell them at a market stall in Hastings or Brighton, and who would be the wiser? And so I take precautions. Whoever it was, he came in, poked around for a time, and went out again without taking anything. And look here," he added, leading the way to the Standish motorcar. "I left that door shut. And the mat below it is rumpled where someone stepped on it."

He lit a third lamp so that Rutledge could see clearly that the door was now ajar, and the mat had been displaced.

"Whoever it was, he came while it was light enough to see whatever it was he wanted to see. Perhaps he had a torch with him. And I was back here by dusk. I'd left at two o'clock to drive to Seaford. I'd had a message asking me to come look at a clutch that was giving the owner

trouble. I brought the motorcar here to work on it over that pit." Rutledge turned slightly and looked at the pit by one of the windows near
the rear of the building.

"That motorcar is out back, right now, if you need corroboration. I
took the lorry with me. If he was watching the garage, then he saw me
leave. If he wasn't watching, he looked for the lorry and didn't find it.
It's always here when I am."

"How did he get in?"

"Look at this building. It's older than my grandfather. The latch on
the rear door was forced. The wood splintered. I should have replaced
it long ago, but there hasn't been enough money to do it right."

"What was the intruder after? If he took nothing."

"I don't know. At a guess he was looking for something that should
have been in the motorcar. It's the only reason I can think of for opening that door. Unless it was sheer curiosity. But Constable Neville had
already searched it for anything that might explain why Rector was
driving it."

It *was* possible. But not likely. What then?

Rutledge asked Trotter for his torch and went to the rear, where the
streaks of dark green paint had been so obvious before.

"Come have a look," he said, and Trotter walked over to where he
was standing.

Someone had carefully buffed away all signs of green paint.

It was as if they had never existed.

Trotter swore with feeling.

"He'll have done the same with his own motorcar. You can be sure
of that," Rutledge said. "He must have seen the scrapes of dark red
paint and realized there would be marks on the Captain's vehicle as
well. Only three people knew about those marks. You, Constable Neville, and myself."

"And I haven't talked about it. You never said anything to Standish
about them?"

"No. On purpose." Rutledge took a deep breath as he passed the torch back to Trotter. "Could you tell, if someone had removed those paint marks?"

"Possibly. It depends on how well it was done. But whoever it was did a fine job here."

Rutledge left soon afterward, and drove straight to the Standish house.

The Captain was not receiving guests at this hour, he was told by the prim housekeeper.

"I'm not a guest," he said, and gently setting her aside, he asked, "Where is he?"

She protested, but Standish came to the staircase and started down. "What is it, Rutledge? Is there news?"

"Just a question that has come up in the course of the inquiry."

Standish thanked his housekeeper and led the way into the drawing room, this time offering Rutledge a seat. "I hope you've found out why Wright helped himself to the motorcar."

"Not at present," Rutledge said easily. "I'm told by someone I've interviewed that a dark green motorcar drove out of Eastbourne heading toward Beachy Head on the night of the storm. We're hoping that Wright might have passed him. If so, he might be able to give us some sense of where Wright was coming from. Constable Neville doesn't know of any motorcar fitting that description. I thought perhaps you might have friends or acquaintances who own such a vehicle?"

Standish frowned. "I know six or seven people with dark green motors. It's a common color. But I can't think that any one of them would have been in Eastbourne on the night of that storm. Three of them live in London, one in Surrey, one in Chichester, another in Arundel."

"If you'll give me their names, I'll get in touch with them."

"I've just thought of someone else. A medical man living in Eastbourne. A Dr. Wilding."

Hiding his surprise that Standish knew the man, Rutledge said, "Is he a friend?" Was this the connection between Wright and Standish that he'd been searching for? Miss Wilding? She had said nothing about knowing anyone else in East Dedham. But then he hadn't asked.

"No, no, I was under his care briefly. The surgeon recommended several local doctors, and I looked them up. Wilding seemed more experienced in such cases."

"Why did you see him?"

"I told you, he was recommended." Standish was abrupt, making it clear he was not prepared to discuss his reasons.

Rutledge had no official cause for insisting. But he thought he knew. The missing hand.

Before he left, Standish gave him the list of names.

Looking them over, he asked, "Have any of these people visited you in the past two or three months?"

"I haven't seen any of them in the past year. With the exception of Wilding, of course. Nor have they visited me." He shrugged awkwardly. "I've not been in the mood for house parties or the like. You were in the war?" He didn't wait for an answer, he took that as a given, because they were of a similar age. "You must know what it's like. There are those who came home to forget, hoping to outrun the past. I've seen them, drinking too much, dancing all night, brittle, seeking oblivion. The rest of us haven't found our place yet. It isn't a world we recognize, and we don't feel we're a part of it. We fought for 1914, but it's long since vanished in the smoke of guns and the blood soaking into the fields of Flanders. Wright felt the same way, I think. He avoided me, as I avoided him. We weren't likely to sit around over a glass of whisky and reminisce." Standish paused. "Well. That wasn't the question you asked, was it? I intended to explain why I haven't kept in touch, and ended up rambling like an idiot. Forgive me."

Rutledge understood what he'd said, better than Standish realized. But he answered only, "Nothing to forgive."

He thanked the Captain and said good night.

But after he'd turned the crank on his motorcar, he stood there, staring into the night.

Hamish said, his voice carrying above the wind in the trees, "Ye ken, it's the living and no' the dead who know the truth. The dead still believe it was worth dying for."

Rutledge got into the motorcar without answering. There was no answer.

He drove down the rutted drive and through the gates, turning back toward East Dedham. But he'd gone less than a hundred yards when his headlamps picked up the figure of a woman just coming out of the lane where he had dropped Jem off to hurry home. Slowing, he drew up near her and called, "Is something wrong?"

She looked to be in her late thirties, and she was wearing a coat over her nightdress.

Turning quickly away, she started back down the lane, embarrassed and wishing him at the devil. And then her need stopped her. Staying out of the brightness of his headlamps, she said, "I can't find my—my son. He's a young lad. Have you seen anyone on the road in that direction?" She pointed toward the way he'd come.

Trying to conceal his own rising alarm, he replied, "A boy? Sorry, no. I just left Captain Standish's house. I'll help you search, if you like."

She drew her coat closer, torn. "I can't think he'd come this far. It's not like him. But I've looked everywhere else."

"Perhaps he's gone out after rabbits," he offered, trying to find a reason that would persuade her to let him help.

But she shook her head. "That's not like him," she said again. "I'm worried—"

"Mum?"

They both heard the voice at the same time. She whirled, hunting the shadows behind her, and then hurried away from the road toward the voice.

"Mum?"

"Where have you been, Jem? I've been worried sick. Do you know what time it is? For heaven's sake, where have you *been*?"

"I woke up thinking there was a dog whining somewhere, as if he was hurt or lost. I went out to find him. I didn't want to wake you . . ."

He couldn't hear the rest, for they were out of earshot.

Hamish said, "It's no' wise for a lass to be out roaming the fields at this hour."

But Rutledge wasn't listening. "I smell smoke."

The wind had veered, blowing from behind him. He got out of the motorcar, unwilling to turn and look over his shoulder, directly into the space where Hamish might have been sitting.

But he couldn't see anything. Neither smoke nor flames. And yet the odor was so strong that he knew it wasn't the smoke from a chimney.

He got back into the motorcar and quickly reversed, racing back to the gates and then up the drive.

Coming to a rocking halt, he got out and pounded on the door.

It was the Captain who opened it.

"What the hell do you think—Rutledge? What is it, man?"

"Step out here. I smell smoke."

Standish went out into the drive, sniffing the air, turning this way and that. "Yes, it's coming—good God!"

Rutledge had seen it in the same instant. A growing brightness in the night sky. And it lit the billowing plumes of smoke rising above it.

"The stable. Behind the house," Standish said, already running back into the hall to shout for help.

Rutledge didn't wait. He turned and ran.

He got there first, realizing that the stable was well alight, and that there was nothing he nor Standish nor the servants could do to save it.

Coming to an abrupt stop, he could feel the heat of the flames on his face, and his first thought was, where had Jem been tonight? And had she done this? But why?

Behind him he could hear voices coming from the rear of the house. And the clanging of a fire bell, carrying on the night air.

Hamish shouted " *'Ware!*"

It was all that saved him. He could sense the blow coming, vicious and with intent to kill, and he managed to jerk away. But not far enough. Whatever it was, cold and hard, it grazed his temple and he went down, dazed, on the edge of losing consciousness, feeling the cold grass on his face as he fell.

"Get up!" Hamish was shouting. "*Now!*"

But he couldn't, he was too busy fighting the spinning confusion that was pulling him down into a well of blackness.

Hamish was calling his name, and he opened his eyes. For one chilling, awful moment he thought that he could see the Scot bending over him, and flung up an arm to shut out the horror of it.

Someone caught first one foot and then the other, and began to drag him toward the blaze.

II

Rutledge realized with a shock that he could feel hands on his
ankles.

Not Hamish, then. But someone else—whoever had hit him—

He fought the darkness now, pushing it away through sheer will,
knowing that if he didn't, he was going to be burned alive.

Catching his assailant unaware, he managed to jerk his left foot free,
drawing it up toward his body as soon as the grip on it slackened. And
then before whoever it was could recover, he kicked hard at the shadowy figure bending toward him.

There was a grunt, half pain, half curse, and his other foot was
dropped.

Rutledge struggled to rise to his knees and then stand, but he was far
from steady enough. Whoever was there, that black shape he could only
half see, growled like a cornered animal and shoved him backward with
all his might. Rutledge could feel the flames now, far too close, far too
hot, and caught at the arms pushing him. It wasn't enough. Letting go,
he aimed a blow toward the figure and struck him in the middle of his
body, knocking him backward. Rutledge went down as well, and rolled.

There were others on the scene now, voices exclaiming, shouting orders.

When he scrambled to his feet and braced himself for another attack, he realized that he was alone. And as his vision cleared, Standish was racing toward him, pulling him away from the fire.

"For God's sake, Rutledge, what the hell do you think you're doing?"

Rutledge shook his head, trying to clear it, and stopped almost at once as it made him dizzy.

"Did you see him?"

"See who?"

"The man—" He coughed as the wind blew smoke over them, and Standish, one arm over his face, dragged him away from the stable.

It was engulfed, now, the old wood feeding the flames. The staff had disappeared, and he could hear them shouting as sparks wafted toward the house.

"There was a man here. I didn't see him clearly. I don't know if he thought I was you or wanted me. He was bent on killing one of us."

Standish glanced at the dark spread of blood across Rutledge's face, but he didn't have time to worry about it. He said abruptly, "It can wait. The house—"

And he was sprinting back toward the kitchen garden.

Rutledge stood there, looking at the stable and the shadows where the fire's brightness couldn't penetrate. But there was no sign of whoever had attacked him.

Turning, he forced himself to race toward the house, to help if he could.

Standish was shouting orders. Other men were there now, from the tenant farms, dragging up ladders and climbing to the roof, buckets of sand or water in one hand. Rutledge helped pass up more buckets as they were needed, until the wind veered again, and the sparks went the other way only to come hurling back soon after.

Wives and children from the tenant farms were there as well, doing what they could to help, steadying the ladders, filling buckets with more sand, more water. And behind them the stable fell in with a *whoosh* that sent sparks flying in every direction, raising a cry of fear from the women present, and angry shouts from the men.

Early on, someone noticed Rutledge's bloody face, but assumed he'd hurt it trying to save the stable, and a woman handed him a wet cloth to wipe the worst of the blood and soot away. But the cut where the blow had landed continued bleeding freely, sometimes blinding one eye until he had a free hand to clear it again.

It was touch and go, a good two hours or more before they could be sure the roof was safe, that the urgency had passed. Behind them the fire continued to consume the stable, but it was dying down, no longer the first shooting flames that towered into the night sky.

The cook, Mrs. Donaldson, brought out a large tray with mugs of tea and cakes she had cut into squares to go farther.

Tea was passed up to the men sitting on the roof, and others came to take theirs. Rutledge had a moment to look around at the tenants. He thought he recognized each family from the description he'd been given. Jem's mother was there, helping drag buckets of water out of the pond and pass them on. She looked tired, a woman who had already worked through the short November day and had been robbed of sleep worrying over her daughter. And now this.

Jem was everywhere, doing what she could and avoiding any contact with Rutledge.

One of the maids was standing by the ruined kitchen garden, where busy feet had disregarded the cabbages and onions and other root vegetables still in the ground. The scent of trampled herbs vied with the heavy smell of smoke and burning wood.

"At least there were no horses," someone was saying to Standish. "I doubt we would have been in time to get them out."

"No." He looked exhausted, his clothes filthy from his exertions, and his hair standing on end.

The other man glanced across at Rutledge, and frowning, said, "What happened to your face?"

"Trying to save the stable," Rutledge said as others turned to hear his response.

It was another hour before everyone went home and the women from the household had gathered up the tea things and taken them inside.

Standish was looking up at the roof, searching for any sign of smoke. Finally he said to Rutledge, who was seated on the lip of the well, "It was a near-run thing."

"Yes."

"How did you know?"

"I was on the road when I smelled smoke. I turned back to find out where it was coming from."

"Yes, well, I owe you for that."

They stood in silence for a time, and then the Captain said, "I have no idea how it got started. There's nothing out there to cause a fire."

Rutledge said, "It was arson. Someone set the stable alight."

"You aren't serious? Yes, you are, aren't you? Who the hell would do such a thing? I can't think why anyone would even want to do it."

"I told you. He wanted to kill one of us. And I think the stable was a way to draw his victim out here in the dark."

Standish frowned. "Yes, you said something—I was too worried about the house to heed any of it. But it was bad timing for it to start. The fire. We wouldn't have noticed it until far too late to do much about it. Hardly the best way of attracting attention."

"Or he knew I'd spread the alarm, and was hoping one of us might come running."

The Captain shook his head. "Doesn't make sense." He gestured around his feet, where the grass was trampled and muddy. "The grass was high by the stable. You didn't know the area. Are you certain you didn't trip and fall, striking your head?"

He hadn't imagined the blow to the head, the hands gripping his feet, dragging him toward the burning stable. But he couldn't tell Standish that he'd been here before, in the dark.

"It would be more comfortable to think so," he said after a moment, considering Standish. This was possibly the second time the man had been attacked by proxy—when Wright was killed in his motorcar, and in the fire tonight. There hadn't been enough light for Rutledge to get a good look at the attacker. He'd been careful to keep his back to the blazing stable. But that could also mean he hadn't really seen Rutledge clearly.

On the other hand, Rutledge's tire had been slashed on a previous visit. And he himself might have been the target tonight. The timing of the fire suggested that.

Turning to look up at the house they'd managed to save, Rutledge said, "But you'd be a fool to ignore what's happening. Wright was driving your motorcar, and I was running to help save your stable."

He thought the Captain was going to ignore the warning.

But after a moment, he took a last look at the carnage that was the kitchen garden, then stared at the roof, scanning it one last time. "You'd better come in, then."

They didn't go to the drawing room but to the study, where Standish poured two stiff whiskies and handed one to Rutledge. It was awkwardly done, with one hand missing, but Standish had learned how to cope.

"Sit down." Standish walked to the windows and pulled the drapes across them, as if he wanted to shut out the night—and anyone who might be standing out there, watching him. Then he went to the hearth to stir up the fire, for the room was noticeably cold.

It was as if he was postponing the inevitable, putting off what he knew he had to say.

Rutledge was patient.

"You should do something about your face," the Captain told him instead. "I'll show you to one of the guest rooms."

"I'd rather get on with this before the headache grows any worse."

"Yes, well." He took a deep breath and went to sit behind the handsome desk, toying with the pens and then the inkwell. "It was during the war," he began. "The eve of the Somme. Were you there?"

"I was." It was curt, inviting no questions.

"There were seven of us. Our orders had come, our leaves cut short. Everyone knew the French were in trouble, but they'd held the Germans on the River Maine; we thought they could hold them again at Verdun. Then the shelling from our own guns began, a fearsome barrage. Always the prelude to an attack." He drank his whisky down and went to pour himself another. When he came back to the desk, he went on: "There was a barn just behind the lines. God knows how it had withstood the bombardment for two years. The house was rubble. But a very enterprising sergeant had seen a chance to make money. Whenever he was in rotation, he'd open the bar and serve any officers who were passing through. I didn't know the others sitting there; I'd never served with them. We were heading back to our sectors and we had a damned good idea that this was a big show. And given what was happening to the French at Verdun—I mean, they'd been fighting the Germans since February, and it didn't look very good by June—we reckoned we knew what was coming. God knows, it didn't scrape the surface of what lay ahead. And so we were drinking the sergeant's wine, getting more than a little drunk, and talking about everything from racing to what we'd do after the war ended. I was never sure how it came about, but we pledged each other that if we survived this attack—survived the war— we'd meet in Paris one year after the victory celebrations and race each other to Nice in our motorcars. All of us expected to have one. We were mad for one. And it sounded like a very good idea. Anything to take our minds off the next morning. We agreed. And five of us survived, much to our own surprise—it certainly didn't appear to be very likely for the rest of 1916 and into 1917."

He fell silent, toying with his glass.

"And so, having survived, you took your motorcar to Paris."

Standish roused himself. "Not this one—not the one Wright borrowed. Another one. I liked it a great deal. I thought it handled well. I felt there was even a very good chance that I might get to Nice first. Ever been there, in the south of France along the sea? There's a plateau before you reach the Mediterranean. And coming down from that plateau to sea level, you drive the devil's own roads. They twist and turn and they hug the edges of the cliffs, with no guards, no markings, and they are treacherous enough in daylight. By the time we got there, it was almost dark, and then a bloody mist came crawling up the precipices, blinding us. I considered pulling off somewhere and stopping until morning. There were villages perched on the edges of the cliffs. Or I could have stopped where the roads were broader, but I kept telling myself the others wouldn't stop, and if I wanted to make even a respectable showing, I wouldn't either. I talked myself into going on. Well, I expect the others must have done the same thing. Not competing so much as—" He searched for the right word. "We'd survived the unsurvivable, and I expect we wanted to prove to ourselves that it wasn't mere luck." He put his hand over his face, pressing it against his cheekbones. "Does it make any sense?"

Rutledge said, "Risking your lives again?"

Standish dropped his hand. "No. Not risking them so much as proving something to ourselves. A matter of courage. We'd made that promise when none of us expected to see the next sunset. My God, Rutledge, nearly twenty thousand men died that first day of battle. It could have been any one of us—all of us. Two were killed later, but we all survived the Somme. It was a triumph of the spirit, don't you see? And making that drive, we raced the devil and won. We didn't race each other."

He rose and went to the decanter, thought better of it, and put the whisky down. "Only it wasn't quite what we expected it to be, that final run. Someone ran me off the road. I went over the edge, and should have died in the fall down the face of the cliff. When rescue came, I was unconscious, my hand badly mangled, and yet miraculously, I lived."

"Who were the other men in that race?"

Standish shook his head. "No. I won't give you their names. I can't believe any one of them would be capable of trying to kill any of the others. Besides, I didn't know them well enough to have made an enemy of them. Certainly not well enough for one of them to want to kill me. I've told you, we didn't even serve in the same sector."

"Were you the only driver to be attacked like that?"

"I don't know," he answered slowly. "They came to the hospital to say good-bye, on their way back to England. But it was rather odd. The others seemed to want nothing so much as to go home. They weren't even eager to set up another meeting in, say, five years' time. If all had gone well, if we'd had a successful run, I think we'd have looked forward to that. As it was, God knew I wanted no part of such a reunion."

"What you're telling me is that none of you trusted the other four."

"No. I don't think it was that." He went to the window and drew the drapes aside to look out into the darkness, then pulled them to again. Turning back to Rutledge, he said, choosing his words, "I think when someone first broached the idea, we were nearly certain we were going to die. If not in the first assaults, then certainly before the week was out. We saw ourselves as doomed. We didn't want to think of home, of family; it was too painful. Here was something we could tell ourselves made living worthwhile. And when we lived through the nightmare of the Somme, we told ourselves that we could do it again. And again. Until the end."

"What about the two men who didn't survive?"

"One of them wrote to us to say he'd be with us in spirit. That he wanted badly enough to do this that he was going to make the journey with us." He gave Rutledge a wry smile. "You'll laugh. But there were times on that long drive south when I thought of him and felt him there in the motorcar with me."

Rutledge said only, "There's no reason to laugh."

"No."

Standish looked away. "I wish to God we'd never made that promise to meet in Paris. But at the time, it felt as if we were defying death."

"And you've never seen these men since that day in the hospital?"

"Nor have they contacted me."

"Wright was followed out of Eastbourne or wherever it was he'd gone. And whoever was driving the other motorcar probably caused his death."

"Good God." Standish stared blankly at him. "But it's not possible. I can't think any one of the other four would—I mean to say, if they followed him, they would have known it wasn't me."

"Not in the dark, in the rain."

"But this wasn't the motorcar I drove last year, when we met." It almost sounded as if Standish was pleading with him, begging him not to connect the crash with the other four men who had survived to meet in Paris. "No, I refuse to believe it."

When Rutledge didn't answer, the Captain said, "Look, Wright took my motorcar without permission. Why? What was so pressing that he couldn't wait until I came back? That's what you need to find out. That's where you need to direct your search for answers." This time when he went to the decanter, he refilled his glass.

"The stable belonged to you."

"Coincidence."

"What about your tenants? Do any of them hold a grudge against you?"

"No, of course not. I've been more than generous with them. They struggled to manage during the war with the shortage of able-bodied men, and it's not much better now. I'd be a fool to blame them. And I'm not the only landowner who has faced this problem."

Rutledge's head was thundering. He set his half-empty glass on the desk and rose. "We're not going to find any answers tonight. Get some sleep, if you can. I'll come back in the morning. We can tell more in daylight."

"I'm going out once more to make certain the fire is no longer a threat to the house. Are you in any shape to drive back into the village? There's room here to put you up."

Rutledge thanked him but refused the offer. This time his host walked with him to the door and saw him out.

Turning the crank, he got into the motorcar and then sat there for a time, looking at the closed door to the house. But his head wasn't clear enough to work out just what had happened and why. In the end, he set out and drove with extreme care all the way back to The Sailor's Friend. This was not the time to find himself in a ditch.

R utledge climbed the stairs to his room, closed the door behind him, and crossed to the washstand mirror to look at his face.

It was enough to frighten children, he thought wearily, and poured water into the basin to wash away the blood. But it had dried and it took him several minutes to rid himself of the worst of it. The cut ran from above his eyebrow to his hairline by his ear, across the bone of his cheek. It was already showing bruising, and he had a feeling his eye might be black by morning.

He couldn't tell what his assailant had used to hit him, but it had broken the skin, and only luck—and Hamish's warning—had saved him from worse.

There had been anger and intent behind that blow, and when it hadn't killed him, whoever had attacked him had tried to pull him into the fire. Anger? Vindictiveness?

Vengeance?

Whoever it was had been only a black silhouette against the brightness of the fire. Try as he would, Rutledge couldn't recall any detail that would help him identify his adversary.

He turned to the sandwiches and tea Josie had brought earlier. The tea was tepid now, but he drank it anyway, his throat still raw from the smoke.

There was nothing more he could do tonight. He undressed, got ready for bed, and turned off the light.

He slept too deeply to hear Hamish or anything else in the night.

Rutledge drove out to the Standish house as soon as the sun was high enough to inspect the still-smoking ruins.

He spent a good hour examining the ground close by the stable, looking for any sign that would indicate how the fire was set. But there was nothing to find. A match, a candle, a bit of smoldering grass or tinder would have been consumed by the blaze long before any alarm had brought people running.

Halfway through his search, Captain Standish came out to speak to him. He had drunk too much last night. His eyes were bloodshot and his hand shook.

He smiled ruefully at Rutledge. "I'm not accustomed to five whiskies before I go to bed. Any luck?"

"None. Not that I expected to find anything useful." Rutledge scraped at graying ash with the toe of his boot. "It was an intense fire, fed by the age of the wood. One wouldn't need to do more than give it a start. A match here, another there. The wind took it as well, once it started. Just be grateful he, whoever he may be, didn't decide to burn down your house instead."

Standish swore. "It might have caught, whether he'd intended it or not. Do you think he'll come back and try just that?"

"I don't know. I think he's letting you know that he knows you're still alive."

"You're harking back to our conversation last night. Maybe whoever it was is punishing me for letting Wright borrow my motorcar. I'm sure he didn't know the Rector hadn't asked."

Rutledge smiled. "That's not as unlikely as you think. Early days."

"Yes, well, for God's sake, find this bastard before he does any more damage. Or kills someone else."

"He might have done that already. I've told you about the rag-and-bone man we found dead at Belle Tout light. Grant."

Standish turned to consider him. "The one who may've argued with Wright? But what does he have to do with me? Why would their killer want to burn my stable?"

"I intend to find out." Rutledge gestured to the blackened ashes, the stark stubs of pieces of wood that hadn't been consumed. Suddenly it reminded him of No Man's Land, and the torn trees that littered the muddy, blackened landscape. "This confused the issue. But that could be exactly what someone had in mind. I have to take that into account as well."

"Then hurry." Standish put a hand protectively over his empty cuff, a measure of his concern. "I don't like what's happening here."

"It's why I came here this morning," Rutledge said, and walked away.

He lingered, however, by the lane where he had seen Jem and her mother, hoping to catch sight of the girl.

Last night, as she was hurrying from one task to another, doing her bit to save the house, there had been no real opportunity to speak to her—and he'd had the distinct feeling that she was carefully avoiding him, for she never came near enough to him to make speech possible.

But the lane was empty. He told himself she would have chores at this hour of the morning, and after a while he drove on.

Where had she been last night?

And more important, what had she seen?

12

As he came into East Dedham, Rutledge saw Constable Brewster in conversation with one of the shop owners. Brewster turned toward the motorcar, and Rutledge slowed.

"There was a fire at Four Winds last night, sir," he said. "I just heard. The—" He broke off as he got a really good look at Rutledge's face. "What's happened, sir?"

"I was there talking to Standish when the fire was discovered. But there was no damage to the house. Only to the old stable where he kept his motorcar."

"Good thing the motorcar wasn't inside," Brewster replied. "Not even Trotter could have repaired that. But I'd have Dr. Hanby take a look at that cut, sir. It's nasty."

"Yes, later. Have a look at this list. Know anything about any of these people? Have they ever been to East Dedham?" A village constable knew his turf, knew who came and went.

Brewster scanned the names. "No, sir, I don't recognize any of them. Who are they, sir?"

"Friends of the Captain's. People he knew before the war." But not the four men whose names he'd asked for.

"Yes, sir. I will say the Captain was never one for large house parties at Four Winds. But he did spend time in London. Perhaps he visited them there."

"Does Standish have a house in London?"

"Not to my knowledge, sir. I've heard he most often stayed at his club." He passed the list back to Rutledge and stepped away from the motorcar as Rutledge thanked him and made to move on.

He went next to find Constable Neville, and asked him the same question, but after studying the list, Neville said, "Did you speak to Constable Brewster about these names?"

"Yes. He didn't recognize them."

Neville nodded. "I don't recall any of them. On the other hand, if the Captain brought them down to East Dedham, I doubt they'd have wandered about. There's not all that much to see here. Except the sea." He hesitated. "What's happened to your face, sir?"

He told Neville about the fire.

Rutledge went back to East Dedham, to the rectory, and spoke to Mrs. Saunders as well. She had flour on her hands, despite having wiped them on her apron when she answered his knock.

Her expression changed as she looked up at him. "Oh, dear, and what's happened? Have you come to blows with Mr. Barnes? I do hope not, the Bishop will be very unhappy. Does it hurt terribly? Is there anything I can do?"

He wished his attacker at the devil for not striking in a less conspicuous place, then assured her it didn't hurt at all, and would be gone in a day or so.

Bringing out the list, he passed it to her, asking if she knew any of the names on it. She read it through, then shook her head. "I don't know any of these men. At least they've never come to the rectory. And Rector never spoke of them in my hearing. Are they important?"

"I don't believe they are," he said, keeping his tone light, not wanting the list to become a subject for gossip. "These are friends of Captain Standish's, and I needed to know if the Rector had been acquainted with any of them as well."

"Yes, sir, I'm sorry I couldn't be more helpful." She glanced over her shoulder, then said in a lower voice, "Himself, now, he's written a letter to his Bishop, he says. I only hope he's not taken a sudden liking to the village."

"I doubt it," Rutledge answered, smiling. "I should think the Vestry would have something to say in the matter."

He left the rectory and turned toward Eastbourne.

He would have to call on Wilding and have a look at the man's motorcar. The more affluent doctors had seen early on the advantages of a motorcar when called out in foul weather, no horse to care for and tend at the end of a long day.

But would he have been stupid enough to follow Wright back to Burling Gap and run him off the road? Or daring enough to slip unseen into Trotter's garage to buff out the green paint on Standish's motorcar?

Hamish said, "If he's an arrogant sort, he willna' expect to be found out."

And there was some truth to that.

What would Miss Wilding have to say about Rutledge's appearance in her father's surgery?

He left his motorcar around the corner from the Wilding house and walked back. Then he changed his mind and continued to the Promenade, going as far as the bandstand. But there was no sign of Miss Wilding walking the dog, Ginger. Retracing his steps, he went back to the house and up the path to the surgery door.

The woman who let him in looked at his face and said, "There are two patients before you. But the doctor will see you as soon as possible."

He'd opened his mouth to tell her his business, then said, "Thank you," instead.

After giving his name, he followed her down the passage to the room where patients waited, took a seat, and looked around. The walls were cream, the furnishings comfortable enough, and the carpet a dark green. Seascapes were hung on the wall, in keeping with the holiday air of Eastbourne, and the other patients, a man and a woman, appeared to be fairly prosperous.

When he was at last called into the doctor's inner office, Rutledge was not surprised to see that Wilding was a man of middle height, dressed soberly in well-cut dark gray clothing, a heavy gold watch chain across his vest. His younger daughter hadn't inherited his attractive features, or his dark hair, silver-streaked now. But she had a grace that her father lacked.

Wilding would have been perfectly at home on Harley Street in London, where the best-known doctors and surgeons had their surgeries.

"Were you in a fight?" he asked, coming around the desk to take a closer look at Rutledge's face. "No stitches, that cut will heal cleanly, I daresay, if you take care of it. Any trouble with that eye? No? Good. I don't think the cheekbone is broken, although it might well feel as if it is."

Rutledge let him finish his examination and return to his chair behind the desk.

"I'll give you something for the pain, as needed. Enough for three or four days. If it troubles you, come back again. Or see your own doctor if you live elsewhere. Which hotel are you staying in?"

"I've come from East Dedham," Rutledge said, "but only in an official capacity. I'd like to have a look at your motorcar." He took out his identification and handed it across the desk. "Inspector Rutledge, Scotland Yard."

Wilding looked bewildered for a moment and then, rising, glared at him angrily.

"You, sir, are here under false pretenses. You will leave here at once."

"Hardly false pretenses." Rutledge didn't move. "There has been a fatal motorcar accident. The Yard is looking for the other vehicle involved, which left the scene rather than stay and offer assistance." There was no need to mention Wright or Standish. If Wilding was guilty of running down the Rector, then he already knew their names. And it was just as well not to bring the Rector into the conversation, for Miss Wilding's sake.

"Are you suggesting that I was a party to this? I've taken an oath, Rutledge. I would have been honor bound to render assistance." He was livid.

"Nevertheless, I shall need to see your motorcar."

The fact that Rutledge hadn't risen, that he had quietly insisted on doing his duty, seemed to reach Wilding, and he got a grip on his fury, the effort showing in his flushed face. "Very well. Come with me."

He walked rapidly out of the office, through the empty waiting room, collecting his coat from a stand, and out of the house into the street without waiting to see if Rutledge had followed him. The motorcar was kept around the corner in a former livery stable that had been converted into spaces numbered for each house that had reserved one. There were lamps burning overhead, and they walked down the row until Wilding stopped at a dark green Rolls, very similar to Rutledge's but newer. He went around to the bonnet and turned the crank before moving the motorcar out into the space next to where Rutledge was standing.

"Look, if that's why you're here, then I shall have words with your superiors in London."

Rutledge was already walking around the vehicle, stooping here and there to search for any indications of a collision. By the time he reached the bonnet again, he had already come to the conclusion that this was not the motorcar he was seeking. There was no sign of a recent buffing, no dents or scrapes that might have occurred in an accident involving another vehicle.

It was possible, as Hamish was suggesting in the back of his mind, that Wilding had had repairs done professionally. But Rutledge was of the opinion that Wilding wouldn't risk going to a garage, where a stranger might see an advantage to removing red paint from a green motorcar.

"There's no indication that your motorcar was involved," Rutledge said, coming to join the fuming doctor. "As for contacting my superiors, Acting Chief Superintendent Markham will be happy to hear from you. I hope you'll explain as well that you were obstructing the course of my inquiry by refusing to bring me here."

Wilding got back into his motorcar, returned it to its allotted space, and then without a word waited for Rutledge to leave before stalking back to his house.

Rutledge watched him turn the corner and then walked to where he'd left his own motorcar. He took his torch out of the boot and went back to the mews. With torch in hand, he searched every dark green vehicle there. If Wilding had chosen to go after Wright, he might have been cunning enough to borrow another man's motorcar. Just as Wright had borrowed the Captain's.

He came up empty-handed.

Walking back to his own vehicle, he was relieved that he hadn't run into Miss Wilding.

And then he saw her, standing at the end of the path just outside her front door, staring this way and that as if searching for someone. She hadn't even brought a coat, and her hair was caught by the wind, blowing across her face. Her skirts were moving with it, flicking around her ankles.

He was about to turn away before she could see him, but it was too late. She cast a worried glance toward the door behind her, then ran down the street toward him.

"I heard my father—he was angry about a policeman coming to his surgery. How could you betray me like that?" she demanded as soon as she was near enough to talk to him. Close to tears, angry herself, she stopped in front of him, barring his path.

"I didn't mention you or the Rector. I came to look at your father's motorcar. Someone ran Wright's vehicle off the road, causing him to turn over and crash."

"You never told me you suspected my father! You lied to me about that as well."

He shook his head. "I had no choice in the matter, I had to clear your father."

"I don't believe you."

"Why would I lie? I can't abandon my inquiry, Miss Wilding, because you object to the manner in which it has to be carried out."

"Did you tell him? Does he *know*?"

"I've already answered that."

She was shivering violently in the cold wind.

"Is there someplace we could go?" He took off his coat and held it out to her, well aware that she wouldn't want him to put it around her shoulders.

For a long moment he thought she would refuse, but her teeth were chattering now, and she took the coat, slipped into it, and hugged its warmth around her. "It smells of smoke."

"There was a fire last night. Deliberately set, as far as we can tell."

"Is that how you hurt your face? Fighting the fire?"

"Yes," he said deliberately, not wanting to tell her the whole truth.

She considered him. "You aren't at all like Constable Plant. He's our local policeman."

Rutledge smiled. "I expect I'm not."

"He would tell me to listen to my father, that he knew best. But Papa doesn't *always* know best. My sister was quite headstrong, and I think he's trying to be more careful about me."

"She didn't get her way about Nathaniel Wright."

"No," she said pensively. "I think that was because in the end she could see the disadvantages of marrying a country parson. Penniless and dull, my mother says. Nathaniel wasn't like that, but they couldn't look beyond his living. If he'd been given a very fine church in a large city, it might have made a difference. More to the point, I probably wouldn't have fallen in love with him if he had."

"Do you think," he asked, "that Wright had come in to see your father that night? To have it out with him? He couldn't have been happy about meeting you without your family's permission to call on you."

"He wasn't very happy about that. But I knew, you see, that my father wouldn't have allowed it. And I wanted to decide for myself if what I'd felt toward him at sixteen had been anything more than a schoolgirl's infatuation with her elder sister's fiancé. It didn't take me very long to realize that he was the man I'd thought he was."

He believed her. Her face was earnest, her eyes holding his. But she hadn't answered his question.

"Did he come to see your father that Saturday night?"

She looked away, but he saw the worry she wanted to hide. "My father went to attend a patient at seven that evening. My sister was here. She waited up for him. Mother and I had gone to Rye to spend the day with her cousin. Nathaniel knew I'd gone there. That's why it isn't likely that he would come to Eastbourne."

But sitting there alone in the rectory, fighting his conscience about the secretiveness of his relationship with Miss Wilding—possibly even worried about his encounter with Grant—he might have decided to have it out with Wilding. And so, with a storm brewing, he'd chosen to borrow Standish's motorcar rather than arrive in Eastbourne wet to the skin from riding his bicycle.

A bicycle that was still missing.

And it was entirely possible that it wasn't Dr. Wilding whom Wright had found at home that night, but his former fiancée, Wilding's elder daughter.

Rutledge said, "Does your sister drive down often?"

"More and more frequently. I've told you Margaret isn't very happy. She learned to drive just to be able to come home whenever she likes. She doesn't care for traveling by train. And Lawrence, her husband, indulges her frightfully. I think she would respect him more if he told her that her place was in London with him."

"What sort of work does Lawrence do that made him more acceptable than a country parson?" he asked, leading her toward the answer he was after.

"He's a barrister. He has chambers near Leadenhall Street, and a fine house in Hancock Square. My mother is quite pleased about that. Two of Margaret's neighbors have titles. Minor ones, but titles nevertheless."

He had what he needed. "You're still shivering, with no hat or gloves. I'll walk you to your door."

"No, it's best if you don't." She took off his coat and passed it to him. "I want to attend Nathaniel's services. Will you take me to East Dedham? Will you send me word? There's no one else."

Her voice nearly broke on the last words, and he found himself promising.

"Thank you." She turned away and hurried up the street to the Wilding house. She disappeared inside without looking back.

He slowly put his coat on as he watched her go, then went to find his motorcar.

He couldn't help but notice that the scent Elizabeth Wilding wore lingered in the warmth of the wool.

He made a decision, as he turned the crank and got into his motorcar, to go on to London from Eastbourne. And there was one other stop he intended to make on the way.

Melinda Crawford had been close to his parents before their deaths, and her affection for them had included their son and daughter. Melinda herself had led a very interesting life. Her father had been stationed in India during the Great Mutiny, and while he was away with his battalion, the rebels had attacked Lucknow, besieging the residency where English women and children and other noncombatants had retired for safety with the small garrison. Before the first siege was lifted eighty-seven days later, young Melinda had been hailed as a heroine, bringing water and cartridges to the defenders. She had grown up to marry a cousin who was also a British officer, and after his death she had made her way back to England by the most roundabout way she could devise, traveling with only her Indian servants. It had been an outstanding feat in itself. Making her home in Kent, she maintained her contacts with the Army and with many men in the government—if rumor was true, refusing the proposals of half of them—and Rutledge had no doubt that she knew more about the conduct of the Great War than any other civilian alive.

As a resource, she was priceless. More than that, he was particularly fond of her.

And so he arrived in time for dinner, to the delight of his hostess and her staff.

Shanta, Melinda's Indian housekeeper, came smiling to take his coat, and he was ushered into the small drawing room.

"My dear," Melinda said, holding up her face for his kiss on her cheek. "This is a lovely surprise. There's just time for a drink before we go in. And the fire is blazing away." After living in the tropics, she kept fires going most of the year, and in this season, what appeared to be a log was burning away on the oversized hearth.

Rutledge winced, remembering the fire in the stable last night, but allowed himself to be led to the best chair and handed a whisky.

"And what have you done to your face?" she asked as he took his first sip. It was very good, a single malt that was as smoky as the Highlands she got it from. He could feel himself relaxing.

"There was a fire last night, a stable being used to house a motorcar. I was on the scene."

"Oh, yes? And who struck you while you were fighting this fire?"

It was no use. Melinda Crawford had seen war firsthand. She wouldn't be palmed off with a tale of ladders collapsing.

He lifted a hand, accepting defeat as gracefully as he could. "I wish

I knew," he told her. "He got away. Whether he's a murderer or not, I don't know, but there's every chance that he is."

"Constables on the beat have their clubs. Why don't you have some means of defense?" It was an old argument, and he had no hope of winning it.

"I ducked. It could have been worse if I hadn't."

"Yes, I see that. It's a good thing you don't have a wife, Ian. She would worry herself into an early decline over the chances you take."

He smiled. "I don't need a wife. I have you to fuss over my wounds." He'd always been afraid that she might discover the one wound, invisible and haunting, that he'd hidden from her and from his sister. Hamish MacLeod had no place in their lives. But sometimes he suspected that Melinda understood more than she let him see.

Satisfied, she returned his smile. "Now, tell me your news. How is Frances faring with her wedding plans? I'm told she's found the gown she wished for. I've asked her to send me a photograph of it."

He gave her what news he had, and asked after the staff.

It wasn't until the port was passed—Melinda made no secret of the fact she enjoyed a small glass—that she asked what had brought him to her, and if he could stay the night.

"I'm in the middle of an inquiry along the East Sussex coast," he said. "And there appears to be a mystery within a mystery. I thought perhaps you could help me find out what I need to know."

"Of course. Tell me the whole story."

And so he did, about the seven men who had pledged to meet after the war and drive from Paris to Nice, an affirmation of survival.

"That's not unusual, you know," she said when he'd finished. "Richard Crawford—Bess's father—told me a story once about three officers in India who vowed they would meet on a certain date to travel to Nepal to hunt tigers. They must have been quite drunk at the time because they drew up an agreement and each signed it in his own blood, cutting his finger with the pear knife and writing his name. Later, one died of dysentery, another of cholera, and the third of gangrene from the prick of a thorn. But their faithful bearers went to Nepal on their behalf, because the arrangements had already been made. When they got there, they were told that villagers claimed that someone had just shot a tiger, and yet there was no one at the lodge, the guides hadn't taken out anyone, and there was no explanation for the tiger's death. This spooked the bearers, as you can well imagine, and they fled back to India as fast as they could go, spreading the account everywhere they stopped." She smiled. "This intrigued Richard. He was a Major at the time, and he happened to have official business in the north. And so he and Simon—you recall Simon? He became Richard's Regimental Sergeant Major? Yes—somehow got themselves a bit of leave and made their way to the lodge near the Nepalese border with India, to look into this tale. It's the lodge where the three men had intended to stay. Everyone swore the incident was true. The odd thing was, when the lodge people had gone out to bring in the tiger's body, it was no longer there, even though the villagers had seen it there, quite dead. The story got around that both the tiger and the hunter who killed it were ghosts."

After a moment, Rutledge said, "You're suggesting that whoever killed the Rector and drove the Standish car off the headland road above Nice is a ghost?"

"Stranger things have happened, but I've never heard of ghosts driving a motorcar. Coaches and carriages, yes, but not motorcars. What is it you need from me?"

He grinned at her. "I must learn the names of those other four men. You have connections in France. I'd like to know who the five were who signed the register in the Ritz Hotel in Paris, around this time last year. If your connection can find Roger Standish's name, he will be able to find the others. And I'd like to know what the French police in Nice put down in their report as the cause of Standish's accident."

"Nice is not a problem at all. I have a dear friend, a retired Naval officer, living there at the moment. If George can't find out about a police report, no one can. As for Paris, Bess is there just now, visiting a friend. The Ritz will be no problem for her."

Rutledge laughed. "By God, you should have run the Intelligence Service during the war."

Melinda cocked an eyebrow at him, and said, quite seriously, "I most certainly supplied them with information now and again, but I had no desire to run it. I'll send wires straightaway. It shouldn't be a matter of more than a day or two for them to find the information you need. And I'll telephone you as soon as I hear."

There was a telephone in one of the hotels in Eastbourne, but none in East Dedham, he told her.

"That does present a problem," she agreed. "I shall find a way, never fear."

Rutledge believed her. Melinda Crawford had never faced defeat.

He spent the night. It was a long drive from Kent to London, and he didn't want to arrive in the small hours, waking Frances. Besides, his head still throbbed, and he'd drunk more whisky and port than was safe.

Fortified with breakfast and promises that Melinda would send him news as soon as she heard, he set out for London.

When he reached the city, he avoided the Yard. What's more, the street was shut off by workmen. The wood-and-stone cenotaph that had been put up in Whitehall to mark the end of the Great War was being replaced by the same design in Portland stone. The King would unveil it during the ceremony to consecrate the Tomb of the Unknown Soldier in Westminster Abbey.

Rutledge needed no monuments to mark the end of the war. No ceremonies, no wreaths, no parades. He had seen the poppies in the fields of Flanders at first hand. He had seen the wounded, the dead, the blackened ruin of northern France. It was forever seared in his memory.

And yet the gratitude of a nation that had watched the flower of its youth slaughtered for four years was touching. It was just that he couldn't bear the images it evoked.

Staying as far away from Westminster as he could, he made his way to Leadenhall and left his motorcar nearby, setting out on foot.

It reminded him of the neighborhood canvassing he'd done as a raw constable, assigned to interview anyone who might have seen something that would help solve the crime that was the center of the inquiry. He'd been good at it, smiling for maids and using his authority when speaking to householders or butlers.

There was a cold wind off the Thames whistling up the lanes leading into the City from the river, and he pulled up the collar of his coat as he walked briskly toward Leadenhall. He quickly realized that Elizabeth Wilding had been more generous than she knew when she described her brother-in-law's chamber as "near" Leadenhall. After a lengthy search, Rutledge found what he was after several streets away: the firm of Montgomery, Applegarth, & Winter.

Lawrence Montgomery was head of chambers and in court for most of the day, he was told by the firm's chief clerk. Rutledge declined to leave a name or a message, which appeared to annoy the clerk, although he hid it well.

From there, Rutledge went to Hancock Square, but his luck had run out.

It wasn't a large square, perhaps no more than a dozen houses around a central garden surrounded by a black iron railing, gates at each point of the compass. He considered knocking on every door until someone directed him to the Montgomery dwelling, but he was reluctant to leave a trail of gossip behind.

He waited nearly a quarter of an hour for a constable to appear. The man walked slowly down the south side of the square, taking in the strange motorcar parked where the street turned.

Rutledge got out and went to meet him. Identifying himself, he asked the constable which house belonged to Lawrence Montgomery.

Striving to hide his curiosity—Scotland Yard was seldom to be found in this rarefied part of London—he pointed out number eleven.

Rutledge thanked him and walked on before the constable could ask questions.

Number eleven boasted an elegant black door with an equally elegant brass knocker in the shape of a stag's head, and a prim maid in black who informed Rutledge that Mrs. Montgomery was presently at Oxford, visiting friends.

"Did she drive, or take the train?" he asked.

"She drove, I believe, sir. Would you care to leave a card or a name?"

"I'm only in town for the day," he replied, "and I was hoping to surprise her. Is she by any chance visiting the Garlands, in Oxford? I might give them a ring to say hello." It was the first name he could think of.

"She didn't say, sir, who she was visiting. I'm sorry."

And that was that. He thanked her and left.

He toyed briefly with the possibility of driving on to Oxford, but he had been too long away from Sussex as it was, and searching the city for one woman could take days.

But the maid's news seemed to verify something that Elizabeth Wilding had told him, that her sister looked for excuses to leave London, coming often to Eastbourne.

There was nothing for it but to head south toward Sussex and the coast without surveying her motorcar.

It was late afternoon when he reached Burling Gap. The sun was bright in a cloudless sky, and he drove to an open space close by the village. Getting out, he went to stand at the cliff's edge, looking down at the flint-strewn strand far below. Then he lifted his head. The sea was the deepest of blues as far as he could see, and the wind ruffled the water, wavelets glittering briefly in the sunlight in a mesmerizing dance. He watched them for a time, then followed the gulls wheeling above a fishing boat halfway to the horizon. To his left was the Belle Tout light, and to his right the Seven Sisters were brilliantly white, their chalk faces topped by an undulating line of green turf. The white cliffs at Dover had nothing on the Seven Sisters.

Just then a bit of the grass not ten feet from where he stood seemed to open without warning, and the yellowing chalk below it, weakened by the sea, peeled away to slide with a roar onto the strand. And the face where the fall had occurred was now blindingly new and white.

Burling Gap, he thought, was surely doomed, and the lighthouse as well. What would the villagers do then? Move inland another fifty yards, or give up their own ways and try to fit into the lives of the inhabitants of East Dedham?

With the sound of the wind blowing off the sea, he didn't hear footsteps behind him until Hamish said, "'Ware!" in warning.

Rutledge turned to find Constable Neville walking toward him.

"Afternoon, sir," he said, coming to stand beside Rutledge.

"Good afternoon, Constable. I've been in London. Any news?"

"All quiet, as far as I can tell." He hesitated. "Do you think it's possible that Mrs. Grant murdered her own husband? There's the money he took from her, but we didn't find it on the body."

"It's possible," Rutledge agreed, turning to walk back to the motorcar. "She's put on quite a show of collapsing in grief, but you know her better than I do. What do you think?"

"It's the belt buckle, sir," Neville replied. "It wasn't taken. And it's a handsome thing, that buckle. You'd think his killer might have considered selling it somewhere. Not in Eastbourne or Pevensey, where it might be recognized. Surely it'ud bring in a tidy sum in a place like Dover or even Canterbury." He bent to turn the crank, and then got into the motorcar with Rutledge. "Just a thought, sir."

"And it would solve one of our problems, with two bodies and suspects thin on the ground," he agreed, turning toward the Gap police station. "Mrs. Grant wouldn't take the buckle. If she killed her husband, it's the last thing she'd want."

"Exactly, sir."

"Do you know who Wright was visiting in Eastbourne?"

"I didn't know that he was, sir. I knew he went there from time to time, when there was no pressing business in the parish. I'd always put it down to getting away from the problems he dealt with every day. About half of my patch goes to St. Simon's. We aren't all Chapel folk. And the gossip runs both ways."

"Surely Wright had someone in East Dedham that he might call a friend. Someone in the Vestry, someone he might talk to when he was troubled, or tired of his own company." Rutledge had asked before, but he'd found it hard to believe that Wright didn't. "He must have been a lonely man, if he hadn't."

"He'd dine from time to time with his parishioners, but from all I've heard, he kept himself to himself. That's not to say he wasn't there if you needed him, and kind into the bargain, but he was not one to be knocking at your door unexpectedly, if you get my drift. This was especially true after he came back from the war. Before 1914, he was a bit more outgoing. He'd step into the pub of nights and spend a little time talking with the men. But he was never one to speak of himself." Neville grinned at him as they drew up in front of the tiny police station. "This didn't stop the local mothers from matchmaking."

Rutledge could understand that. His sister's friends were forever throwing eligible young ladies his way, and he'd learned that invitations to dinners or the theater were often intended to pair him with one or another of them. Marriage was the last thing on his mind, as long as Hamish occupied a corner of it. In spite of the loneliness.

He told Neville about the green paint on Standish's motorcar being removed while Trotter was away.

The constable shook his head. "There's our best chance of proving the crash was no accident. I don't see an end to this business. Not a successful end."

"There are other avenues, but they'll take time. I'm not sure the burning of the stable where the Captain kept his motorcar was happenstance. What was there that someone didn't want us to find?"

"There was no note left for the Captain. And no bicycle belonging to Rector. I was there, I would have seen anything untoward."

"Then perhaps it's a warning." Or an opportunity. Rutledge put a hand up to touch his face, and thought better of it.

Hamish said, "But how did yon fire starter ken ye'd be there?"

My motorcar was in the drive. But he'd already been on the road, and had only smelled smoke by chance. Perhaps the fire had taken a little time to catch hold properly, more time than expected. Whoever it was had had to be circumspect in the way he started the blaze, so as to leave no clues.

But why not the house? Why the stable, if the point was to shock Standish?

Neville thanked him and turned to open the door of his house.

Rutledge watched the door shut behind him and then turned toward East Dedham and Standish's house.

When Rutledge was shown into the study by the housekeeper, Standish glanced up at his face and said, "You look like hell. I hope you're bringing me news."

"Not yet. What did you keep in the stable, besides the motorcar?"

Standish rubbed his eyes. "I haven't slept very well since that night. My servants are uneasy, and it shows. There have been arguments downstairs, and short tempers. Something of value? Is that what you're asking? I can't think of anything in the stable that might be of interest to anyone. Old tack, saddles, my bicycle from when I was ten. I don't know." He dropped his hand. "I shan't be buying a horse. There's nowhere to keep it now. Not until I rebuild. Thank God it wasn't the house. Are you quite certain that fire was set?"

"What else could have started it?"

Standish got up, pacing the floor. "I just don't care to face it. A fortnight ago, if you'd asked me if I had enemies, I'd have laughed at you."

"How does your will stand? Who inherits, if you die?"

"A cousin. I haven't seen him in over twenty-five years—we were both in leading strings, and I made him cry. God knows why, I was too young to remember anything about it. But my mother reminded me some years ago. His father and mine were brothers. His father died in the Boer War, and his mother remarried soon after. She and my mother exchanged letters from time to time, and she seemed happy enough. Her son—my cousin—married well, and has a flourishing career in banking. He had a short war—invalided home with a bit of shrapnel too close to his spine to operate."

"You seem to know more than most about a cousin you haven't seen in a quarter of a century."

"I'm not a fool, Rutledge. I hired a firm in London that keeps an eye on him from time to time. After my father died. This house has been in the family for generations. I shouldn't care to see it go to a ne'er-do-well."

Sensible—and not unusual—to keep an heir under one's eye.

"Who rammed your motorcar in the hills above Nice?"

"Surely you don't believe any of this is connected to Nice?"

"But you've wondered, haven't you, if it was one of your fellow drivers? It changed you, that accident, and not only because of what happened to your hand."

Standish stopped pacing. "I—you see, that race was intended as an affirmation that we'd survived. I've got the scars to show I served my country well. I lost four years in those damned trenches, but I came out whole. I'd not been gassed. I'd not been blinded by shrapnel, I hadn't lost a limb, I hadn't been burned. Yes, I have nightmares, I expect you do as well, and every other poor devil who came out alive. And then this."

He held up his left hand, or where it ought to have been. "I left Nice with this. What sort of affirmation did I have?" His voice and his face were bitter. "It's as if I'd raced the devil, and he'd had the last laugh. 'Missed you in the trenches, didn't I, you poor sod, but I've got you now. Never too late, is it?'"

Rutledge understood, better than most. But he still found it odd that what had happened in Nice had seemed so personal. There was no anger against whoever had run Standish off that dark, twisting road. It was as if the war had reached out long bony fingers from the grave, and that had come close to breaking Standish. He'd ended his engagement, he'd lived here almost as a recluse, and he was haunted by self-doubt.

What's more, Standish didn't want to give the police the names of the other men racing their own personal devils, because he refused to believe they could be responsible. It was ludicrous, when murder was involved.

"Or," Hamish added into the silence, "he doesna' want them to find oot what's become of him."

Startled, Rutledge turned away, afraid Standish might read something in his face.

He'd never told anyone but Dr. Fleming about Hamish—and then in sudden fear and a blind rage at himself for what he considered breaking a second time, he'd gone for Fleming. In the end, Fleming had fought free, and said, "You've faced it, Rutledge. That's one step toward coping. Good man."

But he hadn't felt like a good man. It had taken days to come to terms with what had happened. In the end, he'd seen that it was Fleming's skill that had brought out the truth, and it had been a turning point.

Standish hadn't faced his own truth yet.

"How well did you know the men who raced with you?"

Surprised by the question, the Captain answered, "I've told you. We met that evening before the Somme. I didn't cross paths with any of them again until Paris. You know how it was, so many regiments decimated, making up their numbers from the remnants of others that had fared even worse. I wasn't even sure how many of us would be there in Paris until I walked through the doors of the Ritz and met them in the bar."

A thought occurred to Rutledge. "Did you recognize all of them? Were they the same five?"

"What an odd thing to ask. Of course I did. That evening wasn't something I was likely to forget."

Rutledge dropped the subject. Until he learned the names of the men who had pledged each other to meet in Paris, and spoke to them, he couldn't challenge Standish.

He stood up. "I'll be in touch as soon as I know more. For now, I'd take sensible precautions, if I were you. Stay away from windows in the dark, stay inside after nightfall, don't open the door to strangers."

Standish stared at him. "I still can't understand why I'm in danger. It was you he struck down during the fire. The policeman hunting him. You should take your own advice."

"It was your motorcar, your stable. That's twice. I don't want to hear of a third time."

Standish blinked. "Good God. But surely I've had my three, if you think about it. This hand. The motorcar. The stable. Although it hardly counts, does it, the stable? In the scheme of things." He realized what he'd just said. "In the scheme of things. All right, I'll take care."

13

Rutledge passed through East Dedham on his way to call on Mrs. Grant, and saw Mr. Barnes in close conversation with Edgecombe, Wright's solicitor. Standing in a shop doorway, out of their line of sight, Mrs. Saunders clutched her market basket in both hands, watching the two men.

If she knew the contents of the Rector's will, she was probably wondering if the dead man's gift to his church would influence the Bishop's man to stay.

And that brought him around to the possibility that Wright would most likely have changed his will if he was seriously contemplating marrying Miss Wilding. And Rutledge rather thought he was, awkward as that might be, given the social ambitions of her parents. Perhaps that bequest would have given Elizabeth Wilding a sense of independence and free her from her father's dictates. Wright would have wanted that too. But he hadn't expected to die so soon.

He found Mrs. Grant holding court with a number of neighbors.

After greeting the women, Rutledge asked if he could speak to

Mrs. Grant alone, and her guests reluctantly said good-bye, promising to return.

When the door had shut behind them, he asked, "How are you holding up?"

She wiped away tears and said, her voice husky, "I can't stop thinking of him lying out there, not all that far away, and me, here, saying terrible things about him."

"How much money is missing?"

"I had saved up thirty-five pounds."

A goodly sum for a poor family.

"How did you earn it?"

She looked away. "Doing mending and washing and cleaning houses in East Dedham. I never told him. He was sometimes gone a few days at a time, depending on how far he had to travel to make enough for us to live on. I knew Tim; if I told him what I had, he'd say we could live on that for a bit, or it would tide us through the winter. But I wanted to keep it for a time when he couldn't work any longer."

Rag-and-bone men scraped a precarious living, but it was work suited to some who preferred the freedom it also offered. Still, it had its hardships. Searching through rubbish and knocking on doors, asking if there was anything to collect, these men were out in all weathers, bags over their shoulders, stick in hand, walking miles in a day. Sometimes being paid a pittance for what they brought in to the merchants who used the scavenged goods in their own professions.

"Why do you think he took this money?"

"I was sure he had. Tim was gullible in some ways. Easily talked into any scheme that promised to make him rich. But where did it go? Who took it? That's what I want to know."

He couldn't be certain whether she was telling him the truth—or was incensed that Tim had taken her own hard-earned pounds and now she must wait for the authorities to find them and return them to her.

If Grant had had them on him when he was killed, surely Wright wouldn't have pocketed them. It was out of character. But so was murder, and taking the motorcar. What had gone wrong in the Rector's life to turn him around so completely?

"Who were your husband's friends?"

"And how am I to know that, pray, when he was off to Eastbourne for days at a time, or even over to Pevensey?"

"Where did he stay when he was away overnight?"

"Slept rough in good weather, or found himself a doorway or the like out of the cold."

"Where did he sort his finds?" He looked around at the tidy cottage. Certainly not here. Not a collection of dirty rags, greasy bones, or unwanted bits of metal.

"He'd do it along the strand, if the constable didn't see him. Or in an alley. It was too far to bring it home, then take it back again to a buyer."

"Could he afford lodgings, in Eastbourne?"

"He claimed not. Always complaining about how hard he had to work to put food on the table and keep a roof over our heads."

"What about the women you thought he was courting with his tales of travel? Did he stay with any of them?"

"How should I know? Do you think he was likely to tell *me*? His wife?" Then she ruined the effect of her denial by adding, viciously, "No better than whores, most of them."

"The one who smelled of gardenia scent, who lasted two years. What was her name?"

"I never found out." Her voice was suddenly bitter.

"Surely if you knew that much about her, you discovered her name."

"Well, I didn't. I just knew when he no longer smelled of gardenia. The next one preferred sandalwood."

He tried another tack. "There was one who came to your door. She must have been in love with him to do something so brazen. Who was she? Perhaps we could begin with her name."

"I don't know who she was."

He took a firm grip on his patience. "I think you do."

Cornered now, she said, "Oh, very well. She called herself Delilah. What decent woman would use a name such as that? Likely she was having me on. She was a barmaid at The Jolly Sailor. Tim told me that. But he might have been lying as well."

Now that her husband was dead, no longer philandering, Rutledge thought Mrs. Grant had begun to prefer the role of bereaved widow to that of betrayed wife.

He thanked her and left. Driving on to Eastbourne, he searched for the pub, and found it on a backstreet in a shabby part of town that summer visitors seldom saw. It was busy at the dinner hour, workmen for the most part, looking for a cheap meal. The patrons turned to stare when he walked through the door in his London coat and hat. The decor followed a seafaring theme, with nets slung low from the ceiling, wooden cutouts of fish and lobsters, and even a whale or two vying with dusty models from rowing boats to galleons to clippers. Some of them had been carved by a sure hand. The atmosphere was dark and dingy.

Rutledge made his way to the bar and ordered an ale. The barmaid was fair, slim, and pretty. "I'm looking for Delilah," he said with a smile as he paid for his glass.

"And what would you be wanting with her, if you found her?" she asked, considering his London manners and his educated voice.

"There may be money coming her way," he said.

"And where would it be coming from?" she demanded, suspicious.

"Ah, that's for Delilah to know."

"She's not here," the young woman answered reluctantly.

"Are you sure?" he asked.

"Sure," she answered. "There was a death in her family. She said."

"Indeed? Do you know where I could find her?"

The woman glanced around, making certain she wasn't overheard. "She's gone to her mother's. She said she was afraid."

"Afraid?"

She silenced him with a gesture, adding in a low voice, "Don't cause trouble. Just go."

He pushed his ale toward her with a few more coins. "Where can I find her?"

She gave him the address, her words fast and almost incomprehensible. Then she scooped up the coins and turned away to serve another customer, ignoring him.

He changed his mind about leaving, took his glass, and found himself a chair at a table for two in a corner where he could watch the room. No one showed any interest in his conversation with the barmaid, and he noticed that most men coming up to the bar flirted lightly with her. Satisfied, he rose and left The Jolly Sailor just as two large men came in and hailed friends across the room.

Nor did anyone show an interest in his departure, with an eye to following him.

He walked toward the water, where he stood looking out at the rough sea, and once he was certain that he wasn't being followed, he went to find the address he had been given.

It turned out to be a row of terrace houses, their front gardens littered with odds and ends lying among the dead stalks of straggling plants. He knocked at the door of number seventeen and watched the curtains at the window next to him twitch as someone looked out.

After a moment the door opened.

A white-haired woman in a frumpy black dress said, "What is it you want?"

"I've come to see Delilah," he said. "I think she's in trouble. I want to help."

"She's not here. She took the train to London three days ago."

"I don't believe you," Rutledge said. "I believe she's still here, and frightened."

"You know nothing about my daughter," she told him, her voice cold. "She's got an aunt who is ill. She's gone to care for her."

"Tim Grant sent me."

The woman stared at him, then shut the door sharply in his face.

Rutledge stood his ground, raising his hand to knock again. And keep on knocking until someone came back to the door.

And then it opened. Delilah was plump, pretty, with strawberry-blond hair and a pert nose. Rutledge, in his swift assessment, thought she must be closer to thirty than twenty. Her eyes were red from crying, and she looked as if she'd slept in her clothes.

Too frightened to prepare properly for bed?

"Who are you?" she asked, keeping to the shadows inside the door.

"My name is Rutledge. I'm a policeman, Scotland Yard. I think you may be in trouble."

"Show me."

He took out his identification and held it up for her to see. Satisfied, she reached out, caught his sleeve, and quickly pulled him inside the house.

"Is it true? Is Tim dead?" she asked.

In the close space of the dimly lit passage, Delilah standing there, back to the door, and her mother on the other side of him, he felt a surge of claustrophobia. "Where can we talk?" he asked, and was relieved when her mother opened a door to her left and pointed.

"In here."

He followed her into the front room and stood by the hearth while the two women took the only chairs. A gray-and-white cat was asleep on the couch.

"I've come down from London to look into the death of the Rector of St. Simon's in East Dedham."

"It's true, then? He's dead as well? But what about Tim?"

"I'm sorry. I'm afraid we discovered his body at Belle Tout light. We think it had been there since last Friday evening. Mrs. Grant had reported him missing, but the local constable was under the impression that he might have left her for another woman."

She caught her breath on a sob as he spoke, and fumbled in her pocket for a handkerchief. Her mother got up and put an arm around her.

"You'd better not be lying," she said, glaring at Rutledge.

"It's true," he said. "Why else would I be here looking for Delilah?"

"Her name's Ivy," her mother snapped at him. "Ivy Brown. She only used that in the pub, to keep men from knowing who she really was."

"It was the only name I'd been given," he said quietly. "What was your daughter to Tim Grant?"

"He was going to marry her. There was a position opening in Canterbury, groundskeeper at the cathedral. It was all arranged. They were going to live there."

"He already had a wife."

"That's not true," Delilah said angrily, lifting her face from the handkerchief. "They were never truly married. He told me how it was. He wanted a better life, but she held him back. He'd traveled, seen the world, but she only wanted him to stay in the Gap."

It wasn't the right time to contradict her. "When did you last see him?"

"A Wednesday, my day off at the pub. Must have been the Wednesday—just before . . ." Her eyes welled again, and she was unable to say *before he died*. Her voice was husky as she went on. "He was excited, and he told me a chance had come his way to make a little money, enough to see us set up in Canterbury. What's more, he said, that woman was keeping other sums from him, money that was rightfully his. And he intended to have it. He said chances didn't come his way very often, not like this, and he was doing this for us."

"What sort of chance?" Rutledge asked.

"He wouldn't say. Only that it was a little fiddly, and I mustn't be surprised if we had to leave Eastbourne suddenly."

"Surely that worried you?"

"Well, of course it did. I tried to talk him out of it, I told him that I had a bit put by as well, and we'd manage. But Tim said he'd done worse on his travels and come to no harm, and I was not to worry."

"And you had no idea what it was? He didn't tell you what he was planning to do?"

"No. He said he couldn't tell, that it wouldn't be right. He'd made a promise not to say anything to anyone. There was extra money, if he kept his mouth shut."

"Shut? About what?"

"I've just told you," Delilah said, her voice rising. "I didn't know."

"And yet you've been afraid of something. Or someone."

"There was nothing more from Tim. He didn't come, he didn't send a message. *Nothing.* And then this past Thursday, Betty, the other girl at the pub, found a note under a dish when she cleared a table. It had my name on it, so she handed it to me. She thought it was a love note from a customer, I hoped it was from Tim. Some of the other ragmen come in now and again, they might have brought it for him if he couldn't get away. But I didn't recognize the handwriting. There were only two words: 'You're next.'"

"Who left it? Do you know?"

"Betty wasn't certain. The pub was crowded, we were run off our feet. There'd been a man at that table. He wasn't a regular, she said. But a woman had been sitting there earlier, and several people before that. There'd been no sign of Tim all this week, you see, no word. I was frantic. I wanted to go to the Gap and confront that woman who called herself his wife. I'd done it once, I could do it again. But Mum here said it was foolish, I'd only put myself in the way of trouble, and like as not the blame would fall on me if Tim had left her for good. And him not here to tell me what to do."

"What trouble?" Rutledge interjected into the frantic muddle of words. "Surely you must have some knowledge of what Grant planned. You said it was fiddly."

She glanced at her mother, then turned back to Rutledge. "He said it wasn't really blackmail. He told me it was just an opportunity, a once-in-his-lifetime chance to ask for a little more to keep quiet. He said the person wouldn't know we were leaving for Canterbury anyway. It would mean starting out with enough money to do better." She was suddenly angry. "Do you know what I believe? That jealous harlot he called his wife ruined our future."

"How did she manage that? He wouldn't have told her that he was planning to leave her. Surely not." Not if he was intending to take his wife's savings.

"I don't know. She must have guessed. He always said she kept a sharp eye on him."

Mrs. Brown stepped in. "How had she kept him all these years? By tricking him."

"Even if she learned what he was up to, how would she have managed to find the person Grant was attempting to blackmail? And she would have had to discover that, if she intended to spoil his game."

"He must have told her," Mrs. Brown countered stubbornly.

Rutledge didn't think he had. If Tim Grant was about to abscond with his wife's money and Delilah/Ivy Brown, he would have held his tongue, if only out of a strong sense of self-preservation. Mrs. Grant had her suspicions, but she didn't know the whole truth. He was willing to wager she didn't.

That meant Grant's attempt to blackmail his benefactor had somehow gone wrong and ended in his death.

Wright was dead. If he'd been blackmailed, if he'd killed Grant, he was no longer a threat to Delilah.

But if it wasn't Wright?

"Grant told you nothing at all about this person he intended to blackmail?"

She shook her head. He thought she was lying. She knew more than she felt was safe. Otherwise the ambiguous note left on a table at The Jolly Sailor wouldn't have frightened her so much.

"If you don't tell me what you know, I can't protect you. If I don't know where the threat is coming from, I will be blindsided."

But Delilah was adamant. She knew nothing at all that would help him—or her.

He left soon after, advising Delilah to take precautions. "If I found you so easily, someone else can do the same thing. I'd go to London if I were in your place. Or anywhere else you might have family to take you in. I'm quite serious."

"Find him and stop him, then," Mrs. Brown said. "You're a policeman."

"How am I to do that, if I don't know where to look?" he asked, his question directed more toward her daughter. "If you can't help me, who can?"

"You're a policeman," her mother said again, adamant that it was within his power to do something.

And Delilah turned away so that he couldn't see her eyes. For an instant he wondered if she believed she could force the victim of blackmail to pay her instead. Whether she was an innocent party—or still saw her own main chance.

But Wright was dead.

If Timothy Grant had been blackmailing the Rector—and that could account for the quarrel on the Down that Mrs. Sedley had witnessed—then there was no one left to collect from. No one to leave that threatening message in The Jolly Sailor pub.

But Mrs. Grant was very much alive and it would have been like her to send a threatening message to Delilah. The problem there was that she had been surrounded by friends offering their sympathies ever since her husband had been found. And walking to Eastbourne and back would have taken long enough to make her absence noticeable.

Did this blackmail victim have nothing to do with Wright, except to muddy the waters for Rutledge's inquiry? Someone Grant had encountered in the course of his work? It didn't make this victim any less dangerous.

Still, two unconnected murders so close together in the tiny hamlet of Burling Gap beggared belief.

Was Grant involved in more than one scheme of blackmail? That was a distinct possibility.

Delilah's intentions intrigued him. Rutledge wasn't certain how much she knew—or thought she knew. Had the man who had left the note—he reminded himself that it might also be a woman—come in again? Was that why Delilah hadn't gone back to the pub, because she had already made contact with Tim Grant's victim and set in motion a train of events that would lead to a meeting? She would by nature be suspicious and not put herself in harm's way by walking home from the pub alone late at night. Not after he'd threatened her. And that meant that Timothy Grant had mentioned a sum worth taking risks for. For a bereaved woman who had only just learned that her lover was dead, she had very quickly looked to the main chance.

There was no way to force her to tell him. He would have to come back in the morning and ask the local man to keep an eye on the Browns.

Mrs. Brown followed Rutledge to the door, and as he stepped out into the cold wind, she said, "Was there money on him when you found the body?"

"No more than a few shillings."

She nodded grimly. "Then that bitch got it first."

"I don't think so. She's demanding that the police find her savings and return them to her. Delilah wouldn't know anything about that, would she?"

In the dim light of the entry, he wasn't sure if he saw a calculating look on her face. If Mrs. Grant didn't have that money . . .

If the killer did . . .

Rutledge reached out and put a hand on her shoulder. "Stay out of this. You and your daughter," he warned a second time. "If you know anything that will help me find whoever killed Grant, tell me now. For your own good."

But she stepped back, brushing his hand away, then abruptly closed the door.

Hamish said, as Rutledge turned toward East Dedham in the early winter darkness, "Ye ken, if it's true that yon lass found the message on

Thursday, it couldna' have been left by yon Rector. And there's only one person in East Dedham with access to a motorcar."

Trotter.

Rutledge was uneasy. He debated turning back, making certain Delilah and her mother left Eastbourne. But even as he considered it, he knew it would be no use. Whatever promises they made to him would be worthless.

But there was one question he hadn't asked, and he took the next street that would lead him back to the terrace house.

It was full dark when he got there.

And so was the house. Those on either side had lamps lit in their front rooms, but there was no sign of life in number seventeen.

He got out and went to the door, knocking several times. No one came.

Rutledge tried the door, but it was locked.

It took him a quarter of an hour to find the narrow alley that led behind the terrace houses and make his way on foot to the back garden of number seventeen. But there was no light to be seen here either. Using his torch sparingly, he found the gate and opened it, walking as quietly as he could up to the kitchen door. The garden was littered with bric-a-brac, and he nearly tripped over what appeared to be the stump of a broken birdbath. Muffling his curses, he made it safely to the door, and again tried the latch. But it too was locked.

Either they'd taken his advice and left in a hurry, or they had gone to meet the person who might well have had killed Timothy Grant.

And there was nothing he could do about it.

Retracing his steps, he drove to the Promenade along the water and went down it, then back up it, scanning the benches and the bandstand and any other place where three people might meet quietly.

Where, indeed, Wright and Miss Wilding had met.

It was hopeless. He even stopped at one point, leaving his motorcar in the road, and went to scan the strand below the Promenade. But there was no one. The strand stretched as far as he could see in both directions, and it was deserted. The cold wind off the incoming tide made the hardiest walker think twice about venturing out. Even the gulls had settled for the night.

Had the two women gone in vain, to search for a man already dead?

Or had they found their quarry, and trusted to sheer numbers, two women to one man, to keep them safe?

He turned back, got into his motorcar, and left Eastbourne.

There was nothing more he could do except pray that Delilah and her mother had had second thoughts and failed to keep whatever rendezvous they had arranged. That they'd returned to that dark, empty house and counted themselves lucky to reach it safely.

Still, that sixth sense that had served him well more than once told him that they had found trouble.

He was just passing the bandstand. He glanced up at it and saw a solitary figure there, and something about the way she stood told him that she was waiting for someone. At her feet, a golden-yellow dog lay, patient, on guard.

It was Miss Wilding.

He was about to stop, to speak to her and offer her what comfort he could. But he knew it wasn't wanted.

His last image of her was of dark skirts and bonnet ribbons blowing in the cold wind.

14

There was a message waiting for him in his room at the pub. Rutledge opened it to find a query from Constable Neville.

Mrs. Grant was that upset after you spoke with her. She wishes to know when she can bury her husband.

It could wait until morning, when Dr. Hanby's surgery opened at eight.

Rutledge went to bed, slept without dreams, and as soon as he'd finished his breakfast, went to speak to the doctor. He would be able to arrange an inquest, adjourn it as murder by person or persons unknown, and release the body thereafter. There was no need, in his view, to hold it any longer.

When Hanby's assistant opened the door to him, she wore a long face as she informed him that Dr. Hanby had been called away to consult on an urgent matter. "If you don't require immediate care, you'd best come back tomorrow."

He hadn't met her before, he'd dealt with the doctor's wife. Tall, thin, brown hair streaked with gray, a kind face.

"When did he leave?" Rutledge asked. He'd seen lights on in the doctor's house last evening as he made the turn toward The Sailor's Friend.

"Four o'clock this morning," she told him. "It was very upsetting. There was a message from the doctor in Eastbourne."

Rutledge thanked her and was about to turn away. Instead he stopped her from shutting the door, saying, "Wait. Dr. Wilding?"

"Yes, sir."

"What happened?"

"I'm not at liberty to say, sir. It's a medical matter."

He showed her his identification. "Scotland Yard. It might be important."

His mind was already racing. Delilah. She had met the man after all . . .

Rutledge wanted to swear. It had been the height of foolishness. He'd done his best to stop her, but money to the poor was an escape from want or drudgery. It blinded one to danger, to any risk.

"A suicide, sir. A young lady. Someone walking on the strand saw her in the water and pulled her out. Sadly, she's not coming round as she should."

"A young lady?" he repeated. Who would describe Delilah in those terms?

"Yes, sir, the doctor's daughter. Very sad indeed."

Miss Wilding. He had seen her—debated stopping—and now wished he had.

He thanked her, ran back to the pub, and got into his motorcar.

Morning traffic was heavy on the outskirts of the town, and it took far longer than it should to reach Wilding's surgery. But he changed his mind before he pulled up at the door and made his way instead to the terrace house where Delilah and her mother lived.

He knocked, but no one came, even though he gave the Browns time to dress and answer the door. He knocked one last time, waited again, and left.

Driving back to the Wilding surgery, Rutledge left his motorcar in front of the house and went up the path to knock at their door. He identified himself as Scotland Yard to the woman who answered, and when she tried to stop him, he gently set her aside and went into the waiting room. "Dr. Hanby?" he called. "Inspector Rutledge here."

"He's not in the surgery," the nurse informed him. "He's still in the house."

"Then take me there. It's urgent."

"Dr. Wilding canceled his morning surgery. He's left orders he's not to be disturbed. There has been a family—"

She stopped in midsentence as he brushed past her a second time, found a likely door that led through to the house proper, and took the stairs two steps at a time.

In the passage at the top of the first flight, he turned to the nurse pursuing him and said, "If you don't want me to shout for Dr. Hanby, you'll show me the way."

Out of breath and more than a little anxious, she said, "I don't know why you insist on doing this."

"Because it could very well be a police matter."

"She tried to drown herself, poor child!" she exclaimed. "How can this be of interest to the police?"

But he had been over that in his own mind, from the time he'd driven across the headland in the direction of Eastbourne. His guilt at not stopping the night before was as strong as his anger at Dr. Wilding and his wife for not protecting their daughter when her need was greatest.

And then he was struck by another thought.

He'd driven the length of the Promenade, but there had been no one else about, only Elizabeth Wilding. *Was* it suicide? Or had she been mistaken for someone else? But that was not for anyone's ears. Not yet.

"That's for me to judge. Now where do I find Dr. Hanby?"

She took him down the passage to the third door on his left and knocked gently.

It was Dr. Hanby himself who opened it a crack.

"What is it, my dear?" he asked quietly, then saw Rutledge standing just behind the woman. "Rutledge? What the devil brings you here? What's happened?"

"Step outside, I need to speak to you."

"Can it wait?" He cast a glance over his shoulder. Rutledge could just see beyond him the quiet figure lying still in the bed with a pretty coverlet drawn up to her chest. On either side of her, her parents held her hands, bending low over her.

"I don't believe it can."

Hanby stepped out of the room and closed the door softly. With a nod he dismissed the woman who had brought Rutledge to the sickroom door, and they waited until her footsteps had gone down the stairs and across the entry.

"Now, what is it that won't keep?"

"What happened to Miss Wilding?"

"I don't know that it's any business of yours."

"You were called in."

"Yes, because her father was in a state, and she needed medical care at once. Now what's this about?"

"I need to know if it was suicide or something else."

"Great God, man, is everything murder to you?"

"In this case, yes. Either tell me, or I'll go in that room and ask her parents."

"She hasn't regained her senses yet. Two women found her in the surf, and dragged her out. And none too soon. She was suffering from hypothermia and had nearly drowned before they reached her. One stayed with her, the other went at once to the hotel across the way and got help. The hotel called Dr. Wilding, and when he got there, he saw that the patient he'd been called in to attend was his daughter. He brought her home at once, and his wife sent for me." He cleared his throat. "I'm told there was an unhappy love affair. It's why her father was quite so upset. He blamed himself."

"Who was the man she was in love with?" Rutledge asked. While he himself knew, he wasn't certain that Hanby had been told.

"I don't know. I felt it wasn't my place to ask," he replied coldly.

"Did anyone think to take down the names of the two women who found her?"

"I don't know. Someone told me, but I don't recall."

"Was it Brown, by any chance?"

"I had other matters on my mind. I'm sorry. The hotel might be able to tell you, if it's important. I'm sure Dr. Wilding would like to thank them properly as well."

"There's more to this than an unhappy love affair. I need to speak to Miss Wilding as soon as she's able to talk."

"I've sedated her. With any luck, she'll sleep for a while. She was barely conscious when her father reached her, and she's said nothing since then, to my knowledge. I shan't allow you to go in there and upset her at this stage. Go back to East Dedham and mind your own affairs."

"This is very likely an important part of my work. I'll stay downstairs for as long as it takes to speak with her. Get used to that." And Rutledge turned on his heel and walked away.

Dr. Hanby called to him, but he ignored the summons. By the time he'd started down the flight of steps, he heard the door to the sickroom close.

The first door he opened led into a parlor facing the street. It was a handsome room, done up in creams and a deep rose. There was no fire on the hearth, and the room was quite cold. But one had been laid in the grate ready for use, and he found a match on the mantelpiece and bent over to touch it to the tinder.

It was burning well when a maid came to the door, staring in horror at him as if he'd broken in somehow.

"I'm waiting for Dr. Hanby. A . . . personal matter," he told her.

"Oh," she said, digesting that. Then she crossed to the hearth to see if the fire was drawing properly. "Is there anything I can bring to you, sir?"

"Tea," he said pleasantly, smiling at her. "That would be very nice."

She colored a little, then bobbed a curtsy and left. A little later she came back with a tray that bore the tea things and a plate of sandwiches, another of small cakes.

He thanked her and settled down once more to wait. Several times the same maid went up to the first floor, carrying trays and hot-water bottles, a Thermos of what must have been tea, or more coal for the fire.

It was well after the dinner hour before Dr. Hanby came down the stairs. Rutledge had heard footsteps and was standing in the drawing room doorway, waiting for him.

"I have persuaded Dr. Wilding and his wife to rest a little. Miss Wilding is awake and coherent, though very weak. If you give me your word that you won't upset her, I'll take you up to her room."

"I promise."

"Very well. This way." And he led Rutledge up the stairs to the passage at the top of the flight.

In the lamplight, Miss Wilding looked wan, as if she had been ill for a very long time and was just recovering. Her eyes, closed now, looked swollen. He thought she must have been crying.

Rutledge walked across to the bed and spoke quietly to her.

Her eyes flew open, terror in their depths, and then as she recognized him, she reached for his hand.

He sat down on the edge of the bed and took her hand in his. The fingers were warm now, and they clung to his in a fierce grip.

"I was hoping you would come," she said, and glanced around the room to be sure no one else was there. When she saw Dr. Hanby, she raised her voice to say, "Would you ask Sally for a little more of that broth? Mr. Rutledge will sit with me while you're gone."

Hanby hesitated, unwilling to leave her alone with the policeman.

But Elizabeth Wilding said, "Please?" and in the end, he left, reluctantly shutting the door behind him.

She turned back to Rutledge. "I don't remember very much," she said. "But I'll tell you what I can. I often go to the bandstand now. I know he won't come again, but it's the only place I have to mourn. Ginger is my excuse; she needs more exercise than my father has time to give her, and there's no one else to walk her. Sally can't manage her. And she's company, you know." Her voice was not strong, and he reached for the carafe of water on the table by the bed and poured a glass for her, helping her to drink it.

"I stood there for some time, pretending. And then Ginger was on her feet, staring out toward the strand. I was certain she'd spotted gulls sleeping down by the water's edge, the way she was pulling at the lead, and then she began to bark. I thought she was about to dash down to the water, tearing the lead out of my hands. I didn't want to have to pursue her, and so I wrapped it around the railing. The bark was changing to a deep growl, now, and she was baring her teeth."

Miss Wilding began to shiver. "I'd never been accosted there at the bandstand, but I was suddenly afraid. I knelt down, trying to untangle the lead, and Ginger was frantic to be free, which made it worse. There was a sound behind me, movement, but before I could turn, someone struck me hard across the head. The last thing I remember was Ginger's bark becoming a whimper of pain, and there was nothing I could do. I awoke in my bed, very cold, and I thought it was all a dream until my mother was there beside me, crying, and my father was shouting at the maid to dress herself and come at once. He left for a time, and then he was there again, asking me to forgive him."

"They thought you'd tried to drown yourself."

"What?" She rose up against the pillows. "Suicide? But it wasn't, I'm telling the *truth*," she said earnestly. As his words sank in, she added, "In the water? Is that where I was found? I thought—but where is *Ginger*?" Anxious now, she caught his hand again. "What's happened to my dog? Was she harmed too?"

"I don't know. I'll go and have a look. But first I need to ask. Can you tell me anything about the person who struck you? Man? Woman?"

"I never saw who it was. He—she—didn't speak."

"Do you think he was down on the strand, walking there, at the beginning?"

"Yes, very likely. That must have been what Ginger was on about, but I couldn't see anything. I don't know how someone got behind me. One minute I was fumbling with her lead, and the next I was here, in my bed, frightened by the suddenness of it all."

"I must find this person. Anything you can tell me will help."

Elizabeth Wilding closed her eyes. After a moment she opened them again. "No, I'm sorry. There was no time. Please, what's become of Ginger?"

"I don't know, but I promise you I'll find out." He could hear someone at the door. Dr. Hanby was back. He asked quickly, for her ears alone, "On your honor, it wasn't suicide? This matters, Elizabeth. You must tell me the truth, whatever you choose to tell your family."

"I swear it," she answered in a whisper, her eyes on the opening door. "On Nathaniel's memory."

And then Dr. Hanby was there, saying, "That's enough, Rutledge."

He turned to leave, and Hanby followed him to the door, as if to be sure he didn't hide himself behind the ornate French Provincial wardrobe or under the old-fashioned poster bed.

At the door, Rutledge paused and asked, "The dog. What became of it?"

"There was a dog?" He shook his head. "I've heard nothing about a dog."

Thanking him, Rutledge walked swiftly down the passage and out to his motorcar.

He drove the length of the Promenade, and then back again. There was no sign of Ginger. Unsatisfied, he got out at the bandstand and went to look there.

He heard a whimper, and moving behind the bandstand, where it faced the sea, he saw the dog. Her lead had been snubbed up close to the wall, hardly giving her room to move. Shivering and hungry, she still growled ferociously at him, baring her teeth and trying to break free, even though a length of cloth had been tied around her muzzle.

Rutledge came round to kneel beside her, and by her paw was a broken bit of wood with blood and red dog hair embedded in the rough surface. Rutledge could see dried blood, a darker patch against the fur on the animal's head. Whoever had attacked Elizabeth Wilding had had to stun the dog to tie it up. The leather lead had been wound around one of the thick footings that held up the stand above it. He turned to the dog, unknotted the cloth, and in one swift movement pulled it away. Then he worked at the lead, trying to free it.

Ginger was struggling to rise to her feet, barking madly now. But the footing that held the lead tight didn't move. Rutledge stood back, kicking it, just as someone on the walk beside the Promenade called, "Here, what are you doing to that poor beast?"

It was a constable.

Rutledge said, thinking fast, "She was stolen. Someone tied her up here, where her mistress couldn't find her. It's Dr. Wilding's dog."

The burly constable came up to the bandstand and peered over the rail at the dog below. "Damn whoever did this," he said under his breath, and came hurrying around to have a better look at the situation. "Is she badly hurt?"

"I don't think so," Rutledge replied, "not the way she's behaving." He stooped to work at unknotting the lead. But the dog was pulling too hard against it.

The constable reached out for her.

Ginger, having none of it, threatened to bite both of them. Rutledge managed to lay a gloved hand on her head, calling her by name.

"Ginger? Good dog. Easy, girl, we're doing our best."

After much coaxing, she subsided, cocking her head to one side, watching the two men work at the lead. It wasn't about to budge. And neither man could unwind it.

"She wasn't here the last two times I've made my rounds," the constable informed Rutledge. "I'd swear to it."

"She was muzzled. That length of cloth."

Finally Rutledge took off the belt to his coat, tied it to the dog's collar, found his pocketknife, and cut the lead. That took some doing, the constable holding the belt tightly as he watched the leather slowly shred and then break.

Ginger rose with a bark, nearly bowling over both Rutledge and the Constable. She was intent on running, and Rutledge scrambled to his feet, retrieving the bit of cloth and catching the other end of the belt just as it was snatched from the constable's hand.

The dog was pulling hard at the makeshift lead, and Rutledge had no choice but to go after her. As he kept up with Ginger, he shouted to the constable, "Can you drive? That motorcar. It's mine. Take it to Dr. Wilding's surgery." He added the address, but he wasn't sure the constable heard him. And then he was forced into a run to keep pace with the dog.

They arrived breathless and panting at the door to the surgery, and Rutledge knocked while the dog scratched vigorously at the wood and whined. The younger maid opened the door, the one who had brought him sandwiches. Before she could move, Ginger broke free and dashed past her, coming to a sudden halt in the wide entry, sniffing the air. Then, with a bark, she was away up the stairs, dragging the belt to Rutledge's coat behind her.

He went after her and managed to untie the belt as she danced anxiously outside the bedroom door. He could hear Elizabeth Wilding laughing and crying and calling the dog's name. As soon as Rutledge opened the door, Ginger bolted into the room, leaping for the bed. He closed it again and went back downstairs, going out to the street in front of the house.

The constable was just arriving in his motorcar, clearly enjoying the opportunity to drive it. He pulled to the verge and grinned at Rutledge as he stepped out the driver's door.

"Do your rounds usually take you by the bandstand this time of year?" Rutledge asked as the other man came round the bonnet.

"Not as often, no. But there was a suicide attempt last night. Girl found in the surf. Lucky she was seen in time."

"Do you get many suicides?"

"A few round the holidays."

"Who found her?"

"A mother and daughter, I'm told. They were out walking and saw something dark in the surf. Ran down and pulled her out."

"Who were they?"

"According to the hotel staff, they didn't stay around to be thanked. Well, they were wet to the skin themselves, I expect, and wanting to get home."

He thanked the constable, and when the man walked on, Rutledge went to the hotel just up from the bandstand and spoke to the staff.

The man at the desk summoned the manager who had been on duty during the night.

"Are you a friend of the family?" He was thin, balding, and capable.

"Yes," Rutledge said. "I'm trying to find out what happened to the young woman who nearly drowned."

"There was a woman calling for help as she came through the door. The doorman tried to stop her, as she didn't appear to be a guest. But she was frantic, shouting that she'd just helped pull someone out of the water and needed assistance. I'd come around the desk by then, and I could see she was telling the truth, for she was wet to the waist, dripping water everywhere. I sent two men out there straightaway, got blankets, and followed them. I thought the woman in the water was dead, to tell you the truth." He shook his head. "I didn't give her a chance of surviving. But the older woman, who'd tried to chafe her hands and face while waiting for us, told me there was a pulse, albeit quite faint. We wrapped her in the blankets and brought her here. I took her into the inner office, where there was a little more privacy, and sent one of the staff for hot-water bottles. One of the men went running for Dr. Wilding. He was the closest physician. By that time, I realized that the two women had gone. Good Samaritans," he said approvingly, "not waiting to be thanked."

"You never heard their names? The family will want to thank them."

"Sorry, no."

"Can you describe them?"

"They were not dressed like our guests. The younger woman was wearing red shoes." He said it as if this indicated poor taste. "And their hats were not of the latest fashion."

Delilah and her mother? Impossible to be sure.

He asked several more questions, but he heard nothing that would lead him to the Browns.

Thanking the manager, Rutledge left the hotel and drove to the Browns' house. It was well after ten now, and he was tired.

There were no lamps showing in any of the windows. This time, he decided not to knock. Leaving the motorcar several streets away, he took out his torch and faced the cold wind blowing off the water as he retraced his steps. And this time, he went to the back of the house and found a window that was not properly latched. He opened it with care and climbed into the room.

The first thing he noticed was that the house was cold. There were no signs of cooking in the kitchen and the cooker itself had gone out.

He made his way through the ground floor and then went up the stairs.

The two bedrooms were in disarray. Drawers pulled out, wardrobe doors hanging open, and the beds looking as if something heavy had been dragged across them, leaving the coverlets half on the floor.

The drawers were nearly empty, the wardrobes as well, although there were a few things left behind. Hairbrushes, jewelry, shoes, hats, clothes, and lingerie were for the most part missing. As if someone had packed in a tearing hurry, taking only what was important and aban-doning the rest. Face powder was spilled on the floor in the larger bed-

room, shoes were left where they'd fallen, and someone had shoved the
seat at the dressing table to one side. One of the shoes he saw was red,
and water-stained.

He hoped the Browns, mother and daughter, had made it to Canterbury or some other place of safety.

Rutledge was halfway down the stairs when he froze at the sound of
someone at the house door.

He went softly down the last half-dozen steps and crossed to the
front room, where he could look out the windows there.

A woman in a heavy coat and hat was standing on the walk.

"Delilah?" she called, when there was no answer to her knocking.
"Are you there? It's been days now. I can't cover for you any longer. Do
you want to keep your position or not?" There was exasperation in the
last words. "You must come to work, Delilah. Do you hear me?"

When her words were met with silence, she walked forward and
banged on the door with her fist.

"Delilah? I know you're in there. All right, I tried to be a friend and
warn you. To hell with you, anyway."

And she turned, walking away with an angry stride and disappearing from his sight.

None of the neighbors had opened their doors or shouted from windows.

He waited ten minutes, then searched the house again, this time
looking for anything that might help him find the man Grant had had
business dealings with. Either Grant hadn't trusted Delilah with anything that might be used against him, or he was too smart, knowing he
was about to come into large sums of money—however realistic that
really was—and kept all the details to himself.

Rutledge climbed out of the rear window and pulled it down,
as best he could. And then he made his way down the back garden,
through the dark shadows of the alley, and out into the street again. If
a neighbor had seen him, no alarm was raised.

Once more he arrived at the pub at a very late hour, climbing the stairs to his room. This time there was no Josie to offer to bring him sandwiches and tea. He went down, found someone in the nether regions, and asked for a pot. It was brought up, and as Rutledge was adding the warm milk to his cup, he remembered something.

Constable Neville and others had told him they were Chapel folk, and not Church of England. But where was the chapel they attended, and who was the cleric in charge?

It was far too late to ask anyone. The police station was closed, the shops were shut, and the pub appeared to be empty except for himself.

It could wait until morning, then.

He drank the tea, got ready for bed, and turned out the light. The old building creaked, the stairs and doors sounding as if there were an army of people slipping up in the dark.

He laughed at himself for being a fool, but he slept poorly all the same. Hamish, busy as soon as his eyes opened, was relentless.

After breakfast, he drove to Burling Gap and sought out Constable Neville.

He and a half-dozen other men were standing at the edge of the cliff that ran toward the Seven Sisters, staring down at the sea.

It was particularly rough this morning, ominous gray clouds on the horizon and the wind whipping the sea into a froth.

Rutledge came up to them and wished them a good morning. They looked up, and parted so he too could see what they were staring at.

A good five feet of cliff had fallen down into the sea during the early hours of the morning. Approaching the edge with care, Rutledge looked over. The chalk face was a brilliant white, even in this light. The tide was out, and he could see from this dizzying height that on the strand was a high pile of chalk, sod, and flint stones, marking where the new section of cliff had fallen.

Neville was looking back toward the straggle of cottages. "I can't help but wonder," he said, "where they'll be in another twenty years."

"I'm leaving," one man said, "as soon as may be. As soon as I can find work elsewhere. I'm not waiting."

"Aye, well, you're nearest the sea," another man said. "My wife won't hear of leaving. She says we'll be here fifty years from now."

"Not if we have another winter like last," a third man said gloomily, and turned to walk away.

The others soon followed. Rutledge and Neville made their way back to the police station and shut the door against the wind. The cooker was pouring out heat, and Neville set the kettle on.

"Any word on Timothy Grant's body?" he asked.

"None," Rutledge said. "Dr. Hanby was called away in the night. Last night," he amended. "I've not had a chance to speak to him about Grant."

"Mrs. Grant won't be happy about that."

"Where is an inquest usually held?"

Neville scratched his head. "We've not had one for some time. Not since before the war. I expect it will be in the pub. There's a room in the back, if it's still available. Could be a lumber room by now, filled with odd bits of furniture and dishes and the like."

He sounded as gloomy as his companions out on the cliff's edge.

"Worrying, falls of that size," Rutledge commented.

"The war took most of the young people, one way or another. The older ones are starting to give up. There's a better way of making a living than running sheep here on the Downs. Besides, no one has a large enough flock. They have to club together to sell the wool as it is, and never get the best price."

When he brought in the tray with the teapot, Rutledge asked the question uppermost in his mind. "Where do you attend church services? There's neither church nor chapel here in Burling, and only St. Simon's in East Dedham."

"We Chapel folk meet in houses. Once every two weeks, there's a preacher from down Eastbourne way who comes to us."

"Where do you bury your dead?"

Neville shrugged. "We buried them in St. Simon's churchyard before we went to Chapel. And we still do. Our ancestors are there. The cliffs have always come down. No point in burying anyone out there."

It made sense of a sort.

"Have your people always lived here?"

"Aye, as fishermen and wreckers. There's prehistoric ruins out on the cliffs. They might have been our folk. We like to think so, at any rate." He stirred his tea. "East Dedham, now, only goes back to the Normans. Newcomers, aren't they?"

There was both pride and bitterness in the words.

15

After drinking his tea, Rutledge said, "I'd like to speak to Mrs. Grant again. I've interviewed the woman in Eastbourne who she claims had stolen her husband's affections. He was involved in something, and Miss Brown didn't know what it was. But she was trying to find out, and I have the strongest feeling she knew how to contact the person Grant had worked with. Or he knew how to find her. It's possible she was tempted to try a little blackmail of her own. At any rate, it's likely she was frightened off when he attacked someone else by mistake. If Mrs. Grant knows more than she's telling us, she could be in danger as well."

"But what was going on with Grant?"

"My guess is he was blackmailing someone. Anyone in Burling Gap—or East Dedham, for that matter—who might kill to keep a secret safe?"

"If there was," Neville replied, "I'd have some suspicion of it. That kind of secret changes a man. But, sir, look at this. Who better than a rag-and-bone man to stumble over something nasty while doing his rounds, and try to turn it to his advantage? It's a rough living, what he does."

It made sense. Miss Wilding had been attacked in Eastbourne, and Delilah worked at a pub there. It was where Grant plied his own trade.

When they made their way to Mrs. Grant's cottage, they found Mrs. Mitchell at the door.

"She's not answering," the woman told them. "I've been twice this morning, once with her breakfast, and now to see if she's taken ill from all the distress."

"Let me try," Neville said, and stepped up to pound on the door with his fist. "If she's sleeping, she won't miss that."

They waited in silence for several minutes, listening for the sound of footsteps.

"She wouldn't do herself a harm over Grant's death?" Neville asked.

Mrs. Mitchell gave them a disparaging look. "Not to speak ill of the dead, but he wasn't much of a husband, Grant."

But there was no accounting for affections, Rutledge thought. As a rule, people loved with their hearts and not their heads.

He said, "Try the door."

"I don't like—" Neville began, but one look at Rutledge's face and he reached for the latch.

The door was not locked. Mrs. Mitchell pushed forward to be the first inside, but Rutledge barred her way. "Wait here," he ordered, and she fell back.

He went in, followed by Neville. The cottage was dark, the fires out. Neville found a lamp and lit it. Rutledge had expected to find the room in chaos, but it was no more untidy than it had been on his first visit. The remnants of last night's dinner sat on a small tray drawn up next to a chair, and the gray-and-white cat got up from the couch, stretching and yawning.

Carrying the lamp with them, they walked on into the bedroom. Nothing was disturbed there. But Mrs. Grant was not in her bed. The covers were tossed back, but the bed didn't appear to have been slept in. Rutledge crossed the room to open the wardrobe and found it empty. The drawers in the small chest had been nearly emptied as well.

From the doorway, Mrs. Mitchell said, "There was a valise on top of the wardrobe. It's gone."

Irritated with the woman, Rutledge said, "I thought I'd told you to wait outside."

"And much good that would do you. Didn't know about yon valise, did you? And any woman would have noticed that her hairbrushes are gone, as well as her face powder."

"Then she left of her own volition," Neville said.

"But how did she leave?" Rutledge asked. "Carrying a valise on a bicycle is an awkward business."

"She walked," Neville suggested. "And took the omnibus."

"With no word to anyone about the cat?" Mrs. Mitchell said scornfully. "She thought more of that cat than she did of Timothy."

"She has a point," Rutledge said, scanning the room. But there was nothing here—and nothing in the rest of the house, although they looked—that gave any indication Mrs. Grant been frightened or left under duress.

Except the cat.

As they reached the front room again, Mrs. Mitchell scooped up the cat now winding around Rutledge's legs. "I'll see to her," she said. "As long as need be." And with nothing more to see, she walked out of the cottage and left them there.

"What do you think has become of her?" Neville asked as he set the lamp down where he'd found it and put it out.

"I don't know. We should have a look at Belle Tout, all the same."

They walked on to the lighthouse in silence, and when they reached the grounds began to search. Half an hour later, Rutledge said, "She isn't here."

"I find I'm glad of that," Neville said, his gaze on the corner where they'd found Timothy Grant. "But there's that other woman, the one Mrs. Grant thought her husband had taken up with. Do you think Mrs. Grant has gone to look for her?"

It was possible. But with a suitcase? If a wife went in search of the other woman, she generally went in anger, not taking the time to plan leaving.

Still. Mrs. Grant had been angry with her husband over the other woman, angry with the woman herself. But if she didn't know where to find her, she might have taken a valise, expecting the search to take some time. Betty might not be as forthcoming with Delilah's direction when Mrs. Grant came to call.

The question was, did she have the money to stay in a hotel for an uncertain number of days, if Grant had indeed absconded with her savings?

Hamish spoke, interrupting Rutledge's thoughts. "The other lass in The Jolly Sailor couldna' be sure it wasna' a woman who left the message for Delilah."

It was true.

Neville was looking at him. Rutledge turned away, surveying the light. "If Mrs. Grant killed her philandering husband, and then decided to kill the woman he was about to run away with, she might well have decided not to come back to the cottage."

"But what did she do for money?" Neville asked, echoing Rutledge's own thoughts.

"Perhaps Grant didn't take the money his wife had set aside after all. Perhaps she thought that you might take her demands for a search more seriously if she claimed he'd stolen from her."

"Good God. I never thought of that." As they left the lighthouse and walked back toward the Gap, Neville added, "Why did she make such a fuss about him being missing, if she'd killed him?"

"You hadn't found his body. And she couldn't tell you where to look. Instead she badgered you. It must have worried her, Grant lying there at the lighthouse all that time. If no one found him, she couldn't marry again. Or perhaps she thought the blame might fall on the woman in Eastbourne."

It was a tidy solution. But Rutledge wasn't satisfied with it. He'd met Mrs. Grant. He could imagine her picking up a pan from the kitchen and hitting her husband in a fit of anger over Delilah, then standing over him, realizing he'd broken his neck as he fell. It was even possible she'd managed to drag him to the lighthouse and hide his body there. But how could she get to Eastbourne?

He turned. "We didn't go into the lighthouse. Is it locked?"

"Always has been, if only to keep the lads from exploring and hurting themselves on the stairs up to the light."

They went back and tried the doors and the windows, but no one had been inside since the last owner had left.

Neville sighed. "I don't like it."

"Do lorries come through here? I've not seen them."

"The upper road is more generally used. But yes, sometimes we have one passing through. Or they're here to make a delivery to one of the shops."

"Could she have begged a lift from one of the drivers?"

"It's possible, sir," Neville answered, a ring of doubt in his voice. "You must ask Constable Brewster about that. He might be able to tell you if he heard one passing." He looked toward Belle Tout. "She'll come back. She was that concerned about holding a service for her husband. She won't want to miss that."

"Yes, it's time to see to that."

Rutledge left him at his door and drove on to East Dedham.

He found Constable Brewster in the police station, talking to an older man.

Brewster looked up as Rutledge came through the door, excused himself to the man, and said, "Can I help you, sir?"

"Do you remember a lorry passing through here late last night?"

"As a matter of fact I do. Couldn't miss the sound of him bouncing over the ruts out there in the street."

"Which way was he going, could you tell?"

"At a guess, toward Seaford. That's usually why they come through this way, and not take the main road."

"Would the driver stop and give someone a lift?"

"I expect he would, if he was tired and wanted company to keep him awake. If he liked the look of the person. If he didn't, he'd pass on by."

"Do lorries come through very often?"

"More than I'd care for. They churn up the mud and make the ruts worse. Sometimes they pull over and sleep an hour or two up there on the headland. But that's mainly in summer. Too cold this time of year."

"Do you know if the lorry last night stopped for someone?"

"I was barely awake. Once I knew what the commotion was, there was no need to pay closer attention. I went back to sleep."

Rutledge thanked him and left, although he could see that Brewster would have liked to ask him why he was so interested in a lorry.

He drove on to Trotter's garage and spoke to the man, but he hadn't heard the lorry.

"Sorry, I don't usually take notice, unless they have trouble shifting or their brakes are bad. Now you're here, are you still searching for a dark green motorcar that has red paint on a wing?"

"Very much so. Have you seen anything I ought to know about?"

Trotter shook his head. "My guess is you won't find it hereabouts. If I owned that motorcar, and I knew what I'd done with it, I'd see it wasn't found. If I had to drive it into Wales or Scotland until the hunt was over."

An unwelcome thought. But far too likely.

"Have you been in Eastbourne in the past forty-eight hours?"

"Eastbourne? No, not since midweek. I had work in Newhaven. Why?"

"It's not important."

"Then why ask?"

"A policeman always asks questions. Sometimes the answers are useful."

Rutledge turned back toward the village and saw Jem trudging down the road, hands in pockets, a sack over her shoulder.

He drew up beside her.

"Hallo."

"Hallo," she said, looking up at him. "You look dreadful."

He was certain he did. There was the cut on his temple and possibly a rapidly blackening eye, and he hadn't shaved since yesterday morning, his beard heavy and dark.

"I ran into a tree during the fire. I haven't seen you since then. Your mother was worried about you that night. It's not wise to stay out so late. And it's unkind to worry her."

"I didn't mean to worry her. I couldn't sleep."

"In your wanderings, did you see any strangers about?"

"I don't think so. I wasn't looking to find anyone."

"Are you sure? That fire was set, Jem. And if it wasn't one of the tenants, then it's likely to be a stranger."

Quick to their defense, she said sharply, "One of us? We'd not do such a thing to the Captain!"

"I expect you wouldn't. That's why it's worrying me. Who *would* do such a thing?"

"I don't know. Nobody ever tells me anything about the Captain's affairs. They don't tell me anything at all about anything." Her voice was aggrieved. "They send me away when they want to talk seriously. I'm too young."

"Have they been talking about serious matters of late?"

She shook her head. "Not since the Captain came home. Keeping the estate going during the war was a trial for all of us. Not enough money, not enough hands, no rain, too much rain, what to plant in which field for the coming year. My mum didn't think I knew how she worried, but I did. About my brothers, about the work needing to be done. I tried to grow as fast as I could, but both of my brothers were big, like my father, and I'm never going to match that. I just know it."

He hid a smile. "What have you got in your sack?"

"Onions. Carrots. A little sugar." She reached in her pocket and drew out a shilling. "I found this on the road. Just where I lost mine.

But you found them. You said. I think you didn't want to look for them anymore and tricked me." She held it out to him.

"I expect you aren't the only person walking this road who has lost a shilling."

Jem considered that. "I still think you tricked me. I don't want pity. We're poor, but we have our pride."

Rutledge thought she must have heard that from her mother. "I don't pity you," he said. "You found that shilling fair and square. It would be wrong of me to take it, just to stay in your good graces. I'd rather you stay angry with me."

That seemed to satisfy her. "You're sure?" she asked, her hand still out.

"I found a penny in Eastbourne the other day." It was a lie, but in a good cause. "Near the bandstand. There was no way to find the owner. I kept it. The only alternative was to toss it away again. And that's foolish."

"I've never seen the bandstand in Eastbourne," she said wistfully. "I've never even *been* to Eastbourne."

She was such a bright child, but her life was narrow and would become even more narrow when she married and had children of her own. It was likely she would never see Eastbourne.

"All right, get in," he said. "I'll drive you as far as the lane."

"You really do know the Captain. I saw you helping him the night of the fire," she said, tossing her sack into the back of the motorcar, making him wince. "You went inside with him, even."

"I told you the truth there." He hesitated. "Perhaps you trust me enough now to tell me what you saw the evening my tire was slashed."

"I didn't see anything," she answered promptly. He could imagine that her brothers had taught her well not to carry tales. Had she seen something the night of the fire, despite her denial?

He couldn't think of a way to make her tell him. Threatening to speak to her mother, or to take her to Standish, would only lose whatever tenuous connection he had with this girl. It continued to worry him that she had allowed herself to be seduced by the motorcar into accepting a ride from a stranger, policeman or not. And yet he couldn't very well drive past her, knowing how far she still had to go.

They drove in silence for a time, and then she said, "If someone has lost something, must I tell when I've found it, even if he doesn't want it now?"

"Like the shilling? You told me you'd found it, and I told you I hadn't lost it. We're square."

"That's the policeman's decision?" she asked, staring straight ahead.

He turned and smiled at her. "That's the policeman's verdict."

She turned and smiled at him then, a sweet smile that touched his heart. What was to become of Jem? And yet trying to meddle, to tell Standish that she ought to be in school and have a chance to better herself, might be the worst possible thing for her. She had roots here. She was loved here. That, in the long run, might be the safest and happiest place for her to stay. His London instincts might be the wrong avenue.

Jem got down at the lane and set off at a run, waving to him as she went.

He watched her out of sight, and then turned back to the village.

R utledge had intended to go directly to The Sailor's Friend to shave and change, but he was hailed just before he got there by Barnes.

"I say, what's happened to you?" the Bishop's man demanded. He sniffed the air as he leaned toward the motorcar's window. "You haven't been drinking, have you?" he added in a changed tone, self-righteous judgment strong in his voice.

"I was helping Captain Standish to put out the fire in his stable."

"What fire? I haven't heard of any fire. Was anyone hurt? In need of my services?"

"Fortunately, no."

"I've stopped you to ask if you've made any progress in the matter of the late Rector's death. I should like to see him properly interred before I leave to report to the Bishop."

"There must be an inquest first. I'll speak to Brewster about setting it up. It will have to be convened here in East Dedham. There isn't a large enough room in Burling Gap. And there's the inquest as well for Timothy Grant."

"Who is this Grant? Why wasn't I informed of his passing?"

"He's a Chapel man from the Gap. His body was found at the lighthouse some days ago."

"All the same, I should have been informed," Barnes rejoined testily. "Wait a moment."

He came around the bonnet and got in beside Rutledge. "We'll speak to Constable Brewster together. This time I shan't be left to wonder what is happening."

Rutledge said nothing. Reversing, he turned back toward the police station, and the two men went in together.

Constable Brewster looked up in surprise to see Barnes as well as Inspector Rutledge coming through his door. He got to his feet, looked at Rutledge, and said, "Sir?"

"The inquests for both the Rector and Timothy Grant. Will you set them up? One at ten o'clock tomorrow and the other at eleven. It shouldn't take long."

"Dr. Hanby's still in Eastbourne, sir."

"I expect he'll be back in East Dedham by this evening."

"Yes, sir. I'll speak to Josie, at the pub, about the room."

"Good man." Rutledge turned to Barnes. "Anything you care to add?"

"No, not at all. If you're returning to the pub, I'll go with you."

They went out to the motorcar, and as he got in after turning the crank, Barnes said, "*Two* murders. Or there wouldn't be two inquests. And if they're no longer than you've indicated, you are not able to close the inquiry properly."

Rutledge had had a very long day and night. "I don't attempt to tell you how to serve your flock in St. Simon's, and I don't expect you to tell me how to handle my inquiry."

Barnes stared at him. "Surely constructive criticism is never amiss."

Holding on to his temper, Rutledge retorted, "Then perhaps it will not go amiss for me to tell you that Mr. Wright was a much-loved Rector of that church, and your Bishop ought to take great care in filling his place."

Barnes blinked. "But he was a *thief*. He took another man's motorcar without his consent. Everyone says so."

"When we have all the facts, you may be right to call him that. But not before then." He pulled into the yard of the pub and stopped. "The walk from here will do you good."

And he waited. After a moment Barnes got out of the motorcar and strode away without another word.

Hamish said, "That was no' well done."

"No," Rutledge answered him aloud, "but it was warranted."

Taking the stairs two at a time, he went to his room and spent the next quarter of an hour repairing his appearance as far as it was possible to do so. And then, ignoring the siren call of his pillow, he sat down at the table by the window to bring his notebook up to date.

He still didn't know what had become of Wright's bicycle. Nor could he be sure that Delilah and her mother had gone to Canterbury, out of reach. As for Mrs. Grant, if she went looking for Delilah, she would find only an empty house waiting for her.

If Wright hadn't killed Grant, who had? And where had Wright gone in the hours between taking Captain Standish's motorcar and driving through the storm to East Dedham?

"Precious little for an inquest," Hamish commented.

And it was. Still, there was the farmer—James—who had found Wright's body. And truant boys who had discovered Grant. Then Constable Neville would present his evidence as the policeman responding. Dr. Hanby could attest to the cause of death, and the approximate time it had occurred. And then he, Rutledge, would be asked for the results of his inquiries. He would call for a finding of death by person or persons unknown and ask for a postponement while he pursued additional facts in the case. Acting Chief Superintendent Markham wouldn't be pleased, but there it was. Nor would the Bishop, Rutledge thought wryly.

There was a heavy rain at dawn, but it settled into a foggy drizzle by nine thirty.

Brewster had arranged for the use of the room and sent for Captain Standish, who by this time was in possession of a gray mare, borrowed from a tenant, to conduct the inquest.

The inhabitants of Burling Gap and East Dedham gathered in force, despite the rain, and the room provided by the pub was crowded by the time Standish called the gathering to order and began the proceedings.

Both inquests went smoothly, as Rutledge had anticipated, although their audience was disappointed by the verdicts, having hoped to be presented with a villainous murderer or, at the very least, been given more details than they had already garnered through the gossips. People adjourned to the pub to argue the facts they had just heard and speculate on where they might lead, while others went to the dining room, where lunch was just being served.

As Rutledge was leaving the room, Standish called his name.

"I need to speak to you," the Captain said.

But there was nowhere quiet enough for a private conversation.

In the end, they walked out into the rain and went to the motorcar.

Standish pulled his muffler closer about his throat against the cold, and said, "You like to play your cards close to your vest, do you not?"

"No closer than you have done, refusing to give me the names of the other drivers in Nice."

"They had nothing to do with Wright. Look, he wasn't coming

from East Dedham or one of the sheep farms. He wasn't coming from
the Gap cottages. He could have reached any of those on his bicycle.
He'd done it often enough. No, he'd been somewhere distant. By this
time, you must know where. Why didn't you choose to end this business today, and let us all return to what peace we can find?"

"If I knew the answers, I would have given them into evidence
today. The fact is, while I've learned a great deal about Wright, none of
it has explained his murder. I still don't know why he was on the road
late that Saturday night."

"Then find someone at the Yard who can close this inquiry properly."

"He'll have no better luck than I have. I can understand your concern, Standish. Your motorcar has been wrecked, your stable burned
down, and there's no acceptable reason for any of it. I don't blame you
for being angry. But sometimes these matters take time."

Standish swore. "I'm sorry. Forget that I said that. It's just . . . *wear-
ing* is the word. It's wearing to have to look over my shoulder every time
I leave the house. For all I know, that blow on the head was meant for
me. I find myself looking at my tenants, wondering if one of them has a
grudge I don't know about. I've acted as my own estate manager since
Wilbur died just before the end of the war. He'd been a good man, and
I haven't found anyone to replace him. Did someone feel passed over?
Is it one of the staff my mother let go while I was in France? None of it
makes sense. The Chief Constable sent a message yesterday, wanting
to know what progress had been made. I had to tell him there was very
little. It brought home again how helpless I am. And how the rest of the
villagers must feel, with two deaths on their doorsteps and no notion
still of who was behind them."

Rutledge held on to his temper with a tight leash. He could understand what the shock of losing his hand had done to Standish, after
surviving the war without severe injury. But helpless the man was not.
Blind was a better word. He himself had seen Standish take control
the night of the fire, he had glimpsed what the Captain was capable of,

how he must have commanded those under him in the trenches. But self-pity had driven him to blame everything on that road to Nice. It was little wonder he had been reluctant to give the police the names of his fellow racers—he might well have discovered that they had got on with their lives while he had not.

He forced his voice to pleasantness as he answered. "Hardly helpless, I should think. The village looks to you for leadership, and your tenants look to you to guide them through the hardships they still face. The Chief Constable addresses you as the squire. We'll find this killer in due course. But there's this. Whatever connects Wright and Grant and your motorcar, your stable, we will uncover in the end. Be sure of it." His voice changed, harder now. "Meanwhile, it's your duty to look after your tenants and take care that they aren't caught up in this business. Put them on their guard. And take care yourself. Looking over your shoulder can keep you safe until we do know the truth. It might come faster if you and others were more forthcoming with information. I remind you that that's your duty as well."

Standish said nothing for a time. And then he reached for the handle to open the door. "Harsh words from a policeman. Shocking, in fact."

Without waiting for an answer, he stepped out into the rain and angrily splashed his way to the pub's barn, where his horse had been taken.

Rutledge waited until the Captain rode out and turned toward his house. And then he went back into the pub. Avoiding both the diners and those at the bar, he took the stairs to his room, his mood black.

He opened his door, flung his hat toward the bed, and stopped short.

Melinda Crawford sat in the chair by the window.

16

I gather you haven't had a very pleasant day," she said, regarding him as she held up her cheek for his kiss.

Crossing the room, Rutledge bent to give it, and then turned to take off his damp coat. "I didn't see your motorcar."

"No, I learned that there was an inquest going on, and so I left it by the churchyard, out of sight." She indicated her umbrella, standing in the corner and still dripping. "I walked down, spoke to someone by the name of Josie, and told her I was your aunt, stopping to have lunch with you on my way to Eastbourne. She let me into your room and brought me tea."

"I'd offer you lunch, but the dining room is small, and the gentry went there after the inquest while the rest of the village is still in the bar."

"Never mind, I shan't starve. There's a hamper in the motorcar."

He smiled. Nothing ever seemed to shake Melinda Crawford's composure.

She returned the smile. "That's better. Do sit down, Ian. It's not your fault that you inherited your father's height, but I'm getting a pain in my neck looking up at you."

The smile spread to a grin.

"I take it," she went on, "that the inquest was adjourned, person or persons unknown?"

"Sadly, yes. The village squire has just informed me of my duty to bring the miscreant to justice. He's been keeping secrets, and I hope you're here to unlock them."

"Yes, well, that's why I came. There was absolutely no way to reach you. Do these people know about the telephone and the telegraph? Marvelous inventions, really."

"Does this mean you have the information I asked for?"

"Fortunately, my dear friend in Nice understands the telegraph, and he has sent me some rather interesting information." She held out a telegram while he went to light another lamp against the dismal weather outside, then sat down again.

Rutledge scanned the telegram, then read it more thoroughly.

Melinda Crawford said, "As you can see, Captain Standish went off the road at one of those abysmal switchbacks that bring it down from the heights. There was a heavy mist that night, and the road was unfamiliar to him. He told the doctors there was another vehicle behind him on the road that tried to push him off the cliff and finally succeeded. But the doctors believed the other vehicle was also having difficulty in the fog and trying to keep close in the hope that the first motorcar might lead them both safely down to the coast."

It was all there, in short, almost cryptic sentences, but as clear as Melinda Crawford's interpretation.

"And so as far as the police were concerned, the other motorcar's driver was frightened enough to try to stay close. But did that driver report the crash?"

"No. As you can see, it was a farmer who heard the crash and went to see if the driver had survived. He did, but he lost a hand, had a concussion and two cracked ribs, a broken leg, and a mass of cuts and bruises. He was, in fact, lucky to survive at all. He was in hospital for over a fortnight."

"Do you think it was one of the other drivers who ran him off the road?"

"No one did at the time. But that's something you must find out now."

"Yes, well, it will depend on what Bess can discover."

Melinda delved into her purse and brought out another telegram. "Bess is as prompt as my friend in Nice. See for yourself."

He took the second telegram and began to read.

Here were the five names on the list. Officers all, their ranks given. And Standish's name was among them.

"Holt, Standish, Brothers, Russell, and Taylor."

"Yes. And their addresses."

"Bess has been very thorough," Rutledge said.

"She usually is," Melinda said. "As you well know."

"Thank her for me. And your mysterious suitor in Nice."

"I never said he was a suitor," she retorted.

Rutledge laughed. "My father told me once that much as he loved my mother, he thought you were the most fascinating woman he'd ever met."

"Did he indeed?" she said primly. "Well, your father was sometimes given to exaggeration." She paused. "I bring you other news, Ian. I heard it just before I left for Sussex. Quite by accident, actually. A neighbor had business in Sevenoaks. He was returning home as I was leaving. He stopped to speak to me, giving me news of a friend who lives there. And then he asked if I was acquainted with a Major Holt—I know so many Army officers and men, and my neighbor has met some of them at dinner parties. He told me the Major was killed last night. His motorcar crashed into a tree."

"Good God. Is it the same Holt named here? No, he doesn't live in Sevenoaks, does he? That's in Kent." He was looking at Bess Crawford's telegram. "He lives in Surrey."

"There's nothing to prevent him from traveling to Sevenoaks," she said dryly.

"No." Rutledge frowned. "I shan't be able to speak to him if he's the dead man, and so I hope very much it isn't our Holt."

"You'll have to go to Sevenoaks. I'd volunteer, but I wouldn't recognize this man. And you have the authority of the Yard to pry into another inspector's inquiry."

"I wouldn't recognize him either."

"But you know someone who can."

"Yes."

Melinda collected her things and glanced out the window with a sigh. "As a child, I often longed for rain like this when we lived in India. Now it only makes me long for my hearth."

Rutledge helped her with her coat. "Thank you. As always."

She reached up to touch his face. "My dear boy, I love nothing better than playing detective with you. It brightens my quiet, simple life."

"Indeed," he said, smiling. "And when have you led a quiet, simple life, pray?"

At the top of the stairs, she said, "You can drive me as far as the churchyard. I dislike wet feet."

"Of course."

Halfway down the stairs, she added over her shoulder, "Have you spent much time with Frances recently?"

"I've been out of London for some weeks, except for that one flying visit you know about." He hadn't gone to the house; there hadn't been time. His sister was occupied with her wedding plans, and he hadn't wanted to disturb her. And then, suspicious, he added, "Why? Is Frances all right?"

"Blooming, as you'd expect. Take some time from the Yard when you are back in London. She would like you to help her with the arrangements."

"I thought you were guiding her?"

"I'm not her brother."

And then they were running up in his motorcar to find her own, and any reply was lost in handing her into her seat before turning the crank for the driver.

There was no purpose in returning to his room, and so Rutledge went on to Captain Standish's house. When he was admitted, he had to wait five minutes for the Captain to come walking briskly into the study.

"Rutledge." There were overtones of formality in Standish's manner. It was apparent that he was still smarting from their last conversation.

"I'm on my way to Sevenoaks. I'd like you to come with me. A Major Holt was killed last night in a motorcar crash there. I can't identify him, but perhaps you will be able to."

There was a moment of stunned silence. Recovering, Standish began, "He doesn't—" then stopped abruptly.

"He doesn't live there," Rutledge finished for him. "But that's not to say he wasn't driving through Sevenoaks last evening. Are you coming, or not?"

Standish hesitated.

"I'm asking you to identify him for me. That's all."

"I've seen enough dead men."

"This man's death is not my inquiry. But I need to know if he's the officer with whom you raced to Nice."

"It wasn't a race."

"You're splitting hairs. Are you to come or not?"

"All right," Standish said, goaded. "I'll fetch my coat and an umbrella."

Five minutes later he strode out the door. Rutledge was already waiting in his motorcar. When they had reached the main road, Standish asked, "How did you learn of this man's death? Surely the inspector in charge has already discovered his identity, if you've been told it was Holt."

"I have my sources. What's more, if you'd given me his name earlier, he might still be alive. I could have warned him."

"You can't believe that! Not every crash is linked to that bloody race."

"I'll know more once I see Major Holt's motorcar."

"But Wright had no connection with Nice. Nor did this man Grant, surely."

"Perhaps not. But you lost your hand in one crash, Wright lost his life in another, and now this man Holt has been killed in a third. What if we've been looking in the wrong direction?"

"That's nonsense. Coincidence. There are more motorcars on the roads now than there were in 1914. There will be more crashes. Bound to be."

"Yet you've said that someone tried to run you off the road in the hills above Nice. For all we know, whoever did that is still alive."

"I never saw the motorcar clearly, much less the man. I don't know what possessed him. Perhaps he thought I was someone else. My motorcar was hardly unique. Or perhaps he was an incompetent driver and couldn't control his own vehicle on that godforsaken road."

Hamish said, "He doesna' wish to believe."

"Then tell me why it still haunts you."

Standish fell silent.

The inquests had bought Rutledge a little time. And will-o'-the-wisp or not, the death in Sevenoaks had to be looked into.

As they splashed through yet another patch of standing water on the road north, Standish broke his silence to comment, "Wretched day to be out and about."

Rutledge asked, "Was the Major married?"

"Yes, he married just after the war. I recall him saying something about that in Paris. As I've told you, we had very little in common except the war and the pledge to meet after it was finished. There was no reason to stay in touch."

"More's the pity."

Standish took a deep breath as they passed hop fields and a pair of oasthouses. "To be quite honest, I don't believe any of us wanted to become friends. I think each of us had a very personal reason to make that run to Nice. It was hardly camaraderie that brought us together in Paris. And then there was my crash. It put rather a damper on the conclusion of the race. I think the others felt guilty about that. It wasn't supposed to end that way. We were to get drunk on celebratory champagne or brandy and then go home."

Rutledge didn't reply. It had occurred to him that Standish appeared to be a solitary man by nature, while he himself had learned to become one. They halted for petrol and a late lunch halfway to their destination, but any expectation of outrunning the rain was growing dimmer by the mile. By the time they reached Sevenoaks, night had fallen and the weather was growing more foul by the minute.

"I'm not quite certain I'm ready for this," Standish confessed, staring out his window at the village.

"I must stop at the police station and alert the local man that I'm here in regard to another inquiry, not stepping on his toes."

He found the police station, and leaving Standish in the motorcar—against the Captain's wishes—he went inside and asked to speak to the inspector in charge of the Holt death.

A few minutes later he was turned over to an Inspector by the name of Judd.

"I'm told you've come in regard to the death of Major Holt. Mind telling me why Scotland Yard should be interested in a road accident?"

"Was it?" Rutledge asked, keeping his manner pleasant. "I was told that the Major had died, but not the manner of his death."

"The doctor could smell whisky in the motorcar when he got there. I'd noticed it as well. Usually Constable Crabbe would have dealt with it, but as Major Holt was passing through, I felt it required a senior officer to break the news to Mrs. Holt. She took it quite hard."

"He overturned?"

"No, lost control on a rain-slick road and slammed into a tree."

Rutledge shook his head. "Sad, that."

"It was. The Major was apparently well liked in Surrey. I spoke to the local man there. It seems he'd come to town to look in on a friend who was in hospital. Afterward he stopped by The Hart and had two whiskies before starting for home."

"What was his mood when he stopped there?"

"Taciturn. Well, I understand he was never what one might call loquacious, but he was quiet and somber."

"But not suicidal?"

"Not at all. I never even considered suicide. He was young, married just after the war, and his affairs were in good order. Nothing there to hint at self-destruction. His wife agreed."

"Has she been brought in to identify the body?"

"She was not prepared to come in today. The local man is bringing her tomorrow."

"I think I can spare her that. I've a man in the motorcar outside who knew Holt during the war. I'd like him to have a look at your body."

Judd studied him. "You never said. What's your interest in our victim?"

"I have two cases of attempts on the lives of former officers." Nice wasn't in his jurisdiction, but it bolstered his request to have more than one inquiry. "I'd like to know if this was a third."

"This is my patch. No one has asked for the Yard."

"I've no intention of taking it over. I just need to cross one more possibility from my list."

"Holt is at Dr. Lodge's surgery."

"I don't know Sevenoaks."

"It's in the center of town. There's a large bookstore next door." He gave directions, then said, "It's late to be calling on Lodge."

"I have work waiting for me in East Sussex."

"Oh, very well. If he's awake, he'll let you have a look. If not, you'll wait for tomorrow."

"Fair enough. Where is the motorcar presently?"

"It's where it crashed, not far from Knole. There was nowhere else to take it, and we've had heavy rain all day."

Sitting by the side of the road? Where anyone could get to it? But he said nothing about that, thanked Inspector Judd, and went out to the motorcar.

Standish, tired of waiting, was almost at the station door, intending to come in.

Rutledge said, "We're to drive to the doctor's. By the bookstore."

"I saw a surgery coming in, I think." They hurried back to the motorcar and began their search. Fifteen minutes later they found it. It wasn't next to the bookstore, but a good distance down from there.

The doctor answered the door himself, asking, "What is it you need?" as he peered out at them over his glasses. He was an older man, with gray hair but startlingly black eyebrows and mustache.

The rain was still coming down in sheets, and he opened the door wider so that they could step inside. Standish busied himself with the umbrellas as Rutledge responded. "I'm from Scotland Yard. Inspector Rutledge. Inspector Judd has sent Captain Standish along to identify the crash victim. He knew the deceased during the war and saw him last in Paris not long ago."

It was longer than that, but Standish didn't correct him.

Dr. Lodge took out his watch. "It's late. And I just had an urgent appendix."

"It won't take long. I've brought Captain Standish from East Dedham in Sussex. It would be a kindness to allow him to finish this business tonight. Otherwise Mrs. Holt must be brought to Sevenoaks to identify her husband." His manner was quietly persuasive.

After a moment the doctor said, "This way, then."

He led them down the passage to a door that opened into his surgery rather than his living quarters above. In a back room, windowless and plainly used for storage, a body lay on a deal table, under a sheet.

"Cause of death is severe neck injuries. He struck the tree—it was a large oak—with some force. His head was snapped forward and then back again. I doubt he knew anything more. Death would have been swift."

Dr. Lodge moved forward, and Rutledge followed him. Standish stayed by the door for a moment longer, then came closer as the sheet was lifted.

There was a great deal of head trauma, but the dead man's face, aside from one bloody scrape, was still recognizable.

Standish stared down at the body for a long moment. He started to speak, cleared his throat, and then said clearly, "That's Major Holt. God rest his soul."

Turning, he strode out of the room and down the passage.

Rutledge, standing beside the table, asked, "Are you certain the neck injuries are consistent with the crash?"

"Oh, yes. There's no doubt at all. He was still pinned behind the wheel when he was found."

"No one could have come to the motorcar's door, found him unconscious, and killed him?"

Lodge gave him a sharp glance, then said, "The door was jammed. We had to pry it open to remove the body."

"Thank you, Dr. Lodge. I'll report the Captain's identification to Inspector Judd."

Lodge accompanied him to the door, where Standish was waiting. They picked up their umbrellas, walked out into the rain, and got into the motorcar.

Rutledge stopped long enough to report to Judd that Standish had recognized the dead man and that it was indeed Holt.

"Good. It will spare his widow. She's staying with neighbors. She was in a sad state. Barely two years wed, a happy life to look forward to." He shook his head. "Sad."

Judd walked Rutledge to the police station's door, as if to make certain he didn't linger.

Standish said as Rutledge returned to the motorcar, "I don't think that man cares for you."

"It isn't personal. He doesn't want the Yard poking around, upsetting his own deductions with new questions."

"Much the same way we felt when a senior officer came on a tour of inspection. We were glad to see the back of him. Where are you going? That's not the road to Sussex."

"I'm looking for the motorcar. It's still out here on the road."

"Good God. Holt wouldn't care for that. I could tell he was particular about it."

They drove through the town, coming up on the large houses near the church, and then the turning for Knole. Past the enormous park surrounding the great house, there was a bend in the road, and Rutledge's headlamps quickly picked out a good-sized tree with a motorcar jammed against the trunk.

They were silent as Rutledge slowed and pulled in behind the wreckage.

Just here the rain had tapered to a drizzle. While Standish reached for the umbrellas, Rutledge retrieved his torch from the boot.

They approached the damaged vehicle with care, the wet grass and mud from the road caking their boots as they walked forward.

The color of the Rolls's paint was indeterminate in the light of Rutledge's torch, but on closer inspection, he could see that it was dark green. The bonnet was crumpled, the engine block shoved back almost into the passenger compartment. The lovely Spirit of Ecstasy ornament had broken off and was caught in one of the accordion-like sections. The shining chrome of the radiator was twisted and crushed.

Inside, the driver's seat was shoved sideways, and the steering wheel must have pressed against Holt's chest. Dried blood, mixed with rain dripping through a crack in the roof, was black in the light from Rutledge's torch.

The rear of the vehicle was hardly touched. Rutledge found himself thinking that Hamish would have survived, and pushed the thought aside.

"Dear God," Standish whispered, and stumbled away. Rutledge could hear him retching.

Continuing his inspection, Rutledge moved on.

When he came to the left rear wheel and the boot, he moved closer. In the dark, in the rain, in the light of his torch, he found it difficult to be sure. But he could almost swear that there were scrapes in the dark green paint. And when he moved to the near side, he found the same marks. The tail lamp was twisted to one side, but he couldn't be certain when that had happened. Besides, the scrapes told their own story.

There seemed to be a good deal more glass about than the damage to Holt's vehicle justified. Rutledge squatted for a better look, then picked up one of the larger pieces to examine it.

Had the other motorcar suffered a broken headlamp? This wasn't ordinary glass. It was thicker and slightly ridged on one side.

I might have been wrong about Wright's crash, he told himself, *but not two. Holt must have put up one hell of a fight to stay on the road. And this time the other vehicle must show substantial damage as well.*

Standish came back, wiping his mouth with his handkerchief and saying apologetically, "I never saw the wreckage of my own motorcar. I was in hospital, and the police informed me that it was unsalvageable. It was removed by a firm there in Nice, and that was that. Turned into scrap, for all I know. It would have been worse than this, but where I was sitting . . ."

He couldn't finish the thought.

Rutledge said, "Look here," and pointed out the damage done.

Standish bent closer, peering at the rear lamp and at the shards in Rutledge's palm. When he stood up, he was shaking his head. "There." He pointed to one of the areas of scraping. "That's precisely where my own vehicle was struck from behind. I didn't see it afterward, but I damned well felt it at the time."

"And where the motorcar that Wright was driving had been struck."

"It really is murder, then, isn't it?"

"Yes. And it began in Nice. Do you know of any reason why you and Holt have been targeted? I want the truth this time, not evasions."

"No," Standish replied simply. "I can think of no reason." He took a deep breath. "If it had been one of us—Holt, say—who had brought his personal troubles to Nice with him, I'd have been surprised, but such things do happen. But I brought none. I can swear to that."

"Did Holt ever mention having problems on that high road?"

"No, but then neither did I. I never spoke of it to anyone but the doctors. Not until I told you."

Rutledge considered the matter. If Holt hadn't told Standish—in hospital and gravely injured—it was unlikely that he would have told his wife. He wouldn't have wanted to worry her, and there was no likelihood that whatever had happened in France would follow him home.

"What about Russell? Or Brothers? Or Taylor?"

Standish stepped away, frowning at Rutledge. "How the devil did you find out their names? I thought perhaps the Yard had somehow learned of this crash and sent you word. That that was how you discovered Holt's name."

Rutledge didn't smile. "I've told you. I have my sources," he replied. "Now let's get out of this rain." He strode back to the motorcar, kicked the worst of the mud from his boots, and got in.

Standish stood there by the wrecked motorcar, as if unable to tear himself away. And then he turned and hurried to join Rutledge.

"I don't know how I survived," he said almost to himself as they drove away.

I t was a long journey back to East Sussex. Rutledge was tempted to spend the night at Melinda's house, late as it was, but Standish was with him and he didn't care to introduce them.

Around one in the morning, Standish spelled him for a few hours, but Rutledge's mind was racing too fast for him to sleep.

Did he want Standish with him when he interviewed the remaining three men?

He decided he didn't.

They pulled into East Dedham just as the sun was coming up, and Rutledge drove Standish home.

As the Captain got out of the motorcar, he said, "What are you going to do now? How is what happened in France going to clear up what's happening here?"

"Early days," Rutledge said evasively, and Standish paused, debating with himself.

"Brothers is the nearest. But I don't know what he can tell you that I can't. I don't even know if anything happened to him there in the hills above Nice."

"We'll see," Rutledge answered. "Right now I'm going to sleep for a few hours. Then I'll know what to do."

Standish didn't move toward the house. "I don't know if I wish to go with you or not."

"I think it's better if you don't. Brothers might feel freer to tell me what it is he might know."

"I should have told them. I should have spoken up. It might have made a difference." He shook his head. "In hospital, in pain, I thought it was best not to say anything. I thought, if it didn't happen to them, what was the point? I'd only make their own race less—" He struggled to find the word he wanted. "It might diminish what they had done, as it had diminished my own race. After all, I never finished it."

And then he turned and walked swiftly toward the house door. He went inside without looking back, and shut it firmly behind him.

Rutledge came out of a deep sleep to pounding on his door. He struggled to place the noise, then came wide awake.

"Who is it?"

"Constable Brewster. A message from Constable Neville. He says you'd better come."

Rutledge didn't waste time asking what Neville wanted. He dressed in haste after taking two minutes to wash his face and comb his hair. There was no time to shave. His boots were still damp from constant wettings over the past four-and-twenty hours. He pulled them on over dry stockings.

He went downstairs, where Brewster was waiting for him, and the two men walked out to the motorcar.

The sun was shining, but not with any serious strength, and heavy clouds still lingered on the horizon, promising more rain. The wind had picked up halfway to East Dedham last night, and it still blew fiercely from the sea.

"What did Neville want?" he asked as Brewster turned the crank.

"I don't know, sir. He didn't say."

It was typical of the tense relationship between the two constables. Rutledge swore to himself and concentrated on avoiding the pools of water that marked the worst of the ruts.

He'd expected to go directly to the police station, but as he came into the Gap he saw the cluster of men along the cliff and instead went on, driving as close as he safely could.

Neville, hearing him come up, turned and hurried to greet him, nodding to Brewster.

"There's something you ought to see," Neville told Rutledge.

"Isn't that where the last fall occurred?" Rutledge asked, pointing in the direction Neville had come from. As he got out of the motorcar, he felt the full force of the wind. It would be pushing the waves against the chalk face, tearing at it.

"Yes, it is. One of the worst falls this autumn. But there's something else." He led the way back to the cluster of men, and they parted as Rutledge came forward.

"Beware the edge," Neville said. "It's waterlogged, it could go any minute. And the wind could pull you right over." He pointed out a sounder bit of turf and said, "One of the lads saw it this morning."

Rutledge joined him and looked down. At first he wasn't sure what had attracted so much attention. There was the rubble cast up by the stormy sea and the debris from the recent fall, now gradually being sucked out by the tide. And then as a wave came crashing up on the chalk face to his left, he saw it, bobbing awkwardly in the surf. A brown object that seemed to open and close with the buffeting of the waves.

"What is it?" he asked, just as he understood what he was seeing. "It's a valise. The question is, where did it come from?" But he had a feeling he knew.

"I can't be sure," Neville said, "whether it's brought in by the tide or if it's Mrs. Grant's. I sent Archie—the lad over there—running to ask Mrs. Mitchell if she remembered what Mrs. Grant's valise looked like. She said it was brown." He glanced at Rutledge. "That thing is brown. But then so are most valises."

Brown leather or calf, even brown cardboard. Neville was right.

"We won't know until we can bring it up. The way the surf is pounding it, we could lose it altogether."

"It's not safe to send a man down."

"No." He'd had experience with landslips. They were dangerous at best, deadly at their worst. "Frustrating, standing here and watching it tossed up on the shingle."

"Do you think it's Mrs. Grant's? But why would it be in the sea?"

"The question is, where is *she*?"

17

For a quarter of an hour they watched the valise come apart, one side of it pulled back into the water and the other lying, as if taunting them, briefly at the foot of the cliff, five hundred feet below.

Rutledge, growing more and more impatient, asked, "Do you have enough rope to lower me down there? If we wait any longer, we're going to lose it."

"It's not safe," Neville argued. "For one thing, the edge of the cliff there is too fragile, and for another, we could lose men trying to lower you down and pull you up again." He gestured to either side of him. "With all this rain, the chalk softens. As it is, we're mad to be standing this close."

He was right, but Rutledge chafed at the tantalizing sight of half of the valise lying well within reach. And then it was reclaimed by the waves, rolling about like its other half, tossed from wave to wave like some child's lost toy, disappearing and then bobbing up again.

"I've seen nothing that might be considered the contents of the valise," the man standing next to Neville said. "No shoes or clothing or the like. It could have come from anywhere, tossed away because of a broken hasp."

Rutledge walked back to the motorcar to fetch his field glasses. But even with them he couldn't see anything that would tell him who might have owned the valise or how it had come to be there this morning.

The rough surf, climbing the sloping heap of chalk from the slip, was slowly eroding it. Neville, staring at it, said, "You don't think Mrs. Grant is buried under that fall? It happened the same night she disappeared. If that's her valise, washed out early, will she be next? She'll have to stay in the sea; there's no hope of reaching her to find out what happened to her."

"I don't know," Rutledge responded. "I've been wondering about that myself. I think it might be best to post a watcher along here, in case. Her body might not fare as well as the valise. It could be pulled out to sea in the night, and no one the wiser." He scanned the fall with his glasses, but there was nothing to see. "If she is dead, her killer was damned lucky when he threw her over the cliff. Otherwise she'd have been found straightaway."

"He seems to have all the luck," Neville said with suppressed anger.

Another quarter of an hour, and the sea had successfully reclaimed both halves of the broken valise. They disappeared from sight, and the watchers turned away.

"Well," said Neville with a sigh, "we'll never know. Unless she turns up too. I'll set that watch."

Rutledge thanked him for summoning him, and with a nod to the other villagers went back to his motorcar. The wind had cut through him there at the edge of the cliff, and he could see the other watchers rubbing their hands together as they made their way back to the cottages. He could taste salt on his lips as he drove on to The Sailor's Friend, setting Brewster down at the police station on his way.

He had just pulled into the yard when he saw Mrs. Saunders coming down the hill toward him, a knitted scarf over her head. She hailed him, and he waited for her to come nearer.

"I have found something," she said, waving a folded sheet of paper. "I can't tell if it's important or not, but you'll know."

"Where is Barnes?" Rutledge asked, looking up the hill.

"Reporting to the Bishop. I don't think he cares as much for the likes of us, now that he's been here for a bit. Any excuse and he's away telling the Bishop how backward we are. I, for one, will rejoice to see the back of him. After Rector, God rest his soul, I don't think I could ever grow to like that one. He *hovers*."

Suppressing a smile, Rutledge said, "Where did you find this? I searched the study thoroughly."

"Rector's Bible. His personal one. He always kept it by his bed. I was dusting his room and Mr. Barnes came in asking me to make him a pot of tea. He startled me so, lurking about the way he does, that I knocked the brass candlestick and the Bible off the table. That's when I saw it, stuck between the Old Testament and the New. I don't think Mr. Barnes noticed. I picked it up and put it in my pocket with my back to him."

"Thank you. I'll read it and let you know what it is."

She gave him a sheepish look. "Well, I did read it. In case it was something personal that he might not wish anybody else to know. It's a letter from someone he helped when he was chaplain. You'll see. But you've asked me more than once if Rector had any enemies. I thought it might matter."

With a nod she turned and walked back the way she'd come, and Rutledge found himself wondering if Wright had been aware of how much she cared for him, and her intense loyalty to the man and the position he held.

In his room he took the time to shave, and then he sat down by the window to read the letter.

Chaplain,

I am coming to see you. I have been in hospital again here in Portsmouth, and I fear it has done me little good. You are the only one who ever helped me, and I am hoping you can

*do so again. The doctors tell me that the injury to my brain
is irreversible, that the headaches and the anger will persist
possibly for the rest of my life. I can't bear the thought of that, I'd
rather kill myself and be done with it.*

*I beg you to find it in your heart to forgive me for what I've
done. And find a way to save me.*

*Pray for me, please. I was a good man once. I want to be that
man again.*

Truly your servant, sir.

And the signature was there. *Ralph Mercer.*

He rose, intending to walk up to the rectory and ask Mrs. Saunders
if she recognized the name. But she had read the letter—she would
have said something if she knew who this man Mercer was.

He folded the letter and tried to insert it into the envelope postmarked from Portsmouth. It fit perfectly. What's more, when he
matched the ink on the envelope to that in the letter, he'd have been
willing to wager they were from the same pen. It was true as well of
the handwriting—the same tightly formed letters, the vowels crammed
into the consonants, and the consonants stubby and upright.

It would take a handwriting expert to be absolutely certain, but to
the naked eye, there was no doubt.

Was Mercer the man who had appeared at the rectory shortly after
the letter had arrived, the man with whom Wright had walked to the
church? And afterward, the Rector had told his housekeeper that the
stranger had come about the church organ. But had he?

Who *was* Ralph Mercer?

Rutledge drove to Eastbourne, returning to the telephone he'd used
once before.

He began with Sergeant Gibson in London.

"I need information about hospitals or clinics in Portsmouth for returning soldiers and officers with unresolved issues."

He waited while Gibson went to find an answer. As wounded

men recovered and returned to their former lives—those with broken bones or injuries that healed—most of the wartime clinics had closed, the houses taken over by the Army medical officers returned to their owners. But those with burns, with destroyed faces, with wounds that refused to heal or required repeated surgeries, those with severe amputations, with shell-shock, with brain damage, were still being treated. And he had a feeling from the tone of the letter that Mercer must be among them.

Hamish was pointing out that Mercer had written his letter, had traveled to Sussex and walked to the rectory door, had spoken to the Rector. "He canna' be verra' badly wounded."

"But he could be one of Wright's failures." Rutledge had spoken aloud in the tiny, stuffy room where the telephone was housed.

Gibson said, "Sorry, sir, I missed that."

"I wasn't speaking to you, Sergeant."

"The hospital is on the telephone, as you thought. But I'm not sure it's what you want."

"No?"

"It's for mentally disturbed patients, sir."

"I'll take it all the same."

Sergeant Gibson read it to Rutledge, and then said, "About the names you gave me, sir. There's nothing I could discover that's likely to be of use in your inquiry. All law-abiding men, respected in their parishes."

These were the men whose names Standish had given him, men who had owned dark green motorcars—but who had not gone to France a year ago.

"Thank you, Sergeant. That's very helpful."

He could cross them off his own list. But the critical names now were Russell, Taylor, and Brothers, and for a moment he considered asking Gibson to find out what he could about them. But there wasn't time. He needed to speak to each of them himself, as soon as possible, to warn them, as he hadn't been able to warn Holt.

There was a pause at the other end of the connection, then lowering his voice, Gibson added, "Himself is likely to be confirmed as Chief Superintendent. No longer Acting CS. There has been traffic between here and the Home Office."

It might have been no more than passing on the latest Yard reports. But something in Gibson's voice had suggested a warning. And a dislike.

Rutledge replied, "Keep me informed."

"I'll do that, sir." Another pause. "He *barks,* sir. It doesn't go over well with the lads. Nor the Inspectors either."

A hardheaded Yorkshireman, ACS Markham was not one to ask so much as to order.

"Perhaps he'll mellow, once the position is actually his," Rutledge suggested.

"When the moon sets in the east, sir."

Rutledge thanked him and rang off. He and Gibson had shared nothing, not even friendship. Except for a mutual distaste for overbearing Chief Superintendents. A bond of sorts. *The enemy of my enemy is my friend.*

Rutledge put through the call to the clinic outside Portsmouth, and eventually spoke to Matron, after being passed through a number of underlings.

He gave her his name and his rank, and informed her that Wright had been murdered. That it was necessary to know what business he'd had with Ralph Mercer two months earlier.

There was silence on the other end of the line, then Matron said, choosing her words with care, "Ralph Mercer was an unusual case. There was a bit of shrapnel lodged in his skull, but it was not a significant injury. That's to say, it had not impaired his mental capacity in any way. Nor is it why he has been a patient here from time to time, although he often complained of headaches. Mercer was not his real name. It was the name he has chosen to use, and it was felt that to attempt to correct him, to force him to use his own name, might not be wise."

"I don't follow you," Rutledge said, his throat almost closing on the words.

"No, I'm sure you don't. Ralph Mercer doesn't suffer from shell shock, if that's what you are thinking. During the war, I'm told, his sector was too close to a German tunnel, and when it was blown almost in his face, his men were killed by the force of the explosion. There wasn't a mark on them, they simply died instantly wherever they were sitting or standing. He was the company sergeant, and he was sitting in the cubby hollowed out for use by the officer in charge, and partially protected from the blast, although it damaged his eardrums and possibly his brain. Do you know what I am describing?"

"I was in France," Rutledge said. "I understand." The British had refused to make their trenches more habitable, as the Germans had done. Officers had taken to scraping out a space in the back wall of the trench, hanging a length of canvas across the opening to keep a candle from being seen by enemy snipers, and there they dealt with the business of command, from reading orders to writing letters of condolence to the families of the dead.

"He had no way of knowing," Matron said after a moment, "that the tunnel was so close to his sector. His Lieutenant was nearest the blast, speaking to one of the men, and was killed as well. Mercer felt he was somehow to blame, that he should have been more vigilant, that somehow he should have noticed some sign of what was to come and warned his commanding officer and the rest of the men. He didn't want to be that lone survivor, you see. He felt that Sergeant Miller ought to have died as well. It haunted him. On the other hand, as 'Ralph Mercer,' he had nothing to do with the war, and he could cope to some extent. When that didn't serve, he came to us, and we would keep him until he was himself again. There was a chaplain who helped him a great deal. Last August, when he had an especially bad turn, we kept him for six weeks. And then he felt he wasn't getting the care he needed, and he asked to be released to seek out the Rector of St. Simon's Church in East Dedham. The doctor in charge of his care felt it was wise to allow him to go. I don't know what passed between the chaplain and Mercer, but he returned a calmer man. We were all quite pleased with his improved state of mind. And then, on Remembrance Day, without any warning, he tried to hang himself in his room."

Rutledge could hear the grief in her voice. It was fresh, painful. Losing a patient was difficult enough at any time, but losing one to suicide must be particularly trying to accept. Even attempted suicide. It reeked of failure.

"I'm sorry, Matron."

"I am as well. I had hoped that he might recover, given time. Instead he's signed himself out of hospital. I fear he might wish to try again, expecting to be more successful out from under our eye. What else is it you wished to know about him?"

"I found his letter to the Rector, you see. I think Wright was distressed by it. I didn't know why. Do you have a forwarding address—any way that I can reach him?"

"I'm afraid he didn't leave any. Mercer isn't your murderer, Inspector. But I hope you find whoever it is. The Rector was a good man."

And she rang off before he could respond.

Rutledge put up the receiver and stood there, lost in thought, for several minutes.

And then he went to find Captain Brothers.

The telegram from Bess Crawford had given an address in Maidstone, in Kent, for Captain Brothers.

Rutledge found him on a tree-lined street of middle-class bungalows. The one he sought had black Tudor-style trim, a handsome front garden, and a bow window on either side of the doorway.

When he knocked, a woman dressed in the dark clothing of a housekeeper opened the door to him.

He asked for Brothers, and she in turn asked his name.

Rutledge told her, adding that he had come from Scotland Yard on an urgent matter.

He was taken down the passage to a sitting room, and after several minutes a fair man of medium height, a scar across one cheek, came through the door.

Wary, he said, "You're from Scotland Yard? I'd like to see some identification."

Rutledge handed it to him, and Brothers looked it over carefully. Lifting his head, he handed it back and then said, "What is this urgent business that brought you here?"

"Major Holt is dead. And Captain Standish is in danger. I've come to ask you to tell me what happened in Nice a year ago."

"Nothing happened," Brothers replied curtly.

"Standish was nearly killed when his motorcar was forced off the road. His injuries, in fact, were severe, including the loss of a hand. That's hardly to be considered 'nothing.'"

"You'd better sit down," Brothers said after a pause in which he seemed to battle his own reticence. Rutledge watched it reflected in the Captain's eyes and saw the decision form. "It's a long story and not a very pleasant one."

"You were one of the five men who met in Paris and then drove to Nice?"

"I was. I'd had to borrow my brother-in-law's motorcar. At the time I didn't have my own. But that was all right. None of the others seemed to think it mattered." He crossed to a sideboard where a drinks tray held pride of place. "Whisky?"

"Yes, thanks."

He poured two generous glasses, and handed one to Rutledge.

"It was an uneventful drive. Russell, I think it was, had chosen the route, and he provided maps for all of us. In Paris we studied them carefully, asking questions, jotting down notes. I enjoyed the planning. Oddly enough, it was rather like planning an assault, although without the consequences. We didn't meet along the way; we were on our own, and I rather liked that too. I hadn't come for the camaraderie so much as to keep my promise. You've heard about that part? The night before the Somme offensive? Yes, well, it seemed such a gallant thing to do. Flouting death, making an adventure out of our survival. I don't think any of us came home from the war with any dreams left. It had been a damned hard four years, and I was tired to the bone. I walked into the house, tossed my bag into a corner, undressed, and slept the clock around. Worried Mrs. Dawson, she thought something was wrong. Were you in the war?"

"Yes."

"The Somme?"

"Yes."

"Madness, that. It was when we all lost hope. I was surprised to find myself still alive in the autumn, when it was finished. Four months of hell. And after the Armistice, we came back to a bleak world. I didn't get in until well into January. It was winter-dark, everyone appeared to be as exhausted as I was, and nothing seemed to be the same. Besides, most of my friends had been killed or badly wounded. Lonely. Depressing. A shortage of everything. The drive to Nice had been a talisman while we were fighting. 'I survived—I'll drive to Nice with the rest.' But it wasn't something that was actually going to happen. After nearly a year at home, the race seemed to offer a respite from the present. At any rate, when the time came, when I took William's motorcar and set out for Paris, I had come to the point of doubting myself, doubting the Armistice, doubting the England I'd come back to. I had lost the man I was during those four years of war. I thought I could find him again."

He got up and refilled his glass. Rutledge had hardly touched his own.

"It will sound odd to you, but in a way that drive was a reaffirmation of my own courage. Looking back on the war, I seemed to have scraped through. So many men had serious wounds—or they died of horrendous ones. I'd been wounded, of course, but I was back in the field in a matter of days. I hadn't earned the right to compare myself to them. Do you understand what I'm saying? Yes? Well, this was another test, in a way, alone in my motorcar and reliving four years of hell, trying to come to terms with the killing and the night attacks, and the snipers and the shelling, and torn bodies everywhere, telling myself I had deserved to survive. I'd *earned* it. Don't laugh. But that's what was going through my mind."

"I have no intention of laughing," Rutledge said somberly.

"At any rate, all went well, or so I thought. I'd begun to take an interest in the journey for its own sake, the scenery, villages where I'd stopped for meals, the people I'd met. And then—then I was driving one of the most hellish roads I'd ever seen: twisting, narrow, poorly banked, nothing but a deep drop on one side, and in many places, no room to pass. Imagine driving that as a heavy mist came up the side of the mountain, and all you could see was a drifting white veil obscuring everything, swallowing your headlamps, dampening all sound, leaving you as blind as if you'd lost your sight."

He got up and walked to the window. With his back to Rutledge, he gave an account of what happened next.

At the end, he turned around, his face strained. "I was sure I was going to die. It was a bloody miracle that I didn't. I don't think I've got over it yet. I still don't know whether my skill saved me—or his was not quite good enough to kill me."

Rutledge drank a little of his whisky, then said, "And the others?"

"That's the odd thing. No one mentioned a similar experience. And I was sure as hell not going to tell them what happened to me."

"All of you must have put on a good front. Standish didn't drive off the road in that fog. He was pushed off by another motorcar. He thought he was the only one to have been targeted, and he said nothing. Just as the rest of you said nothing. He felt he'd already spoiled the trip for you without adding feverish claims of attempted murder."

"Gentle God," Brothers whispered. "I didn't know. I went to see him in hospital, and he was not a pretty sight, I can tell you. All the more reason to say nothing to him about what I'd been through. I'd survived. I knew how bloody lucky I was." He looked away. "And yes, for a while up there in the hills, I believed it was one of us trying to run me off the road. Foolishness, but at the time it seemed the only explanation."

"Have you seen any of the other men since Nice?"

Brothers shook his head. "No. I think what happened to Standish sobered all of us. Or maybe it was what happened to each of us on that road. But in the name of God, who did that to me, to Standish?"

Rutledge didn't give a direct answer. "Have you heard? Holt has died in a motorcar crash. In the driving rain, he lost control and struck a tree. That's how it appears. The evidence tells a different story, pointing to someone deliberately trying to run him off the road. Someone tried to kill him, and succeeded."

Brothers stood there, staring at him.

"And," Rutledge went on, "someone who borrowed Standish's motorcar was also murdered. It isn't clear whether the crash killed him, or he was found alive and killed. But there's little doubt that two vehicles were involved."

"Oh God."

"Which of you could have done such a thing? Holt is dead, that puts him out of the running. Standish, you, Russell, or Taylor?"

"I don't know. You'll think me mad, but while I was driving through that mist, I thought about Everett. He'd wanted to make it to Paris. Instead he died of gangrene. He wrote me a letter just before he died, telling me he'd be there in spirit with us. I had the strangest notion that he was driving that other motorcar. A ghost in a ghost motorcar. But I tell you, it was all too real. There was nothing ghostly about the force with which he—whoever he was—tried to send me off the road."

"Are you quite sure Everett is dead?"

"What? Yes, of course he is. Why do you ask?"

"It's my responsibility to check every fact."

"I received a letter from his mother. After Nice. She wrote to say she was told by the Sister who took care of her son that he had fought to live and drive with us. It had given him the strength to endure a number of surgeries with courage and patience. And his mother wanted to know if the race had been all we had expected it would be. What could I tell her? The truth? It would have been cruel."

"I agree. Who else, then?"

"My God, Rutledge, who could have had such a grievance against all of us? This speaks of madness, not anger."

"I don't believe it has anything to do with madness. If you think of anything else that could have a bearing on any of this, write to me. There isn't a telephone, I'm afraid." He gave his direction in East Dedham and then finished his drink. Rising, he said, "Thanks for the whisky. And be careful, man. Stay off the road, make certain your doors are locked. Warn your housekeeper not to open your door to anyone she doesn't know well."

"What if it's one of the others? Russell. Taylor. Even Standish."

"I doubt it's Standish. I don't know the others."

"Nor do I. Not well. But why in heaven's name would either of them try to kill us?"

"I don't know. I'd rather hoped you might."

"It has to be one of us, doesn't it? I mean to say, who else was in Paris *and* in Nice?"

Rutledge was halfway to the door when something Brothers had said stopped him.

"What do you mean, *who else was in Paris and in Nice*?"

"Just a manner of expression. But oddly enough, I *did* see someone else in Paris. It was the sergeant who'd converted the barn into an officers' mess. I hardly recognized him. But I'm sure that's who it was. At least I was certain at the time."

"Do you recall his name?"

"Sorry, I don't. Interesting story there, though. He deserted some five months after the Somme. Spring of '17 that would be. Word got around that an officer had run off with the sergeant's wife. Apparently she gave him a name, and it's possible he shot that man in the back in the retreat following an attack. There was no way to prove it, you know how chaotic retreats were. But she told him later that she'd lied, that it was another man. He killed *her* then."

He felt like swearing. "Had any of you met this man's wife?"

Brothers shook his head. "I can't speak for the others, but I've never set eyes on her. He'd shown us a photograph of his wife that night before the Somme. A very pretty woman, though I got the feeling she was no better than she ought to be. A very provocative pose."

"Do you think any of the others, one of the seven drinking that night before the battle, could have dallied with the man's wife?"

"God knows, Rutledge. I was never sent back to England on leave. I can't speak for the others. But look here, if the man was in Paris, he can't have killed Holt."

"Enough time has passed. He might have decided that no one was looking for him at the ports." As they had done for deserters, till well after the end of the war.

"Yes, I see." He shook his head. "I'm afraid I'm not much help. God knows I wish I'd never agreed to meet and race. I thought afterward that we were putting ourselves in danger again, when we should have been grateful we lived to see the war end. What possessed us that week of driving, to take such a risk? I don't think I'll ever understand it."

"I expect you didn't believe you'd live to see Paris. It was something to take your mind off tomorrow, when death was staring you in the face. Soldiers make all kinds of promises then. Bargaining with God. Even the Crusaders swore they'd build churches if they lived."

"It would have been safer to build a church," Brothers answered him sourly.

R utledge had arrived in Rye too late to call on Russell and found a room for the night in the Mermaid Inn.

He slept without dreams for once, came down early for break-fast, and walked in the town for a time, finally climbing the hill up to St. Mary's Church to watch the gulls coming in from the sea. Then he went down one of the cobbled lanes to where he could look out at the water below. In the early-morning light it sparkled, and for once the wind didn't carry its usual chill. He had always liked Rye, with its long history. It had Saxon roots, had once belonged to a Benedictine abbey in France, and later became one of the original Cinque Ports, a chain of protection on a coast far too close to England's traditional enemy, France. Warships anchored in the protection of the River Rother, and when they were withdrawn, smugglers and fishing fleets found it just as useful.

When at last the church clock struck nine, he turned and went down the cobbled Mermaid Street to the Russell house.

It was easily found, ivy climbing its walls and framing the bow window with its crisp lace curtains. They formed a backdrop for a black cat curled up on the white window ledge next to a crystal vase filled with silk flowers in shades of rose and cream and lavender. When Rutledge lifted the knocker, the cat lifted its head and stared balefully at him, its amber eyes accusing him of disturbing a well-earned nap. He was smiling at it when someone answered the door. She was an older woman, an apron over her dark dress, her soft white hair in a knot at the nape of her neck. Her eyes were blue, and just now bright with curiosity as she examined the stranger on her doorstep at this hour.

"Yes?" she asked.

"Good morning," he said, smiling. "My name is Rutledge. I'm from London and I'm looking for Lieutenant Russell. Does he still live here?"

The brightness faded. "I'm so sorry," she said. "He died a month ago. Did you know him in the war?"

"We had mutual friends," Rutledge answered, stifling his own cu-riosity. "I didn't know."

"I was just putting the kettle on. Would you care for a cup of tea? I enjoy talking about my son. It helps ease my loss."

She was far too trusting, and it worried him.

He followed her through to the kitchen, where the kettle was now on the boil, and she said, "If you like, I'll bring a tray into the front room."

"I'm comfortable here," Rutledge said, and she nodded.

"Cedric was such a lovely little boy. He'd sit at the table there while I made dinner, and tell me all about his school day. The war changed him. I expect it was true of any number of young men."

He let her talk while the tea steeped and she brought cups and saucers to the table. And then he sought a way to turn the conversation to how her son had died.

Before he could think of one, she brought it up herself.

"As I told the other young man, Cedric was depressed after he came home from the war. I couldn't tell you why." She poured the tea into their cups and sat down across from Rutledge. "It was her fault, you know. That woman. I tried to tell him what she was, but he was besotted with her. She promised to write, but she never did. He feared something had happened to her. My belief is that she soon found someone else. Then he went off to Paris, some foolishness about motorcars and Nice. He said it would help him. But it didn't. He came home in an even darker mood."

It was a rather convoluted account, but Rutledge was able, after a fashion, to understand what she was saying. Was this woman the sergeant's wayward wife?

He found it hard to believe. For one thing, there was the matter of time.

"How long had your son known this woman?"

"He met her in 1917, when he was sent home to recover from his wound. I have no idea how they met; he never said."

Still. There were any number of women like the sergeant's wife, looking for a better life.

He could wait no longer. His teacup was nearly empty, and he would have to go.

"How did your son die?" he asked as gently as he could. "An old wound?"

"He killed himself," she said, her eyes welling with tears. "He left me a lovely note, telling me how much he loved me, and how terrible the war had been, and how Nice had shown him that death was still waiting for him. And he thought it best to be done with it, because he was no good to anyone in the place he found himself."

Rutledge had been prepared for anything but suicide. He wanted to ask how, to be sure it wasn't the same hand behind *this* man's death. He was trying to find the words when she told him.

"He took his service revolver out on the Weald, where I wouldn't be the one to find him. And he shot himself. He was careful not to mar his face, because he knew I'd have to identify him. But he was still dead."

She turned away, pretending to set the milk jug and the bowl of sugar to rights, although they didn't need her care.

"I'm so sorry," Rutledge said quietly. "I didn't know. I wouldn't have intruded on your grief if I had." The Weald, rolling and once wooded, came down to the sea at Rye, very much like the Downs at the Gap, although it had once provided timber for building and the charcoal industry that had also flourished here. Russell had left his body to the mercy of strangers, to protect his mother.

"No, you haven't intruded," she said. "My friends and neighbors mean to be kind, but they're uncomfortable with my grief. It wasn't that way during the war, you know. We read the lists of wounded and killed and went to offer whatever consolation we could to those whose sons and fathers and brothers were named there. In the war it was as if we all suffered the same pain and sorrow. I expect suicide is different."

He reached out and touched her hand where it lay on the table. "He must have loved you very much."

"But not enough," she said with a sad smile. "Not enough."

He set his cup on the tray and rose to take his leave. She went with him to the door, thanking him for coming, for remembering to seek out her son, even though the war was over.

Rutledge was at the door, ready to step out into the sunlight, when Hamish jogged his memory. Something she had said when he first arrived . . .

The other young man.

He said, "You told me that someone else had come to call. Perhaps I know him?"

She frowned. "It was just a fortnight ago. He didn't give his name, not at first," she said. "And then I asked him outright, thinking I might remember it from Cedric's letters. He said it was Standish. That he was my son's commanding officer. Captain Standish. Later I wondered about that, and I went to find the letter of condolence from his commanding officer. And it was signed by a Captain Newland."

"I expect," he said carefully, not to alarm her, "that your son had also served under Captain Standish at one time, and he remembered him. I don't seem to recall Standish, myself. I was never under his command."

"I think there's a photograph of him in Cedric's things. It must have been a party. There were eight men in an old barn, the oddest place you can imagine. Do you have time? I'll look it out for you."

Suppressing his excitement, he said, "I should like that very much."

She went down the passage to another room and came back with a small box tied up in white ribbon.

"I'd given Cedric a camera for Christmas 1914. Before he went to France. It was a Brownie 2, from America. I found it in a shop in London. I thought perhaps he'd like to remember his experiences, and that later I could share them with him. But he didn't want me to see the photographs. He said they brought back too many memories. Still, there were a few that he showed me. Of places he'd been, people he'd known." Untying the ribbon, she took out a handful of photographs and passed them to him.

He steeled himself to find photographs of the Somme, but then he remembered that these were to share with Mrs. Russell.

Half a dozen men around a downed German plane, grinning at the camera as if they personally had shot it down. As they might well have done. A church half destroyed by shell fire, and a rosebush to one side of it, still struggling to bloom. A dog his company had adopted, playing tug-of-war with a bit of rag. A line of ambulances in the distance, silhouetted against the sky as they drove toward a base hospital. Half a dozen nursing Sisters standing outside a ward tent. To his surprise he recognized Bess Crawford among them, smiling for the camera. And after that, a shadowy photograph of a barn, and a makeshift canteen or mess hall.

A trestle-table bar and a half-dozen scavenged bits of furniture offering seating. One table cluttered with an assortment of cups and candles in tins, as well as several empty bottles, and six men standing around it. He could make out three familiar faces. Standish. Brothers. Holt.

At his shoulder, Mrs. Russell said helpfully, "Cedric took this photograph. The next one shows him."

Rutledge looked at the next one. The same setting for all intents and purposes. Only this time Holt was missing, and another man had taken his place.

"Yes, there he is," she said. "Look, in the middle. But of course you know him, don't you?"

The young Lieutenant standing there was of medium height, his hair dark and his smile contagious. The photograph was grainy, the camera struggling with the low light. He had an arm around Brothers's shoulders, and what appeared to be a teacup in his other hand, raised in salute. Rutledge could just see the resemblance to the woman beside him.

"Yes, of course," Rutledge told her. "And Standish?"

"There at the bar. He's wearing a different uniform. Probably for the party, don't you think?"

"I'm sure," Rutledge said, not wanting to contradict her. "He was pretending to serve the others."

"That's right!" she said, pleased. "Don't you think that's a particularly good likeness of Cedric?"

"It is." He looked through the other photographs, but these were the only two from the barn on the eve of the Somme. "I wonder, could I borrow this photograph? I think the others would like copies, if I can have them made."

"Oh no, I'm so sorry! I couldn't bear to part with it."

Rutledge understood, although he had to swallow his disappointment. He could have forced her to allow the Yard to borrow it, but that would have been cruel.

"I understand." He handed the photographs back to her, thanking her for the tea and for letting him see these memories of her son's war, saying good-bye.

He was already on the sunlit cobblestones, turning back toward St. Mary's, when the door opened again.

Mrs. Russell stuck her head out the opening. "Mr. Rutledge? I understand so little about cameras. I don't know if they will be of any use to you, but Cedric also has kept the negatives in this box."

18

Rutledge drove directly to the Gap and East Dedham, the precious negatives in an envelope on the seat beside him. He had wasted three hours looking for a shop in Rye that could make copies for him. He had found one, but the owner was in Canterbury for the next three days, and only he, it seemed, understood the mysteries of the darkroom.

Dusk was already falling when he arrived in the Gap, the days growing shorter far too fast. He went first to the police station to find Constable Neville.

"Any news of the valise or Mrs. Grant?" he asked, walking in the door.

"Nothing to report. As the weather improved, the tide hasn't been as high, nor the waves either. But the valise is gone, probably at the bottom of the sea by now. As for Mrs. Grant, I was there only this morning, looking over at the fall, and it appears to be very much the same to me. Shame we can't put a party with shovels down there, but it's still such a large fall to shift, and we'd only have a few hours at a time to work."

"Keep watch, all the same."

Neville reached into a drawer and pulled out a sheet of paper. "The police along the coast are asking about a body that came ashore near Hastings. My first thought was of Mrs. Grant, but it's male, and there's no one missing here. Nor at East Dedham." He passed the sheet to Rutledge.

"Doesn't appear to be anyone we want to find," he agreed as he read the description of any identifying marks and then looked at the black-and-white drawing. "The sketch here is not very good, he'd been in the water a day or two. But I think recognizable, if you had someone in mind." He read on. *Cause of Death: Broken neck.*

He hadn't yet met with Taylor, as Hamish was reminding him.

Looking at the date given here, he realized that the man had died the Wednesday after Wright's Saturday-night crash.

"If he jumped from the hill just beyond Hastings, the rocks there might account for the neck being broken," Neville was saying. "But still."

"Yes. Still. There's one man unaccounted for in my own inquiries, but he would be younger than this. Approximately fifty, it says. I'll show this to Captain Standish. Nothing may come of it, but we'll have made certain. Has Constable Brewster seen it?"

"I expect he got one as well. Hastings trying to clear up loose ends."

"Probably that's all we were intended to do," he answered as he started for the door. "Apropos of nothing, I've been to Rye, once a seafaring town. And it reminded me. Where did the name of The Sailor's Friend come from? There's a grave by the same name in the churchyard. You didn't have that much of a fishing fleet here, did you?"

"There was no safe place to draw up the boats," Neville said. "But it has nothing to do with fishing. It's connected with an early parson at St. Simon's, who urged the building of a lighthouse here. We'd had some appalling wrecks along this coastline in his day."

"Makes sense," Rutledge agreed, leaving.

He drove on to Standish's house. The housekeeper showed him into the dining room, where Standish had just begun his dinner.

"It's early, but the staff has been invited to an engagement party in East Dedham, and I gave them permission to go. There's little enough to amuse them in the village. Take a seat. There's more than enough for two, and I'm afraid we're on our own. The dishes are on the sideboard, and we're to help ourselves. Ah. I heard the outer door close. But I expect everything has been thought of."

Rutledge demurred, but Standish said, "You can't stand there questioning me while I try to eat. Sit down."

He'd missed his lunch. He took off his coat and set it with his hat and gloves in the entry, then came back and served himself a parsnip-and-apple soup from the tureen on the sideboard.

Standish had been right, there was more than enough for two, and even though only one man had been expected to dine, there were extra plates and silverware and wineglasses for half a dozen. Old habits, Rutledge thought, died hard. A house accustomed to entertaining would never be caught short.

As he sat down to Standish's right, the Captain poured wine in his glass. "How old is Taylor? Any idea?"

"Thirty? Thirty-two?"

"Now finish your soup, and we'll talk before the next course."

The soup was excellent and he gave it his full attention. Then he turned to Standish and said, "I've found Brothers and Russell."

"Have you indeed?" Standish asked as he was about to refill his own glass.

"Brothers was quite helpful. And rather worried, when he heard about Major Holt. He told me what had happened to him in France. It was very similar to your own experience. Except that he was fortunate enough to find a village where he could pull off. And the other motorcar went on. Still, Brothers was wary the rest of the way to Nice, certain the driver would be lying in wait farther along."

Standish set his glass down. "Are you quite serious?"

"I am. He told me he wished he'd never set foot in Paris."

The Captain shook his head. "I feel much the same way. And Russell?"

"He went out onto the Weald and shot himself. He left a suicide note. I expect it's true, what his mother told me about his death."

"Good God," Standish said blankly. "I've had my lows, but I've never—but then, Lieutenant Russell was young in 1916. That's to say, he was most likely two-and-twenty, but *young*. If you follow me."

"If he was an only child, reared by his mother, he might well have seen very little of the harshness of life."

"Precisely my point. I don't remember, but I'd wager he hadn't gone to public school."

"Apparently it was the grammar school in Rye."

"Yes, well. There you have it."

"There was an unhappy love affair near the end of the war. His mother didn't approve of the woman, apparently, and then the woman broke off the relationship when he'd recovered and was sent back to his regiment. The odd thing was, he was afraid for her."

"Wartime romances seldom prospered."

"Could she have been the wife of the sergeant who set up a canteen for officers in the barn?"

"God knows. Lieutenant Russell was in his sector. Whether he was on terms with the sergeant, I can't tell you. I saw photographs of my own sergeant's new baby. He was showing them to everyone he could lay hands to. He also carried a postcard of Gladys Cooper in his wallet."

Half the men in the British Army had carried her likeness. A strikingly beautiful actress, she represented all that men were fighting for, home and hearth and someone waiting for their return. Those who had no sweethearts found that her face filled their dreams very nicely. Those who did saw in Gladys Cooper an idealized version of English womanhood, out of reach but not out of imaginings.

"Why do you ask?"

"Because Brothers swears he saw that same sergeant in Paris while you were there. And he'd heard that the man had killed his wife's lover—an officer—by shooting him in the back during a retreat. His wife told him too late that she had lied to him, given him a wrong name. Rumor had it he then killed her. He deserted soon after that. But he might have seen Russell in Paris, and gone after you on the road. Only he may not have known—or cared—which motorcar Russell was driving."

"Are you sure of this?"

"I'm sure of nothing. But the pieces of the puzzle are coming together." He got up to serve himself the next course. "There's another piece that's intriguing. Mrs. Russell tells me you came to her house to offer condolences on the death of her son."

"I came there? Nonsense, Rutledge. I haven't been in touch with any of these men. I've told you that."

Rutledge took out the negatives he had brought back from Rye.

"Have a look at these. I know, they are small and not the clearest, but I want you to put a name to each face."

"Where the devil did you get these?"

"Look at them first."

"Ah. I remember now," Standish said, squinting as he held them up to the lamp. "Russell had a camera. They were forbidden, you know, but he wanted a souvenir of the moment. We weren't too happy about it. He promised to send us each a copy of it. And never did."

"Did he take photographs in Paris, or Nice?"

"He may have done. I know I wasn't in them."

"Can you see the men's faces clearly enough to recognize them? It was easier in the actual photographs, but even they weren't very clear. I barely recognized you."

"Let me see. That's Everett. He died of gangrene." He'd begun from the right, naming each man. "Holt isn't in this one, of course. He must have taken the photograph for Russell."

"Is he in this one?"

Standish set down the first negative and took the second from Rutledge. "It's difficult to tell with any certainty. The lighting was terrible. But it was a barn after all, and we only had candles. Ah. I think that's Holt. God rest his soul."

"Mrs. Russell pointed to that man, identifying him as Captain Standish."

"Who? Oh, that's the sergeant you were on about. You can see me standing there, second from the right this time."

"The man who came to her door was the sergeant. He was using your name."

"What in God's name for?"

"I expect to confirm that Mrs. Russell's son was well and truly dead."

"But why kill Holt? And what does this man have to do with the Rector?"

"I still think he mistook the Rector for you."

"But that's mad. I had nothing to do with his wife. I wouldn't recognize her if she walked through my door."

"My guess is that he's back in England, in spite of the charge of desertion against him. And he knows that he nearly ran two out of five men off the road, and actually sent a third man over the cliff, looking for Russell. And Russell got through, got back to England safely, without a scratch. The sergeant's tidying up loose ends. I expect there's a reason he wants to come back to England now. Inheritance? A woman? Or perhaps he's tired of hiding out in France. If any of you had recognized him there in Paris, you could have reported him to the Army. And one of you might have seen his face behind the wheel of his motorcar."

"That means he's planning to live somewhere in this part of England. Where he might encounter us at any time." Standish pushed his plate aside. "I find I've lost my appetite." He sat there for some time, staring out the windows. The darkness outside mirrored the scene in the dining room, and all he could see was his own reflection staring back.

"What sort of man is the sergeant?"

"I can't tell you anything important. I know he was good at making things work. Witness that officers' mess, as he called it. It was remarkable, what he'd found to furnish it. He must have raked through the ruins of dozens of houses or shops to find what he needed. We all turned a blind eye, of course. The wine was good."

"Was he already looking for the man who had interfered with his marriage?"

"The devil you say!" He turned back to Rutledge. "Do you think he was?"

"He'd have had a larger clientele if he'd opened the mess to the ranks. But I suppose officers paid better. I don't know."

Standish went to the sideboard, filling a glass with the port that was waiting there.

"He was polite. 'Sir' this, 'sir' that. Jovial in a respectful way." He came back to the table. "What you'd expect from the ranks. What all of us expected from them."

"Did he ever ask personal questions?"

Standish rubbed his chin. "He did. It never seemed like prying, mind you. Just—I remember we were drinking to the fact that all of us came from the southeast of England. Surrey, Kent, Sussex. We'd never met, you understand, but we had something in common. The sergeant was amazed, he was asking how far apart we were. We gave him a rough idea of the miles from Rye to Maidstone to East Dedham—I hadn't realized what he was after. He asked if we'd ever been to Tunbridge Wells. The old garrison town. Holt, Brothers, Russell, and I had. Taylor was from Chichester. He hadn't been there; his family was from Hampshire originally, in the other direction."

"Tunbridge Wells. Where he lived? Which he might now be coming back to?"

"I don't know." He hesitated. "I think he mentioned that his grandmother was from the town. Damn it, I see now he was a clever bastard! We had no idea."

"And you don't recall his name?" Rutledge picked up the negatives and put them back in his pocket.

"No. I don't know that I ever knew it. He was simply 'sergeant' to us. *Sergeant, another bottle of wine. Sergeant, the candle's nearly gutted. Good night, Sergeant.* All the staff in a mess hall are men from the ranks. Career officers before the war probably knew them by name. We never had the opportunity to learn them."

It was true. And half the regiments had incomers, as the original complement was killed or wounded. There was seldom the same camaraderie that he'd heard Melinda Crawford talk about, when the regiment was posted to the Empire and men and officers got to know each other from years of serving together.

Rutledge had hardly eaten his own meal. He rose, helped himself to the port, and said, "I'd be careful if I were you. If we're right, you and Brothers are still very much in danger. Taylor as well."

"I realize that now."

"I must call on Taylor as soon as may be." Rutledge drank off his port and set the glass on the table. "Thank you for dinner. I'm afraid your cook will think we didn't care for it."

"It's time I got a dog. If only to finish off the food I leave on my plate."

Rutledge smiled. "It would be wise for other reasons as well."

Standish followed him to the entry, and Rutledge shrugged into his coat. Picking up his hat and gloves, he said, "Would you know the sergeant again, if you saw him? Brothers recognized him in Paris. Or thought he had."

"If you'd asked me before tonight, I'd have said no. But I've just looked at that negative. I think I might now."

Rutledge said, "His face is farther away than the others. And in shadow. Easier for you than for me. He reminds me a little of Trotter."

"At the garage? No, I don't think so. I remember this man as taller."

Rutledge shook his head. "There are no strangers here in East Dedham. Except for the Bishop's man."

Standish laughed. "Barnes? From what I hear from my staff, he's only passable in the pulpit and he's appalling as a person. They want the Rector back. Wright and I had very little in common, but he was a good man." The laughter stopped short. "*Did* he die in my place? I refuse to believe it. I don't want that on my soul."

"It isn't. It's on the soul of whoever ran him off the road."

He opened the door and went out into the night. As he bent to turn the crank, Standish closed it behind him.

The wind had dropped, and overhead he could see a sweep of stars. Out on the road, he was thinking about Standish and the others that night in the barn, and what had happened in Nice three years later, when his headlamps picked up a figure on a bicycle some distance ahead of him. It was wobbling about on the road as if the rider was drunk, and he sped up for a closer look.

It was Jem, on a man's bicycle much too large for her.

She heard the motorcar coming up behind her and risked a glance over her shoulder. She lost control as she did, and the bicycle swayed wildly under her. It crossed to one side of the road, veered to another, and crashed into the undergrowth, throwing its rider.

Rutledge sent the big touring car surging ahead until he was even with the scene. His heart in his mouth, he was out of his door before the vehicle stopped rocking from the sudden braking.

The bicycle's front wheel was spinning madly, and he heard a whimper from shadows cast by the brambles and briars.

"Jem? It's Rutledge. Are you all right?"

"I don't know," she answered in a quavering voice.

He stepped closer, reached down, and lifted the bicycle clear of the barely seen figure underneath it. Turning, he set it on the road out of his way. Then, ignoring the fingers of last summer's dried wildflowers and trailing vines and long branching twigs, he knelt beside the girl.

"Where does it hurt?"

"You shouldn't have come up behind me like that!" she said, her fright turning to anger.

"I didn't know who you were. Now, where does it hurt?"

"My arm. And my shoulder. Oh—don't touch it."

He couldn't tell whether she had broken a bone or just bruised something. "You can't lie here all night, waiting for the sun to rise. Give me your good hand and I'll lift you out."

"I can't move," she said plaintively, and all he could think of was that Dr. Hanby might still be in Eastbourne.

"Is it your spine? Your back?" he asked, trying to conceal his worry.

"No. It hurts my shoulder to try, and my hand is scratched. I want my mother." The last words were on a sob.

"She's not here," he said, making an effort to sound as normal as possible. "So you must make do with me. Besides, if I go to her door and tell her how badly hurt you are, I'll frighten her out of her wits."

"She thinks I'm in bed," Jem said in a small voice.

"Then let's see if we can get you back there before she knows you're gone."

By this time, the initial shock was beginning to wear off. She fumbled for his hand, saying, "I don't want to worry her."

Rutledge moved carefully, slowly, lifting her first to a sitting position, and then, after a minute's rest, to her feet.

She stepped away when he reached out to run his hand over her shoulder, but he could see from the way she carried it that it hurt. "Can you lift your arm?" he asked, very worried now and wondering if he could leave her alone here while he went to find her mother.

She managed to do it after two attempts, wincing at the effort but trying to be brave.

"I don't think anything is broken," he said as he made her move it several times more. "Is the pain worse now, or better?"

"Better."

He led her to the motorcar and she sat down gingerly in the passenger's seat.

"There's a good lad," he said bracingly. "Just like your brothers, strong and brave."

She smiled then, waveringly but a smile.

He went to the boot, looking for something to clean her scraped hand. In the light from the big headlamps, he could see the right one was bleeding a little. In the end, he gave her his handkerchief, and she looked up at him several times to see if he minded how she was soiling it.

He watched her use her left arm as she was working on her hand, grimacing as both hurt, but unaware that she was actually showing him that nothing was broken or torn. There was a scratch on her arm and one under her chin. It could have been far worse. He began to relax.

Waiting until she had finished working on the hand and shyly handed him his handkerchief, Rutledge asked, "That's a large bicycle for a lad. Your brother's?"

She tried to slide out of her seat, but he was blocking her escape.

"Your brother's?" he asked again. "Jem, why are you riding it at night?"

"I found it," she said defiantly. "All right?"

"Found it—where?"

"It was in the orchard. Hidden by all the high grass. Nobody claimed it for days—I didn't touch it. I didn't take it away. Sometimes I rode it at night, but I didn't *steal* it."

The police had conducted a long and thorough search for this bicycle. Mrs. Saunders would have to identify it to be certain, but he could understand what Wright had done. No one from the house was likely to go into the orchard this time of year. Especially not at night, through the high grass. He could leave it there, retrieve it as soon as he brought the Captain's motorcar back.

But Jem, running wild when she could, had come across it and hidden it for her own use. It was probably the nicest bicycle she would ever have, well cared for by the Rector, who depended on it and would have taken it back to the rectory if he'd lived.

"It belongs to the Rector. Mr. Wright."

But he had probably never come to the Standish house riding it. Until that one night. How would she know?

A mystery solved.

"I must take it with me, Jem. You know that."

"You told me when I found the shilling that I could keep it, that I had no way of knowing who had lost it. Well, that's just as true of the bicycle." Her mouth was set in a stubborn line.

"But I know who lost it," he told her gently. "And even though he's dead, I must take it back to his house. It isn't yours to keep. Besides, it's far too big for you. Witness tonight's crash."

He thought she might cry then, but she drew her sleeve across her eyes and stared up at him ferociously.

"Don't pity me. I didn't *know*."

He stepped back, going to the bicycle. "Will you help me lash it to the boot?"

He couldn't fit it in the rear seat.

For a moment he didn't think she would. Then she to came where he was holding the bicycle, ran her hands longingly over the handlebars, and said, "Where's the rope?"

She couldn't do much, her shoulder was still hurting, but he'd reasoned that helping him might make her disappointment less painful.

When it was done, he thanked her, held out his hand, and solemnly shook hers, careful of her scrapes.

"Can you find your way home from here? I can see the lane, not more than twenty feet away. I'll watch you go."

She shook her head. "I don't need to have you watch. I can find my own way home." She paused. "You won't tell my mother, will you?"

"She'll see the bruises and scrapes."

"I'll tell her I fell out of a tree in the orchard. I always climb the trees there—"

She broke off as a shot rang out in the night's stillness, and Rutledge didn't need to ask what it was. A revolver. And the sound had come from the house.

Standish. Had he killed himself? Like Cedric Russell? He'd sent the staff away. He'd seen Rutledge leave . . .

He ran for the driver's door. "Go home," he told Jem sternly. "Go in and lock the door. Do you hear me?"

"What was it? A shot? But who's shooting at this hour?"

"It doesn't matter. The Captain cleaning his revolver. I'll have a look. Now *run*."

This time she didn't argue. As he was reversing to return to the house, he could see her moving as quickly as her stiffening body could manage. She would hurt tomorrow.

As soon as she reached the lane, he was gunning the motor a second time in a matter of minutes, back to the drive, and up it to the door.

Leaving the motor running, Rutledge got out and, ignoring the brass knocker, pounded at the wood.

"Standish?"

"I've got a shotgun. Come through that door, and you're a dead man."

"Standish, it's Rutledge. Don't be a fool."

There was a moment of silence, and then he could hear Standish drawing the bolt and opening the door.

"What the hell are you doing here?" Standish demanded. "Inside. Shut it. *Now*." He was still holding the shotgun.

Rutledge did as he was instructed, shoving the bolt home as Standish gestured with his weapon.

"The drawing room. Stop at the door."

Rutledge walked to the doorway and looked inside the pretty room.

A vase lay shattered on the carpet, and broken glass was scattered under the window.

"He missed," Standish said in fury. "I don't know how, he had a perfect target."

He broke the shotgun and set it against the wall. "Did you see anyone as you came up the drive?"

"No—"

Jem.

Rutledge turned to Standish. "I'll have a look."

"You aren't armed."

"Nevertheless."

He ran to the door, swore as he was stopped by the bolt, and fumbled at it before he had it open.

Rutledge had always had a very good sense of direction. He didn't waste time driving back to the road, but on foot cut across the lawn and into the trees, heading in the general direction of the lane.

His mind was focused on the girl, out in the dark alone while a murderer was on the loose. That added wings to his fear.

He was never sure later what had warned him—the sixth sense that had kept him safe all through the war, or some slight sound. He had been running in a direct line, and now he altered that, slightly to his right, thinking to head Jem off.

The shot was almost point-blank, and he ducked reflexively, but he had already heard the whisper as it flew past his ear.

Jem was safe for now. The killer was still here. There would be enough time for her to reach her cottage safely.

Cursing himself for not bringing his torch, he swerved in the direction he'd seen the muzzle flash, and was almost on the man. But the shooter dodged to the left and set out again, Rutledge no more than twenty paces behind.

Then Rutledge lost him in the hedge alley where the shadows were deeper.

He heard him to his left and turned toward the sound, tackling the man moving fast toward the first line of trees.

They went down hard, and a shotgun went off nearly in their faces.

"Standish?" Rutledge said.

"What the hell are you doing, Rutledge?"

"I lost him in the hedge alley. I thought you were in the house."

"So I was, until I heard the second shot. I swear I saw him heading this way."

Rutledge helped the man to his feet but kept the shotgun. "Is the other barrel loaded? Right. Go inside. Stay there until I come back."

"Like hell I will—he missed me by inches. I want him as badly as you do."

But it was too late now. They listened and cast about for several minutes. The shooter had gone.

"He's in a hurry," Rutledge said. "He's no longer willing to wait to set up a motorcar crash; he'll kill you now, any way that he can."

They turned back toward the house, and Standish stopped by Rutledge's motorcar. "Where did that bicycle come from?"

"It belonged to Wright, I think. It was—"

He was saved from answering by a scream, high-pitched and terrified.

Standish whirled, looking back the way they had come.

"It's the child of one of your tenants. I'd swear to it. Which way? Hurry, man."

"Follow me." In the dark, the park was treacherous underfoot, brambles and vines catching at their feet as they ran. They reached the bottom of the lane, and some thirty paces on they could see the flint cottage belonging to Jem's mother.

The door was wide open, lamplight spreading down the steps and across the edges of small gardens outlined with stones, marking the path.

They reached the door at the same time, and Rutledge stepped inside. Jem's mother was lying on the floor.

"*Oh God.*" Standish was across the room, kneeling beside a slim fair-haired woman. There was blood on her face and in her hair from a blow to the head. "Mrs. Meadows? Can you hear me?"

Rutledge knelt beside him, searching for a pulse. "She's alive," he said. "Where's her daughter?"

They searched the small cottage, Standish calling the girl's name. "If you're hiding, it's all right to come out now. It's Standish, Jem. And Rutledge. You're safe."

But Jem didn't come out from behind the bed or under the kitchen table. They looked into the back garden, calling again.

"He's taken her." Rutledge cursed himself for not seeing her home, knowing it still wouldn't have been enough to save her. Whoever it was had come here, to the cottage, and attacked her mother to get at Jem.

"Why?" Standish asked as he hurried back to the front room and knelt again by Mrs. Meadows. "I don't understand."

"I expect it was because she'd seen his face. I don't know of any other reason why he would come to the cottage." But how had he got here? And how had he taken the girl away? In the dark green motorcar that Trotter had been searching for?

Rutledge went to the pump and drew water in a small copper pot, found a towel in a cupboard drawer, and brought them back to Standish. "Stay with her—if she wakes up, see what she has to say. I'll search for her daughter."

Without waiting for an answer, he left, moving up the lane at a fast trot, searching for Jem. Or her body. He could remember that scream, terrified, chilling.

19

He reached the road without any sign of Jem and turned back toward the Standish drive. Stopping only long enough to untie the bicycle, he left it by Standish's door.

And he began to search, driving this road and that, making his way toward the village, driving the streets, quiet at this hour of the night. He got out, took his torch, and quartered the churchyard, then went to the dark rectory and circled it.

Where else? The Downs. There were sheep pens here and there, but it was empty land, no place to put a child. The cliffs overlooking the sea . . .

Rutledge ran for his motorcar, and driving fast, came to the headland. It was too dark to see a body down there. Even against the white of the chalk, the shadows were confusing, their shapes strange and unlikely.

He searched Belle Tout, then went to find Constable Neville.

The constable was washing up after his evening meal, his shirtsleeves rolled up to his elbows. He listened intently to Rutledge's account of the missing child.

"Jem Meadows? Everyone keeps an eye out for her. There's no one here who would harm her, much less her mother. Jem's lost her brothers and her father, a plucky little thing, and even here in the Gap, we admire her spirit."

Rutledge put his hands up, rubbed his eyes, then dropped them. "She has to be somewhere."

"I'll call out every able-bodied man, and we'll search. Speak to Constable Brewster. He'll do the same in his patch."

Rutledge wasted no time. Back in East Dedham, he went in search of Constable Brewster. He found the man by the pub, coming out after having a beer. Explaining what he needed, he said, "How do you summon people at a time like this?"

"Rector rang the church bell."

"Then let's be about it." They hurried to the church, and Rutledge, torch in hand, found the ropes to the bells tied up in the tower. Too high to reach, to keep them out of the hands of children and mischief makers.

He found the table where the booklets about the church and other pieces of literature were kept, swept them to one side, and between them, Rutledge and Brewster carried the table to the tower.

"There must be an easier way. Rector would have known."

"There's no time to search," Rutledge told him, and climbed up. He caught the bell ropes, and leaping down, he gathered them in his hands and began to pull them.

He'd seen bell ringers, pulling down on the ropes in a long motion, then letting go. He tried that, and first one bell and then the next began to toll. Not in an orderly fashion, but regular enough to bring the village men in a hurry.

Brewster went outside to wait for them, and soon Rutledge could hear voices as people gathered. Brewster began to explain what had happened, and then he sorted the gathering crowd into search parties.

Barnes came down from the rectory, willingly joining one of the groups. By this time, Rutledge had abandoned the bell ropes and was outside, adding to what Brewster had said.

"Whoever he is, he's armed, dangerous. And the child is at his mercy. If you see anything, use caution—keep watch, and send one of your number to find me. If she's found, we'll ring the bells again, to bring you back in. Good luck. Find lamps, torches, rope—anything you might need—and take it with you."

"There's the cliffs," a voice from the crowd asked. "What about them?"

"I've looked. It's too dark and too far down to be certain of anything. Let's pray we find her anywhere but there."

He watched them sort themselves out as Brewster gave them instructions. *This surely isn't the first time they've done this,* he thought.

For they were starting out in an orderly fashion, silent and intense.

Rutledge had no choice but to wait in the pub for reports, wishing himself out in the field. But these men knew the ground, they could cover it more thoroughly than he could alone, and someone had to hold the fort in the interim. That someone had to be him.

Mrs. Saunders came, sat with him for a time, and then brought him a whisky from the bar.

"You've not had much sleep of late," she said, handing it to him. "You'll be grateful for a bit of courage to see you through the night."

He knew she was right. But who could have done such a thing? Where was this elusive sergeant, and why had he taken Jem?

Absorbed in his thoughts, he slowly realized that Mrs. Saunders was talking to him.

"I'm sorry," he said. "My mind was with the searchers."

"Not a bit surprising." She nodded. "I was just saying, it's a good thing it's not rain coming down in sheets. If they keep moving, they'll stay warm enough."

"I should have thought to send blankets with them. She'll be cold. Jem."

"It would only slow them down. They'll tend to her when she's found, you needn't worry about that. Most of them have children of their own." She chuckled. "I see you know she's a lass, and not a lad.

Rector wasn't happy about that, but he said it was safer for her. She's as footloose as her brothers. Gave the Bishop's man quite a start the other night, coming out of the cemetery. It was late, he'd just come in, and there she was bowling out of the gate on a bicycle, he said. I didn't know she had one. I expect the Captain gave her one to keep her out of mischief."

"It was the Rector's. The bicycle. She found in the orchard at Four Winds and didn't tell anyone. Not even her mother. At least I think it's his. I'll bring it in for you to have a look."

"It's a wonder she didn't break her neck on the thing. It's much too big for her."

"It belongs to the rectory, if it was Wright's. Perhaps you can convince Barnes to ride it."

She chuckled. "That one? Not very likely. Besides, he has his own motorcar."

Rutledge turned to her. "He what?"

"He has his own motorcar."

"He wasn't driving it the day he came here."

"That's true. He went to see the Bishop and he brought it back. It's kept in the shed behind the rectory."

His wits were working fast, now, Hamish alive at the back of his mind.

"What color is it?"

"A pretty dark green. You can see your face in the paint, it's that shiny."

Barnes? Who once ran a mess hall in a barn in France? *Damn* the man. Right under his *nose*.

"He's the Bishop's man. Do you ever remember him calling on the Rector before? Sent down by the Bishop?" he asked her.

"The Bishop usually sends Mr. Ferris to attend to church matters. An older gentleman, quite nice. But I expect he couldn't spare him for this long a time."

Hellfire and damnation!

Rutledge was on his feet, heading for the door. "Stay here. If they find her, sound the horn on my motorcar. I'll be back."

She said, "You haven't finished your whisky."

But he was gone without answering. He took his torch from the front seat of his motorcar and set out for the rectory at a run. Rounding the house, he found his way to the shed set well behind the house, beyond the gardens, the clotheslines, and the coop where once there were chickens.

The hinges on the shed doors were rusty, but he shoved them open and stepped inside, turning on his torch.

There sat the motorcar, a rich dark green, just as Mrs. Saunders had told him. He stared at it for all of a minute, praying that it was what he had been searching for ever since he'd seen the scratches on Standish's boot and wing. He walked into the shed, stopped at the bonnet, and shone his light on the gleaming paint of the right and left wings and two undamaged headlamps.

He went closer, examining the headlamps first. He would have sworn one was newer than the other.

Turning to the wings, he ran his hand over them. Smooth as glass, the finish as perfect as it had been when the vehicle was on show for prospective buyers.

Or was it? Was there a slightly different texture in the wings?

He touched the doors, went back to brush his fingers over the boot, and did the same for the top of the motorcar. Then he went back to the wings.

He would have wagered that it had been repainted, and very recently. But only the wings, he thought. There was a thickness on both of them that wasn't quite the same as the layer upon layer of paint that the factory could apply, let dry, buff, and apply again.

Imagination? Wishful thinking?

Hardly evidence. Yet.

He felt the wings again, looking for something else this time. Roads in England were abominable—loose chippings, trailing tree branches, and overgrown hedgerows were just a few of the hazards a driver faced. And the tiny pits where the paint had met with chippings were missing.

He did the same with the headlamps. The struts that held them in place, large as they were, were rough on the left side, new and smooth on the other. What's more, the bonnet was still slightly warm.

He'd been right.

But where had Barnes gone to have this bodywork done? Certainly not to Trotter. The local man had no facilities for repainting a motorcar, even if he could have replaced the headlamp. And he would know he was aiding a man wanted for murder.

Brighton, then? London? Back to the factory? Where no one would have heard about motorcars being run off the road, their drivers killed, and a murderer could make up any story to satisfy curiosity.

Not even Sergeant Gibson, who appeared to have endless resources when it came to tracking down obscure bits of information, would be able to find out where the work was done without taking endless hours and numbers upon numbers of men knocking on doors, asking questions of mechanics over half of southern England.

Barnes had taken a grave risk, hiding the motorcar away in the shed under their noses. Taking it out only when he felt it was safe. Rutledge himself had never seen it. It hadn't been left out front when the man arrived that first day. But Barnes had brought it here at some stage.

Neither Brewster nor Neville would suspect the Bishop's man, dark green motorcar or not.

But where was he, the real Bishop's representative, who must have been sent to deal with the death of the Rector of St. Simon's? Was he also dead? Or had Barnes somehow seen to it that word never reached the Bishop that Wright had been killed? Come to that, why had Barnes stayed so long in East Dedham?

Rutledge had no time to consider that. Jem was still missing, and only Mrs. Saunders was waiting at the pub for any news from the men out searching.

Shutting the shed door on the motorcar, Rutledge hurried down the sloping lane to The Sailor's Friend.

As he was walking, Hamish said, "Ye didna' recognize the sergeant in yon photograph."

It was true. But the sergeant had the shapeless haircut of the ranks, and all that could be determined looking at his features was that he had a high forehead. His eyes were in shadow, and there was nothing that would set him apart from half a hundred other men. Barnes's hair now gave him the appearance of a gentleman who went regularly to his barber, and his manner was that of an educated man. Even his voice was upper middle class, his way of carrying himself that of a man of means. His clothing fit the image as well. If he wasn't the Bishop's representative, how had he come by clerical attire?

Somehow in the years since he deserted, this man had remade himself. But why had he chosen the church?

Rutledge had almost reached the door of the pub when he heard a horse coming fast down the street of the quiet village. The rider turned into the pub yard.

"Mr. Rutledge? Sir? I recognized you from the night of the fire. The Captain sent me. Mrs. Meadows has recovered a little, but I'm to bring the doctor back with me. She's in a state over her daughter."

"We're searching for the child now," he said, catching the gray's bridle. "Has she told the Captain anything that might help us?"

"She's not very lucid, given all she's been through. But she told us that Jem had been at home when they heard the last shots, and the girl was fearful that something had happened. Her mother tried to stop her, but she said she had to go, that a friend was in trouble. And then she came back, flying into the house, telling Mrs. Meadows to run, that someone was after her. Mrs. Meadows stood her ground, thinking Jem was overly excited, and then this man, his face hidden, came through the open door. He struck her down without a word. She didn't know what had happened to Jem. It was the first thing she wanted to hear as soon as she regained her senses."

Rutledge said with more confidence than he felt, "Tell her I don't think this man will hurt Jem. He's hidden her away, and we should find her very soon now." Lies, all of them, but necessary.

The horseman looked down at him anxiously. "Is that true? What I'm to tell her?"

"It's what we know now. If it changes, I'll send word."

"Thank you, sir." He gathered the horse under him as Rutledge stepped back, and set out at a fast trot for Dr. Hanby's surgery.

Rutledge stood there, watching him go.

The motorcar was still in the shed. Barnes was out searching with the rest of the men from two villages. The man felt safe. Only Jem had really seen his face in the dark at Standish's house. And if she was never found, he would stay safe.

Time passed with agonizing slowness. Mrs. Saunders sat with Rutledge for a while, then went to organize the women of East Dedham to prepare tea and food for the searchers as they came straggling in.

And he was left alone with his thoughts.

He'd said nothing to her about Barnes, for her own protection.

When he'd returned from the rectory, she'd asked if anything was wrong, and he'd forced a smile and said all was well, that one of Standish's men had come into the village to fetch Dr. Hanby to Mrs. Meadows.

"A precaution. She's anxious for her daughter, and that's not good after a blow to the head."

"He's not there to sedate her, if the searchers find the girl's body?"

"I hope not. It wasn't the intent in sending for Hanby."

Satisfied, she talked about the Rector for a little while longer, and then went to make herself useful preparing for the cold, tired men who would soon be coming back.

"Pray God . . ." she said as he helped her on with her coat and she tied her bonnet closely against the cold air. "Pray God she's found and soon."

Unable to endure the wait, Rutledge found pen and paper in his room and sat down at a table in one corner of the bar, using his notes to write down everything he'd discovered, learned, or suspected. Some of it repeated earlier reports for the Yard, but he wanted to be thorough, to leave nothing out. He enclosed the negatives and gave the address of Mrs. Russell, the owner of the actual photographs in Rye. He included the addresses of Standish, Holt, Brothers, and Taylor.

Reading it over, he decided it was as complete as he could make it. He'd found an envelope as well, and he put the pages inside and sealed it, writing his name across the flap, to ensure that no one tampered with it.

The village women arrived, carrying baskets and hurrying into the pub kitchen. He could hear them talking in somber tones as they worked.

By the time the first of the search parties came in, weary, cold, with nothing but acute disappointment to show for their hours of tramping across the Downs, trays of food and large kettles of hot water were waiting.

Gathering around Rutledge, they told him precisely what ground they'd covered, and he wrote it down.

A second party came in a quarter of an hour later, and he sat with them as well, drawing them out, hoping they would remember a place they hadn't looked. Even as he did, he knew it was useless, that they had been thorough. Many of them must have children of their own, for there was a tension in them as they reported, and a sense of failure.

As one man put it, "We'll go again at first light. We're bound to see more then."

Barnes was with the third party. Hamish had warned him as the Bishop's man came through the door, and Rutledge found a reason to turn away before Barnes could read his eyes and learn that he had been found out.

This group had searched the coast from where the Iron Age habitation had been excavated by archaeologists almost to Beachy Head.

"Nothing," said their leader, whom Rutledge had recognized as the butcher, shaking his head, a worried frown between his eyes. "Of course there was no way to see anything down on the shingle, you were right about that. That'ull have to wait till morning. A few hours' sleep, and at first light, we'll have another look." He was a big man, broad-shouldered, his sandy hair streaked with gray. "If she's down there," he added grimly, "there'ull be no need for haste."

"No," Rutledge agreed, and let them go to the fire to warm themselves and partake of the food and tea.

Barnes lingered, giving Rutledge a chance to single him out, but Rutledge ignored him, his eyes on his notes, marking search areas on a rough map someone had just handed him.

Barnes left. Rutledge let him have a head start and then slipped out the kitchen door to follow him. But he went up to the rectory, and once he was inside, lamps bloomed in the passage by the stairs and then again in one of the bedrooms on the next floor.

Rutledge had hoped that the man might lead him to Jem. And he hadn't. Unless she was in the rectory, and it would be damning evidence if searchers found her there.

He was sorely tempted to make his way into the house and take Barnes into custody there and then, but the man couldn't be made to tell him where the child was.

It was dark, cold, and she must have been quite frightened by now. He refused to think about the possibility that she'd been hurt. Barnes would have had to keep her quiet, wherever he took her, and Jem would have fought hard.

Another search party was coming in, and he hurried back to the pub to speak with them. But they could only shake their heads, asking for news themselves.

He sent them to the kitchen for food and something to drink to warm them.

On the heels of their departure, he heard someone at the outer door and turned to see Constable Brewster walking into the pub, holding something in his hand. Rutledge could feel hope surging, praying for word, anything that would tell them where to look.

But Brewster dashed that, saying, "There's a telegram for you, sir. Just brought to the station."

Gibson? Rutledge thanked the constable and took the telegram from him, tearing it open straightaway.

But it wasn't from the Yard. As he looked first at the name below, he realized that it was from Brothers.

Wish you good hunting. Discovered Taylor is on the telephone and decided to put call through to him. Reluctant to speak to me until informed Holt killed. He and Holt came back on same ferry Calais to Dover, and talked. Both had difficulties on that road, not same as mine. Taylor had brake problem, discovered just before descent to Nice, thank God. At last hotel stop Holt told someone spotted attempting to meddle with motorcar. Gendarme gave chase. No damage then, but vehicle in mist tried to send him over, until it lost a tire and pulled back. Taylor hasn't seen Russell since Nice. Passed warning to him.

Brewster, hovering, asked, "Good news?"

"In a way, yes. But no help in finding Jem Meadows."

"Too bad. I'll go back to the station and wait there."

When Brewster had gone, Rutledge went to sit in a dark corner of the room, leaning his head back against the wall and closing his eyes. There was no prospect of sleeping. He could think of nothing but Jem in the hands of a murderer, and how helpless he was to do anything about it.

Josie came in and said, "Sir? This will help a little."

He opened his eyes to see her holding a pillow from somewhere, a fresh pillow slip on it. He thanked her and took it, grateful for her thoughtfulness.

"They tell me in the kitchen that there's been no news."

"No."

"I know who Jem is. I've seen her coming to the shops on errands for her mother. I wish there was something I could do besides make tea and cut the bread for sandwiches."

"The men appreciate it," he said. "It helps them keep up their spirits."

She sat down, wanting to talk, and he listened to her chatter for a time, half his mind out on the Downs with the searchers.

And then something she was saying registered, distracted as he was.

"What did you just say?"

She'd been telling him about the pub. Apparently her mother had worked there before her, and her grandmother before that. "'Only I'd married the owner'?"

"No, before that."

"Oh. About the Reverend Mr. Dolby. He was pastor here over two hundred years ago. We learned about him in school. All those ship-wrecks along the Gap coast horrified him. Villagers did what they could to save people on board, but Mr. Dolby had to bury too many of them, and felt he must do something to warn ships off the rocks. They can see the white chalk cliffs, of course, even at night, but if they venture in too close, they wreck."

"Yes, I've heard that. You said he was the sailor's friend. I've seen his grave in the churchyard."

She nodded. "We take care of it. We always have."

"I could tell. Now, explain to me again why he's the sailor's friend?" He was intent, leaning forward, all his attention centered on Josie.

That rattled her. "There was talk about putting a light here. Well before Belle Tout. But nothing came of it."

Rutledge smiled encouragingly. "And after that? I'm not sure I understood what you were describing."

"I expect I didn't explain it well. I've never seen it, you see. He dug a tunnel. All he had was a chisel and an ax. And he went right down through the chalk, following a fissure, until he came out right above the sea. Then at night he set lamps in the opening, to warn ships away. It was an amazing feat, and nearly as successful as a lighthouse."

He could hear the echoes of a classroom lesson as she told him the story.

"Is it still there? Dolby's tunnel?"

"Oh yes. It's not safe any longer. The chalk has crumbled. But my father has a photograph of himself as a lad, standing in the opening. I'll bring it in tomorrow to show you, if you like."

But he couldn't wait until tomorrow. "Come and point out on the map where this excavation into the chalk began."

"I think it's been closed up, to keep the sheep from falling down and breaking a leg. We were always warned away as children." But she followed him over to the table and studied the rough map. Running her finger across it, she moved to the lighthouse and then a little to the side of it. "It should be here. Close by, at any rate."

But Rutledge thought it must be a bit farther away, because he hadn't noticed it when he'd been at Belle Tout with Neville.

"Fascinating story," he told her. "Thank you. I'd asked Constable Neville about The Sailor's Friend, but he didn't think to tell me the whole of it. Now, if you'd do me a favor? I must go out for a little while. Will you wait here and see to any of the search parties? Show them the map and ask them to mark where they've been. I wouldn't bother to mention the cave. The team from that area has already come in." He pointed out the marks on the map.

Happy to be helpful, she agreed, and he set out for the butcher's shop.

The man was heavily asleep, and his wife had difficulty waking him. He came down in his nightclothes to where Rutledge was standing at the foot of the stairs, and said, "What's this about? Have they found her?" His hair was tousled, and he looked like he had been up all night, deep bruises under his eyes.

"Sadly, no. I have to ask. Did you search Parson Dolby's cavern?"

"We never called it that when I was growing up," he said, clearly thinking Rutledge had awakened him for nothing. "It was Parson's Hole. The lads preferred it. And yes, we searched. What do you take me for? Barnes volunteered to go down. Nothing there."

Rutledge felt cold. "Thanks," he said, and was out the door and into his motorcar before the butcher finished what he had to say, that Rutledge would be better off in bed himself, not waking people who had just managed to fall asleep.

He drove for the headland, Hamish busy in the back of his mind, warning him it was a foolish thing he was attempting to do alone.

"Yon lass said it was crumbling. Wait for help. Or find yon constable at the Gap."

But there was no time. He wanted to be there and back before Barnes got wind of what he was about. Josie might hold her tongue— and might not.

Rutledge drove as close to Belle Tout as he could, then got out of the motorcar, leaving his hat but taking his torch and the rope he'd used to lash Wright's bicycle to the boot. Days ago, it seemed now. But far longer than that to a child in such a place.

He walked up the sloping ground, casting about until he saw what he was looking for.

There was an iron grille over the hole, grass and wildflowers growing in and around it. He thought at first that it was going to be too heavy to lift.

Hamish said, "If yon parson came every night to light his lamp, it couldna' be beyond the strength of one man."

And the searchers had lifted it before him—Barnes as well.

Reaching through the grille, he gripped the cold bars with his gloved hands and heaved to one side.

The grille moved, but not far enough. A second try, and his torch showed him a black pit below his feet.

But the parson had had a good grasp of engineering. Chalk steps led into a sloping tunnel, and as each level dropped, more steps led down to it.

He stood there for a moment, listening to the sea rolling in. The night was still black, and there were no stars, only heavy clouds.

Then he knelt and shouted down into the tunnel, calling Jem's name, listening for any response, all his faculties alert. He waited, but there was no sound from the darkness. He tried to tell himself she might be too afraid to answer, unable to recognize his voice.

Still, the silence was ominous.

He rose to his feet, turned on his torch, and started down into a black void.

The steps had eroded with time, and he had to be very careful not to miss his footing. He moved slowly, keeping his light shielded, glancing from time to time back the way he'd come. At least the roof of the tunnel was still high enough that he could manage, tall as he was. And that gave him hope—a man could carry a slight girl's body down here more or less easily. But how had Barnes discovered this place? Had someone told him? Or had he stumbled across it at some point when he was out in the night?

Rutledge was reminded of the body found in the lighthouse back garden. Barnes—and Grant. Where had they encountered each other? Not in France. Eastbourne? Had Grant, the rag man no one noticed, seen something he thought might be used to blackmail a stranger? But what?

If Barnes had killed Grant, why not drop his body down here? Perhaps he hadn't known just where the opening under the grille went. Not then.

His foot slipped on the next set of chalk steps, and he nearly went down. Barnes, he thought grimly, must have worked in the tunnels in France, if he'd brought Jem down here. No one else would have dared venture so far.

Going still deeper into the chalk, he began to feel claustrophobic, his breathing roughening, and his sense of being caught where there was no air, where the walls seemed to be closing in, raised the specter of being entombed here forever. The wild urge to retreat while he could consumed him. It was willpower alone that kept him going, and the thought of Jem.

Another level down. Surely he must be near the sea by now?

But he knew he wasn't. He couldn't hear it yet. He still had a long way to go.

Down again, the ground slippery underfoot where the chalk was damp. And the roof over his head had begun to sink a little with every yard, choking him with a desperate need to get out of there.

Two more levels. Dolby must have been mad to try this, he thought. Had the spirits of so many dead sailors watched him as he worked, one man determined to prevent the next wreck? And yet the people living here had benefited from the wrecks, the silks and tobacco and wine and brandy and whatever else the ships carried. Gunpowder? Muskets? The Gap dwellers would have been grateful for such gifts, meager as their incomes must have been.

He had to stand for a moment to catch his breath. There seemed to be no way forward, no way back. Rutledge fought the horror of being buried alive again, only this time in a world of white, not the smothering black earth of Flanders. But it was the same, taking away his air, making his heart thunder in his chest, the hand holding the torch wet with perspiration, his coat seeming to weigh him down, and his body feeling trapped.

Clenching his teeth, he moved down another level—and this time he was rewarded with the distant sound of the sea.

Just ahead, the tunnel turned slightly, which was ingenious on Dolby's part because it would stop the sea from pouring in here during storms, tearing at his precious efforts. But where was Jem?

He reached the bend, one hand on the wall to steady himself, and walked carefully around it, uncertain what he'd find.

And there, twenty feet from him, was the arching opening that led to the sea. He had come to the end.

He saw Jem, then. A dark mound all too close to the edge. The tide must be coming in, he thought in one part of his mind, because the sound of the whispering as the water ran out again was loud.

He moved toward her as fast as he dared. The chalk here was damp, uncertain underfoot, and he couldn't judge how steep the drop might be just beyond her. And then he had reached her, kneeling beside the still, dark figure, afraid now to touch her, an unreasoning feeling that she was dead.

She had been wrapped in what appeared to be a rug from a motorcar and left at the very edge of the opening. Beyond was the moving mass of the sea, and darkness. He couldn't see her head or her face, only her shoes. The waves were loud in his ears as he put out a hand and felt the cold beaded moisture on the rug.

She didn't move.

He drew her back from the edge, and setting his torch to one side, he began to fumble with the rug, turning her over with great care, shutting his mind to what he was about to find.

He was almost knocked backward as she kicked out, catching him in the chest as he was bending forward. A muffled sound came from the depths of the rug.

Relief washed over him.

She drew her knees up, preparing for another kick. He moved clear, saying, "It's Rutledge. Stop. I'm trying to help you."

This time he heard a distinct whimper, and he hurried to unfold the rug. And suddenly there she was, her eyes large in her pale face. The effort needed to kick him had left her struggling for breath around the gag in her mouth.

Silently swearing with such intense fury that his hands were shaking, sending the torchlight dancing around them, he reached for the edges of the handkerchief and pulled it free. She lay there gasping, still unable to move, and running the torch light down her thin body, he discovered that her hands and feet were bound.

He stood up to fish out his pocketknife, then knelt again to cut the rope around her feet before cutting those around her wrists.

"Mummy? Is she all right?"

"She's alive and waiting for you," he told her.

And Jem began to cry, sobs shaking her thin shoulders. He reached out and lifted the straw-colored hair from her face. It was then that he saw the cut, deep and caked with blood.

He wanted to kill Barnes with his bare hands, but that would have to wait.

Jem was on her knees now, crawling past his outstretched hand and reaching for him. He held her until the sobbing stopped, then set her on her feet and said bracingly, "All right, lad, can you walk?"

She had been bound for hours. The circulation in her legs was not the best, but with his help she took a first tentative step and then another. "Where are we? Is that the sea I hear? We're awfully close."

"Parson Dolby's Hole," he said, but she looked up at him in the light of his torch and said, "Who?"

"You need to spend more time in school, my lad, instead of wandering about the countryside, missing your lessons. Or you'd know." He draped the rug over her shoulders. "Give me your hand."

She did, fearfully, following him. "I don't like this place," she said, and he could feel her shivering.

"Do you remember being brought here?"

"I don't think so. Why is it so dark?"

"It's a tunnel. We must climb up it." He went ahead, still holding her hand, and they made it up to the first level, then started toward the next.

Jem was tiring now, he could feel the pull on his hand as she forced herself to keep up. He slowed his pace, trying to conceal the driving force of his anger from her, his need to confront Barnes.

In the end he carried her the rest of the way, but when they came to the upper end of the tunnel and he set her on the ground, Jem looked around with interest. "That's Belle Tout," she said, pointing. "And your motorcar."

"Can you walk that far?" he asked as he dragged the grille back over the opening to the tunnel.

She had regained something of her swagger. "Of course I can."

But it was rough going, and she climbed into his motorcar with an effort, lying back against the seat, beyond exhaustion. "I want to go home," she told him plaintively.

He pitied her, and what she had been through this night. But there was danger for her still. "Not just yet. You aren't safe. I must find the man who did this to you, and I want you to be out of sight for a time. Do you think you could point him out, even in a crowd of men?"

"Yes, I can," she told him firmly. "I thought he'd shot you. And the Captain. I thought you'd walked into a trap, and I wanted to help."

"You were very brave." He took the turning to the Gap, pulling up in front of the police station there.

Constable Neville was still awake. He'd been out with the first party to return, and now he was waiting for the last to appear. But they were searching between the Standish estate and the cliffs. It would take them longer to come in.

He was at the door as soon as Rutledge quietly knocked, opening it and staring in astonishment to see Jem at his side.

"Indoors," Rutledge said to her, and as soon as she stepped across the threshold, he had the door shut. "You know Constable Neville?" When she nodded warily, he added, "You'll stay here and mind the constable until I come back. Will you promise?"

"I want to go home," she said again.

"Not yet." He turned to Neville. "Keep Jem out of sight. Are all the searchers in? No? I don't want anyone to know that she's been found and is alive. Not for another few hours. There's something I must do."

"But surely I can send word to her mother."

"I meant no one, Neville."

"You can't let Mrs. Meadows wait and worry. That's unkind."

Jem had walked to the nearest chair, climbing into it and leaning back, her exhaustion catching her up.

Rutledge lowered his voice, his back to the girl. "It's unkinder still to have to tell her mother we lost Jem a second time. He bound and gagged a child, wrapped her in a rug that would slowly smother her, and left her to die alone, where no one would find her. She can identify him, Neville."

"Who took the child?" Neville asked, barely above a whisper. "Do you know? Did she tell you?"

"I'd guessed it was Barnes."

"Surely not?" Neville asked, shock clear in his face as he glanced from Jem to Rutledge. "He's a man of the *church*."

"He was with the search party that covered this part of the coast. When they reached Parson Dolby's Hole, he volunteered to search it. And he told the others that there was no sign of her. Ask the butcher. He'll confirm it. What's more, I've found his motorcar. Green, with recent damage." Rutledge took out the envelope he'd been carrying in his pocket and passed it to Neville. "It's explained in here. And it goes to Scotland Yard if anything happens to me."

Neville was about to argue, but Rutledge was already out the door.

He heard Jem calling to him. "Mr. Rutledge? Will you fetch my mother? Please?"

"Straightaway," he promised, though he knew it wasn't possible. Not yet.

It was after four in the morning, the sun not yet up, the sky even darker than usual with the heavy cloud cover. Rutledge walked to the cliffs, looking out at the Seven Sisters, a ghostly white sweep against the blackness of the sea and the night. When he finally had his anger under control, he turned back to his motorcar.

20

The last of the search parties was just coming in as he passed the pub, the men tired and depressed, knowing they were going to have to report their failure. The church bells hadn't rung, and so they were all too aware that Jem Meadows hadn't been reported found.

He waved to them and went on to the rectory. He left his motorcar closer to the churchyard, out of sight, and walked the last fifty feet, keeping to the shadows, and then swinging wide to the far side.

The rectory was still dark. He made his way around it to the shed, opened the door the barest crack, and shone his light inside. It was reflected in the gleaming paint. Barnes's motorcar was still there.

He moved back to the kitchen and tried the door. Mrs. Saunders had left it off the latch. Who would break into a rectory? Rutledge opened it carefully and stepped inside the short passage that led to the kitchen, nearly tripping over the line of boots and catching himself with a hand against one wall. He hadn't used his torch; he wasn't sure that Barnes had slept. He could just as well be keeping watch in his bedroom, or more likely, from the parlor window, where he could see the searchers return empty-handed.

Barnes was no common criminal, and he'd served in the Army. He wouldn't come quietly when Rutledge ordered him to give himself up.

There was something Barnes wanted very badly. But what? Revenge?

He saw a door next to the dresser, and he opened it quietly to find what he had hoped was there, back stairs spiraling up to the bedrooms above. He climbed them and walked as quietly as he could down the passage. He listened at each door for an anxious cough, a movement to ease tension—anything that would tell him where Barnes was waiting.

He went down the line of doors, then retraced his steps, softly opening each one and shining his torch inside. Barnes was armed, and Rutledge was careful never to make himself a target.

He came up empty-handed. Finding his way again to the back stairs, he returned to the kitchen, moving quietly still, letting his hearing tell him what he needed to know. His eyes had adjusted to the darkness, but he had no feeling for where to find a chair, where there was a cabinet, a pail, a carpet sweeper. He had to rely instead on Mrs. Saunders's reputation for tidiness and order.

Safely reaching the door that led from the kitchen into the main part of the house, he had only just opened it halfway when he caught what sounded like the soft chiming clink of crystal against crystal as someone lifted the top from a decanter.

Waiting must not have been easy for Barnes. He was pouring himself a drink from the Rector's store, no doubt counting each hour as he listened for the church bells to tell him that the girl had been found. As long as she was still hidden, he could continue with his pose as the Bishop's self-righteous representative.

Rutledge moved silently along the side of the staircase until he could see through the balustrades to the far side.

The parlor door was standing wide.

There was no chance of rounding the staircase and reaching the doorway without being seen—without drawing fire.

Rutledge had no weapon. And there was nothing to hand that

would remotely match Barnes's revolver. If he hadn't reloaded, there were still three shots left. If he had, there would be six chances of finding his mark.

Much as he wanted Barnes, he wasn't prepared to take the risk. There was still too much to be done to be sure this man went to the gallows.

He cast about for anything that would serve him, and he saw the lamp sitting on the table not two feet ahead of him. Where anyone coming through the front door would find a light at hand.

The question was, where was Barnes standing? By a window? Or by the hearth, where he could most certainly cover the door as well?

There was nothing for it but to try.

Rutledge had taken three strides toward the table and the lamp on it when the door opened on a draft of cold night air, and someone stepped in.

There was no time to think. Either the newcomer was someone from the village, and about to be shot—or it was Barnes, who had gone out earlier and was just returning, and someone else was in the parlor.

Rutledge lengthened his stride, caught the person in the doorway completely off guard, and slammed into him, knocking both of them down the short flight of steps and onto the hard, cold ground. And in the same instant, shots rang out from the parlor, the second one breaking the window glass and spitting into the earth just by Rutledge's ear.

"What the hell—?" Brewster exclaimed.

Rutledge rolled, carrying Constable Brewster with him, to the far side of the path to the door, and for the moment out of range.

Scrambling to his feet, Brewster backed up to the flint wall of the rectory, his eyes wide in his white face and his mouth open.

Rutledge was there beside him in an instant. "Go the long way around," he was saying rapidly, "well out of range. Get help. He's armed, as you can see. Don't let anyone take chances. I just want the rectory surrounded. Off you go."

"But who is it?"

There was no time to explain. "Barnes," Rutledge said in his ear. "Now *go*."

Brewster stood his ground. "It can't be, you must be mad."

"For the love of God, get out of here while you can. And bring back enough people to do as I asked."

"There's a man at the police station. He's off his head, wanting to know if it's true that Wright is dead. He was told by someone, but he didn't believe whoever it was, and he's here to find out. I came to fetch Barnes, to see if he could do something with the man."

"Never mind the man, he can wait. Go on, find help, quick as you can." He put his hand on Brewster's shoulder and pushed him toward the side of the rectory.

"But you don't understand—he's threatening to kill himself—"

He was cut off by a roar of sound as Barnes came round the house in his motorcar, driving full out, careering as he turned past the rectory lawn, heading fast toward the pub and the way open to the main road, just beyond. He turned to fire one last shot in the direction of the two men standing by the rectory wall, and Rutledge felt flint chips dig into his face even as he jerked away.

The motorcar was going too fast. Barnes lost control. It jumped the low wall around the churchyard and went hurtling into the stones marking graves. It smashed into a table tomb, standing waist high above the ground, and stopped, hung up on it, front wheels spinning, motor gunning.

Abandoning Brewster, Rutledge raced for the churchyard, leaping the wall, ignoring the broken stones and sunken graves.

Barnes was climbing out of his motorcar, dropping down to the ground. He was clearly dazed by the shock of the crash. He clung for an instant to the frame, then saw Rutledge barreling down on him. He whirled, reached into the motorcar, retrieved his revolver, and fired point-blank at the man from London.

The hammer clicked on an empty chamber.

Disbelieving, Barnes fired again, and then Rutledge was on him, pulling him away from the motorcar, and with all the force of his shoulder behind the blow, he hit Barnes squarely on the jaw.

Barnes went down in a heap at Rutledge's feet, and it took all the will Rutledge had to stop himself from kicking the man. Only Hamish, hammering at him, and the thought of the hangman stopped him. Instead he picked up the revolver and set it on a gravestone behind him.

Breathing hard, Rutledge stepped back and looked down at Barnes. When he was certain the man could hear him, he spoke the formal words necessary to take him into custody.

Brewster was shouting and running toward him, but he didn't turn. He waited—hoped—that Barnes would try to stand up, giving him a reason to hit him again.

But Barnes lay there on the damp, bruised grass, looked up at Rutledge, and said, sneering, "All your possible evidence just got turned into scrap." He inclined his head toward the wreckage of the motorcar. And then he raised his voice so that Brewster could hear every word. "I don't understand why you're doing this. You have no proof of murder, or anything else. It's not my fault you're incompetent at your job."

Brewster came to a halt ten feet from Rutledge. He had heard Barnes, and he turned to the man from London. "You struck him—a *man of the cloth.*"

"He *shot* at you, damn it." Rutledge turned back to Barnes. "The girl survived. We have a witness who can identify you. It's enough to be going on with."

He reached down and hauled Barnes to his feet, saying as he did, "Do you have your handcuffs, Constable? Good. Use them."

And he waited while Brewster reluctantly did as he was told, then followed them out of the churchyard and down the hill. Trotter could deal with the motorcar later.

Men were hurrying toward them, having heard the shots, and Rutledge called as they came nearer, "Jem Meadows has been found safe.

She can identify this man as her abductor. And Constable Neville is holding the rest of the evidence against him. Will one of you see to the ringing of the church bell?"

They parted for the little procession, asking questions, demanding answers. But Rutledge said only, "He's not what he appears to be, this man. Go home to bed while the constable here and I sort this out. Then you'll be given all the information we have." It was the voice he'd used commanding men on the battlefield, and many of these villagers had been in the war. They listened.

Still, they disbanded slowly, wide-awake, tired, confused, talking among themselves.

As the three men arrived at the police station and opened the door, Brewster remembered his other problem. Rutledge ignored him, saying to the man who leaped up from his chair, "Who are you?"

Outside, muffled by the closed door, the church bells began to ring, a wild jangle of sound that could be heard across the parish.

"The name's Mercer. The chaplain isn't dead. They are lying to me on purpose. It's a conspiracy, I tell you. I just saw him barely a fortnight ago. I asked the ragpicker to give him a message. I was in trouble in Hastings, and I needed help. There was no one else to send. But he didn't deliver it. Not until too late. They kept me in jail for days, saying I'd stolen the money, but I'd saved it. To repay the chaplain. Honest work, and no trouble, then they found me sleeping on the strand, called me a thief—I hate being shut up in small places, you don't know, you don't understand."

Brewster was about to say something, but Rutledge ordered him to take Barnes to the cell in the rear. Then he turned to Mercer.

"You saw the Rector a fortnight ago, you say. What day was it?"

"Saturday. It was a Saturday. He had to be back here in time for the morning church service. But he took me to Eastbourne for the train and waited there with me. He wouldn't take the money. He said I should use it wisely."

"How did he come to you?"

"In a motorcar. He said it wasn't his, but he'd explain later. I didn't want him to find himself in trouble, but he said not to worry."

Rutledge hesitated, knowing what the truth would do to this man. He glanced at Brewster, then said, "I'm sorry. He's dead. Mr. Wright. It was—sudden. He didn't suffer."

Mercer sat down, his head in his hands. "I didn't want to know. I didn't want it to be true."

"He was a good man." Rutledge put a hand on his shoulder. "Do you have anywhere to sleep tonight? There's a room in the pub. I'll see to it. Then where will you go?"

"To Portsmouth."

To the hospital.

There was nothing Rutledge could do.

"Constable Brewster? See that Mr. Mercer here finds a room at The Sailor's Friend. I'll be along shortly."

Brewster was reluctant to leave, but in the end, he ushered Mercer out of the police station and started toward the pub. Rutledge watched the two men go, then went back to the cell where Barnes was waiting. His chin was already bruising. Rutledge had no regrets.

He said, standing in front of the cell's heavy door, "There's no one here but you and me, Barnes. I'd like to know why."

Barnes smiled coldly. "I'm sure you would."

"You killed Holt, you maimed Standish, and you got to Russell too late. Why? What had they done to you?"

Barnes shook his head. "You think yourself clever. Perhaps you'll find out. But not from me."

Rutledge turned away. He had one more duty to attend to: returning Jem to her mother as soon as possible.

He watched their reunion, the tomboy suddenly a little girl who had been through more than any child should have to bear, clinging to her mother and crying against her shoulder.

After a time, he explained to Mrs. Meadows that her daughter would have to give evidence at the trial to come, adding, "She's very brave. And she will do it well."

"But how did Jemima come to know you?"

He had been afraid of that question. Mrs. Meadows had warned her daughter not to speak to strangers. Now, on the spot, he had the choice of giving Jem away or telling only a part of the story. Careful not to catch Jem's eye, he said, "She found something the police have been searching for. The Rector's bicycle. I should think there will be a reward for that." He himself would see to it that there was.

"Is this true, Jemima?"

"I did, Mama." She was careful not to explain exactly how this had been accomplished.

"Then thank you, Inspector, for returning my daughter to me. She has not been an easy child to rear, but I wouldn't change her one bit."

He extricated himself as quickly as he could, explaining that there were other duties waiting for his attention. But the truth was, he was still angry at Barnes, and it was suffocating him.

Standish, relieved by the news, sat down in front of his hearth, head back against the carved roses on the chair. "God, I'm glad it's over."

"Not quite. There's still the motive to uncover. Barnes won't talk. But I know someone who can find out. He has his means."

"The man's a monster. Someone will have to write to the Bishop, explaining about Barnes. I expect that will be my duty. I'd seen him a time or two, you know. At a distance in East Dedham. And I failed to recognize him at all. He's changed. He could pass as a gentleman now."

"We'll have the inquest and bind him over for trial. But there's still much we don't know about the man."

Before leaving, Rutledge said, "You do realize that Jem heard the shots and came running to the house, to help in any way she could. Putting herself at risk. That's loyalty of a sort few men can command."

He didn't wait for an answer. There was Grant to deal with, and his missing wife. Nor did he know what had become of Delilah and her mother. And he could expect no help from Barnes.

E ast Dedham was quiet as the sun rose over the headland, a cold morning. Men who had spent much of the night searching for Jem Meadows, and the women who had fed them, were still asleep.

Rutledge, who had seen the first fingers of dawn fill the eastern sky before he sought his own bed, found it hard to shut down the facts circling themselves in his head. In the end he went down to breakfast as soon as the dining room opened. Josie, yawning hugely, came to take his order.

She was full of excitement over the rescue of Jemima Meadows. It helped to dampen the fatigue she must have felt after a very long night.

"I was just dropping off to sleep when the bells began to ring. I was that excited, I ran downstairs and threw open the door to be sure I'd heard them."

She was also full of the news that Barnes had abducted the girl. "A man from the church—I can't believe it's true. And I'm told nobody knows why."

He didn't satisfy her curiosity. Instead he asked how well she knew Mrs. Grant.

"I don't know her at all," Josie answered him. "She lives in the Gap. They don't come here, and we don't go there."

Not much help there, he thought, and finished his breakfast when she disappeared into the kitchen.

He hadn't searched the bedroom Barnes was using at the rectory. But a man like Barnes would leave no incriminating information there. Not with Mrs. Saunders's propensity for cleaning and scrubbing. He wouldn't take a chance that she might pry farther than a mop and broom and duster reached.

Rutledge remembered something that Chief Inspector Cummings

had said to him early on in his career. Before the war changed him, changed everything.

Go back to the beginning. Not to sound idiotic—but that's where it began.

This business had begun in France, just before the Somme offensive.

A farm where the shelling had destroyed everything but the barn. A makeshift officers' mess. An undertaking by seven men to meet in Paris when the war was over. Two of them died before the Armistice. Five made it to France.

No, *six* men made it to France, one of them a deserter.

Rutledge stood up so quickly he jarred the table, sloshing tea into the saucer.

Brothers had seen the sergeant—Barnes—in Paris.

Was that the beginning, and the night before the Somme only a prelude?

He took the stairs three at a time, caught up his coat and hat, was pulling his driving gloves out of his pocket as he went out the pub door.

It was a fine morning to drive to Maidstone. But Rutledge hardly noticed it.

It was teatime when he walked into Brothers's house.

Brothers rose from the table, his cup in his hand. "What's happened?" he asked sharply. "Has there been another death?"

"I've come for information. You told me you believed you'd seen the sergeant in Paris. Did he see you?"

"I don't know." He considered the question. "Yes, there's a good chance he did. We didn't speak, of course. He was with someone."

"Where were you?"

"The five of us—Holt, Standish, Russell, Taylor, and I—were going out to dine at a restaurant Taylor knew of. I was the last one out the door. The sergeant was inside the hotel, just crossing the lobby when I glanced back."

"What was he doing?"

"Crossing the lobby, I've told you."

"All right. Describe him."

"I wasn't actually certain it *was* the sergeant. I hadn't seen him since '16." Brothers set his cup down, motioning Rutledge to a chair as he resumed his own seat. "What's this all about?"

"Humor me. I'll explain afterward. Why weren't you certain it was the same man?"

"He looked different. The way he was dressed. Odd for a deserter: expensive dark clothes, his hair longer, well cut, and a mustache. The kind officers often sported. I've always been rather good with faces. It's why I find it so easy to remember the dead." He looked away, pain in his face.

Rutledge gave him a moment to recover. "Was he wearing a clerical collar?"

That brought a smile from Brothers. "Hardly. No, he looked more like an officer, except that he wasn't in uniform."

"Who was he with?"

"There was a very attractive woman on his arm. I'd forgot about her, actually. I was paying more attention to the man. A few years older, possibly, and dressed like old money, if you know what I mean. Fashionable but understated."

"Were they guests at the hotel?"

"I think they came to dine there. I don't know why I was so sure of that, but there was a handsome motorcar outside, a uniformed chauffeur at the wheel. They must have come in just before we came down, or we'd have met them at the door."

"What else can you tell me about the woman?"

Brothers tried to remember, closing his eyes. "That's all. I was looking at the sergeant. I saw her more as an extension of him, if you follow." He opened his eyes. "They were on good terms. Comfortable with each other, as if they'd known each other for some time."

"English or French?"

"I have no idea. Wait, the motorcar was English. Why is this important?"

Rutledge told him.

"Ah. It makes sense. My God, Rutledge, surely she didn't know about his *past*."

"No. Nor do we know how to find her. I wonder if she's still important to him. Is she in England? Or still in France?"

There was no answer to that question, and Rutledge left with a feeling that he had nearly run out of possibilities to explore.

He drove back to East Dedham. It was dark when he arrived, and he left his motorcar at the pub, walking up to the rectory. Someone had patched up the broken windows. There was no light that he could see, but he went round to the kitchen. A lamp was burning there, and when he drew closer to the window, he could see Mrs. Saunders sitting at the large table, doing her mending.

It was another hour before she went off to her sister's house, and he was free to go in. As before, the kitchen door was off the latch, and he made his way inside.

He found the room that Barnes was using without much trouble. It was neat, no clothing, no shoes or cuff links or stockings cluttering up the chairs and the table. He cast his light about, careful not to let it reach the windows, and decided to begin in the wardrobe.

Nothing but clothing on the hangers or in the drawers. Shoes, well polished, were in tidy rows beneath the trousers and coats and shirts.

He took the valise down from the top of the wardrobe and went through it. It had been emptied before it had been put up there.

The desk near the window was as helpful as the wardrobe. Nothing of a personal nature at all.

Rutledge moved on to the table by the bed. The drawer held reading glasses, a case for them in embroidered velvet, a pen, a small diary, and two handkerchiefs.

He opened the diary and found some notations. A date in December, the words *Dover* and *The Saucy Belle*. A ship, expected in Dover next week. Other notations were dates that had passed. Luncheons or dinners, a party or two. Among them he found the date that Barnes must have returned to England. Calais, *The Mermaid,* a little more than a month earlier.

Replacing the diary, he knocked the glasses case off the table and stooped to retrieve it.

It was an ornate case, beautifully crafted and sheathed in velvet. It wasn't until he turned it over that he saw the small metal plaque on the back of it.

To Michael, with all my love, Kathleen

Rutledge looked inside the case. There was the name of a jeweler in Canterbury, not far from the cathedral.

He'd had very little sleep, but it didn't matter. He stopped at the pub, ordered sandwiches and tea to take with him, and set out for Canterbury.

B y the time the shop opened, Rutledge was waiting at the door. He had stopped only long enough to purchase shaving gear and a fresh shirt, take a room at the nearest inn to make himself presentable, then order a hurried breakfast.

An older man, perhaps fifty, with graying hair, greeted him and asked how he could serve him.

Rutledge smiled. "Inspector Rutledge, Scotland Yard." He handed the man his identification. "I need to find the person who purchased this case. Can you assist me with that?"

The man looked around, as if fearful that someone had overheard the request from the Yard, although the shop was empty. "I remember it well," he said, taking the case and looking it over. "It was a special order from Paris. Lady Kathleen Marshall bought it for a friend. I only know his name as 'Michael,' I'm afraid."

"Where can I find Lady Kathleen Marshall?"

"She lives in a lovely manor house not far from town. I don't believe she's there at the moment. Her husband was Sir Wilfred Marshall. He was killed at Passchendaele, and she went to France last year to see his grave. She met someone there who had served with him, and she went back this summer to visit him." He fiddled with a small sign on the counter in front of him. "I hear through other family members that she will marry this man, Michael, at Christmas."

"Are you certain about this?"

"Yes. My source is very reliable. Sir Wilfred's mother, in fact. Rings have been ordered."

The shop door opened, and the man looked up. Two women entered, and he said, "Will that be all, sir?"

"Is the family happy about this?"

The jeweler said quietly, lowering his voice, "I'm told they asked her to wait, and she did. This summer she told the family that she had made her decision."

"They have been quite open with you."

"We have served the family since my grandfather's time," he said, and with a nod he turned away to speak to the newcomers.

Rutledge went to the local police station to find out how to reach the Marshall house.

It stood on a ridge from which he could see the distant cathedral, and the tall brick walls around the house were entered by a pair of ornate wrought-iron gates, the family's crest in the center of each. A brick path led between boxwoods to the white door, set in the same rose-colored brick. The house was tall, three-storied, Georgian, with white facings at the windows.

There was money here, he thought, a great deal of it, and whatever Kathleen Marshall's widow's portion was, it was more than Barnes would see in a lifetime.

He walked to the door, lifted the brass knocker in the shape of an ornate *M*, and waited. A maid answered, and he asked for the Dowager Lady Marshall. He had to produce his identification, and then waited again before the maid conducted him to a bright sitting room where a fire burned cheerfully on the hearth.

"Inspector? I can't imagine why the Yard is calling on me today."

He turned to see a well-dressed woman in her late fifties, graying gracefully, step into the room. Her features were classical, a high brow, straight nose, marked by very intelligent gray eyes.

"Good morning," he said. "I've come to ask a few questions relating to an inquiry. And I'm looking for the owner of this glasses case."

"Why, Kathleen had that made for Michael. Is he all right? There hasn't been an accident, has there?"

"The truth is, I wonder if you have a photograph of him?"

"I think I do. But will you tell me why you require it?"

"He has been arrested for murder."

She stared at him. "*Murder?* I'm so sorry, I don't quite understand."

"Could I see his photograph, please? If there's any mistake on my part, I'll gladly apologize and leave."

She went to a table between the windows, long skirts hiding its legs and an array of photographs in silver frames covering the top. She reached for one, decided on another, and brought it to him. "This is Kathleen with Michael. It's rather good of both of them."

The woman was pretty, perhaps closer to thirty than five-and-twenty. Her hair was done in a fashionable style, and the walking dress she wore was well cut. She was standing in front of Notre Dame, smiling, and the man beside her, dressed like a gentleman, holding a malacca cane, had removed his hat for the photograph.

Rutledge was staring at the features of the man who had claimed he was the representative of St. Simon's Bishop, the same man who had taken Jem Meadows to a deserted cave and left her to die.

Lady Marshall was watching his face closely. She said, "You do recognize him, I see."

"Sadly, yes."

"Surely there is a mistake?"

"I'm afraid not."

"What has he done?"

And so Rutledge told her.

21

Lady Marshall listened to Rutledge, questioned him, and finally rose, saying, "There's one solution to this problem. Will you drive me to this East Dedham, and let me see for myself this man you are calling a murderer?"

"It will be my pleasure," he replied, concealing the fact that this very request was what had brought him here to this house.

He waited in the sitting room for her to change and pack a small valise. The maid who had admitted him brought him tea and little cakes.

Half an hour later, Lady Marshall came down, apologized for keeping him, and went with him to the motorcar.

She didn't speak for some time, and then she began to talk about the man she knew as Michael Reston.

"He's American, you know, although he was brought up in Yorkshire by his aunt after his parents went through a particularly nasty divorce. His father was one of the railroad barons, but his mother was left nothing when his father died, the family was so vindictive. And he's had to make his own way. That's very commendable, you know. I can't

hold it against him. Even after those horrible death duties, Kathleen
is quite wealthy, and he was worried about the differences in their incomes. He suggested a legal agreement limiting his access to any funds
or inheritance she might have. Of course Kathleen wouldn't hear of it.
She has given her whole heart to Michael."

He said nothing, neither defending nor damning the man he'd taken
into custody. But he had a feeling that the marriage, only weeks away,
had made it imperative for Barnes to silence the men who remembered
him and his wine in a barn somewhere in France.

After a time, she added, "You're quite certain, are you not, that you
have the right man? I wonder why."

He remembered Jem bound and rolled in a rug, left to die. And
Miss Wilding, possibly mistaken in the dark for Delilah, fished out of the
sea. Whatever lay between Barnes and the five men who ran their motorcars to Nice, a woman and a child were not party to that. Mrs. Grant
might well be added to the list, if her body was under the cliff fall. Timothy Grant, Wright, Holt—they too must belong on that list.

"Because," he said finally, "I have seen the bodies."

She glanced across at him, then fell silent.

They arrived in East Dedham in a wintry rain, cold and dreary.
At the police station he helped his passenger down and escorted her
into Constable Brewster's world. He thought she had never set foot in
a police station, much less a cell.

"We have kept the prisoner here because there isn't a cell in the
hamlet of Burling Gap," he explained after presenting the constable
to her. Brewster, overawed, had little to say as he handed Rutledge the
key to the single cell and watched them walk down the short passage
and open the door.

Barnes was on his feet; had risen, Rutledge thought, as soon as he
had heard the door begin to open. And then he stood there, stunned,
as Lady Marshall followed Rutledge inside the cramped space of his
cell.

He recovered quickly. "I am so sorry," he said to her, "that you should be drawn into this. I've tried to tell this man I'm not at all the person he's after. But he refuses to hear me. I think he's desperate, and I'm the stranger in the village—I have no one to speak up for me."

Rutledge could see the pity on Lady Marshall's face. "My dear," she began, then faltered.

He left them then, and went to ask Brewster to fetch Mrs. Saunders. He waited until she came, breathless, at the constable's heels, her black umbrella running with rain.

"Will you make an identification for me?" he asked. "I wouldn't have brought you out if I didn't feel it mattered. And then Constable Brewster here will take your statement about the day Mr. Barnes arrived at the rectory door."

She gave him an uncertain smile. "I'll do my best. I've had such a fright, knowing that that man had been in the same house with me. I never liked him, you know."

"I know," he said, and gave her his arm to lead her back to the cell.

She was taken aback to find an elegant woman standing there when she stepped into the small space. She curtsied, then looked to Rutledge for guidance.

"This is Mrs. Saunders. Housekeeper to Mr. Wright, the late Rector of St. Simon's. The man you know as Michael Reston came to her door shortly after the Rector's death."

Mrs. Saunders needed no prodding. "He said he had been sent by the Bishop. That he'd come to take over until such time as the Bishop could send us a new Rector. He called himself Barnes."

"There's no truth to that," Barnes exclaimed.

"Then why are your belongings in a wardrobe in the second-best bedroom in the rectory?" she retorted. "It's a house of mourning. We don't take in paying guests. You can come and see for yourself, my lady. I don't tell lies."

Lady Marshall turned to Barnes. Her face was pale, but her spine was straight and her voice level as she said, "I have to believe her, Michael."

"I will take you to the child he attempted to silence. She can tell you her own experiences," Rutledge offered. "Or to Captain Standish."

"That isn't necessary. I'd like to go home now. I shall have to explain this matter to my daughter-in-law. And I don't know how to begin." She turned and walked out into the passage, never looking back at Barnes.

"It's all lies," he shouted after her. "Why won't you believe me?"

Rutledge turned to usher Mrs. Saunders out, but she said, looking the man in the cell straight in the eye, "You're evil. Rector preached forgiveness, but you'll find none from me. Nor from *her.*" She marched out with the righteousness of a woman whose good nature had been taken advantage of.

Behind them, as Rutledge shut the door, they could hear Barnes shouting, cursing Rutledge until he was out of breath.

Rutledge asked Brewster to see Mrs. Saunders to the rectory and to take her statement there. Then he went out to the motorcar. Lady Marshall was already sitting in her seat, her expression inviting no conversation. He turned the crank, then got in beside her.

"I'm sorry," he said.

"No, you're not. You wanted to see that man humiliated."

"I wanted to see justice done. Will you come to the inquest?"

"I shall not. I believe there's a train in Eastbourne. If you could drive me to the station, I'd be grateful. I don't think I can manage returning to Canterbury in your company."

He reversed the motorcar and started back the way he'd come. "You will understand later that I had very little choice in the matter. There is still another murder, possibly two, that I must lay at that man's door. And another count of attempted murder. He was making certain that when he came to live in Kent, there was no one alive who could point him out as a sergeant they had met in a barn in France."

"Surely there were dozens of men who served with him."

"Would you believe them, if they came to your door? Five officers would have been a different matter. Especially since one of them had actually seen Barnes with your daughter-in-law."

"I wanted her to find happiness again. This will break her heart."

He had no argument to counter that, except to say, "I can't prove it. Not yet. I've just learned his name. But I have been told he murdered his first wife. Lady Kathleen is well out of this engagement."

He saw Lady Marshall to her train and safely aboard. But standing there by her carriage, she said, "I will not have my daughter-in-law testify in court."

He watched other passengers stepping aboard. "It could be necessary."

"Then I shall speak to my solicitor about finding someone we know to defend Michael."

"That's your choice to make," he replied coldly, but he thought it was her shock and anger speaking after such a betrayal, and her anxiety over how she was to explain this sudden turn of events to her daughter-in-law or call off a wedding whose invitations had most certainly already gone out. On reflection, she would do her best to keep the family name out of the whole sordid business, and leave Barnes to his fate.

She went aboard and he made sure her valise was stored away and that she had the quieter window seat.

He watched the train, wreathed in smoke, pull out of the station, then went to send a telegram to the Bishop, asking him to come to East Dedham. And he sent another to Gibson, asking him to set in motion a search for Mrs. Grant, late of Burling Gap.

When it was finished, he went to stand along the Promenade, watching the sea roll in across the shingle.

Hamish, speaking over the sound of the waves, said, "She was verra' upset. Yon lady."

"She had to see for herself. And I needed to be sure. He's used so many different names. God knows, we may not be at the end of his killings. But I think eventually he would have killed Kathleen Marshall for her money."

Rutledge had one more stop to make, the house where Delilah and her mother lived.

To his astonishment, Delilah herself opened her door the barest inch, until she saw who it was standing on her step.

She flushed, stared at him for a moment, glanced over her shoulder, and then said, "Come in, then."

Rutledge walked into her front room. Her mother was there, as he'd expected, but the other woman, sitting in one of the comfortable chairs as if perfectly at home there, was Mrs. Grant.

Mrs. Grant rose, her face turning as red as Delilah's, and she began before he could speak, "We were just talking about you. It's like you were conjured up by what we were saying."

"And what was that?" he asked, appropriating the only other chair in the room, leaving Delilah to join the cat on the couch.

"Well," said Mrs. Grant, casting glances at the other two women. "I came to Eastbourne to find Ivy, here. And it took time, mind you. She and her mother had gone to stay with a cousin over on the next street, afraid for their lives. I was after finding out if she'd killed my Timothy for rejecting her for me. But I discovered he was cheating on both of us with *another* woman, and you could have blown me over with a feather when Ivy and her mother were strolling down the Promenade one evening, and they saw a man trying to drown the hussy. Ivy knew him by sight from The Jolly Sailor, but I didn't know who he was, and she didn't know his name. We're of the opinion that *he* must have killed Timothy."

Blackmail hadn't been mentioned.

"You didn't go to the local police?" Rutledge demanded. "Why not?"

"We didn't think they'd believe us," Mrs. Brown retorted. "But what if it was the same man my Timothy had quarreled with out by Belle Tout? What if *we* were next?"

He turned to Delilah. "You were meeting that man to blackmail him. You lied to me when I was last here."

Mrs. Brown spoke up. "We thought we'd have a look, see if he came to the bandstand. I don't know if *she* was also thinking about extorting a bit of money, but when we saw him knock her down and carry her to the water, we waited until he left and went to find her. But she was unconscious. We took her to the hotel, and they wouldn't give us the time of day when we came back two days later to find out who she was."

"She was an innocent bystander," Rutledge said coldly. "She had nothing to do with Grant or this man. And he left her dog tied up there. God knows how, but he must have mistaken her for Delilah."

Ivy exclaimed, "I don't believe you. We were afraid to go back that night, but we went to the bandstand the next morning, and the dog wasn't there."

"And both of you, and Mrs. Grant here, have been wondering how you could find out who he was." He was angry and disgusted. "And then blackmail him for trying to kill the young woman."

They denied it vociferously, but he knew they were lying. He stood up, cutting their protests short.

"Get your hats and coats. You're coming with me."

It was several minutes before he could convince them that he wasn't taking them to the police station in Eastbourne. In the end, they did as they were told, and with some trepidation, they followed him out to the motorcar.

They were silent all the way to East Dedham, growing more and more apprehensive as time went by. He had nothing to say to them until they reached the police station.

"I want to know if you recognize the man I'm about to show you. I want no lies, or you'll be back in Eastbourne gaol before I'm finished with you."

He didn't wait for them after stopping the motorcar and leaving it by the door. They trooped after him. Mrs. Grant, who knew Constable Brewster, glanced away from him as they passed.

Rutledge opened the inner door and stepped to one side.

"Is this the man you intended to blackmail?"

They crowded into the small space and stared at the man who had risen to stare back at them.

"It's the new Rector," Mrs. Grant said in astonishment. "What's he doing behind bars?"

"He's the man from the pub," Delilah added.

"And from the bandstand," Mrs. Brown answered. "I'd swear to it."

Barnes stood there, staring them down, saying nothing.

"Will you give Constable Brewster statements to confirm what you've said?"

It would mean the end of their schemes. But a cell was a sobering place, and he rather thought that face-to-face with Barnes, they might well be having second thoughts about blackmail and the man glaring back at them. They nodded vigorously, their winter hats bobbing in unison.

"But what's *he* here for?" Mrs. Brown asked.

"You'll find out after you've given your statements." He ushered them out of the room, and then turned toward Barnes. "It's over."

"I won't hang. They'll set me free. You'll see. And when they do, I'll come for you," Barnes said in a low voice that wouldn't carry.

"I'll be waiting," Rutledge told him grimly. "It would give me the greatest pleasure. Whether you are alive or dead."

And then he went out to make certain the three women had kept their word this time.

S tandish came to speak to Rutledge shortly after he'd returned the Browns and Mrs. Grant to Eastbourne with a flea in their ears for dabbling in blackmail.

He said after greeting Rutledge, "I went to see Jem. To thank her, and to be sure she and her mother are all right. I'm hiring someone to help them with the tenant farm."

"That's good news. You might even consider giving her a bicycle for finding Wright's. She's earned it."

"You were right about this hand. I've used it as an excuse long enough. Maybe something good has come out of evil. At least in my case. There are fences that need mending. And they aren't all on the land."

Rutledge wondered if that might mean Emily Stuart—an unlikely fence, perhaps, but decidedly in need of mending.

"Do you think there's strong enough evidence to hang Barnes? We need to be sure of him, Rutledge. He can't get off. Not after what he's done."

Rutledge considered the question, his face grim. "Honestly? There's no unbreakable link between Barnes and Wright—or even proof that he killed Holt. For one thing, his motorcar has front-end damage now, and even if we located the mechanics who had repaired it after earlier attempts, it's circumstantial. There's Grant. Barnes knew about Delilah, one of the man's dalliances, which tells me he'd used Grant, but we can't be sure he killed the ragman. I expect Barnes encountered him in Eastbourne and discovered where he was from. East Dedham is too small to walk into the village and begin asking questions. Very likely he paid Grant for information about the village and you. But when Grant tried to blackmail him, Barnes got rid of him. Or he may have intended to kill him anyway. An experienced barrister will call these charges speculation."

He remembered Lady Marshall's threat to hire a barrister, without regard to what this man had done. She would have regretted her words, after sober reflection. She was too intelligent not to. There would be sympathy for her daughter-in-law, deceived by lies and false promises, but none for the family's continued support of the man who had made them. Still, as the arresting officer, he would have to take that threat into account, however unlikely he believed it was.

"But there's Jem," Standish pointed out.

"She'll do very well as a witness. But she's eleven, and she can be confused by clever questioning. What's more, her mother didn't see Barnes and can't confirm her daughter's identification. We have the butcher and the men in his search party who can confirm that Barnes claimed he searched the Hole, but he can swear he didn't go far enough. There's a woman in Eastbourne whom Barnes attempted to kill. She didn't see his face. The two women who rescued her did. It forms a pattern, although attempted murder isn't a hanging offense. We can show that Barnes lied to Mrs. Saunders and the people of East Dedham about who he was, but not why he had lied. The inquest won't be a problem. The question is, can we convince a jury that he has killed without conscience?"

"There's his military career—his desertion."

"Unsavory, yes, but it won't hang him. Not two years after the end of the war. There must be some evidence that he killed his first wife and her lover. I intend to find out. But I rather think he covered his tracks there as well. He's a clever bastard."

"Damn it, you're Scotland Yard. Make certain he can't wriggle out of this. I don't care how clever he's been, surely you can be even more clever. It's your duty."

Rutledge stood there, accepting the rebuke. But he knew, better than Standish ever could, that evidence was elusive, proof not always certain. There had to be another way. He'd grappled with it in the night, and driving, and looking in his mirror shaving. As far as he could see, he'd exhausted every avenue.

They'd been talking in Brewster's police station, Standish by the table that served as Brewster's desk and Rutledge with one foot on the rung of the constable's chair. As Standish turned to leave, his frustration apparent, his bad arm knocked against the desk and sent a pile of papers to the floor. They drifted like snow, settling in an untidy heap. Standish swore. "Clumsy!" he said, but it was Rutledge who bent to retrieve them and return them to the desk.

"How did you come into the village? I'll gladly take you back to the house."

"No, I brought the horse. But I've told Trotter to hurry with the repairs of the motorcar. I'd stopped driving. I should start again. I'm told

it can be done, even with one hand. I spelled you, coming back from
Sevenoaks, without running us into a ditch."

And he was gone. Rutledge, reaching for his coat, hung over the
back of Constable Brewster's chair, happened to see the topmost sheet
on the pile he'd put back on the desk.

It stopped him in his tracks.

22

Rutledge reached out to pick the sheet up, as if half fearful it would vanish before his eyes. It had had no meaning the first time he saw it. Now? Knowing what he did?

It was the notice from Hastings about the body they had found and failed to identify.

Hamish, in the back of his mind, warned, "It's no' a certainty. For all you know, they could ha' put a name to the dead man by now."

Still. Rutledge read the description again. Older man, possibly in his fifties . . .

He shoved his arms into his coat, reached for his hat, and was out the door on the run, not bothering with his motorcar.

Reaching the rectory out of breath, his heart pounding, he knocked at the door, praying that Mrs. Saunders was there and not at her sister's.

She came at last, looking up at him with alarm. "He's not escaped, has he? Barnes?"

"No." He willed himself to speak calmly. "Could we step inside, out of the wind?"

"I'm so sorry. Do come in." She led him to the parlor and offered him a chair. He sat, and asked her to do the same. Then he asked the question that had brought him here.

"I wonder. Do you know this man?"

It was cruel, he knew, to hand her the sheet from Hastings without any warning, any preparation for the shock it could cause. But he dared not prompt her.

She looked at the drawing, frowned, and said, "I don't know . . ." Reading the description and looking again at the sheet, she put her hand to her mouth to stifle a gasp. "Oh, please. Is this why you brought it to me? Tell me I'm wrong. This isn't Mr. Ferris? Surely it isn't."

"I'm afraid it could be."

"What a loss he will be to the Bishop. Oh, my dear, I don't think I can stand many more such shocks."

"Did he come often to the rectory?"

"From time to time, of course. On church business. More often once Rector went to France, to make certain all was well."

"And he stayed here?"

"Yes, and it was always a pleasure to look after him."

"Do you possibly recall what sort of valise he carried?"

"Just an ordinary brown calf. Like Rector's own."

The valise that Neville had seen, tossing in the surf? After Barnes had removed the clerical garb that he wanted?

"Do you recall Rector ever having a photograph taken with Mr. Ferris?"

"Rector never did, no. But I do believe there's one that Mr. Stapleton took with Mr. Ferris and sent to Rector in France. To show him all was well."

"Do you think the Rector kept that photograph? Brought it home again with him?"

"I should think he did," she said doubtfully, looking around the room as if it were hiding there. "Why would he not?" Then she brightened. "Of course, it would be in his trunk. Where he kept his uniforms and the like."

She led him to the attic, musty and dim in spite of the lamp he carried up with him, and the trunk was at the top of the narrow steps, well within reach. Mrs. Saunders opened it reluctantly, still viewing the trunk as the Rector's belongings, which she would never have searched in his lifetime. It was Rutledge who took over and delved into the contents. Here were the chaplain's uniforms, folded away in tissue paper, along with a tattered Bible, a camera, and a box. He offered it to her to open, but she shook her head. It held souvenirs, among them a brass rifle-cartridge casing engraved with a cross and a regimental badge, a silk handkerchief made from a flare's parachute and embroidered with a scene from a village, and beneath those, a chocolate tin. Again he offered it to Mrs. Saunders, and this time she attempted to open it, but it had rusted a little. She handed it to Rutledge.

It took him a minute or two to coax it apart, but the lid finally rested in his hand.

Mrs. Saunders leaned forward to see what was inside.

There were a dozen or so photographs, and Rutledge took them out to sort through them. One of a British biplane sitting in a field, another of a tank burning near a trench, and quite a few of men, labeled on the back with their names. Among them, Rutledge found what he was after.

He recognized Stapleton first, bearing less of a resemblance to an apostle here, and with him a graying man smiling at the camera. Mrs. Saunders, at his shoulder, said, "Mr. Ferris."

"I should like to keep this for a few days. Would you mind? I'll give you a receipt for it."

"No, just bring it back, if you please. I don't think Rector would mind my having it."

"No." He took out his wallet and carefully set the photograph inside.

They closed the trunk, and as they descended the stairs, he said, "Thank you, Mrs. Saunders. I'm so sorry to have brought more bad news. But I have a feeling that Barnes waylaid Ferris and killed him, in order to take his place."

"But why did he do such a mad thing? A man of the church?"

Because Barnes was arrogant; because Standish was more of a hermit than a man, and harder to kill. Once he'd learned that Wright and not Standish had been driving that motorcar, he'd had to find another way of reaching the Captain.

Rutledge said only, "I think he was eager to find someone who lived here. And it seemed to be a safe enough place to hide while he was searching."

"But he went often to report to his Bishop. He said."

"That's what he told you. But not what he did."

Rutledge stayed longer than he'd intended, out of concern for Mrs. Saunders, but as soon as he could decently leave, he went back to the motorcar and set out for Hastings.

He'd been there before, on another inquiry. He knew the town well. Going directly to the police station, he asked to speak to the officer in charge of the drowning described in the notice that had been circulated around Sussex and Kent.

After a moment, someone came out to meet him, and Rutledge was relieved to see that the man was new to him.

"Inspector Gage. You're Rutledge? Scotland Yard?"

"I am. I've come from East Dedham, where I'm currently investigating a motorcar crash. The Rector, Nathaniel Wright, died in it."

Gage nodded. "I've heard about that. What brings you to Hastings? Do you know who our dead man is? I can't believe he has anything to do with your inquiry."

Rutledge smiled, trying not to lose hope. "Then you've identified him?"

Gage reluctantly shook his head. "Sorry. No."

"What do you know about him?"

"Come into my office. We can talk there."

It was cluttered, smelled heavily of cigar smoke, and boasted only a pair of chairs. Rutledge took one and waited.

"Odd case. A man was fished out of the surf early one morning. It appeared that he'd drowned, but the doctor reported a broken neck. And no water in his lungs. The doctor also told us there was no chance our body was a suicide off the headland, not enough damage to support the possibility. I don't much care for suicides, too damned much work. That left us with murder. We'd sent round a query trying to identify the man, hoping any next of kin could help us, but so far no one has come in to claim him."

"Go on," Rutledge said.

Gage smiled. It was more a grimace. "The query did bring us one lead. A constable over to Pevensey thought he could place our body. He'd seen someone he believed was the dead man, talking to another man outside the shops. Our body was wearing a clerical collar, and he got into a dark green motorcar with the other man. They drove away together. We asked around Kent if anyone had lost a clergyman, but no one had."

"Did you send round again to Sussex as well?"

"Sussex?" he asked, as if Rutledge had said Calcutta instead of the next county. "Of course we did, but no flock without its pastor there either."

"Why was this clergyman in Pevensey? Any word on that?"

"That's where it gets murky. A constable in a village outside Canterbury reported that a priest who fit the description had been visiting at the home of the late Sir Wilfred Marshall. He was a family friend, there to arrange the marriage of Lady Kathleen Marshall, and he left two days before our body came ashore. We wrote to his Bishop, but had to scratch his name from our list."

"What was his name? This visitor to the Marshall house?"

"Farrier?" Gage dug around in the papers on his desk, then shrugged. "It hardly matters anyway. According to the Bishop, Farrier is alive and well and attending to church business."

"How was the body clothed, when you found it?"

"A shirt and trousers. No shoes or coat. Good quality. Not shoddy. No indication he was in holy orders."

"How did the clothes fit him?"

Gage considered Rutledge before answering. "Well enough. A tad tight in the waist, as if he'd gained a stone of late. He was a bit on the paunchy side."

"When the priest met with another man driving a dark green motorcar, were they quarreling?"

"Quarreling? I doubt it. The priest got into the motorcar, didn't he? In fact, the constable was of the opinion they knew each other, and the priest was surprised to see the other man."

I'll just wager the priest was surprised, Rutledge thought to himself. *He wasn't expecting to find Barnes in Pevensey. And Barnes must have got the shock of his life when the priest told him that Wright had been killed, not Standish, and he, Ferris, had been sent to deal with St. Simon's Church until a replacement for Wright could be found.*

Gage was watching him. "Any of this make sense to you?"

"I'm not sure. Can you confirm the name?" He had to be certain.

"Look, the Bishop in Sussex told us he's alive and well. Farrier."

Rutledge had a feeling Gage was being obstructive on purpose. He considered showing him the photograph from Wright's trunk, and decided against it. A waste of time. Gage had already made up his mind.

But Gage *had* seen the body. He brought out the photograph and held it out.

"Did your body look like either of these men?"

Gage barely glanced at it. "No."

"Take a closer look."

He studied it for a moment. "All right, yes, the younger one." Then his gaze shifted to Rutledge's face. "Now, where did you find that?"

"In an Army officer's trunk." He could tell Gage didn't believe him. But he knew now that Gage had recognized Ferris. His eyes betrayed him.

"What's his name?"

"Ferris."

"Who is he, when he's at home?"

"A missing priest. What's the name of the constable in Pevensey?"

"Arnold. If you can shed any light on our dead man, I'd be grateful." The words were polite, but Gage's eyes were dark with suspicion now.

"Believe me, I'll be happy to share whatever I learn with you," Rutledge said, rising and taking his leave.

Pevensey wasn't far. It too was on the sea, a wide sweep where it was likely that William of Normandy had come ashore to face Harold of England in 1066. Rutledge stopped for petrol, then drove on. His body was demanding sleep, but his mind was racing with possibilities and refused to pay it any heed. He ignored everything but finding the police station in Pevensey.

Constable Arnold, he was told, could be found along the High, making his daily rounds, and Rutledge went in search of him.

He spotted the man, gray-haired and sturdy, standing outside an ironmonger's shop at the foot of the High, talking with a young woman who was pushing a pram.

Rutledge found a place to leave his motorcar and walked back. The woman had gone into one of the shops, leaving the pram on the street, and Arnold was keeping an eye on it.

He watched Rutledge approach, recognizing someone with a purpose, and a stranger at that. When Rutledge was near enough to speak to, Arnold said, "Looking for something, sir?"

Rutledge smiled. "If you're Constable Arnold, I've found what I was after." He took out his identification. "I've come to ask you for more information about the priest you saw some days ago, getting into a dark green motorcar with another man."

Arnold took a deep breath. "I had a feeling there was something odd about that. But no one would listen. Not even the inspector in Hastings."

"What was odd?" Rutledge asked.

"I don't think the priest liked the other man, sir. They were polite, speaking to each other. But there wasn't what you might describe as warmth between them."

"And yet the priest got into the motorcar with him. How long did they talk before this happened?"

"A good ten minutes or so, sir. I was standing there watching them. The priest had just stepped out of the tobacco shop but didn't walk on. I thought he might be uncertain which way to go, and so I crossed the street intending to speak to him, seeing that he was a stranger. There's an omnibus that runs between Hastings and Eastbourne, but it doesn't stop just there. Before I got near enough to speak, a motorcar came down the street, slowed, and then stopped. He stared at the driver, and the driver stared at him, got out, and said something to him. The priest replied, and they spoke for a bit. While the driver of the motorcar tried not to show it, he got a shock, speaking to the priest. It was then he must have offered the man a lift, because the priest wasn't agreeable at first. They discussed that too."

"Did the priest have a valise with him?"

"That's why I thought he must be waiting for the Eastbourne omnibus. A brown one. Leather, rather smart."

"If you saw him again, could you identify the man who gave the priest a lift?"

Constable Arnold considered the question. "I can," he said finally.

It occurred to Rutledge that Arnold was of the same generation as Neville in Burling Gap. A man who knew his patch with a thoroughness that came from years of keeping an eye on everyone in it.

The woman stepped out of the shop just then and thanked the constable, walking on with her pram.

Rutledge brought out his wallet and showed the photograph to Arnold. "Could the priest you saw be either of these men?"

Arnold studied it. "Not the older one."

"That would be Stapleton."

"But this one could very well have been him." He was pointing to Ferris.

"Will you come with me to East Dedham? There's someone I want you to take a look at."

"What's this about, then?"

"I'd rather wait until you've seen this man."

Arnold took out his watch. "I'm finished at five o'clock. Will that do?"

And Rutledge had to be satisfied with that.

He found a place along the shore where he could look out across the water toward Pevensey, and slept for several hours. It helped. And then he went back to retrieve Constable Arnold.

They rode in silence for the most part, the headlamps picking out the road. As they neared the Gap, Arnold said, "This man I'm to see. Is he alive or dead?"

"Very much alive."

When they reached the police station in East Dedham, Rutledge left his motorcar in the road and took Constable Arnold inside, introducing him to Brewster, who was just finishing the last of his tea.

"There's a man in the cell, at the end of the passage," Rutledge said then. "I'd like you to take a look at him. If you know him, I'm interested in what you have to say. If you don't, I'd want you to tell me that too."

"A cell? What's he taken up for?" Arnold asked.

"For one thing, we believe it's a matter of mistaken identity."

Arnold nodded and walked on. Rutledge and Brewster, listening, heard his footsteps recede down the passage and then come to a halt in front of the cell where Barnes was being held. Several minutes passed, but neither the Pevensey constable nor the prisoner spoke. Then the footsteps returned.

"That's the owner of the green motorcar, sir. I'd take my oath on it."

"And you saw him drive away with the priest?"

"Yes, sir, I did."

Rutledge felt a swelling sense of satisfaction.

"He isn't the priest, by any chance?"

"No, sir. I'm quite sure of that. The priest was older than the driver. Graying and a little stooped. Your photograph matches him, although I'd guess he was a bit younger when that was taken."

"Will you give me a statement, setting out all you've told me? Identifying the man in the cell and the priest in this photograph?"

For answer, Arnold sat down at Brewster's desk and took out a pen. Brewster handed him paper, and then said quietly to Rutledge as the constable began his statement, "That's Mr. Ferris in the photograph. And Mr. Stapleton."

"Yes, and I shall want a statement from you, describing what was done here tonight."

"I'll be happy to, sir. But I'd like to know the point."

Rutledge took him outside, out of Arnold's hearing, and explained what he'd learned.

Brewster's broad face changed as he listened. "Then you've got proof, now," he said when Rutledge had finished.

"For one death. Yes," Rutledge agreed.

He drove Arnold to Hastings, and presented his evidence to Inspector Gage.

"And the Bishop never knew there had been a switch in the two men?" he asked.

"He had every reason to believe Ferris was at St. Simon's. And Mrs. Saunders, the housekeeper, believed that Ferris must have been unavailable. She took Barnes at his word."

"It was a dangerous game he played."

"I don't think he expected to find himself in East Dedham that long. The Bishop will have to send someone here to make a formal identification of your body."

"Aren't you the clever one?" Gage said, and then added, "It makes my life easier, all the same." It was the nearest he could come to gratitude.

Rutledge returned Constable Arnold to Pevensey, thanking him for his good eye.

"It's odd, you know. There's something that isn't quite right, but you can't put your finger on what it might be. And it sticks in your mind afterward. That's why I recalled the incident so clearly. And the men."

"It's a very good thing you did." Rutledge watched him walk away. And he found himself thinking that Gage, with his promotion to Inspector, had lost touch with the constable he'd once been.

It was quite late when he got back to East Dedham.

But he was no longer bone-tired. Instead, it was with a brisk step that he walked back into the police station and went down the passage to where Barnes was asleep on his cot.

Without compunction, Rutledge woke him.

"I can't prove beyond a shadow of doubt that you killed Wright or Major Holt. I can't prove you ran Captain Standish off the road high above Nice. Not with any certainty. Not if you have an astute barrister."

Silent, Barnes regarded him with what was surely a smugness born of his belief in his own cleverness.

Breaking his silence, he said, "You're setting me free. Thank you. I shall speak to my solicitors about ruining what's left of your career."

Rutledge let him enjoy his momentary sense of triumph.

And then he went on. "But I can show evidence that you abducted Jem Meadows, and tried to drown Elizabeth Wilding, mistaking her in the dark for Ivy Brown. And I can now prove beyond a shadow of a doubt that you killed Mr. Ferris and took his place at the rectory. It doesn't matter, you can only hang once. But hang you will for that. Good night, Sergeant Barnes. I wish you pleasant dreams of the rope."

He turned on his heel and left the cell, left the station.

There was still much to do, the inquests to complete. But Rutledge felt vindicated. He had wanted to kill Barnes with his bare hands, there in the chalk tunnel that was Parson Dolby's Hole. But now the law would see to that for him, and there would be justice done, of a sort. It wouldn't bring back Holt or Wright, Ferris or Grant, it couldn't restore Standish's hand, or even shorten Jem Meadows's nightmares. It would not bring back Elizabeth Wilding's happiness. Such tragedies couldn't be undone.

There was never any way to restore what had been lost.

At least the world would be shown who was behind that loss, and know that it was over, once and for all.

It was the best that he, Rutledge, could do to make amends.

He went to Dr. Hanby's surgery and arranged the release of the Rector's body, to allow the Bishop or possibly even Stapleton, who had known Wright, to make arrangements for a funeral.

And before he could leave East Dedham, he had a promise to keep to Elizabeth Wilding.

Acknowledgments

Our gratitude—as always—to Pauline and Brian, who found the crooked road we needed for the Rector's car crash.

Everything else grew out of that find, because we had our setting on the cliffs.

And our thanks to Linda, who found a missing link. Her sharp eye and willingness to scramble about like a mountain goat to get just the right photograph often saves the day.